VALOR TALE

VALOR TALE

David Earl Williams III

To order additional copies of this book, contact:
Xlibris Corporation
1-888-795-4274
www.Xlibris.com
Orders@Xlibris.com
35263

Contents

I dedicate this book to those who want to succeed in life and make better of themselves to fully evolve into a more intelligent and satisfied being. To those who knew I would make my life better than it was, to those who helped me and motivated me always, for being graced by God and receiving the gift of life itself. To all those who are dear to me,
this is a big thanks to you all.

Prologue

In the early years of the country of Mesovilla, there was peace and order. Ran by a senate that was the head of the democratic society, the natives' lives was simple. As the years went on, turmoil began to build up, gradually tearing the country apart. An outbreak of chaos ran rapid throughout Mesovilla. Many heinous acts took place that could no longer be dealt with by the law. The outpour of cries from the people reached the Senate to stop these acts of madness. Instead, the Senate turned their backs on the people and left all as it was. With this act of abandonment, thus began the Great Liberation. The country went through fifteen long years of war. Many lives were lost, but finally when it ended, the war-torn country retained order.

After the reconstruction of Mesovilla, a new government was formed. No longer was it a democracy; this country was now under the new order of martial law. This new form of government would prove to be effective for many years to come. It had seemed law and order was in effect as time went on. The corruption this time came from within the government itself. Blinded by power and greed, the unjustified acts of the government caused the people of Mesovilla to detest and fear them as well. With another war brewing within the provinces of Mesovilla, confusion swept the nation on which side to join. New Havenport had turned against the Helix capital and threatened to use a biological weapon to gain supremacy over the Helix capital. The Great Civil War lasted eight long years; the war had ended with a single nuclear attack on New Havenport and ended the threat of a biological attack on the homeland capital.

Order had again reigned, and stricter laws were passed. Freedom was now an illusion. As the years passed on, the corruption within the government continued. Among the people, there are very few who have risen up against the government. These freedom fighters defend the rights of the innocent. They are their voice and the fighting spirit of what true order and freedom is. They are the Aurora

Blade. Like before, the country of Mesovilla erupts into further turmoil. Though this time, the corruption is deeper than they could have imagined. There will be many challenges to overcome as the event unfolds before them. What fate lies ahead for them all now?

Valor Tale Cast of Characters

Dew Wilder

 Character Designer: Michael Nguyen

Age: 24
Height: 175 cm
Weight: 68.9 kg
Weapon: Bo staff
Birth date: January 8th
Birthplace: Twin Pines
Occupation: Leader of Aurora Blade
Blood type: O+

Dew is the main protagonist of the story, and he is the leader of the Robin Hood like thieves, called—The Aurora Blade. Once served as a member of the Swat Trooper Elite during the Great Civil war; he fights against the corrupt government of Mesovilla to put an end to the reigning oppression that hangs over the people, and to restore the freedom that long ago existed. Dew had lived with his grandfather after his parents' untimely death involving a car accident. Dew had always looked up to his grandfather as his role model, and had always dreamed of some day emulating him; as his grandfather had served in the Swat trooper Elite in the past. Rena is Dew's Sifu who he had learned the art of bojutsu from; he also has a crush on her as well. His childhood friends being, Hopkins and Emily Arrlington lived next door to him. They would ditch school at times to go exploring around the town and even up to Mt. Illini looking for adventure. Dew would unfortunately lose his grandfather to death as he himself had been in a car accident. Since that day, he had promised himself to continue on living to succeed in the name of his family. Out of the group, Dew is more selfless than the others, and assesses the situation carefully before jumping ahead. He is truly a leader.

Lorenzo Arana

Character Designer: William Irvin Wade

Age: 30
Height: 177.5 cm
Weight: 79.3 kg
Weapon: Brass Knuckles
Birth date: July 21st
Birthplace: Helix
Occupation: Aurora Blade member
Blood type: A-

Born into poverty and losing his parents' to the Liberation War, him and his brother Steve were left homeless. Spending most of his youth with his brother, they would mug and pick pocket people to survive just another day of the growing harsh society that Mesovilla was becoming. On one fateful night, during a mugging went wrong; his brother was killed by a Swat trooper and he himself was thrown off of a bridge as he attacked the Swat trooper in vengeances. His unconscious body would be found by a man name, Aquagonla, who later on after being in his care taught him the art of Kenpo. Being the originator of the Aurora Blade, Lorenzo everlasting hatred for the man who murdered his brother had begun to consume him through his actions of terrorizing the locals instead of fighting against the corrupt government. To cause a drastic change in his attitude was the passing away of Aquagonla. On his death bed, Lorenzo vow to control his hatred and fight for the people as it was intended in the first place. He had then realized his errors and corrected them from there on out. Lorenzo tends to suffer from depression here and there due to witnessing his brothers' murder. Now second in command of Aurora Blade, he is indeed a worthy ally to have.

Rena Cullen

Character Designer: William Irvin Wade

Age: 46
Height: 170 cm
Weight: 60.3 kg
Weapon: Scythe
Birth date: December 14th
Birthplace: Demmin
Occupation: Teacher
Blood type: O-

Rena had moved to Twin Pines at the age of twenty nine to start a new life after her marriage had gone rotten and husband who dedicated his life to his work as well. In the end, leaving the kids in his custody is some thing she regrets daily. Meeting Dew and his grandfather three years later, she becomes aquatinted with the two and then offers to teach Dew the art of Bojutsu as a token of their friendship. During the times when Dew's grandfather had to leave town to attend to business elsewhere, she had become Dew's caretaker as well. She had trained him every waking morning and when he had came from school, every evening as well. She was quite pleased in Dew's progress in learning the art of Bojutsu, just as she quick as she learned from her father at a young age. Dew refers to her as Sifu (Cantonese for teacher). She has a vast knowledge in the fields of marital arts and science. She reunites with Dew during an altercation with some Swat troopers at her school house in Helix. She then continues to aid him and the others in their struggle to liberate the people from the oppressing government. Rena is a bit conservative on the information she receives, and tends to not divulge any of it until the last moment; as if she was hiding some thing. She catches on quick to the things that happen around her, than her younger companions do. Though she is unaware of the crush that Dew has on her. She is mainly helpful to the group when they are in need of her assistances in battle.

Cooper Tyler

Character Designer: William Irvin Wade

Age: 25
Height: 172.5 cm
Weight: 74.3 kg
Weapon: Mop
Birth date: November 23rd
Birthplace: Demmin
Occupation: Janitor
Blood type: O+

Coming from a family of military heritage, Cooper just like Dew in some ways, grew up wanting to join the Swat Trooper Elite; which his father was a member of at the time. Being too young to enlist, he would in the mean time work for a local cleaning service as a janitor to learn some responsibility in the work force. Through day in and day out, he would continue day dreaming about the thrill of what battle would be like. Some time later after his father had retired from the Swat trooper Elite; he had realized his father was becoming ill. His father was dying from Cancer; Cooper would spend as much time handling the load of work and attending to the household chores as his mother took care of his father day and night. Before his father had passed away, he had told Cooper to take care of his mother and live up to his name. So with his passing, Cooper had then enlisted into the Swat Trooper Elite to do just that. Months after passing his basic training, he got word on his home providence being attacked, which leads to his mothers' death. After being assigned to a unit lead by General Landmore; he met Dew who he befriended and both began to share the same hatred towards their duties. After being injured in a raid on a New Havenport lab facility, he was honorably discharged and found work in the Helix capital as a janitor. Since the misfortunate events in his life, he has used the job to hide his grief and guilt of not keeping his word to his late father. He eventually meets Dew again joining him in his fight against the Helix capital. Cooper tends to observe the actions of his companions, he is steadfast, and up holds a great concern for the well being of his friends as well, especially when it comes to Elvir.

Krista Naples

 Character Designer: William Irvin Wade

Age: 23
Height: 162.5 cm
Weight: 57.6 kg
Weapon: Boomerang
Birth date: August 11th
Birthplace: Llivisaca
Occupation: Tour Guide
Blood type: AB-

Born in the providence of Llivisaca; her father had died prior to her birth from over dosing on Crystal Meth. This left her mother who was a schizophrenic, suicidal, and drug addict herself to raise her and her brother, Ketcy all alone. Often neglected and abused by her mother, Krista would find love and develop a strong bond from her brother. Ketcy had taken care of Krista as she was growing up, while their mother was too consumed in feeding her drug addictions. Krista would often run away from home to escape the miserable surroundings to have a piece of mind. Eventually she would return home every time to be with Ketcy. On one early morning, Krista and Ketcy had discovered the lifeless body of their mother lying on the living room floor after over dosing on heroin. With out any other known relatives to go to, Ketcy then took any job he came across to support him and his sister; which barely kept a roof over their head. Out of desperation to provide a better means of living for Krista, Ketcy had joined the local notorious gang known as,—The Black Mantis. The rewards were bountiful, and the two lived a comfortable life from there on out. Krista then would follow behind her brother foot steps and join the gang. As brother and sister, together they would begin to build the foundation that would lead to the gang rise of power and control over the providence. As the years passed by, Krista began to realize that her brother was becoming corrupt by this new life style. For her, this way of life was not giving her any kind of satisfaction in hurting others to make their lives better. Krista then decided to leave the gang, and start her life anew. Her decision didn't go well for her brother who was the leader of the group now; he had in the end denounced her as his sister and only family. Using her knowledge about Llivisaca inner cities to the country side, she ended up working for a local tour guide agency to make an honest living. She meets Dew and the others after being assigned to them to give them a tour of the city. She is the most optimistic and cheerful of the bunch.

Vilmer Oilla

 Character Designer: Michael Nguyen

Age: 49
Height: 180 cm
Weight: 88.4 kg
Weapon: Grappling Hook
Birth date: June 8th
Birthplace: Cumbersome
Occupation: Mountaineer
Blood type: B+

Well known across the country side of Mesovilla; Vilmer was the first person in history ever to climb the tallest mountain in the world, Mt. Illini (8,868 m). With the accomplishment of this feat, he had gained the fame and respect from others as he had always dreamed about when growing up. Although with all the acclaim for his merits, he was struck with an overwhelming feeling of guilt and sadness. When he had started the ascension up the mountain, he was accompanied by a very good friend name, Aldous who he had knew since the days of attending the university with. During the ascension, the two decided to take a break at the midpoint of the mountain. Setting up camp, Aldous had gone for a cigarette break as Vilmer was resting inside the tent to recuperate from the long climb. The weather at this moment had begun to worsen, and due to the rough winds, Aldous was blown off of the mountain hanging onto the edge of it for his life. Vilmer would hear his screams for help and rushed to his aid. The weather had become unbearable as he tried to help his dear friend back onto the mountain. The end result had caused Vilmer to lose his grip on Aldous hand, in this; Aldous fell 4,434 m below to his death. The memory of watching his friend fall to his death had played over and over in his mind; this had caused him to continue on upward to finish the climb in his name. But every time he ascended higher, he felt that he had robbed Aldous of his chance at fame. After the incident, Vilmer never climbed again and isolated himself from society to atone for the death of his friend. However, a little boy name, Konrad who had looked up to him after hearing the stories of his climb; would occasionally visit him like he was an uncle. Konrad is Vilmer's only friend until he meets Dew and the others later on. For being the oldest of the group, Vilmer possesses great physical strength, flexibility, and kinesthetic awareness for his age; along with his vast experience of climbing and medicines.

Elvir Bouzigard

Character Designer: William Irvin Wade

Age: 21
Height: 155 cm
Weight: 55.7 kg
Weapon: Duel Daggers
Birth date: March 16th
Birthplace: Minerva
Occupation: Thief
Blood type: O-

Born into an upper class family in the providence of Minerva to her mother who was a native resident of the area; father who was a former senator and currently head of Bouzigard financial institutions all over the province. He had moved to Minerva to acquire the land that was giving to him by the old government of Mesovilla shortly before the Liberation War. Growing up, she had received the best schooling and care that a rich family could provide. Unlike any other child who would be spoiled rotten and uncaring if they were in her position; Elvir looked passed all the materialistic things that were given to her, only wanting love from her workaholic father. Unfortunately her father was too busy most of the time to attend to his daughter and wife. This pushed Elvir further away from him and much closer to her mother. A couple years would pass by and Elvir mother would end up catching a fatal disease that had caused her to be bed ridden. Elvir attended to her every need and spent as much time with her; for her father, he was too consumed with his work to do this, though he did hire the best doctors to treat his wife. As time passed on, Elvir mother condition had worsen and the pain had become unbearable. She ultimately took her own life after nothing else had helped to make it better. Elvir was broken hearted by this event and blamed her father for the cause of her mother's death. Elvir disgusted by her father lack of love and concern, left home and denounced her blood line. She would later check herself into the local orphanage and find the love and care that she had always wanted in the end from the caretakers. When she was much older, she ventured off into Llivisaca and eventually joined the Black Mantis Society; she would find herself going down the same path as her father was becoming consumed by greed and caring about herself. She eventually meets Dew and the others joining their cause. Elvir comes off as being useless and even disliked by the others in the group, contrary to this; she is always dependable to assist them when it is needed. She becomes close to Cooper as the story progresses.

Thornton Videl

Character Designer: Michael Nguyen

Age: 36
Height: 183 cm
Weight: 74.3 kg
Weapon: Bastard Sword
Birth date: October 9th
Birthplace: Helix
Occupation: Ex-military (high ranking enlisted)
Blood type: A+

Thornton is the main antagonist of the story and Dew's rival as well. He was the one of the leading superior of the same unit that Dew and Cooper were apart of during the Great Civil War. Sent by the Helix capital to retrieve a deadly virus, Thornton and the others raided the chemical facility that held possession of the viral. This would be in New Havenport, the province that Helix was at war with. The team would successfully and peacefully get the viral in their possession only because of the intrusion of the scientist daughter who pleaded with Thornton not to kill her father. He surprisingly shocked the other member of his unit by letting the scientist live, abiding to the wishes of the woman. Thornton would then develop feelings for this woman, and they would become closer to each other in time. With the war coming to an end, Thornton and the scientist daughter would run off with the viral to prevent the capital of Helix plans of misusing it. The governor of Mesovilla found out about this and had the whole unit and other soldiers killed off out of frustration. Thornton would eventually come face to face with the governor; finding himself in trading the viral in exchange for the life of his beloved. With the exchange gone sour, his beloved was killed while protecting Thornton from being harmed. Thornton had then lashed out at the governor injuring him, but in the end being shot by a swat trooper with a shot gun; Thornton flew off the roof top of the chemical facility to the water below. To cover up the events of what happened in New Havenport, the governor had ordered a bomb raid to wipe the province off the map in which this ended the civil war. Since then, his where abouts are unknown.

Chapter 1

The Cry for Freedom

Narrator.　　Our story begins in the martial-law province of Helix. As our hero Dew and his gang of Robin Hood-like thieves called the Aurora Blade—Lorenzo, Paca, and Lynch—sneak about in a district warehouse where all the collected tax money is being audited.

Lorenzo.　　*peeking from behind a crate.* Damn . . . look at all that money they got. Those bastards seemed satisfy with themselves.

Lynch.　　I bet they are.

Dew.　　Any of you see where they're storing the money at?

Paca.　　*looking into binoculars.* It looks like all the money is being loaded into those metal crates.

Narrator.　　As Dew and the gang continue observing, Schwartz Cromwell, the secretary treasurer of Mesovilla, enters the room.

Schwartz.　　SWAT trooper, are you almost finished? Governor Videl wants all the money accounted for before we deliver it to him. Did you make sure we counted it all?

SWAT trooper.　Yes, sir, we did account for it all. We're almost done though, sir.

Schwartz.　　Hurry it up then.

SWAT trooper.　Yes, sir. (*He then turns to the other SWAT troopers.*) You heard the man; let's get this done immediately.

SWAT trooper 1.　Yes.

Narrator.　　As the SWAT troopers begin to load the crates in a faster pace, Dew and his men go in for a closer view.

Lorenzo.　　What now?

Dew.　　Move out.

Narrator.	Dew and his men attack the unexpected SWAT troopers standing watch, easily taking them out. Now Dew confronts a bewildered Schwartz.
Schwartz.	What the?!
Dew.	How rude of me; let me introduce myself and my associates. We are the Aurora Blade, defenders of the innocent, keepers of the peace. We steal from the rich and give to the poor. You know, just like Robin Hood type of stuff. My name is Dew Wilder, and don't ever forget it.
Schwartz.	Wilder? Ha-ha . . . I'll be sure not to forget that.
Narrator.	More SWAT troopers arrive to confront Dew and the gang.
Schwartz.	Looks like the cavalry has arrived. This is where I depart.
Dew.	Going so soon?
Schwartz.	I must, unfortunately. See you all later, if you live, that is. (*Then he turns to a SWAT trooper.*) Kill them. (*He then walks off.*)
Narrator.	Dew and the gang battle against the SWAT troopers and easily defeat them. After the battle, Dew then walks up to one of the crates.
Paca.	So how are we going to get all this money out of here?
Dew.	We aren't.
Lynch.	What do you mean?
Dew.	We're leaving it here. We don't have time; we've been discovered, and there are probably more of those guards on the way.
Lorenzo.	What now?
Dew.	We're going to blow this place up along with the money.
Lynch.	What?! Have you lost your mind?
Dew.	No, but if you think for a moment, do you seriously think we can get this all out? Like I said, we don't have time, no chances. There's no other way.
Lorenzo.	I agree.
Narrator.	Dew then takes out an explosive charge from a knit bag he has on the side of his belt. He places the explosive device on the crates. Dew sets the charges. They quickly head outside to the harbor as they escape the warehouse, which then blows up into flames. Dew and his gang watch the fireworks from a nearby bridge.
Lorenzo.	Ha-ha-ha . . . Someone is going to be pissed off about this in the morning.
Lynch.	I could have taken at least something. (*sigh*) So much money gone . . . What a waste.

Dew.	It was all for the best. At least now with this, the government can't get their hands on it. This will be a smack in their face now.
Paca.	A huge smack.
Dew.	All right, guys, let's get out of here.
Narrator.	As Dew and his men run off, a helicopter appears over the burning warehouse.
SWAT trooper.	No pay raise now, huh?
Schwartz.	Don't bet on it. All that money . . . gone. (*He looks out of cockpit window of the helicopter.*)
Narrator.	Then the warehouse begins to explode into larger flames as the fire trucks arrive.
Schwartz.	The Aurora Blade.
Narrator.	As the pilot circle around the burning warehouse, Schwartz bursts out in laughter.
Pilot.	Sir, what is so funny? Are you all right? (*concerned*)
Schwartz.	Ha-ha-ha . . . Yes, I'm fine. Let's go. (*raspy voice*) Aurora Blade (*he whispers to himself*) . . . he-he-he-he . . . so it begins. Soon . . . he-he-he-heh.
Narrator.	The helicopter flies off. Two years have passed; Dew and the Aurora Blade are yet again on another mission. We find our heroes sneaking around in the Mesovilla Museum of Art, second-floor basement.
Dew.	That wasn't so hard at all. (*looking around*) Easy intrusion.
Lorenzo.	You think this would get old after a while? No, I never get tired of doing this. Time to piss the government off again tonight.
Dew.	Yeah, yeah. Not so loud. Not trying to draw attention yet.
Lorenzo.	Sorry, man. I'm just pumped up as always.
Paca.	Don't we all?
Lynch.	*looking around the corner, then turns to Dew.* Looks all clear from here, man. There won't be too many worries of security here; they're all on the upper levels anyway.
Dew.	Ok then. Let's get going, ya.
Narrator.	Dew and his men advance through the museum undetected, passing all security cameras and patrols. Finally reaching the third floor of the museum, they come to a stop.
Dew.	I had a thought just now.
Lorenzo.	Yo, homes?
Dew.	We'll be able to get more stuff if we all split up.

Paca.	Sure, that will work.
Lorenzo.	That works for me.
Dew.	We'll meet up at the usual spot then.
Lynch,	*walking off.* Whatever.
Lorenzo.	What's wrong with him?
Paca.	I don't know. He's been acting strange as of late.
Lorenzo.	Hmm . . .
Dew.	We'll deal with that later. For now, gather what you all can. Until then, later. (*then runs off*)
Narrator.	Now separated, Dew goes at it alone to the sixth floor. Reaching his point of destination, Dew approaches the display room where a display case on a pillar in the middle of the room lays a red gem. Red infrared beams surround the display case.
Dew.	What do we have here? Looks to be of value. This will be a piece of cake.
Narrator.	Dew uses his agile skills to get through the infrared beams and remove the gem from its place into his hands.
Dew.	A piece of cake . . . ha-ha-ha.
Narrator.	An alarm goes off, causing all exits to be sealed off.
Dew.	Damn!
Narrator.	Then a security bot hovers down from the ceiling to come face-to-face with Dew. The security bot lunges at Dew, and he jumps out of the way. Dew battles the machine and defeats it. After destroying the security bot, he looks around for a way to escape. He notices a ventilation shaft opened nearby in the corner. Dew quickly rigs the room with explosives and hears the SWAT troopers' footsteps coming toward the sealed door. Dew then quickly enters the ventilation ducts and crawls his way out as the SWAT troopers attempt to open the sealed door to the display room. Dew ends up crawling out of the ledge of the building. The SWAT troopers finally enter the display room, and this triggers the explosives to go off and incinerate them. And the impact of the explosion causes Dew to leap to a rooftop of a nearby building.
Dew,	getting up on his feet. That was close. Mission completed though. (*He dusts himself off.*) Whew.
Narrator.	Dew then leaves to rejoin his friends, who are waiting for him at the park nearby.
Lorenzo.	There you are. A little late, huh?

Dew.	Sorry for that. I had to deal with a few minor problems back there. I'm here though. So what did you all get?
Paca.	I can say a lot of stuff. The people back at the village will be happy now.
Lorenzo.	I got a lot of shit too.
Lynch.	A few trinkets, nothing more.
Dew.	Hmm . . . We did well tonight. Let's get going.
Lorenzo.	Say no more. I'm way ahead of you on that thought.
Narrator.	Dew and his men then run off down the bike pathway as the museum burns in flames. After walking a bit, they come to an old water well. They enter a secret passageway leading to Tranquil forest. They are greeted by the villagers, who are rebels themselves aiding Aurora Blade in their fight against the corrupt government.
Villager.	Welcome back.
Villager 1.	I see you all made it back in one piece . . . ha-ha.
Dew.	Nice to see you too. (*Then he pats the villager on his shoulder.*)
Lorenzo.	We took a lot this time.
Villager.	I like the sound of that.
Lorenzo.	I guess Governor Videl will take us more seriously now?
Dew.	If he hasn't now, when will he?
Lynch.	Hah.
Lorenzo.	I know that I'm starving.
Paca.	Me too.
Narrator.	Dew and the others go to their hideout to grub down on some chow. Meanwhile, back at Videl Mansion Estate, Gov. Zircon Videl sits quietly in his chair turned to the window at his desk in his office. Killbin, Videl's loyal advisor, enters the room.
Killbin.	Sir, it seems the Aurora Blade have struck again. This time it was the Mesovilla Museum of Art.
Narrator.	Zircon sits there in his chair, still turned to the window as his secretary/bodyguard, Peoria, serves him a cup of tea.
Zircon.	*Heh* . . .
Killbin.	Sir, those terrorists have shut down most of your operations. What are we to do?
Zircon.	*Tsk, tsk, tsk* . . . Hmm . . .
Narrator.	The sheriff of Helix, Gwinnett Hepworth, enters the room enraged.

Gwinnett.	Governor Videl, what the hell is going on here?! My damn men are getting slaughtered by those terrorist bastards.
Zircon.	Hmm . . .
Gwinnett.	Are you listening to me? Say something you—
Zircon.	*turns his chair to face Gwinnett.* How dare you come in here and yell at me! How dare you challenge my authority and question me. I'm running this country here! Don't ever mock me again. Things are going as planned. This is what I exactly expect them to do. I know what I'm doing.
Killbin.	What are we going to about this problem though?
Zircon.	I don't see them as a problem. We'll play with them a bit more, and then you'll see.
Killbin.	Is that wise, sir? I mean, they did cause Schwartz to have a nervous breakdown. He hasn't been ever right since then.
Zircon.	His personal issues don't interest me. They won't be too much of a threat for long. Gwinnett, I want you to double security in all sections of Helix for now.
Gwinnett.	With what men? I don't have too many left on the force.
Zircon.	Work with what you got.
Gwinnett.	Did you not hear me the first time? We can't—
Zircon.	Just do it!
Gwinnett.	*rolls his eyes.* Fine then.
Zircon.	Killbin, thank you for the update. Very intriguing . . . You both may leave now. (*then turns to the window again*)
Killbin.	As you wish, sir.
Gwinnett.	*Humph.*
Narrator.	Killbin and Gwinnett then exit.
Zircon.	Silly little pawns. They just don't know . . . hah!
Narrator.	The next day, Dew and the gang return to town in disguise, checking out their next hit—the Town Square Bank. As they observe further, they notice the increase of SWAT troopers patrolling the area.
Lorenzo.	More grunts than usual, eh?
Paca.	This makes me want to rethink this one now.
Dew.	Don't say never.
Lynch.	Oh then, Great Leader, tell us how we'll pull this one off then? (*sarcastically*)
Paca.	Somebody has a sense of humor today.
Lynch.	Yeah, really?

Paca.	Yes, really! Do we need to talk about something? You haven't been yourself lately.
Lynch.	Me? I'm fine, don't worry.
Paca.	I dunno . . .
Lynch.	It's a good thing you still care though.
Paca.	Huh?
Lorenzo.	Hey, that's enough.
Lynch.	Sorry.
Dew.	*dazed*. This place . . .
Lorenzo.	Dew, something wrong?
Dew.	Oh, nothing . . . You know, let's worry about the plans later. Just because they increased the security here in the day doesn't mean it'll be like this in the night. We all need a break.
Paca.	Break, already? We just got here.
Dew.	I just need some time alone. Plus with the layout that Lynch given us, this will be no problem.
Lorenzo.	Okay. So we'll meet back here then, later tonight?
Dew.	Yes. I'll catch you all later. (*then walks off*)
Paca.	What got into him?
Lorenzo.	I don't know. I wonder about someone else as well.
Paca.	Yes, me too.
Lorenzo.	We'll all meet up later then.
Paca.	All right.
Lynch.	Yeah.
Narrator.	As Dew leaves his friends, he continues farther down the street for a bit. After walking a few blocks, he comes to a run-down schoolhouse.
Dew.	This place brings back memories.
Narrator.	Dew then enters the schoolhouse and sees an old friend and teacher, Rena Cullen, who at the time is searching through some books on the shelves.
Dew.	Some things never change, I see.
Rena.	Huh?! That voice sounds familiar. (*then turns around*)
Dew.	Long time no see there, sifu.
Rena.	Well, if it isn't you. How are you doing? (*She walks up to Dew and hugs him.*)
Dew.	Pretty well, actually. Yourself?
Rena.	Making it. You look nice; you've grown up so well.
Dew.	You're still looking young and vibrant.

Rena.	I'm flattered. He-he-he . . . still the same Dew I remember. So you actually remembered to come and see me again?
Dew.	You didn't think I would?
Rena.	No, I just thought you would forget and live life. Who remembers the past when the future is promising?
Dew.	*whispering to himself.* I wish that were so true though.
Rena.	What's that?
Dew.	Nothing.
Rena.	Hmm . . . If I knew you were in Helix, I would have contacted you sooner.
Dew.	I was clueless myself. It's funny; I just happened to pass by here and had the urge to come about here. Who would have ever known this would happen?
Rena.	Must be fate.
Dew.	Maybe.
Rena.	Do you remember when you were younger; I used to bring you here to learn bojutsu?
Dew.	Of course, it seems like yesterday.
Rena.	Still practicing it?
Dew.	I never stopped. I learned from the best.
Rena.	No need to flatter me. It's all right though, you probably forgot about it all. I must say it's refreshing to see you again though, my pupil. Time goes by so fast, and here we are again.
Dew.	Yep.
Rena.	So what have you been up to as of late?
Dew.	Nothing much.
Rena.	Really? I'm curious . . .
Dew.	About what?
Rena.	It's nothing; it would be rude of me to ask you such a silly question. Forget about it.
Dew.	Go ahead and ask away.
Rena.	Well, I was wondering, did you ever settle down yet?
Dew.	No. My life is mostly business now and rather too busy for that.
Rena.	I see.
Dew.	What brings you back here?
Rena.	I got tired of living in Twin Pines, so I decided to come here for a while and try teaching again. No too much business as of late. I think I made a mistake doing that though. I only say that because of the insane taxes we have to pay here.

Dew.   Tell me about it.
Rena.   It's a shame; our country used to be in such order. It's now in so much
                anarchy these days. You really don't know what is right anymore.
Dew.   Well, that's why you have people who fight against our oppressing
                government like the Aurora Blade does.
Rena.   That's true. They at least have honor and pride. I admire that.
Dew.   You do?
Rena.   It's just that, when can a person take enough garbage from an
                unfair society? I see why the people protest and oppose them.
                It's interesting to see a group of brave souls stand up against
                a force so corrupted. No matter how much the media slanders
                them, the Aurora Blade still keep fighting. It's impressive, don't
                you think?
Dew.   You sound so passionate about it.
Rena.   Well, yes. I respect people who stand up for their rights. We all
                can learn something from them.
Dew.   *You'll be surprised.* I see your point.
Rena.   Not much going on here today, so I was doing some cleaning up
                here.
Dew.   It's been so long.
Rena.   You're job must keep you busy a lot, huh? It's not like you're
                going around killing people . . . ha-ha-ha.
Dew.   I wouldn't say that.
Rena.   It has been quite a while. *Humph.*
Dew.   Yeah . . . I guess I'll let you get back to what you were doing.
Rena.   Leaving so soon?
Dew.   Unfortunately, duty calls.
Rena.   Try to come back and visit me when you have time, all right?
Dew.   I'll do that. Take care for me. (*then exits*)
Narrator.   Dew walks out the schoolhouse. He notices two SWAT troopers
                entering as he left. The SWAT troopers approach Rena . . .
Rena.   May I help you?
SWAT trooper.   Yes, you can. We've come to collect the weekly taxes.
Rena.   Again? I just paid last week for Pete's sake.
SWAT trooper 1. Well, it's time for this week's taxes to be collected.
Rena.   I hardly made any money this week though. Could you perhaps
                come at the end of next week? I shall pay you in advance.
SWAT trooper.   Sorry, ma'am, if you wish to keep this dump of yours open, pay
                now or forfeit your property over to us.

Rena.   That's ridiculous. No, I won't.

SWAT trooper 1. Don't want to pay? I think this will be worth of value then. (*He reaches for Rena's neck and rips the amulet hanging from her neck. She smacks the SWAT trooper.*) Urgh!

SWAT trooper. Ha-ha-ha. That had to hurt.

SWAT trooper 1. *grabs Rena's arm.* Oh, aren't we cheeky? Damn, bitch, you won't get away with that. I think the teacher needs to be taught a lesson.

Rena.   Let me go!

SWAT trooper. Ha-ha-ha.

Narrator.   Dew enters the room.

Dew.   Perhaps you should listen to her and let her go.

SWAT trooper. *startled.* Who are you?

SWAT trooper 1. This doesn't concern you. Leave now.

Dew.   I think differently. (*draws his bo*)

Narrator.   The SWAT trooper lets go of Rena's arm.

SWAT trooper 1. You want to intervene in official police matters? Fine then, we'll deal with you, street rat. You'll learn your place.

Dew.   Enough chatter; more action.

Narrator.   The two SWAT troopers rush at Dew, but they are easily defeated within moments. After that, Dew checks the unconscious SWAT trooper's pocket and retrieves Rena's amulet for her.

Dew.   I believe this is yours. (*giving Rena the amulet*)

Rena.   Thanks. (*She takes the Amulet back from Dew and puts it around her neck.*) I was wrong to doubt you. I see that you have kept up your skills after all.

Dew.   I told you. It's going to get ugly from here on out. We should leave like now before more of those creeps come.

Rena.   You're right. Let's go then.

Narrator.   Dew and Rena run out of the schoolhouse as two other SWAT troopers walk up. They dash pass them, and this alerts the SWAT troopers.

SWAT trooper 3. What the?!

Narrator.   The SWAT trooper that was defeated by Dew drags himself to the door to his men.

SWAT trooper 1. Stop them . . . ugh. (*then passes out*)

SWAT trooper 2. Those bastards!

Narrator.   The two SWAT troopers are in pursuit of Dew and Rena, who continue running through alleyways.

SWAT trooper 2. Stop!
SWAT trooper 3. There they are! Don't let them get away!
Narrator.   As Dew and Rena continue to flee from the SWAT troopers, they eventually come to a dead end.
Dew.   Dead end, damn.
Rena.   What now?
Dew.   Lemme see. (*takes a look around and notices a manhole*) I got it. (*then runs over to the manhole*)
Rena.   What are you doing?
Dew   *removes the sewer lid then turns to Rena.* You coming or rather stay here?
Rena.   This is the only way? Gross . . . live or let die. I'll take my chances down in the sewers then.
Dew.   Great.
Narrator.   Dew and Rena leap down the manhole just before the reinforcements arrive.
SWAT trooper 3. Where'd they go?
SWAT trooper 4. They went into the sewers.
SWAT trooper 3. You want to go down there?
SWAT trooper 4. Hell, naw.
SWAT trooper 2. They're end over their heads now. That sewerage leech will take care of them. They're good as dead down there. Let's go.
Narrator.   The SWAT troopers walk off. Meanwhile, Dew and Rena are wandering around in the sewers . . .
Dew.   Whew, it smells down here.
Rena.   No kidding. So what now?
Dew.   The only thing I can think of at the moment is keep walking until we find an exit.
Rena.   Okay.
Narrator.   Dew and Rena then begin to continue venturing through the sewers. After wandering through the long corridors of the sewers, they eventually find an exit. They both come to a stop.
Rena.   It took us a while, but we made it.
Dew.   Let's see where this takes us.
Narrator.   Dew and Rena then run toward the ladder leading up to the manhole until the room begins to shake violently.
Dew.   What the hell?!
Rena.   What's going on?
Dew.   I don't know, but it doesn't sound good.

Narrator.	Suddenly, a large leech pops up from the sewerage water to stand between them and the exit.
Rena.	?!
Dew.	Great, a diseased turd . . . It looks like we'll have to fight our way out then. C'mon!
Narrator.	Dew and Rena battle the sewerage leech; in the end, they are successful in defeating it. After that ordeal, Dew and Rena climb up to the surface.
Rena.	Isn't this funny?
Dew.	What's that?
Rena.	My house is right here, Dew. Oh, the luck.
Dew.	Who would have known?
Rena.	Well, since we're here, I guess if you want to, you can come in if you like?
Dew.	Why not? I'll need some rest after that.
Rena.	You're not the only one.
Narrator.	Dew and Rena then enter her house.
Rena.	All this excitement in one day . . . I'm too old for this.
Dew.	You? No.
Rena.	Ha-ha-ha. I'm tired though. Dew, make yourself at home. I'll be back. (*walking off into the kitchen*)
Dew.	All right then. (*walking over to the couch; then he sits down*)
Rena.	*yelling.* You thirsty?
Dew.	No, thanks . . . this day . . . ha ha ha.
Rena,	*walking into the room.* Dew, I appreciate your help back there. I don't know what could have happened to me if you weren't around then.
Dew.	Anytime, sifu.
Rena.	I owe you one.
Dew.	It's okay. No need to.
Rena.	Maybe you should stay here for a bit. You know until nightfall.
Dew.	I suppose I should; those bastards are probably still looking for us. I will then. Thanks.
Rena.	Great. Well, I'll be in the kitchen. Not hungry, are you?
Dew.	No, I'm fine. I'm just tired, that's all.
Rena.	Let me know if you want anything else. (*then exits*)
Dew.	It's nice to sit on a comfortable couch for once. (*then begins to lie down*) I think . . . I'll . . . take . . . a nap . . . for (*then closes his eyelids*) . . . a little . . . while. (*snore*)

Narrator.	Dew falls into a deep sleep on Rena's couch. He begins to dream of his experience when he was a youth of twenty-two years old in the SWAT trooper elite during the Great Civil War four years ago. The war wages on between the Helix capital and New Havenport. The scene starts off as an armored jeep drives up onto the battlefield.
Hopkins.	The day finally comes.
Cooper.	Here we go.
Thornton.	Nothing like a good war. It's been a while since I've seen action. (*then turns to Dew*) Hey, boy, you nervous?
Dew.	Not really.
Thornton.	Not really? You are; don't deny it. I see it in you.
Dew.	Whatever.
Thornton.	Ha ha ha . . .
Dew.	What's so funny?
Thornton.	I've been doing this for so long; I just look at you, and . . . boy, you have no idea what you're about to get yourself into. You may be calm now, but we'll see how much that change.
Dew.	Maybe. You never know.
Thornton.	Sound so sure of yourself there. That's good though. At least you'll die ignorant. Ha ha ha.
Dew.	Don't really care.
Thornton.	Now with that frame of mind, you won't last too long on the battlefield.
Dew.	What else is new?
Thornton.	You're something else.
Dew.	Maybe your ignorance will get you killed.
Thornton.	Trying to be funny?
Dew.	Maybe I am.
Thornton.	You stepping up to me, Small Fry? I rank higher than you, Lance Corporal. Watch your tongue with me.
Dew.	Should I now, Sergeant? So you can talk smack to others and then not expect it back?
General Landmore.	*turns to Dew and Thornton.* That's enough from both of you! You two better get your shit together right now. We have an important mission ahead of us. I don't need you, two, fighting one another. One team, one direction.
Thornton.	Of course, sir.
Hopkins.	Sir, we're at the checkpoint now. Shall we begin the mission briefing now?

General Landmore. That's fine. Let's do that then. All right, everyone, listen
           up. The mission is quite simple. While our troops are out there
           fighting off the New Heavenport forces, we will insert ourselves
           upward to the chemical facility on Mount Darien. From there,
           we will infiltrate the complex from that point.
Hopkins.   Sir, what about the security there?
General Landmore. After further surveillance over the complex, it should be no
           problem for us with the backup provided for us once we reach the
           facility, which will provide as distraction to the sentries there,
           and we can get in and out easily.
Cooper.   I don't have to worry about getting killed now.
General Landmore. Take great caution though. Just because we have some
           backup doesn't mean we can let our guard down. Don't expect
           this to be a walk in the park. You're all not in boot camp anymore;
           nor is this some training exercise either. Reality is harsh, and
           there are no second chances here. Keep that always in mind.
Dew.   Not too comforting, but true.
General Landmore. Our primary objective is to retrieve the SKT virus vial
           from the facility. Earlier this year, we had interrogated a New
           Heavenport scientist who was captured during the raid of another
           chemical facility just west of the complex on Mount Darien. He
           had confirmed that the virus vial was being stored in the lower
           levels of the facility.
Dew.   SKT?
Thornton.   You don't know what it is? What did you think we were coming
           here for? You must be one of the few that falls asleep during the
           briefings. There's always one that does. Ha-ha-ha . . . you're full
           of surprises.
General Landmore. If you didn't know what it was before, you'll hear it again.
           The SKT stands for systematic karyotype takeover. It was first
           tested on guinea pigs in earlier experiments. The test data from
           that resulted that the virus could attack the DNA structure and
           alter the host.
Dew.   Mutation, huh?
Thornton.   You're paying attention this time. Good boy.
Hopkins.   Here we go again.
General Landmore. As I was saying before I was rudely interrupted, before the
           war broke out, Helix and New Heavenport were working on this
           project, the SKT viral development, for military usage. Now

since then, Governor Videl is worried that they may use this as a weapon against our forces and the other nations. It's a great importance we get this as soon as possible in our hands. We received word earlier in the week that the New Havenport forces were planning to unleash it into our nation's capital. We're not sure how this would be possible as we have the shoreline under heavy manning, yet there are a few rebel forces back on our homeland. So we're here to prevent the major loss of innocent lives. You four were selected by the elite for your expertise. I'm fully confident that you'll succeed. Like I said, let's make this easy and come out all alive. Leave no man behind. For now, gentlemen, stand by until further instruction.

Hopkins.	Roger that, sir.
Cooper.	Waiting for death. I should have never joined the military.
Thornton.	Can't run off now.
Cooper.	Don't remind me.
Thornton.	This is so boring. So the real fun begins. Can't wait until we see some action.
Dew.	Easy, killer.
Cooper.	Hey, Dew.
Dew.	Yeah?
Cooper.	You know, being out here makes me miss home more and more. You ever feel like this?
Dew.	I know how you feel.
Cooper.	This shit sucks.
Dew.	Well, just hang in there, friend. Once this is over, be glad you're alive and look forward to that.
Cooper.	I'm not afraid of that, but just second thoughts. That's all.
Dew.	We all do.
Cooper.	So what were you doing before you joined?
Dew.	Not much. I lived with my grandfather most of my life since the death of my parents. I was a baby then. Had a few jobs here and there, easy life I guess. I only joined the military to fulfill my grandpa's dreams. If he was only here now . . . yep. What about you?
Cooper.	I was a janitor back in the mainland. It was a decent paying job, but wanted to do more with my life. So I joined the military, also to fulfill my late father's dream as well. So we're not so different, are we? (*then smiles at Dew*)
Dew.	No, not at all.

Thornton.   You two sound like schoolgirls chatting away . . . hah!

Cooper.   What about you, Sergeant?

Thornton.   I have nothing to tell you. I can tell you this: I love war, and nothing pleases me more than the feel of battle, nothing else.

Dew.   Typical stiff.

Thornton.   *Heh.*

Hopkins.   Sir, I just received message from the troops. They're on their way now. Should we advance on?

General Landmore. Proceed forward.

Narrator.   Then the armored vehicle begins to drive upward to Mount Darien, leaving the waging battle that is going on. Dew then begins to wake up from his slumber.

Dew.   I wonder (*looks at his wristwatch*) . . . damn. (*He pops up on his feet.*) Where's Rena? Rena! (*yelling*) I guess she's gone. I hate to leave without saying good-bye, but I must go.

Narrator.   Dew then exits the house and rushes to the Town Square Bank, where he rejoins the others. Dew enters an alleyway behind the bank then climbs up a ladder leading to the rooftop of the bank.

Lorenzo.   Dew, there you are.

Lynch.   We were about to go in without you.

Lorenzo.   What took you so long?

Dew.   Sorry about the wait again. I had to see an old friend of mine. So is everything set up?

Paca.   Yes.

Lorenzo.   You weren't lying about the security at night; there's hardly anyone on patrol here. By the way, we took care of jamming the cameras. Should be another easy night.

Dew.   What about the security cameras?

Paca.   We've already took care of that too.

Dew.   All right then. We're all ready I see.

Lorenzo.   Dew, me and you will descend from this point. I've got Paca staying here just in case there is some trouble. Lynch will be stationed across the street.

Dew.   That works for me. It's fun time. Come on, let's do this. (*then starts to walk off with Lorenzo*)

Lynch.   I get so tired of this.

Paca.   Tired of what?

Lynch.   Just all of this. (*then starts to walk off*)

Paca.	Lynch.
Lynch	*stops and turns to face her.* Yes?
Paca.	You seem so different lately. What's wrong?
Lynch.	I've been asking myself that every day.
Paca.	Something is wrong; we need to talk about this now. It's important.
Lynch.	Not now; we got a job to do. We'll talk afterwards.
Paca.	Lynch, are you sure?
Lynch.	Yes.
Paca.	Don't get too stressed out, okay, sexy?
Lynch.	I'll try not too. (*then exits*)
Paca.	Lynch . . . (*sigh*)
Narrator.	Dew and Lorenzo successfully enter the bank after descending from the ceiling. They encounter a few guards venturing through the bank but dispose of them with ease. After a while, they finally reach the vault room.
Lorenzo.	Here we are.
Dew.	This was easy . . . hmm.
Lorenzo.	What's up?
Dew.	I feel like I forgot something.
Lorenzo.	What's that?
Dew.	Oh, forget about it. Must not be too important. No worries. Well, looks like this is going to be a simple one.
Lorenzo.	Aren't they all after a while? Let's get what we come for.
Dew.	Not here for nothing. We'll make this fast. I have a strange feeling all of a sudden about this.
Narrator.	Dew pulls out a combination decoder and places it on the vault. After a few moments of deciphering the code, the vault unlocks and opens up.
Dew.	Easy.
Lorenzo.	Too easy. Shopping time. (*grabs a bag*)
Narrator.	Dew and Lorenzo begin loading the valuables into their bags. Gathering what they could, they finished up loading the bags up with riches and begin to leave.
Dew.	Let's get out of here.
Lorenzo.	About that time again, partner.
Dew.	I'm going to call Paca and Lynch. (*grabs his handheld radio from his pocket then speaks into it*) Paca, Lynch, mission complete. We're coming up. How are things looking up there?

Narrator.	Dew waits for a response over the radio, but no response is given.
Dew.	*talking into radio handset.* Lynch, Paca, respond.
Lorenzo.	Why aren't they answering?
Dew.	Odd. Something must be wrong.
Lorenzo.	Well, let's get out of here then.
Narrator.	As they try to rush to the exit, a gang of SWAT troopers appear to block their path.
Dew.	?! (Then stops)
Lorenzo.	*looking around.* What's this?! I knew this was too easy for a heist. Must have been a setup.
Narrator.	Gwinnett then enters into the room.
Gwinnett.	Must have been . . . heh-heh-heh. So we meet at last. You're that famous terrorist group everyone is talking about. How nice to meet you all face-to-face finally.
Dew.	Can't we share the same pleasure of meeting you?
Lorenzo.	We're not terrorists either.
Gwinnett.	So many of my men, dead because of your actions. Did you think you were going to leave with all that money? Not on my time.
Lorenzo.	Where's that governor of yours at?
Gwinnett.	The governor is a busy man; he doesn't have time to waste on scum like you.
Lorenzo.	Scum? It's like your type to say something like that. You're the true scum, money-hungry bastard.
Gwinnett.	I'm hurt.
Dew.	Some kind of man the governor is. What "true leader" makes his people pay outrageous taxes and arrest the innocent for stupid reasons, humiliating them and treating them like animals? Is that just an easy way for him to have cheap labor? He's nothing more but a mere dictator.
Gwinnett.	I know how you feel; he's not my favorite person either now. Trust me when I say that I despise his guts. The money though, it is good pay.
Lorenzo.	Sellout.
Gwinnett.	This is getting old now.
SWAT trooper 6.	Sir, can I shoot them? (*pointing the rifle at Dew and Lorenzo*)
Gwinnett.	You, men, must be getting eager? Well, I've enjoyed my time with you. Men, finish them off. (*then exits*)

Narrator.	As Gwinnett exits, Dew and Lorenzo battle the SWAT troopers. They defeat the SWAT troopers.
Dew.	I knew I felt something wrong.
Lorenzo.	We don't have time to think about this. We need to leave.
Narrator.	Dew and Lorenzo flee from the area trying to escape until more SWAT troopers arrive pursuing them. As they continue to run from the SWAT troopers, they split up to lose them. Dew is able to exit outside the back of the bank back into the alleyway. Dew sees Lynch on the other side of the fence that closes off to the next street over . . .
Lynch.	*shouting.* Dew, come on! Hurry!
Narrator.	Dew runs over to the fence and attempts to jump it as Lynch reaches his hands out to pull him up. Suddenly, Dew is popped in the back of the head by one of the SWAT troopers' rifle butt. Dew falls down unconscious to the ground.
SWAT trooper 7.	We've got him now. Take him away.
SWAT trooper 6.	Yes, sir.
Narrator.	Then the SWAT trooper drags the unconscious Dew away. Dew awakes in a prison cell to find himself captured along with Lorenzo and Paca.
Dew.	*feeling the back of his head.* Ooohh . . . damn that hurts. (*rising up*)
Lorenzo.	I see you're awake now.
Dew	*turns to Lorenzo.* You all got caught too?
Paca.	Looks like it.
Dew.	Wait, where's Lynch at?
Paca.	I think he was the only one to get away.
Lorenzo.	Lucky . . . that was a tad bit easy. Someone must have tipped us off.
Dew.	Probably (*feeling the back of his head*) . . . argh. That stings.
Paca.	Things were going smooth. How could this've gone wrong?
Lorenzo.	I couldn't tell you.
Dew.	I don't want to think about that now.
Paca.	What now?
Dew.	The first thing to do is, we'll have to find away out of here.
Paca.	I wonder why Lynch didn't come back for us.
Lorenzo.	Who knows?
Narrator.	A SWAT trooper enters into the room along with a janitor . . .

SWAT trooper 9. All right, you. Sheriff Hepworth wants this office clean and the floors mopped.

Janitor. Yeah.

SWAT trooper 9. The men have been leaving trash all over the place; do a good cleanup in here. I'll be back. (*then exits*)

Janitor. Great. Might as well get to work then.

Narrator. As the janitor begins to sweep the room with a broom, Dew glances over at him.

Dew. *That voice . . . he looks familiar.*

Paca. The question is, how do we escape?

Lorenzo. We'll find a way.

Paca. Any ideas, Dew?

Janitor. Dew?! *It couldn't be him.*

Dew. Give me some time to think.

Janitor. *turns to face the prison cell.* Could it be? (*Then he drops the broom to the floor.*) Is it you, Dew?

Dew *turns to face the janitor.* Huh?

Janitor. Dew, I can't believe it. It has been a while.

Dew. Cooper?! Well, I'll be.

Cooper. You lived after all. How have you been?

Dew. At the moment in a runt, but fine now. Ha-ha-ha . . . who would have known? Today has been full of surprises for me.

Cooper. Funny how fate plays its role. I would have never imagined seeing you here in this place.

Lorenzo. You two know each other?

Dew. Yes, he's an old friend of mine.

Cooper. I see you're a part of that group everyone keeps talking about. Ironic. From soldier to freedom fighter, what a change in life, huh?

Dew. I was never a patriot.

Cooper. Like I ever was.

Dew. Ha-ha-ha. I see you went back to doing the job you "loved" so much.

Cooper. You got jokes.

Dew. Hah, only good humor.

Cooper. I know. You got yourself in a jam, I see.

Dew. Somewhat.

Cooper. If I recall, I owe you a favor? I think I can help you out here.

Dew. How so?

Cooper.   I'll get you all out of there.

Dew.   You sure? Those SWAT troopers . . .

Cooper.   Don't worry about a thing, We're old pals. I'll be fine. I never forgot what you did for me. I'll get you, guys, out.

Dew.   Thanks.

Narrator.   A SWAT trooper enters into the room.

SWAT trooper 9.   Hey, what are you doing over there?

Cooper.   I was (*bends over to pick up a waste basket*) . . . I was picking up this trash here.

SWAT trooper 9.   Oh . . . I almost forgot to tell you. Clean the bathrooms as well.

Cooper.   Okay. (*He whispers to Dew.*) I'll be back. Promise.

SWAT trooper 9.   Come on now, we don't pay you to stand around with your finger in your ass.

Cooper.   Of course not.

Narrator.   Then Cooper exits the room with the SWAT trooper.

Lorenzo.   I hope he does come back. I can't stand being caged up here.

Dew.   He'll come back. I know so.

Narrator.   Another SWAT trooper with two escorts enter the room armed with rifles and approach the cell.

SWAT trooper 1.   All right, you, let's get moving. (*then opens the cell*) You have a date with the judge. This way please.

Paca.   The judge? I don't like the sound of that.

Narrator.   Dew and gang are escorted out of the cell to a courtroom. They approach the stand to come face-to-face with Judge Clymer, head of the justice department.

Paca.   What now?

Dew.   We'll see.

Lorenzo.   Something smells fishy here.

SWAT trooper 1.   The Honorable Judge Clymer.

Judge Clymer.   Silence in the courtroom. I'm tired at the moment and would like to make this fast. Tell me the reason for this session.

SWAT trooper 1.   This is case 208: *The People of Helix Capital v. The Aurora Blade*. The charges against them are the following: violation of government property, manslaughter, and grand larceny.

Lorenzo.   We did all of that? They make it sound so bad . . . hah.

Paca.   No jury?

Escort 1.   He is the judge and jury.

Clymer.   Oh, it's this case . . . May the first witness proceed to the stand.

SWAT trooper 1. Euh, Your Honorable One.

Clymer. Yes, what is it?

SWAT trooper 1. About the witnesses . . .

Clymer. What about them?

SWAT trooper 1. Well, first of all, sir . . . there are no witnesses; none alive that is.

Clymer. I see. So you have me waken up out of my sleep, in the middle of the night to hold an emergency hearing. No witnesses though? Hmm . . . I suppose I could throw this case. Then on the other hand, I find you all . . . GUILTY! GUILTY! GUILTY! Heh-heh-heh.

Lorenzo. That was a speedy trial.

Paca. Guilty?! That wasn't fair at all.

Clymer. It is only fair; you all deserve it. Scum like yourselves are a waste of time. You should not be allowed in our society. You destroy our pure values with your so-called justice. You're nothing but terrorists and surely get no more of my time.

Lorenzo. Pure values? Don't make me laugh. Crooked fucks like you with power take away what is true and right from the people.

Clymer. The people? Those who follow the rules will be spared; those who defy us will suffer. Silly people have no free will; it's all imaginary. We chose how the people live, not them.

Lorenzo. Simple minded people you mean? Keep dreaming. You'll never control free will.

Clymer. I've heard enough of your opinions. I made my decision. I sentence you all to death. Prison would be too good for trash like you. SWAT troopers, kill them!

Escort 2. In the courtroom, sir?

Clymer. You heard me. Do it!

Narrator. The SWAT troopers are about to execute Dew and friends, until Cooper appears behind the SWAT trooper swinging his broom to the unsuspecting SWAT troopers head. The SWAT troopers fall to the floor knocked unconscious.

Dew. Cooper, it took you awhile.

Cooper. I had to make my appearance at the right moment. Timing you know. (*then uncuffing Dew and the others*)

Dew. Thanks.

Clymer. Damn!

Lorenzo *grabs Clymer by his collar*. Now it's time to get down to business.

Clymer. W-w-wait . . . mercy. (*shaking with fear*)

Lorenzo.	Not feeling too powerful now? Where's your free will at now? (shaking clymer)
Clymer.	If you kill me, you won't get away with it.
Dew.	You think you're governor cares about you? Only himself, that's the only person he thinks of. You must get paid well to so easily sell yourself?
Clymer.	I get paid pretty well, I must say.
Paca.	Soulless.
Clymer.	Stupid freedom fighters. Do you think you can change all of this? The right of freewill and freedom of speech died a long time ago. There's no reason for it. Ha-ha-ha.
Lorenzo.	Disgusting. (then throws Clymer to the floor) Money is all that's important to you; you are lost.
Narrator.	Suddenly more SWAT troopers burst into the courtroom . . .
SWAT trooper 4.	Freeze!
SWAT trooper 5.	Trying to escape? Not going to happen. (pointing his rifle at Dew and the others)
Dew.	That's the idea.
Lorenzo.	Bring it on.
Cooper.	Let's mop the floor with these guys.
Narrator.	Dew and friends battle the SWAT troopers, quickly finishing them off.
Clymer.	I'm impressed, doing in the SWAT troopers like that. Humph. You lads made your point clear. He told me this would come down to this.
Lorenzo.	What are you babbling about?
Clymer.	Let's see if Videl's weapon really works.
Dew.	Videl's weapon?
Narrator.	Judge Clymer pulls out a virus vial out of his pocket and then injects himself with it.
Clymer.	Heh-heh-heh. Let us see what this will do. Can you Defeat . . . me? I give you . . . the . . . death penalty!
Dew.	Huh?!
Clymer.	transforming into a mutated scorpion-moth. Silly . . . fools!
Lorenzo.	This is some crazy shit.
Clymer.	Ha-ha-ha. Aaaaaaaaaarrrrrggghh!
Narrator.	Dew and his friends battle the mutated Clymer, eventually defeating him, only now left with questions.
Paca.	What did he do to himself?

Cooper.	That was tripped out.
Lorenzo.	What just happened?
Dew.	It couldn't be . . . impossible. How?
Lorenzo.	Dew, what is troubling you?
Dew.	I'm all right . . . this is getting too strange. Forget about it. We don't have time to think about this now.
Lorenzo.	You're right. So best thing to do is to get out of here.
Narrator.	As the others leave, Dew follows behind as he stops to look behind at the mutated Clymer's corpse.
Dew.	SKT . . . (*then exits*)
Narrator.	Dew and the others quickly rush through the prison to end up finding a stairway. Descending down a few floors, they are confronted by Gwinnett.
Gwinnett.	So we meet again after all. Leaving so soon?
Dew.	You look surprised.
Gwinnett.	I underestimated you, Aurora Blade. I can see why you, guys, are such a pain in the boss's neck. Ha-ha-ha. Hey, janitor, what are you doing here? Get back to cleaning those urinals!
Cooper.	Do it yourself.
Lorenzo.	Move it, bub.
Gwinnett.	I can't simply let you all leave so easily. You're sadly mistaken.
Lorenzo.	Your funeral, pal.
Gwinnett.	Ha-ha-ha . . . feisty hoodlums. I see you punks think it's that easy. It won't work to intimidate me.
Dew.	We'll just have to go through you then.
Gwinnett.	*Heh* . . . No getting past this point. Time it money.
Narrator.	Dew and friends battle Gwinnett and successfully defeats him knocking him unconscious. Cooper then starts to check Gwinnett's pockets.
Paca.	What are you doing?
Cooper.	Looking for his key card. I just thought about it. We can't leave this place without it. All the doors open only if you have authorized access to certain doors.
Paca.	You don't have one of your own?
Cooper.	No, I'm always escorted when I come here to clean.
Dew.	That makes sense. Good thinking about the key card.
Cooper.	We'll need this. (*taking the card key to the garage entry way from Gwinnett*) So sorry, but got to go.

Narrator. As the four continue down the stairway, they finally reach the garage to be greeted by more SWAT troopers.

SWAT trooper 9. HALT! (*He pulls out his rifle.*)

Lorenzo. Shit.

SWAT trooper 6. Give yourselves up; nowhere to go now. (*pointing the rifle at Dew and the others*) Hands up!

Narrator. Suddenly, a car out of nowhere speeds up and hits the SWAT troopers to the ground. The car then stops and the window to the driver seat lowers down.

Rena. How's it going, Dew?

Dew. Rena?!

Lorenzo. Who's this?

Rena. Hurry up and get in before the reinforcements show up.

Dew. How the—

Rena. Well, come on!

Narrator. Dew and the others quickly jump into Rena's car just before the SWAT troopers storm the parking garage. They drive off as the SWAT troopers open fire on them. The gun fire cease as they drive off into the distance. Gwinnett enters.

Gwinnett. Fools! They got away . . . damn!

SWAT trooper 3. There goes my paycheck now.

Gwinnett. *Argh!* No matter; it's not over yet. Heh-heh-heh. (*then walks off*)

Narrator. The scene switches to Dew and friends, who are speeding down the highway after escaping from the prison.

Rena. *driving*. Interesting life you live, Dew. I would have never expected this of you . . .

Dew. You make it sound like it's a bad thing.

Rena. I didn't mean it like that, but you surprised me again today.

Dew. How did you know where we were at? I didn't mention once I was part of the Aurora Blade.

Rena. I had suspected something was different about you. When we were fighting off the SWAT troopers earlier, the way you fought. I can see you kept up your skills well. Then you left a blueprint on my couch as well.

Dew. I Knew I was missing something. Some giveaway, huh?

Lorenzo. So that's where you were earlier.

Rena. I heard that they had caught you, guys, on the radio. So I put two and two together and figured it out. Just because I'm getting old, doesn't mean I don't notice things.

Lorenzo.	If you could, could you drive a little faster please?
Rena.	Friend of yours, Dew?
Dew.	Yes. This is Lorenzo, she's Paca, and my old war buddy of mine, Cooper.
Rena.	That's right; I remember you did leave to join the military during the civil war.
Dew.	*That was only six years ago when I first joined. It all seems like it happened yesterday.* Hmm.
Cooper.	*looking out the backseat window.* I guess no one is following us.
Paca.	That's a relief.
Narrator.	Suddenly, a large tank appears right behind Rena's car, rushing toward them.
Cooper.	Okay, I stand corrected.
Dew.	Sometimes . . .
Lorenzo.	No one is following us, huh?
Cooper.	Not at the time.
Rena.	I'll try to lose them.
Narrator.	As Rena continues driving down the highway, they come to a roadblock.
Rena.	Darn, the road is barricaded (*then slows down the car and stops it*),
Lorenzo.	Why we stopping?
Rena.	We can't go any further, obviously.
Dew.	I suppose we'll have to get out and make a run for it.
Cooper.	This brings back memories.
Paca.	Every time . . . quite the predicament.
Narrator.	Dew and the others get out of the car as the tank approaches them, coming to a stop. The tank hatch opens up, and Gwinnett appears with a megaphone in hand.
Gwinnett.	Heh-heh-heh. *You all* didn't think you would see me so soon, eh? After I dispose of you, Dew and your merry men; I'll finally get that well-deserved raise I've been waiting for and the governor to get off my back. Since my police force couldn't deal with you vagabonds properly; I guess if you want something done right, you have to do it yourself.
Dew.	Let's finish this.
Lorenzo.	Ass kicking time.
Cooper.	Shall we go?
Gwinnett.	I'll crush you all into dust. Heh-heh-heh. DIE!
Narrator.	Dew and is friends battle Gwinnett while he is controlling the heavy-armored battle tank; he begins to fire missiles at them

only to miss. In spite of the moment, Dew takes advantage of the tank's misfires, and with it destroys the tank, which begins to be engulfed in flames.

Gwinnett.   Dammit, this can't be happening?! NOOOOOOOOO!

Narrator.   Then the tank burst into larger flames, then explodes, in the process destroying the barricade that once blocked Dew and his friends' exit and killing Gwinnett.

Cooper.   Toasted.

Rena.   I guess we won't have to worry about him no longer.

Dew.   No, not after that.

Lorenzo.   What a way to die.

Dew.   We should get going now.

Rena.   I agree. Let's go.

Narrator.   Dew and the others get into Rena's car and drive off. Later on that night, a conference is being held at the governor's estate. Zircon and his men are all gathered around at a table.

Killbin.   Sir, I'm pretty sure you're aware of the current situation?

Zircon.   Yes, I am. Learning about what happened earlier tonight does not bother me too much.

Killbin.   How can you say? Sheriff Hepworth and most of the uptown precinct have been taken out.

Zircon.   Sheriff Hepworth and the rest of them served their purpose and were loyal. We have to expect a few sacrifices. Then I say, he should have been careful about going off by doing such a stupid thing on his own.

Killbin.   Hmm. Also, sir, we had found Judge Clymer's body. Well, what seems to be left of him, that is. The autopsy report stated by the doctors, it seems he had, or was injected with some kind of viral agent. They've never seen nothing like this before. It was like some sort of temporary mutation he underwent.

Zircon.   Interesting . . . (*whispering to himself*) So it did work.

Killbin.   This alerts me a lot, sir. This plague could be a health issue to the public. The situation with the rebels is worse as it is as well. What are we planning to do about this?

Zircon.   Like every grave situation calls for extreme measures.

Schwartz.   Extreme measures you say, sir? I'm rather interested in hearing more about your course of action.

Zircon.   Yes, just getting to that about now. By the way, Schwartz, nice to have you back at work again. I hope the time off helped you recover from your nervous breakdown you had.

Schwartz.	I'm glad you asked. Yes, the time off helped a lot too.
Zircon.	I have a plan. This is our ace in the hole. As from this point on, the Aurora Blade will be no more.
Peoria.	How so?
Zircon.	We're going to hit them on their home field, their stronghold.
Killbin.	But Sir, we don't have any kind of intelligence's about their base of operations. I doubt if one even exist.
Zircon.	There is one, my friend. How do I know this? you may ask.
Schwartz.	Pray tell.
Zircon.	Not so much myself, but someone else does.
Narrator.	Lynch then enters the room.
Lynch.	That would be me. Nice set-up here, Mr. Videl.
Zircon.	Thank you. Nice to see you again as well, Lynch.
Schwartz.	Glup! H-h-he's one of those terrorists. Why is he here?
Zircon.	Calm down, Schwartz. It's okay, take a breather. He's works for me. This is all apart of my plan. From day one I've observed this situation and waited until I received all the info I could. Why not make allegiances with the enemy to gather some leverage in this war against the Aurora Blade? Tomorrow we will destroy their stronghold, which is located in Tranquil forest. Once we lure the leader and a few of his men into our trap, we'll send an air raid over the area to begin the invasion. Once they've all been wiped out by our surface piercing bombs, that will be one less trouble to worry about.
Killbin.	Tranquil forest is our nation's treasure. How will we explain to the public the destruction of the forest and deaths of innocent lives there?
Lynch.	There are gas lines that surround the rebels' stronghold that generate power to the village.
Zircon.	We can say simply that they blew themselves up knowing they were close to being defeated.
Killbin.	Reconsider this, sir. The innocent people . . .
Zircon.	No one is innocent these days.
Schwartz.	The public will believe such a story too. Let them hear what they want to hear. Marvelous.
Killbin.	This is wrong.
Zircon.	No second thoughts now, Killbin. We'll go as planned. *Once the Aurora Blade is gone, the world will be mine.* Heh-heh. Meeting adjourned.

Killbin.	It's not right. (*then exits*)
Schwartz.	*facing Zircon.* He's being too passive toward this situation. He seems a little soft hearted.
Zircon.	I'm not too worried about him. He'll be fine. He has no choice but to be. He'll be dealt with later. Lynch, make sure things go well tomorrow.
Lynch.	Of course, as long as you keep your promise.
Zircon.	You have my word.
Lynch.	Very well. (*then exits*)
Schwartz.	May I be excused, sir?
Zircon.	Yes.
Schwartz.	Thank you. (*then exits*)
Narrator.	Schwartz then begins to walk down the hallway until the room begins to fill up with smoke. A figure appears in the shadows.
Schwartz.	Oh, it's only you?! It's about time you came.
???.	Did you find anything of importance yet?
Schwartz.	If it's about the SKT virus, nothing at all as of yet.
???.	I know he has at least one of the virus vial. I'm growing impatient.
Schwartz.	Don't worry; you'll have your chance. Give me more time. Work with me here.
???.	Time is of the essence. I shall give you that. Don't fail me; I'm doing my part.
Schwartz.	As long as you do that, I'll keep my end of the bargain. Remember who's in control now.
???.	Ha-ha-ha. (*then disappears*)
Narrator.	Meanwhile, back in Tranquil forest, Dew and the others arrive at the Aurora Blade hideout.
Dew.	Home sweet home.
Lorenzo.	Glad to be back here. I'm beat.
Rena.	So this is where you live now. A little shabby, but I guess it will do.
Cooper.	Just like you, Dew. You know how to pick 'em.
Paca.	Better than nothing.
Lorenzo.	Since we're all here now, it makes me wonder what Judge Clymer did to himself.
Paca.	That was too strange.
Cooper.	Why does this remind me of something?
Dew.	*It couldn't be . . . how can it?* No . . .

Rena.	Somebody please explain to me what is going on? I wasn't there at the time.
Cooper.	I don't know myself.
Rena.	Dew, do you know something about this?
Dew.	*SKT*. This is crazy.
Lorenzo.	Yo, Dew. Hey, are you listening? Dew . . . Dew, hello?
Dew.	Huh?
Rena.	Are you feeling all right, Dew?
Dew.	Nothing's wrong at all . . . nothing, yep.
Rena.	Something must be troubling you?
Dew.	I'm fine, it's nothing really. (*then walks off outside to the front porch*)
Cooper.	Something is bothering him.
Rena.	I wonder about.
Cooper.	Makes me wonder about something too.
Lorenzo.	What's that?
Cooper.	The thing with you, guys, . . . why are you doing all of this?
Lorenzo.	Why you ask? I suppose for the innocent . . . to preserve freedom as well. Myself personally, I have a personal reason why. It was twenty years ago. I lived at the time with my brother, Steve. He took me in after the death of our parents during the Great Liberation. He seemed more like a father than a brother. Our only means of survival on the streets were hustling and pick pocketing. It wasn't normal living, but we got by though. So one day, me and my brother were on one of our little missions. This day I remember the most, because this was the beginning of the rest of my life.
Narrator.	The scene changes to Lorenzo's past; Steve and Lorenzo are hiding in the bushes in the park, watching people passing by the bridge. They wait to rob their next victim.
Steve.	We've got to wait for the right moment.
Lorenzo.	I haven't eaten in days.
Steve.	Don't worry lil bro; we'll get some money soon. You all right?
Lorenzo.	I will be.
Narrator.	As they continue watching, a couple walks by.
Steve.	All right, here we go. Stay here.
Lorenzo.	I will. Be careful.
Narrator.	As the couple continues to walk, Steve lurks up behind them. He then snatches the woman's purse and runs off with it.

Woman.	Oh?! My purse.
Man.	You punk. Police! Police! Police!
Narrator.	As Steve runs off with the woman's purse, the man cries are heard by a SWAT trooper patrolling the area nearby.
SWAT trooper.	What's this? (*Then he sees Steve running.*) I see . . . this could be some fun.
Narrator.	The SWAT trooper begins his pursuit after Steve who is halfway across the bridge.
SWAT trooper.	*running after Steve.* Hey, you, stop! Stop dammit!
Steve.	*still running.* Shit!
Narrator.	The SWAT trooper continues after Steve and eventually catches up to him, tackling him down from behind to the ground.
SWAT trooper.	Are you deaf? Should have stopped. (*pinning him down*)
Steve.	*struggling.* Get the fuck off of me, you pompous pig! *Argh!*
SWAT trooper.	A rough one I see. Boy you just made my night. (*still holding him down*) You're going to go away for a while, boy.
Lorenzo.	*running towards them.* Steve!
Steve.	*still struggling with the SWAT trooper.* Lorenzo, get back!
SWAT trooper.	You might want to listen to him, little boy. (*turns his head to Lorenzo*)
Lorenzo.	No, get off of my brother! (*He runs toward the SWAT trooper and kicks him in his face.*)
SWAT trooper.	Urgh! (*He gets up and takes his night stick out. He whacks Lorenzo in the chest with it.*) Little punk!
Steve.	Fucker!
Narrator.	Steve rushes toward the SWAT trooper and jumps on him. They begin to grapple with one another. During the struggle, the SWAT trooper pulls out his hand gun and shoots Steve in the chest. Lorenzo gets up and runs over to Steve, who lies on the ground coughing up blood.
Lorenzo.	*checking on him.* Steve?!
Steve.	R-run.
Lorenzo.	No, I won't . . . I won't. Don't die.
Steve.	Sorry . . . lil bro . . . go . . . *ugh.*
Lorenzo.	Steve!
SWAT trooper.	Damn kid . . . he was foolish. That just to show you crime doesn't pay. Hah!
Lorenzo.	BASTARD!

Narrator. An enraged Lorenzo jumps onto the SWAT trooper and then bites his nose leaving a deep gash. The SWAT trooper throws Lorenzo off him down below into the lake under the bridge.

SWAT trooper. *feeling on his nose. Oooww* . . . damn gutter trash. (then walks off)

Narrator. Later on, we find Lorenzo floating in the water unconscious as it roams violently, carrying him to a landfill, washing him onto shore. A man who happens to be walking by observes this.

Aquagonla. What this?! Oh god (*He runs over to Lorenzo's aid. He then checks on his vitals.*) He needs medical treatment. Hold on, you, I'm here for you.

Lorenzo Narration. I was found unconscious lying in a heap of garbage after I had washed up on shore. The man that saved me, name was Aquagonla, a former instructor of kempo. He took me in; he taught me everything. After years of training, my skills had improved. I pushed myself to become better. I would never rest until he is dead. Yes, it was, Zircon Videl, he was that tyrant who took my brother's life. My lust for vengeances had grown too, all to repay the man who killed my brother. We had formed the group Aurora Blade. I found people to join who were tired of the unjustified laws and oppression they were suffering under. Years went on and my master was getting old and frail. I had returned to find him on his death bed. He called me over to his side before his . . . passing.

Lorenzo. Master, it hurts me to see you in this condition.

Aquagonla. Ha . . . this is the way of life. All things must eventually die.

Lorenzo. Master, stop talking like that. You'll be fine.

Aquagonla. You jest . . . it's all right though . . . it's my time to go. Don't fret it . . . you do have to remember to control your anger. Don't let it destroy you in the end.

Lorenzo. Aquagonla, I—

Aquagonla. Say no more. Remember my teachings, young man . . . never give up, fight for what you believe in . . . find your peace, and live in bliss.

Lorenzo. Yes, master, of course.

Aquagonla. Take care, my child. I will see you . . . in the afterlife . . . *ugh.*

Lorenzo *sighs.* Master.

Narrator. The scene switches back to the present time.

Lorenzo.	After my master's death, I kept my word to fight for the good and fight and not stop. I later met Dew after an encounter with some SWAT troopers. He was impressive with the way he fought. We crowned him leader of the gang later on. Stealing from the rich, giving to the poor, all that to be known as the Saviors of Helix.
Cooper.	Interesting.
Rena.	I wonder where did Dew go.
Paca.	He must be outside on the porch. He always goes out there to think when he is bothered by something.
Rena.	I'll go check on him then.
Narrator.	Rena then exits outside to the front porch to find Dew leaning against the railing thinking to himself.
Rena.	Dew, are you doing all right?
Dew.	*looking up at the midnight sky*. Rena . . . I'm fine. (*then turns to face Rena*) Why do you ask?
Rena.	What's really bothering you?
Dew.	Not a thing . . . I just needed to be alone for a moment.
Rena.	Okay, Dew. I'll be inside if you need me. (then exits)
Dew.	This night . . . it reminds me of . . .
Narrator.	Dew starts to daze off. The scene shifts to his home back in Twin Pines nine years ago.
Dew.	Grandpa, are you busy? (*He enters the room.*)
Grandpa.	*sitting down in a rocking chair as he is reading a book*. No, not at all. (*then puts the book down on his lap*) Come on over here with your grandfather. What's on your mind there?
Dew.	Oh, I wanted to see how you were doing. (*then sits down on the couch*)
Grandpa.	I'm all right. So, how do you feel about going into the service? You excited, I bet. You have grown up a lot.
Dew.	The years have gone by fast.
Grandpa.	You know, our whole family has been all about the military. It makes me happy to know you want to do this for yourself. Gain a new aspect on life, and it'll mature you more too. I'm proud of you, but are you ready for this?
Dew.	I have no doubts.
Grandpa.	You got your whole life ahead of you. Maybe after your enlistment, you can find a nice girl and settle down with. Good old living there.
Dew.	I don't know . . . I guess so.

Grandpa.	Well, you're not an ugly man; I don't know why you don't have a girlfriend now.
Dew.	It'll just complicate things right now.
Grandpa.	Sound like your father to me. He said the same thing and met your mother. I remember when I was in the military, it was good then. It should be good for you too. I know you will do all right.
Dew.	Grandpa, don't worry, I will be fine. I'll be back to see you again. I'll make you proud . . . I will.
Grandpa.	You always do. (*then he gets up to hug Dew*)
Narrator.	The scene shifts back to the present time. Dew notices Lynch running toward the hideout.
Dew.	Lynch.
Lynch.	Dew, I see you're all fine.
Dew.	Yes, we are. Where have you been this whole time?
Lynch.	I was coming to look for you, but I got chased off by those SWAT troopers.
Narrator.	Lorenzo then walks outside.
Lorenzo.	What's all the commotion out here? (*He looks at Lynch.*) Lynch, welcome back. Thanks for leaving us hanging back there, asshole!
Lynch.	I'm sorry.
Lorenzo.	Sorry are you? You're a sorry piece of—
Dew.	No more arguing. We're all tired, and we need some rest. It's been a long day as it is.
Lorenzo.	What about the mission tomorrow?
Dew.	We'll brief on that in the morning. I need to go for a walk. (*then walks off*)
Lynch.	What's wrong with him?
Lorenzo.	I could be asking you the same thing now.
Lynch.	I'm sorry, Lorenzo. I know I've been slipping up lately, but it won't happen again.
Lorenzo.	You're lucky Dew is so forgiving. Me personally, I'm not. (*then goes back inside the hideout*)
Narrator.	Paca walks outside to the porch.
Paca.	Lynch, you're back.
Lynch.	I'm glad you made it back safe. I'm so sorry I ran off like that, I didn't mean to.
Paca.	Forget about it. I'm happy you're back.
Lynch.	At least you're all right.

Paca.	We still have to talk.
Lynch.	We do. I wanted to ask you something. I've been meaning to ask you this for a while.
Paca.	Yes, Lynch?
Lynch.	I know I've been acting different lately, and I'm sorry for that.
Paca.	It's okay, I'm not worried about that. I need to tell you something first.
Lynch.	No . . . I need to tell you this. I mean, ever since I joined the Aurora Blade, we've been giving to the poor and all. Yet what have we gained out of this in return?
Paca.	What we've gained? Satisfaction of helping the less fortunate.
Lynch.	Paca, can't you see? We haven't done anything for ourselves. Day in and day out we help others, but what about us? I cannot do this forever. I want to provide a better living for us.
Paca.	Lynch, this is a good thing we are doing.
Lynch.	That's true, but we're not saviors. We're people, normal people like anyone else. Paca, I don't want my children growing up in this type of life style. We deserve much better than this. We deserve riches and better surroundings. I'm tired of being chased around like a rat. This place isn't a suitable living for anyone.
Paca.	What do you think we've been fighting for this whole time?
Lynch.	Is it getting us anywhere? Paca, I love you with all my heart. I don't think I can continue doing this.
Paca.	Is it me?
Lynch.	No. It's all the fighting for nothing. I just want a better life. I'm tired of all this fighting. Let's run away from it all.
Paca.	What about the others?
Lynch.	It seems selfish, but just me and you. Forget about all of them, this is about me and you.
Paca.	We can't leave them all like this. I'm sorry. My parents died fighting for a better world. Now I must do the same to complete their cause. I won't leave yet.
Lynch.	Dammit, Paca. We don't have to go through this. Why can't this be easy?
Paca.	It never is.
Lynch.	These people do not care if we live the next day or day after. As long as the cause is completed, that's all that matters to them. I won't do this any longer. I know where I stand, with you or not.
Paca.	How can you say such things? Is it that way now?

Lynch.	No, but you know you don't want to live this lifestyle either. I don't want to leave you; please don't make me do that. Paca . . .
Paca.	Lynch, I have something to tell you. I don't know how to say this.
Lynch.	What's wrong?
Paca.	Lynch . . . I'm . . . I'm pregnant.
Lynch.	What?! When did you find out about this?
Paca.	It was a week ago. I wanted to tell you sooner, but now was a good time.
Lynch.	I'm a father . . . Paca, I'm sorry for the way I've been acting. So sorry, baby. Forgive me.
Paca.	I love you, Lynch.
Lynch.	I love you too.
Narrator.	Paca and Lynch hug. Meanwhile Dew is walking along the beach shore alone. Rena then follows behind him.
Rena.	*running*. Dew.
Dew	*stops and turns around*. Rena.
Rena.	I see you're taking a walk now. You hold all those thoughts in without talking about it, you'll pop like a firecracker now. ha-ha-ha.
Dew.	I couldn't sleep just yet. Must be of all the excitement building up. This usually helps when I have a lot on mind, coming out here to the beach.
Rena.	Does it now?
Dew.	Yes. I listen to the waves crashing against the rocks and the humming of the ocean breeze. It's quite soothing, actually.
Rena.	It's so pretty out here. I haven't been out in nature like this for a while. (*then sits down on the sandy ground*) It's beautiful out here.
Dew.	It is. (*then sits down*) You all can stay here tonight with us. This place is safe. So many people come here for refuge and to help in our cause. They sacrifice their lives for us. I wonder why. Is it because of how corrupt society is? Or is it just to escape daily life? I care for these people, like if they were family. They're all outcasts like me. I get tired of fighting sometimes. When is enough, enough? Why do I continue to fight?
Rena.	Because you care.
Dew.	It's hard sometimes, but I manage though. How long will this all last?

Rena.	Dew, don't think so much about it. You are doing a good thing, and many people fight with you for the same thing. It's because it's right. No worries, friend. Things will be fine. I'm going to go back and join the others. (*then gets up on her feet*) Just get some sleep, okay? You'll feel better in the morning.
Dew.	I'll try. Thank you, Rena, for talking to me. It helped. Rena . . .
Rena.	Yes, Dew?
Dew.	I knew for some reason we would see one another again.
Rena.	I knew we would too. Six years is a long time . . . I guess we'll have a lot of catching up to do? We all learn a little more about one another every day . . . heh. Well, good night, Dew. See you in the morning. (*then walks off*)
Dew.	Good night to you, my dear Rena. Funny how this is all coming together. I would've never thought of such things . . . all in one day. Life is a trip . . . hah. What's next?
Narrator.	Dew then looks into the midnight sky, and then he dozes off into slumber. Once again the scene shifts back to Dew's past six years ago. The armored jeep makes its way up Mount Darien's pathway to the chemical facility. The armored jeep comes to a stop after reaching the midpoint of the mountain. The armored jeep door opens.
General Landmore.	*jumping out with rifle in hand.* Move out!
Thornton.	Party time. (*jumping out with rifle in hand*) This will be a good day.
Narrator.	Then the rest of the team follows behind General Landmore and Thornton as they venture through the massive jungle toward the chemical facility. Getting closer to their objective, a horde of sentries appear out of nowhere and begin firing on Dew and the rest, causing them to take cover behind the trees.
Thornton.	Damn . . . I thought these assholes were being kept distracted by our backup?
Hopkins.	I thought so as well. They've couldn't have made it past our men. It doesn't make sense.
Cooper.	Nothing ever does.
Dew.	This is fun. (*sarcastic tone*)
Thornton.	How long are we going to stay here in this one spot? We got to do something.
General Landmore.	Take cover. I doubt any of you want to get shot now. We don't know how many of them there are.

Thornton.　　The mission though . . .

General Landmore. Lay low.

Thornton.　　This is stupid . . .

Narrator.　　The guns continue blazing across the jungle terrain, hitting the tress as Dew and the other continue firing back at the sentry's.

Hopkins.　　I'm running out of ammo. (*reloading his rifle*)

General Landmore. This isn't going to be easy, I see.

Hopkins.　　Hey, Dew.

Dew.　　*shooting at the sentry's, then turns to Hopkins.* Yeah?

Hopkins.　　Remember when we were younger, when we were almost killed by that mountain lion?

Dew.　　Yeah. What about it?

Hopkins.　　You remember how scared we were?

Dew.　　Who could forget something like that? (*Then he quickly returns fire to the sentries*) What's your point?

Hopkins.　　I'm afraid more now at this point than at that moment. Glad your grandfather was there to save us.

Dew.　　Not here now though. I know what you mean.

Thornton.　　What a tragic childhood experience that was for the both of you. You sure do pick a fine time to share that with us when we're getting shot at. Could this get any better? (*sarcasm*)

General Landmore. Less talking, keep shooting!

Cooper.　　After this clip, I'll be out. (*reloading his rifle*) There's too many of them.

Thornton.　　So much for the backup. I had enough of this. (*then moves from behind the tree into the open*)

General Landmore. Thornton, what are you doing? Get back here! That's an order!

Thornton.　　Some orders have to be ignored and broken.

Cooper.　　Has he lost it?

Narrator.　　As Thornton runs right into the opening, the sentry's catch them in their sights and open fire on him. Thornton pulls out his long sword and deflects the bullets as he continues rushing toward them. The sentry's then drop their weapons to engage in close quarter combat with him. He kills a few of them as the others run off to retreat.

Thornton.　　Fools. You all can come out now. They're all gone.

Cooper.　　Aghast.

Hopkins.　　Impressive. Indeed it is.

General Landmore. Dammit, Sergeant! What the hell is wrong with you? Why did you not listen to me? You could have gotten us and yourself killed.

Thornton.   Well, we're all still alive, aren't we, General?

General Landmore. *Argh* . . . reckless. Disobey my orders again and see what happens.

Thornton.   There is no fate worse than death.

Dew.   You are insane.

Thornton.   Just be glad you're still alive, Wilder. Well, for now that is.

Dew.   Whatever . . .

General Landmore. We still have a mission to complete. Let's get going. (*then walks off*)

Narrator.   The men continue through the jungle and finally reach the chemical facility and enter the unguarded entrances with caution. Now inside the complex, Dew and the men continue to patrol the area. Cooper then begins to converse with Dew.

Cooper.   Dew.

Dew.   What's up?

Cooper.   *walking.* So is that true about what you were saying earlier about your grandfather? You know, about the whole thing with the mountain lion?

Dew.   *walking.* Yes.

Cooper.   Amazing. He must have been very important to you?

Dew.   He was. When he was younger, he was apart of the SWAT trooper elite as well.

Cooper.   He had to be trained pretty well to fend off a mountain lion. I know we sure didn't get that type of training.

Dew.   Yeah . . .

Cooper.   Did you ever see yourself doing this when you were younger?

Dew.   Not really.

Cooper.   *whispering to himself.* Reminds me of myself.

Dew.   Say something?

Cooper.   Just thinking aloud.

Dew.   Oh, so you have any family and friend waiting for you back home?

Cooper.   No one.

Dew.   Sorry.

Cooper.   It's all right.

Hopkins.   Dew.

Dew.   Yes? (turns his head to face Hopkins while walking)

Hopkins.   I wonder what Emily is doing right now.

Dew.   Thinking about you most likely.

Hopkins.   She's supposed to be getting married soon. I wish I could be there to watch her on that altar in her white wedding gown. I hope she's all right.

Dew.   She's doing better than us right now, I know that. She's a strong woman. She'll be fine. You'll see your sis soon. Hang in there, friend.

Hopkins.   You and her would have been a good couple together.

Dew.   Perhaps. I can't change that now. I'll accept love when it comes my way. Someday . . . all in due time, you know.

Hopkins.   No need to rush you. You're right. Thanks for the motivation as always.

Dew.   No problem.

General Landmore. *walking.* That's enough of the yapping. Don't get too comfortable; the mission isn't over yet.

Dew.   Yes, sir.

Narrator.   The team continues wandering through the faculty for a while. After some time, they reach the second-floor basement, coming to the SKT viral research lab being guarded by two sentries. Dew and the others take a peek from behind the corner of the wall.

Hopkins.   Sir, it looks like there are only two of them there.

General Landmore. Two? Something isn't right here. This is too easy . . . Stay alert.

Cooper.   So what's the plan to get past them? (then accidentally drops a rifle magazine) Shit!

Sentry 1.   What was that?!

Thornton.   Good job, idiot.

Sentry 2.   Go check it out.

General Landmore. Forget about this, the stealth mission is over. Let's take care of this quickly before anyone else comes.

Thornton.   Now you're talking, sir.

Narrator.   Dew and the others jump out to face the two sentries' . . .

Sentry 1.   Intruders!

Sentry 2.   These must be the guys who are here for the vial. (pulling out his rifle)

General Landmore. We're coming through. Get out of our way!

Dew.   Duty calls.

Thornton.   Move it or lose it; your choice.

Sentry 1.   Die, you dogs.

Narrator.   Dew and the soldier's battle the sentries, easily taking them out. Then they enter the dim-lit lab with caution as they armed themselves with their rifles.

Hopkins.   Kind of quiet in here, huh?

Thornton.   Too quiet.

General Landmore. Be ready for anything.

Narrator.   As they investigate the room, suddenly, a figure is seen running to the other side of the room.

Hopkins.   What was that?!

Cooper.   Something is over there.

Narrator.   The lights turn on, and the mysterious figure turns out to be Dr. Kenneth Voight, the creator of the SKT virus, with a gun in hand.

Voight.   So you're the fools they sent here to retrieve my work.

General Landmore. Dr. Voight, I presume?

Hopkins.   Dr. Voight, hand over the vial, and no one will get hurt.

Voight.   Hah! I won't. My precious lifework isn't going to waste.

General Landmore. I assure you, you won't get hurt. All we're here for is the vial. Just hand it over to us.

Voight.   You take me for a fool? That tyrant will not have this in his hands. You're right about one thing though. No one will get hurt, except you! (*Then he points the gun at Cooper.*) Ha-ha ha!

Narrator.   Dr. Voight is about to fire at Cooper until Dew quickly knocks down Cooper to the ground, nearly getting hit by the bullet. Thornton pulls out his long sword and has the tip of it pointed at Voight's jugular.

Voight.   ?!

Thornton.   That was a sorry attempt there. Give me a reason why I shouldn't end your life here now? I have no problem doing that. Try me.

Dew.   *getting up.* Cooper, you all right?

Cooper.   *getting up.* Yeah . . . that was close.

General Landmore. Thornton, what are you doing? This isn't apart of the mission. He lives.

Thornton.   Do you hear anything?

Voight.   If you're going to kill me, do it then. What's holding you back?

Thornton.   You must not care for your life.

General Landmore. Thornton, this is the last time I tell you this. Listen to me!

Voight.   Set me free.

Thornton.   As you wish.

General Landmore. Thornton, don't do it! That's an order.

Hopkins.   Thornton.

Narrator.   Thornton is about to strike down Voight until Elizabeth, Dr. Voight daughter, enters the room.

Elizabeth.   Stop! Don't kill my father. (*running over to Thornton*) Wait!

Thornton.   Huh?! (*He turns to face Elizabeth.*) W-who are you?

Elizabeth.   My name is Elizabeth. I'm his daughter. Please don't hurt him. There has to be a better way to resolve this.

Thornton.   There never is a better way. You wouldn't understand that. I have to do this.

Elizabeth.   *getting on her knees*. Please, I beg of you . . . spare his life. Take me if you must.

Voight.   Elizabeth, no!

Elizabeth.   Just don't kill him, sir.

Thornton.   He must mean a lot to you? Fine (*sheathes his sword*), I'll spare him. Now please, get off of your knees. There will be no bloodshed today. Not in front of a beautiful woman anyway.

Elizabeth   *rises*. Thank you. Father, give them the vial.

Voight.   If I do that—

Elizabeth.   Father, please.

Voight.   This is a mistake, but fine. (*then pulls out the SKT virus C vial from his front pocket*) Here, take it. (*giving it to Landmore*) You have what you want, now leave us alone.

General Landmore. Mission completed then. Men we're going back to camp now. Move out! (*Then he walks off.*)

Hopkins.   I'll never understand you, Sergeant. You disobey orders from our superiors, but you listen to a girl? Just when you think you know someone. (*walks off*)

Cooper.   Thanks, Dew. I thought I was a goner for a moment. I owe you one. (walking with a limp) Ouch!

Dew.   You, okay?

Cooper.   Yeah.

Narrator.   Cooper almost collapses to the floor until Dew catches him . . .

Dew.   Got ya.

Cooper.   I think I sprained my ankle. Argh . . . I can walk on my own.

Dew.   I doubt it. You're going to need help, I see. (*then puts Cooper's hand on his shoulder to help him walk*) Does this help?

Cooper.	Yeah . . . thanks, man. Looks like my leg is done for. I hope they send me home. You think they will?
Dew.	Probably. For your sake. That's a good thing.
Narrator.	As Dew and the others exit, Thornton turns around and glances at Elizabeth with fiery passion as she looks at him in bewilderment.
Thornton.	Such a strange feeling . . . What is this?
Hopkins.	Sergeant, come on. Hurry!
Thornton.	Hmmm. (*then walks off*)
Narrator.	Dew and the men exit the lab. The scene switches back to Tranquil forest as we find Dew lying in the sand asleep. A villager approaches Dew and wakes him up.
Villager.	Hey, Dew.
Dew.	*waking up*. Huh?
Villager.	The others were looking for you.
Dew.	*Mmm*, that was a nice nap. (*then yawns*) Thanks for waking me up.
Villager.	No problem. (*then walks off*)
Dew.	Another dream . . . I wonder why I've been having those dreams though. I've got to figure this out some other time.
Narrator.	After finishing up his thought, Dew walks back to his hideout to join the others. Dew enters to find Lorenzo, Lynch, and Paca waiting for him.
Lorenzo.	There you are. We got a little worried about you. Did you sleep well?
Dew.	I suppose . . . well we can start on the brief now.
Lynch.	No time like the present.
Cooper	*walks in*. Sounds interesting.
Rena.	Can we join in for this?
Dew.	Cooper, Rena?!
Lorenzo.	I don't think you coming along with us on this mission is such a good ideal.
Cooper.	You never know; you might need help.
Rena.	He's right. I mean we might as well. I can't go back to the school now after yesterday. Plus, I still owe Dew for saving my life back there.
Cooper.	We're fugitives now; let's share the glory.
Dew.	You, guys, are crazy, but are you sure you want to do this? It'll be dangerous.

Cooper.	Nothing new to me. You know that.
Rena.	I think we've made up our minds on this.
Dew.	I can't turn down good help. I think this can work out. Okay then, we'll be doing this all together.
Lorenzo.	If you say so.
Lynch.	I'll begin the brief then. (*then pulls out a blueprint*) I had some of our men do some intel a few months back on our next target. We'll be hitting up the foundation of the Helix capital treasury, which is the Videl National Mint. We had to take our time planning this out carefully. The security is extremely tight, and it's almost nearly impossible to enter the premises without security spotting you, so they say.
Lorenzo.	How will we get in?
Lynch.	After observing the place more from inside, our insertion point will be from the sewers.
Rena.	That brings back memories.
Lorenzo.	Why there? Wouldn't they have some kind of security posted there or at least traps of some sort?
Lynch.	There were, but we've taken care of that already. All parts of that section, security cameras and alarms, have been disabled. From there out, it should be easy.
Lorenzo.	Something doesn't seem right.
Dew.	Seems like a solid plan. I believe we can pull this off. Let's do this then.
Cooper.	Who's going then?
Dew.	It'll be me, Lorenzo, Rena, and Paca.
Lynch.	Dew, let's have Paca stay here.
Paca.	Huh?
Dew.	Why?
Lynch.	We don't need everyone coming with us for this mission.
Paca.	Lynch, its fine. I'll—
Lynch.	No, I need you here . . . I think someone at least needs to stay behind to watch over the base.
Dew.	All right.
Cooper.	I'll stay behind as well. I'll make sure everything stays in good condition.
Paca.	Cool with me then.
Dew.	Fine then. I guess we're all ready to go?
Rena.	I am.

Lorenzo.	Works for me.
Dew.	Come on, let's go.
Narrator.	Dew and the others exit; Paca stops Lynch before he leaves.
Paca.	Lynch, why didn't you want me to go? Do you think I'll slow you all down in my current condition?
Lynch.	Yes. I just want to make sure you and the baby stay safe and unharmed.
Paca.	Lynch, it's okay.
Lynch.	Listen, no matter what happens . . . remember this, I love you.
Paca.	I love you too, but why are you talking like this?
Lynch.	We'll have a better life soon.
Paca.	What do you mean by that?
Lynch.	I can't tell you that now. Please, just trust me on this. It's for the better.
Paca.	I trust you.
Lynch.	I have to go now; see you later. (*then kisses her and runs off*)
Paca.	Be careful!
Narrator.	Meanwhile at Videl Mansion Estate, Zircon is sitting in his chair at his desk thinking to himself. Peoria enters the room.
Peoria.	Sir, preparations for the raid is in progress.
Zircon.	Excellent. How are the bomber jets coming along?
Peoria.	They're being loaded up as we speak. All SWAT troopers are assembled and awaiting in position.
Zircon.	Update me when the trap is set up; then we shall deploy the troops.
Peoria.	Yes, sir.
Zircon.	Heh-heh-heh. Such a perfect plan . . . Soon enough, I will have it all.
Peoria.	Sir, they just got done with loading the ammo onboard the aircrafts (*listening to ear piece*). Now fueling is in progress.
Zircon.	How long will this take?
Peoria.	Twenty-two-minute standby.
Zircon.	That's fine. No rush yet. (*then smiles*) *Heh.*
Narrator.	Meanwhile, Dew and the others reach the underground entry point of Videl National Mint.
Dew.	Here at last.
Lynch.	This is it.
Lorenzo.	It looks like all the surveillance cameras and security personnel have been taken care of . . . hmm.

Lynch.	Can you believe it?
Lorenzo.	Something still doesn't seem right here.
Dew.	We're here now; let's just finish this.
Lorenzo.	Yeah.
Dew.	Rena, you okay?
Rena.	Yes, why wouldn't I be?
Dew.	Just concerned.
Rena.	I'm fine, but thank you though.
Lynch.	You all ready to go?
Dew.	Sure. Come one everyone, let's go.
Lorenzo.	Let's rock.
Narrator.	Dew and his team enter the mint. As they advance farther through the complex, they encounter a few guards on patrol, easily defeating them. Time passes and they finally reach the main vault area.
Lorenzo.	This place is like a maze. It took us long enough to get here.
Dew.	Why am I beginning to feel uneasy about this all of a sudden?
Rena.	Is this where they keep all the collected tax money at?
Dew.	Yes, every last cent is stored in that vault.
Lorenzo.	Well, let's get it open then.
Lynch.	I don't think it's going to happen.
Lorenzo.	Why's that?
Lynch.	I wasn't able to get any info on the vault code.
Dew.	Now you tell us this?
Lorenzo.	You never fail to amaze me. Well, how else are we going to crack this thing open now?
Lynch.	I didn't think we would make it this far. Hah.
Lorenzo.	What do you mean by that?
Lynch.	I have to admit something to you all. It's a secret though.
Dew.	Say what?
Narrator.	SWAT troopers then enter the room surrounding Dew and the others.
Lorenzo.	Ambush?!
Lynch.	Don't be so blind; this is all a set up. Can't you see that now, my friends?
Dew.	It's obviously clear now.
Rena.	They had trusted you. How could you?
Lynch.	They've trusted me too much. Ha-ha-ha.
Lorenzo.	You rat bastard!

Lynch.	It's true. It has been me all this time setting you all up. Dew, did you think that the bank heist we tried to pull off was really that easy? It was a perfect way to test to see how gullible you all were. The results as were expected. I didn't want it to all come down to this, but I was forced to make the right choice.
Dew.	Right choice?
Rena.	You must be doing this for the money?
Lynch.	That too, but it's deeper than that. Let me explain something, ever since I had joined the Aurora Blade, I wanted to make a difference. I wanted to help those who had needed help. Fight for the poor, rebel against the rich. This was the life I chose, such a noble thing to do. After day by day of fighting to liberate the people, I began to question myself, what do I get from this? I had no self-satisfaction, just disappointment. I looked at my surroundings and got sick of the never-ending cycle of fighting for a lost cause. I realized the things we were doing made us no better than the government we fought against. The only thing that kept me going was Paca. Her heart is so pure and kind; she keeps my mind sane. You, Dew, you are a scam artist, not a hero. Do you think I want her and my child to live this type of life?
Dew.	Child?
Lorenzo.	Paca is pregnant? Why didn't she tell us this?
Lynch.	She didn't want to slow you all down. You're all self-concerned, only caring about your own well-being. I want a normal life for us. We will have that soon enough. All this time I've wasted will be worth it, in the end. You have to admit, this plan went perfectly well to lure you all here, huh?
Dew.	Lure us?
Lynch.	As we speak, Governor Videl has ordered a full, wide assault on Tranquil forest. Then bomber jets will be deployed afterwards. Our great stronghold is going to be obliterated.
Lorenzo.	All because of you. Traitor!
Dew.	You've allowed thousands of innocent people to die today, just to get your due? Damn you, you coward! Paca will die too. You know that?
Lynch.	She'll be fine. She will be taken away to safety during the raid.
Lorenzo.	Is that your governor's promise?
Lynch.	He's promises are better than yours.

Dew.	You actually believe that he will do that? Lynch, I can't believe you.
Rena.	Desperate man . . . don't you have any guilt?
Lynch.	I do, and this hurts me to do this to you all. For Paca, I must do this though. Our future! I'm sorry this has to be this way, but it's time to look forward to a better life now. Farewell, my old friends. (*then exits*)
Narrator.	Now Dew and friends battle the SWAT troopers and dispose of them quickly.
Lorenzo.	Damn, Dew, we've got to get back to Tranquil forest. The others need our help.
Dew.	No kidding.
Rena.	I doubt standing around here dwelling on the thought is going to help.
Lorenzo.	I hope we make it back in time.
Dew.	No time to think about it now. Let's go.
Narrator.	Dew and friends then exit. Meanwhile, back at the Videl Mansion Estate . . .
Peoria.	All preparations for the attack are completed. Anytime when you are ready, sir.
Zircon.	Begin the attack.
Peoria.	Yes, sir (*then picks up the handheld radio and pushes a button*) All troops move out.
Narrator.	The SWAT troopers begin their movement toward Tranquil forest. A villager sits at the front gate of the village stronghold. The wind blows calmly, and the birds are chirping.
Villager.	Such a nice day. (*yawn*) Good day.
Narrator.	Suddenly the whole forest begins to get quiet.
Villager.	Huh? I wonder why it got all quiet all of a sudden.
Narrator.	As the villager looks over the front gate, all of a sudden a swarm of SWAT troopers appear, charging toward the stronghold.
Villager.	Oh, dear. (*then sounds a siren*) Man your arms! (*screaming*)
Narrator.	The villagers then scurry to arm themselves with weapons. Cooper and Paca step outside the hideout to see what all the noise is about.
Cooper.	What's going on?
Villager 3.	*running past Cooper*. The SWAT troopers are coming! We're being invaded!
Paca.	Lord no . . . Could it be . . . Lynch?

Narrator.	The SWAT troopers rush through the front gate of the village stronghold; then the villagers begin engaging them in battle. As the battle proceeds on, more SWAT troopers raid the village as the villagers desperately try to fight them off. The bullets blaze through the air piercing one another, violently knocking them down to the soil, painting it crimson red with blood. Cries of agony, the smell of sulfur in the air consumes the battlefield. As all this is happening, Dew and friends arrive outside the main gate of the stronghold.
Dew.	Dear god. It's already started.
Lorenzo.	Dew, we've got to hurry.
Dew.	You're right. I hope Cooper and Paca are okay. Let's go.
Narrator.	Dew and the others enter through the main gate and assist their comrades already engaged in battle. After a long period of fighting in the mist of chaos, Dew and the other run into Paca and the other villagers.
Lorenzo.	Paca.
Paca.	*waving to Lorenzo behind a wall.* Lorenzo, you, guys, over here!)
Narrator.	They run over to Paca.
Dew.	Are you all fine?
Paca.	*reloading her rifle.* Couldn't be better.
Villager 4.	I see you're all still alive. This has turned out to be a swell day.
Dew.	You can say that again.
Villager 5.	Damn. There are too many of them. (*reloading his rifle*)
Paca.	*shooting at a SWAT trooper, then ducks.* I'm about to run out of ammo in a moment. Dew, where's Lynch at? Is he all right?
Lorenzo.	Paca, he . . . I don't know how to say this. He . . .
Dew.	He is helping out the others. Don't worry, he's fine.
Rena.	?!
Dew.	Paca, get out of here with the others. We'll take care of this.
Paca.	Dew, you may need help.
Lorenzo.	Listen to the man. Please go!
Paca.	Okay.
Dew.	Rena, stay here and nurse the injured.
Rena.	Got ya.
Dew.	Lorenzo and I are heading to the watchtower to aid any survivors we find. Later. (*then runs off*)
Rena.	Be careful.

Paca.	We'll do our part too.
Narrator.	Dew and Lorenzo head toward the tower and encounter a few SWAT troopers on the way up to the top, easily defeating them. As they ascend farther up, they run into Cooper.
Cooper.	Dew, Lorenzo, I'm glad to see you again. Quite hectic here, huh? Reminds me of old times.
Dew.	It sure does. Cooper, we're heading up to see if there is anyone else that needs our assistance. Keep guard down here.
Cooper.	No problem. This is like the time when we went through Mount Darien.
Lorenzo.	Mount Darien?
Dew.	Come on, Lorenzo, we've got to go. Cooper, if anything happens that comes to worse, escape.
Cooper.	Yeah. Take care.
Narrator.	Dew and Lorenzo head farther up, reaching the top level of the tower. As they walk around they come across a corpse. Lorenzo goes over to the fallen watchtower guard to check on him.
Lorenzo.	*checking the watchtower guard's pulse.* Hmm, dead. Poor bastard. (*sigh*)
Dew.	No use being up here then. We should leave.
Narrator.	Suddenly a helicopter appears over the tower and begins to slowly lowering down. The helicopter speaker system then clicks on.
Zircon.	Very brave of you two gentlemen to venture up here. So at last I meet the trash that has been causing me so much trouble. *Tsk, tsk, tsk . . .* silly fools.
Lorenzo.	Zircon, you heartless creep. Call off the air raid!
Zircon.	I can't do that now. I see my puppet couldn't get the job done right. Well, it doesn't matter. You'll all die soon.
Dew.	You'll be murdering innocent people.
Zircon.	Innocent people? Ha-ha-ha. They're all guilty as you are. Society must have stability and order. The less of the masses, the better it is.
Lorenzo.	You ignorant fuck.
Zircon.	Enough chitchat. I'm a busy man. Enjoy the last moments of your lives. Peoria, go!
Narrator.	Peoria then jumps from the helicopter to the top of the watchtower.
Peoria.	It's nice to have finally met you all. So you're the vermin I'm about to exterminate.

Lorenzo.	You?! You have to be joking? Hah!
Peoria.	Death is a reward, honor it.
Lorenzo.	In your dreams, girly.
Peoria.	You are underestimating me. Ha-ha-ha. I shall pave the floor with your blood. Now you shall die!
Narrator.	The helicopter flies off.
Dew.	I guess she is serious.
Lorenzo.	I don't like chicks with attitude.
Narrator.	Dew and Lorenzo fight Peoria, who is armed with a baton, but they manage to defeat her. After the fight ends, the sound of missiles approaching the village is heard. Peoria manages to escape as Dew and Lorenzo flee to catch up with the others. Meanwhile, on the surface of the village, Rena assists the remaining villagers into the underground shelter under the entrance to the watchtower.
Rena.	Are you all right?
Villager 5.	Yes, thank you (*then enters into the underground shelter*)
Paca.	Lynch. (*then starts to run off*)
Rena.	Paca, where are you going?
Paca.	Rena, I have to go find Lynch.
Rena.	Paca, stop!
Paca.	I'm not leaving without him. Go, I'll be fine. Tell everyone, I'm sorry. (*then runs off into the battlefield*) LYNCH! (*shouting*)
Rena.	Paca, no.
Narrator.	Dew, Lorenzo, and Cooper enter the scene.
Dew.	Rena.
Rena.	Dew.
Dew.	Is everyone safe?
Rena.	Yes, but Paca ran off to look for Lynch. I tried stopping her.
Lorenzo.	Dammit! I've got to stop her. (*starts running toward the tower entrance*)
Dew.	Lorenzo, no. (*pulls on his arm*) The bombs.
Lorenzo.	I don't care about that!
Narrator.	As Lorenzo starts to head toward the tower entry, the door slams shut and automatically locks itself.
Lorenzo.	What?! (*Then he starts banging on the door trying to open it.*) Paca, don't do this. Paca, open the door. Paca, please.
Cooper.	Lorenzo, come on. Hurry!
Lorenzo.	No, I can't! Don't worry about me . . .

Narrator.	Dew pulls Lorenzo by his legs into the underground shelter, and then the hatch shuts. The missile then hits, disintegrating the forest to ash. As the forest is covered in a cloud of black smoke and flames, Zircon's helicopter flies back over the destroyed forest.
Zircon.	That takes care of that. Everything is going so well. Hmm, that young man, he looked familiar from somewhere.
Pilot.	Sir?
Zircon.	Oh, pilot . . . we may go now.
Pilot.	Yes, sir.
Narrator.	Then the helicopter flies off. Meanwhile, on the surface of the wrecked Tranquil forest, Dew and the others open up the hatch of the underground shelter, climbing up to the surface.
Dew.	Everyone all right?
Cooper.	I'm still alive and kicking.
Dew.	Rena, you good?
Rena.	Yes, thank you.
Lorenzo.	Why? (disbelief)
Dew.	What's wrong?
Lorenzo.	We should have been here sooner . . . damn!
Dew.	We tried our best.
Cooper.	There was nothing else we could do.
Rena.	Lorenzo, don't be so hard on yourself. At least we saved who we could.
Lorenzo.	We should have saved Paca. This is fucked up.
Dew.	Lorenzo, calm down. I'm sorry myself. I shouldn't have trusted Lynch like that.
Lorenzo.	It's too late for that now. It won't bring Paca or anyone else back. *Did it have to come to this*? That bastard killed my brother, and now friends. (sigh) NO MORE! Damn you . . . (*then punches the ground*) Zircon! (*Then falls to the ground and begins to cry*) NO MORE!
Dew.	We'll get him back for this.
Rena.	What are we going to do now?
Dew.	There's nothing left here now. We'll have to set camp elsewhere, until we figure this out. It wouldn't be a good idea to go back to the city right now.
Cooper.	That wouldn't be the smartest thing to do. No use staying here anymore.

Dew.	So it is happening again. This is personal now.
Narrator.	As Dew and the others begin to leave the destroyed forest behind them, heavy black smog covers the scenery. Two weeks pass. Our story shifts to Dew and friends, who have camp set up in the outskirts of Tranquil forest near a river bank. Since the incident, Lorenzo has begun drinking heavily. Dew and Rena start to worry about his current condition, and they decide to go check up on him, only to find him lying on a bed of branches surrounded by empty alcohol bottles as he chugs down one
Dew.	Lorenzo.
Lorenzo.	Huh? Who . . . who is that calling me? (*hiccup*)
Rena.	Lorenzo, it's us.
Lorenzo.	Dew, Rena is that . . . you? Ahh . . . come here, my friends, and . . . h-have a . . . drink with me. (*getting up*)
Rena.	No, thanks.
Dew.	Hey, Lorenzo.
Lorenzo.	That is my name. What, you don't think I know my own name? (*Hiccup*) Ha-ha-ha. You know what? There . . . is nothing better than . . . good old vintage alcohol to wash away . . . your problems! (*Burp*) Whew . . . that wreaks. (*Begins to staggers and falls towards Dew who catches him.*) Thanks friend, you're always . . . there for . . . me.
Dew.	Lorenzo, are you listening to me?
Lorenzo.	I hear you, loud and clear!
Dew.	I know it has been hard for you to get over what has happened as of late. Trust me; it has been hard for us all too. But drinking yourself to death isn't going to change a thing. C'mon man, we have to look pass this mess and move on forward.
Lorenzo.	It's a lovely day, don't you . . . think? Wait . . . I don't know. I can't tell. I'm so wasted. Heh-heh-heh.
Dew.	Damn, Lorenzo! Snap out of it already! This isn't like you.
Lorenzo.	Leave me alone. (*then pushes off of Dew and falls to the ground*) Can't you see I am hurting here? No . . . all you care about is your damn self. Selfish Dew always worried about his own well being.
Dew.	What?!
Lorenzo.	I failed to save Paca and the others because you had stopped me in doing . . . so. They're all dead . . . because of you!
Dew.	You fucking drunk! I can't believe you, how dare you say that?! You know there was nothing more we could have done to save

	her and the others. You have some nerve to blame me for all of this . . . Fine then, be that way. I know what I am going to do. I am going to take some action against the government.
Lorenzo.	All by yourself? Hah!
Dew.	If so, yes. I do have the others who will help me, and we will do it with out you. Screw this hiding out shit. You can stay here and drown yourself in alcohol and self pity. I could care less now. Rena, lets go, there is no need to talk to this person any longer. (*then walks off*)
Rena.	Dew, wait. Lorenzo, I know you didn't mean that.
Lorenzo.	Forget about him. He can go piss off. So . . . Rena, do you want a drink?
Rena.	No thank you. I must go after Dew now. Lorenzo, all I ask from you at this moment is to please come to your senses. Not for Dew and me, but for those who have died. Think about it (*then walks off*)
Lorenzo.	Bah! Who needs you? I don't need any of you. You hear me? None of you!
Rena	*runs over to Dew.* Dew, are you okay?
Dew.	I'm fine. Why wouldn't I be?
Rena.	Dew, you know he didn't mean what he said to you. He is obviously stressed out and down about what has happened. Don't take him seriously.
Dew.	Are you making excuses for him now? I am just as bothered about all this as he is. He had no right to lash out at me like that. I hope he does come to his senses soon. After his little comment, I should have been harder on him.
Rena.	Dew, stop. That's not the point. Don't get so angry at him.
Dew.	*Humph* . . . you're right. I should know better. I suppose I was wrong for losing my patience. It bothers me to see him like this, that's all.
Rena.	He'll come around sooner or later. Patience, my friend.
Dew.	Hmm . . . you're right.
Rena.	Let's leave him alone for now. I have a good feeling things will get better.
Narrator.	Dew and Rena exit. Lorenzo lies on the ground passed out and begins to dream of when he was younger training under his mentor, Aquagonla. The scene shifts to the beach shore area of Tranquil forest seventeen years ago, as a young Lorenzo walks up to Aquagonla, who is in an Indian stance meditating.

Lorenzo.	Hmm.
Aquagonla.	. . .
Lorenzo.	Master, what are you doing?
Aquagonla.	. . .
Lorenzo.	Are you sleeping? (*then tries to touch him on the shoulders*)
Aquagonla.	Don't . . . I'm meditating.
Lorenzo.	Oh. (*pulls his hand back*) For a minute there, I thought you were dead or something.
Aquagonla.	Don't be silly. (*still meditating*) So tell me, what do you want?
Lorenzo.	Nothing, master, I was just curious about what you were doing. That's all.
Aquagonla.	Young minds are always so curious. In time, age will change all that. Like they say, "Curiosity killed the cat." Hmm . . . I wonder. (*opens his eyes and looks and turns his head to face Lorenzo*) What are you curious about my young apprentice?
Lorenzo.	Well Master, since I have been here in your care for awhile. I have noticed that you know some martial arts. I like how it looks.
Aquagonla.	My kenpo?
Lorenzo.	Yes . . . I would like to learn that from you.
Aquagonla.	Heh-heh-heh.
Lorenzo.	What's so funny Master?
Aquagonla.	I thought I would never hear that again from someone else's mouth. Why would you want me to teach you? I'm curious.
Lorenzo.	I want to avenge my brother's death.
Aquagonla.	Ah, I see. At least you are honest about your intentions of wanting to learn from me. With that, I must decline your request.
Lorenzo.	Why?
Aquagonla.	If I were to teach you the skills that I know so you may avenge your brother's death; what makes me believe that you will not use these skills to harm others in the end?
Lorenzo.	I wouldn't do such a thing.
Aquagonla.	Hah! You say that now, but how do you know for sure? The anger that inhabits your body will eventually consume you turning into lust for power. I mean, if you want to do this out of retribution, you are no better than the man who murdered your brother.
Lorenzo.	I am sure that nothing like that will ever happen.
Aquagonla.	Learn this young pupil; fighting is not all about the glory of victory, or some thing as trivial as revenge. It is about protecting

the ones who are dear to you, yourself and the principles of life itself.

Lorenzo. I see. But I still beg you to train me in Kenpo. Give me your guidance and the discipline I need.

Aquagonla. Totally out of the question.

Lorenzo. Master, please!

Aquagonla. I don't know. You're too small, and your arms are puny. You might quit on me.

Lorenzo. No, I won't. I shall train my hardest. I will.

Aquagonla. Hmm . . . I see your determination. Not too many children at your age have that in them. Very well then, I shall train you. From me, you will learn to amplify your anger and use it in the purest form to fight against injustice. It won't be easy, but it will be worth it in the end. Remember this my young apprentice, when the times get hard, never quit. When the training is taking its toll on you, never quit. Never quit at any thing; because if you do, you are wasting your time pursuing whatever that purpose is in the first place. Do not forget these words . . .

Lorenzo. I won't forget, and thank you Master for this opportunity. I will not let you down.

Narrator. The scene shifts back to the present time. Lorenzo awakes out of his drunken stupor as he lies on the ground thinking to himself.

Lorenzo. Have I given up? How could I do such a thing? I've let myself and the others around me down. I will not stop here. (*then punches the ground and gets up on his feet*) I won't let myself fall into depression. I will keep fighting.

Dew. Lorenzo?!

Lorenzo. Dew.

Rena. He's awake.

Lorenzo. Dew, I wanted to tell you something.

Dew. What's that?

Lorenzo. I apologize to you for my behavior as of late and I am sorry.

Dew. I see.

Lorenzo. Yeah. I feel really terrible about everything, and I can only be angry at myself. I should have not lashed out at you Dew. That was wrong of me.

Dew. Lorenzo.

Lorenzo.	I am done regretting things and now it is time to move on from the past. We can from here work together and make things better than they are now. So Dew, you forgive me?
Dew.	I do, and I am sorry for getting angry at you.
Lorenzo.	Don't be, I deserved it. I needed to be reminded of my purpose in life. So, thanks.
Narrator.	Dew and Lorenzo then shake hands.
Rena.	Well it is good to see you two getting along again.
Cooper.	Yes it is.
Rena.	So, what happens from here?
Lorenzo.	Only one thing to do and that is to take action against the government.
Rena.	How will we do that?
Lorenzo.	I don't know, I haven't put much thought into that yet. But I will, soon.
Rena.	Oh.
Cooper.	Actually you guys, I have an idea.
Dew.	What's that?
Cooper.	While you all were hiding out here, I went back into town and heard word from the locals that the governor is going to throw a party at his mansion estate tomorrow night. That would be a good time to make our appearance then.
Rena.	That doesn't seem like the logical thing to do.
Cooper.	I am not finish explaining myself. When I was sent to do some cleaning at the prison before I ran into you all, I came across a stack of expired ID cards that happened to be tossed away in the trash. Instead of discarding them, I kept and used them as coasters at my house. In this situation, we can use the ID cards to get onto the mansion estate for tomorrow night's ball. The security personnel will probably do a scan on the cards to make sure they are valid once we arrive there.
Dew.	How can we use the card if they are expired?
Cooper.	Good question you ask, and now I will give you a simple answer. I had to modify the pictures and the expiration date on the ID cards so it would look more legible. So from there, we'll get inside the mansion and carry out our mission.
Dew.	Not a bad ideal, Cooper. Where did you learn how to do this?
Cooper.	It's just a few jack of the trades I picked up when I was in the military.

Dew.	I didn't learn that one. Ha-ha-ha
Lorenzo.	Hmm . . . sounds good to me. I wouldn't have thought that one up. Good thinking.
Cooper.	Thanks.
Lorenzo.	Well, no turning back now. We're all in this together, until the end.
Rena.	That thought never crossed my mind once.
Dew.	So tomorrow night it is then.
Lorenzo.	We all should get some rest then. I'll prepare our inventory then.
Dew.	Cooper, thanks for the info and your help. Glad you stuck around.
Cooper.	Anything for a friend.
Narrator.	Meanwhile, at Videl Mansion Estate . . .
Killbin.	Sir, the preparations for tomorrow night's ball is all set up.
Zircon.	Excellent to hear that. It will be a good festival then.
Killbin.	Yes it should be. Sir, may I ask you a question? This has been bothering me for quite some time.
Zircon.	Ask away my friend.
Killbin.	Does it bother you at all a bit that all those people died the way they did?
Zircon.	Heh-heh-heh. I don't seem to give it a second thought. You have to expect a few causalities when you're at war with terrorist. Now that the terrorist have been eliminated , it is time for peace and order to prevail again. It is sad that it had to come down to the way it did, but it was for the best of the nation.
Killbin.	For the best?
Peoria.	What's wrong, Killbin? Are you feeling guilty about all of this?
Killbin.	I think—
Schwartz.	Before you finish that thought, I have to ask how the security will be at the ball?
Zircon.	The security will be doubled for extra precaution. We don't need any gate crashers trying to get in.
Schwartz.	Outstanding. Well, at least we won't have to worry about the Aurora Blade crashing the party.
Zircon.	No need to worry about them anymore. Heh-heh-heh.
Narrator.	A SWAT trooper enters into the room.
SWAT trooper.	Excuse me, sir. I'm sorry to interrupt you, but you have a visitor.
Zircon.	Who is it?

SWAT trooper. It's, Mr. Lynch.

Zircon. Ah . . . well then, let him in.

SWAT trooper. Yes, sir. (*then exits*)

Narrator. The office door opens as Lynch barges in seething with anger.

Lynch. Zircon!

Zircon. Well, long time no see, Lynch. How are things?

Lynch. How are things?! If you only knew.

Zircon. I sense that you're angry. Come now, after all those riches I gave you, I thought you would be a happier man.

Lynch. DAMN YOU! (then *punches Zircon's desk*) You can take it all back. Those riches mean nothing to me anymore.

Zircon. Having a change of heart now? Heh.

Lynch. I have no heart no more.

Zircon. Inconsiderate of you. I kept my promise, and you got what you wanted.

Lynch. No, I didn't. My love of my life, who would have been the mother of my unborn child, are both dead. The deal was to make sure she would be kept safe. You broke our truce. I should have never trusted you.

Zircon. You have such nerve coming in here by giving me your sad story. We had tried to bring her back, but it was then already too late. I'm sorry for what had happened, but life does go on.

Lynch. You emotionless swine! I should kill you here! (*pulls out a knife*)

Narrator. The SWAT trooper enters the room.

SWAT trooper. *raises his rifle and points it at Lynch*. Drop the knife now!

Zircon. No harm done here. You may lower your weapon, SWAT trooper. I think Mr. Lynch was just about to leave. I would put that knife away if I were you. We don't need any more bloodshed now. I just had my carpet cleaned in here today.

Lynch. Argh . . . fine then. (*puts away his knife*) I may not be the man to make you suffer. But sooner or later, some one will. (*then exits*)

Zircon. Silly man . . . You may be excused, SWAT trooper.

SWAT trooper. Yes, sir. (*then exits*)

Peoria. Sir, do you want something done about Lynch?

Zircon. No. He's not of a major concern to me at the moment. However, he will be dealt with later. Hmm . . . for now, I would like to be alone in thought. You're all dismissed.

Schwartz. As you wish. (*then exits with Lynch and Killbin*)

Zircon.   Good times. It's nice to finally have everything going according to plan. Soon it will be time. *Hee-hee-hee.*
???.   *whispering.* Zircon.
Zircon.   Huh? Someone just call my name just now? Hmm . . . I must be hearing things.
???.   *whispering.* Zircon.
Zircon.   There it is again. Who is calling me? Answer me. Hello?
Narrator.   The room begins to fill up with smoke. Suddenly a figure appears.
???.   Long time no see, Zircon. Ha-ha-ha.
Zircon.   W-who's there?
???.   Ha-ha-ha. You don't remember me, after all these years? Shame on you.
Zircon.   Who are you? What do you want?
???.   I'm broken hearted; you don't remember the man you left for dead? The sins we commit.
Zircon.   The man I left to die? No . . . It couldn't be. How?
???.   I'm afraid so. Your time will be soon. I'm coming for you, dear brother. Judgment!
Zircon.   You're supposed to be dead . . . (*gulp*)
???.   Isn't that a bummer. Time for you to die! (*then approaches Zircon*)
Zircon.   Get away from me! No, Stay back!
             NOOOOOOOOOOOOOOOO!
Narrator.   A SWAT trooper busts into Zircon's office to find him curled up into a ball shaking in fear.
SWAT trooper. Sir?!
Zircon.   T-there was a man in my office trying to kill me.
SWAT trooper. *looking around.* There's no one here, sir. (*then lends Zircon his hand to get up on his feet*)
Zircon.   *getting up.* There was someone in here a moment ago. I'm not making this up.
SWAT trooper. It doesn't look like it was. Sir, whoever it was couldn't have gotten in here past me and security. Are you feeling all right, sir?
Zircon.   Strange . . . Perhaps I need some rest. It's been along day. I'm fine.
SWAT trooper. Do you need any further assistance, sir?
Zircon.   No, but thank you. You may go. No harm done.
SWAT trooper. Of course. (*then exits*)

Zircon.	I must be working too hard . . . silly imagination. ha-ha (*exhales deeply*)
Narrator.	Meanwhile, back at the riverbank near the destroyed Tranquil forest, Lorenzo is gazing into the moonlit sky. Dew walks up to him.
Dew.	I see you're still awake.
Lorenzo.	I am not tired yet. So came out here to do some thinking.
Dew.	Oh. (*then sits down next to Lorenzo*) What's on your mind there, friend?
Lorenzo.	A lot of stuff, and things I have noticed differently about you as of late.
Dew.	What's that?
Lorenzo.	You've changed a bit.
Dew.	I have changed? How so?
Lorenzo.	That woman, Rena. It seems you and her are close.
Dew.	Hah . . . she was a teacher of mine when I was younger. A very good friend too.
Lorenzo.	Is she? It seems more than that to me.
Dew.	No way. We're just friends, that's all. Do I make it seem like we're more than that?
Lorenzo.	No, but I notice how protective you are of her. I think it's cute . . . ha-ha-ha.
Dew.	I don't know what you're implying.
Lorenzo.	I'm saying it's cute. You have calmed down a lot since she has been with us.
Dew.	I guess a good friend will do that to you, eh?
Lorenzo.	A good friend . . . ha-ha-ha. I think it's time for me to hit the sack. Feeling that sleep coming over me. Well, I'll talk to you in the morning boss. Later. (*then gets up and walks off*)
Narrator.	As Lorenzo departs, Rena approaches Dew.
Dew.	What's he talking about? I'm still the same person.
Rena.	Dew.
Dew	*turns around to face Rena*. Rena.
Rena.	I see you're still up. Couldn't sleep?
Dew.	Nope.
Rena.	Must be the excitement, huh?
Dew.	I guess.
Rena.	I really don't get a chance to look up at the stars too often. Yet tonight, the stars are beautiful. Don't you think, Dew?

Dew.   I suppose.

Rena.   What's wrong?

Dew.   Nothing really. I'm just thinking of what tomorrow will bring us all.

Rena.   Don't think so hard about it. Don't want to strain your mind now.

Dew.   Rena, I need to ask you something.

Rena.   Go ahead.

Dew.   Have you ever thought of someone who you hold dear to your heart and would do anything for?

Rena.   Well, yes. A very long time ago that was.

Dew.   Have you ever come across a situation where you could never tell that person how you really feel for them, due to being just friends?

Rena.   Maybe I have. Dew, it sounds like this person is special to you.

Dew.   She is, but she may never know this.

Rena.   Oh, I see. Well, all I can tell you is give it time, and when the moment is right, let the lady know how you truly feel for her.

Dew.   I see . . .

Rena.   Hope this advice helps you out?

Dew.   It does and thank you for it.

Rena.   I'm going to get some rest now. Don't stay up too late now. Good night, Dew. (*then walks off*)

Dew.   Good night, Rena.

Narrator.   Rena then walks off, leaving Dew as he sits alone near the rumbling riverbank.

Dew.   Rest well, my dear Rena.

Narrator.   Then Dew picks up a pebble and begins to play around with it. He throws it into the river and then lies down looking up into the moonlit sky, slowly dazing as he falls into slumber. The scene shifts back to six years ago on Mount Darien. Six months have passed since Dew and the others retrieved the SKT virus vial. The soldiers have set up camp near Mount Darien, occupying the area after causing the New Havenport troops to retreat. A light breeze blows as Dew approaches General Landmore's tent and then enters.

Dew.   Sir, request permission to enter. (*saluting*)

General Landmore. Enter. (*He salutes back, and then Dew drops his salute.*) So what brings you here at this hour?

Dew.   I wanted to ask of something from you, sir.

General Landmore. Which is?

Dew. Have you heard anything about Cooper? Is he all right?

General Landmore. All that I've heard about the status on him is, he won't be coming back with us anytime soon. Lucky bastard. Seems like that sprained ankle of his turned out that he snap it out of place. Well, he's fine though.

Dew. I see.

General Landmore. You two have become good friends I've noticed. Well, at least you don't have to experience the death of a friend in front of your face. So how are you fairing?

Dew. Alive.

General Landmore. That's how I like to see it. You remind me of your grandfather.

Dew. I do?

General Landmore. Yes. He was a great person and soldier as well. He raised you well. Is that all you wanted?

Dew. Basically.

General Landmore. Before you go. Have you seen that sergeant of yours around lately?

Dew. No, sir.

General Landmore. He's been disappearing a lot and acting different. Hmm . . . Carry on.

Narrator. Dew exits the tent and then takes a stroll down the murky lakeside. Walking for a bit, he finds Thornton sitting on a tree stump thinking to himself as the water calmly flows down the stream. Dew approaches him.

Thornton. *has a rose peddle in his hand, looking at it.* Sweet loving woman, come to me again.

Dew. Sergeant. (*walking up*)

Thornton. *turns his head facing Dew.* Dew, how nice to see you.

Dew. So you've been here the whole time?

Thornton. Somewhat of it.

Dew. You know the general was looking for you?

Thornton. I'm pretty sure he was. I usually don't get a chance to talk to a lot of people. How about me and you talk for a bit?

Dew. You want to talk with me?

Thornton. Why wouldn't I? Just because I'm a man of war, that doesn't mean I can't socialize. Whatever differences we have on the battlefield, shouldn't stop us from talking to one another like gentlemen.

Dew.	I suppose so.
Thornton.	Let me ask you something, Dew.
Dew.	What is it?
Thornton.	Have you ever been in love?
Dew.	I guess so. Why?
Thornton.	I mean unconditional love—the type of love that you would do anything, well almost anything, for a person.
Dew.	I have.
Thornton.	All my life, the only thing I lived for was myself. I realized that there is always one person that makes another whole. I've never felt so alive, until now. It's a nice feeling.
Dew.	You met someone? Wait . . . it's that girl, the doctor's daughter, isn't?
Thornton.	Perhaps . . . curious I see. Well, Dew, at least you know I'm not a shallow jerk after all. Hah . . . (*getting up, and then starts walking off*) If any one ask, you didn't see me. (*then exits*)
Dew.	Hmm . . . love.
Narrator.	The scene changes to three nights later. Dew is standing watch, patrolling the area around the campsite, armed with an M4 assault rifle. Dew continues to walk around as another sentry passes him by. Dew takes a rest as he leans against the barracks wall. He puts his rifle down next to him and then looks at his wristwatch.
Dew.	Hmm . . . two hours left. Good. Damn my feet hurt. All this walking for nothing. I hope my watch relieve comes on time. That's all I need now, to be relieved late.
Narrator.	As Dew takes a breather, he happens to hear a woman's laughter coming from the woods. Dew picks up his rifle and goes to investigate it. As he walks farther into the woods, he sees Thornton and Elizabeth sitting near a pond holding hands. Dew hides in the bushes nearby and goes in for a closer view.
Elizabeth.	My beloved, it feels so good to see you again.
Thornton.	I'm glad you made it out tonight.
Elizabeth.	Me too.
Thornton.	How are you doing?
Elizabeth.	Better now that I'm with you.
Thornton.	Is that so? Ha-ha-ha. I feel the same way about you too. (*sigh*)
Elizabeth.	What's wrong?
Thornton.	It may have been just a few days ago we saw one another . . . I'm happy, so happy to see you again.

Elizabeth.	Are you?
Thornton.	Uh-huh.
Elizabeth.	Me too.
Narrator.	Thornton embraces Elizabeth as they begin to kiss one another. Thornton then pulls back as he stares into Elizabeth's eyes.
Elizabeth.	Gentle, loving man, with those passionate eyes you steal my heart and soul away.
Thornton.	I've completed my mission then. Yeah!
Elizabeth.	So true. I'm so happy that I was able to sneak out for you tonight, and every other night as well. I know we've only known one another for a while, but I have to tell you . . . I like being with you, Thornton.
Thornton.	I understand. I feel the same way.
Elizabeth.	There are things you should know about me . . . things we should talk about. I wonder if I told you about my past, would you accept me?
Thornton.	Elizabeth, it doesn't matter to me about your past. I only care about you and what we have now. This is all that matters.
Elizabeth.	We come from different worlds. We're on opposite sides in this war. I worry about you getting hurt; I don't want to lose you.
Thornton.	You won't.
Elizabeth.	Thornton, I . . .
Thornton.	I have to ask you something.
Elizabeth.	Yes?
Thornton.	I thought about this for a while. Ever since we met, you had made me so ever grateful for a lot of things and life as well. Maybe it fate and destiny for us to meet. I don't care about the war; I care about us. You've replaced that missing void in my heart with love.
Elizabeth.	Thornton . . .
Thornton.	Let's get married and run away from him. I'm tired of fighting. I want to live a normal life now, with you.
Elizabeth.	*giddy*. Do you mean all of this?
Thornton.	Yes, I do, with all my heart.
Elizabeth.	Won't they come looking for you if you run off? Are you sure you want that? My father will never approve of us and he won't stop until he finds me either.
Thornton.	I know it's all of a sudden, but I feel this is the right thing to do. Elizabeth, I want this. I love you!

Elizabeth.	Thornton, I love you too. Yes, I will marry you too. I can't say no to a wonderful man like you. I think of you every moment. When I stare into your eyes, I feel safe with you. You make me whole.
Thornton.	Make us one?
Elizabeth.	Yes, one.
Narrator.	Thornton and Elizabeth then kiss as the moonlight shines on them.
Thornton.	Always a wonderful feeling.
Elizabeth.	That was nice.
Narrator.	Thornton and Elizabeth stare into each others eyes for a moment.
Thornton.	Must be that time again?
Elizabeth.	I hate that I have to leave you now. (*sigh*) I wish I could stay with you. Always.
Thornton.	We will be together more soon, my love.
Elizabeth.	That sounds good. I must be going now. Take care, my love.
Narrator.	Thornton watches Elizabeth as she walks off into the forest. Thornton then walks off himself. After observing this, Dew then exits the area as a dark figure steps out the shadows. A week has passed by as the war continues to wage on. Dew is in his rack sleeping until he hears a loud rupture of noise coming from outside the barracks. Dew and Hopkins are waken up by the noise. They both get up to investigate it.
General Landmore.	Sergeant, answer me!
Thornton.	I have nothing to say to you, sir.
General Landmore.	Where have you been as of late?
Thornton.	Around here. (*then starts to walk away*)
General Landmore.	Don't walk away from me, dammit!
Thornton.	Hah!
Dew.	What's going on out here?
Guard.	Don't worry about it. Go back to your rack.
Hopkins.	Not as of yet.
General Landmore.	That wasn't a very good answer. You're not leaving here until you give me a real answer, Sergeant.
Thornton.	Don't worry about it.
General Landmore.	I guess you wouldn't want to tell me now? Not my business, especially when you're sleeping with the enemy.
Thornton.	?!

General Landmore. I know you've been seeing Dr. Voight's daughter, sneaking out at night and all. What have you told her?

Thornton.   I haven't told her anything of importance. How do you know about us?

General Landmore. I had some of the men follow you. You've been reckless. I wonder though how close you two have gotten.

Thornton.   It shouldn't matter to you.

General Landmore. It does when we're out here on the battlefield fighting. We're at war with these people for God's sake. I won't let you deceive yourself anymore or put us in jeopardy because of some girl.

Thornton.   Deceiving myself? No, we have all been deceived. No more lies; you and me know both why we are really here and the purpose of all of this. This war is a sham.

General Landmore. Insubordination.

Thornton.   Whatever. To hell with you. (*then starts walking off*)

General Landmore. If you walk off on us, we won't stop until we hunt you and her down. (*walking up on Thornton*) Traitor!

Narrator.   Landmore grabs Thornton's shoulder, but Thornton counter grapples him by twisting his hand, bringing him violently to the ground. The SWAT troopers in the area rush over to restrain Thornton as Dew and Hopkins watch in shock.

Dew.   Wait a sec.

Guard.   *stepping in front of Dew.* Stay back!

Dew.   Hey . . .

Hopkins.   Dew, don't. We can't do anything.

Dew.   Damn.

SWAT trooper. helping Landmore up. Sir, are you okay?

General Landmore. *getting up.* I'm fine.

Narrator.   The SWAT troopers restrain Thornton with handcuffs.

General Landmore. Don't you have some balls on you! Sergeant, you've done it now. That's an account of striking a high ranking officer and conspiring with the enemy. Your ass is going to court-martial for this. You will never see that woman again. I will make sure of that. You fucking piece of shit, you are going to get it good, NOW!

Thornton.   Ha-ha. Does that turn you on, Sir? I bet it does having me put away. It's fine though. Lock me up, but you will see how much your government really cares for you in the end. You're all just a bunch of pawns; you just don't know.

General Landmore. What?! You disgust me. Take this traitor away.

Narrator. The SWAT trooper then drags Thornton off to the brig.

General Landmore. Nothing left to see here. Return to your barracks.

Dew. Hmm . . .

Guard. You heard the general; that's an order!

Narrator. Dew and Hopkins then return inside the barracks. Meanwhile back at the chemical facility on Mount Darien. Elizabeth is attempting to sneak out until she is confronted by her father.

Voight. Elizabeth.

Elizabeth. Father?! (*turns to face Voight*)

Voight. Where are you going at this time of night?

Elizabeth. For some . . . fresh air. It got stuffy in here.

Voight. Really? You don't need to lie to me. I know what you have been up to as of late.

Elizabeth. I don't know what you mean?

Voight. You were with that soldier, weren't you?

Elizabeth. I don't know what you're talking about.

Voight. Don't lie to me.

Elizabeth. So if I am?

Voight. It matters a lot, actually. I didn't raise you to be gullible. Don't you understand we are at war with these people? He is the enemy.

Elizabeth. You're wrong, Papa. They're our country men; we're at war with our own government.

Voight. Confused child, don't you see they are the same as that governor? They serve under him; they aren't our country men.

Elizabeth. I don't care about none of that. I love him. He's different than they are.

Voight. You love him?! Ha-ha-ha.

Elizabeth. Why are you laughing?

Voight. I would have never thought that you would hurt yourself like this. The mere thought of you lying to me and with him sickens me.

Elizabeth. I'm happy for once in my life, and you don't see that. You kept me sheltered from the world all my life, from hurt, and finally, I see that you didn't do it for my safety, only your insecurities.

Voight. What? How dare you! I' am doing all this to prevent you from making a mistake. You're different form most people, and you know this. I won't allow you to deceive yourself due to you lusting over some man.

Elizabeth. Stop it! I love him, and he loves me. Why can't you see that?

Voight.	He's playing you like a fiddle.
Elizabeth.	You're wrong.
Voight.	I had enough of this. For what I am about to do is in your best interest. You're prohibited from ever seeing that man again. Do I make myself clear to you?
Elizabeth.	No, Father. I refuse to let you stand in the way of my happiness. I see now you don't really love me. You're selfish!
Voight.	WHAT?! (*then slaps her*) You said enough as it is. I—
Elizabeth.	How would you know what love is? All you do is stay here in this place and work. That's why Mom left you! All you loved was work, nothing more. You vulgar!
Narrator.	Elizabeth then runs out of the door crying down the mountain trail.
Voight.	*shouting*. Elizabeth, get back here! Elizabeth! Maybe she's right. Have I forgotten what it feels like to care?
Narrator.	Three days has passed by. Thornton is in confinement in a holding cell guarded by a sentry. Dew enters the brig and approaches Thornton's cell. Thornton stares ominously at Dew.
Guard.	What are you doing here?
Dew.	I'm visiting, obviously.
Guard.	We're you given permission to do so? The generals' orders were to have no one talking to this man. I'll be nice today though. You can go ahead.
Dew.	Yeah . . . (*then turns to Thornton*)
Thornton.	Oh, it's you. I would have never thought you of all people would come and see me.
Dew.	Sergeant.
Thornton.	What do you want?
Dew.	I just came by to see if you're all right.
Thornton.	Aww . . . I'm touched. Thanks for your concern though. Heh. So what's new out there?
Dew.	The same old, same old. The war so far has gotten pretty ugly. We've lost two hundred men in the last three days.
Thornton.	Let me guess, claymore mines?
Dew.	Yes.
Thornton.	Our modern day military with all their expertise and technology seems to be falling apart. Poor souls . . . Well, may they find peace in the end. Well, I'm alive and stuck in this dump. I consider them lucky in my book.

Dew.	The governor is making a visit here today. I don't know why, but we've been preparing for that as of late.
Thornton.	He's coming here, huh? Ha-ha-ha . . . I know why.
Dew.	What's going to happen to you?
Thornton.	They'll probably try to keep me locked up like some kind of animal. Typical of them wanting to keep the truth from getting out. Hah!
Dew.	Are you afraid you won't see Elizabeth again?
Thornton.	Ha-ha-ha . . . There is no fear in what is about to come. Soon enough, we'll be free.
Dew.	What are you talking about?
Thornton.	I wish to be left alone now. I have a lot to think about.
Dew.	Okay. If you need anything, I'll get it for you. (*then starts to walk off*)
Thornton.	Dew.
Dew.	Yes? (*turns around to face Thornton*)
Thornton.	Thanks.
Dew.	No problem. (*then exits*)
Narrator.	Thornton then sits on his cot in his cell pondering to himself. As he does this, he hears a faint whisper calling his name coming from outside the cell window.
Thornton.	Who's that?
Elizabeth.	*whispering*. Thornton, Thornton, it's me.
Thornton.	Elizabeth (*then runs over to the cell window*) . . . I'm glad to hear your voice again. I've missed you so much. How were you able to get into the camp site without being spotted? How did you know I was being kept here?
Elizabeth.	I was getting the feeling something was wrong when you didn't show up to meet. Then I overheard these two soldiers talking about you. I snuck into the camp wearing one of their uniforms.
Thornton.	How were you able to do that?
Elizabeth.	By chance, one of them were going for a swim. So he left his uniform unattended and I took it. Must have been luck. You all right?
Thornton.	I'm fine now since you're here. I'm stuck in this cell though.
Elizabeth.	Thornton, I've made a decision.
Thornton.	What's that?
Elizabeth.	I left my father's care. It's time to start my life over now . . . I want us together forever. Me and you.

Thornton.	Good. I need to get out of here though. I can't escape. That SWAT trooper is guarding this place well.
Elizabeth.	Hmm . . . Thornton, don't worry about it. I have an idea. Just sit tight. I'll be back. (*then runs off*)
Thornton.	Elizabeth, where are you going? Elizabeth—
Narrator.	The SWAT trooper enters the room.

Guard. Huh? Hey what are you doing?

Thornton	*turns his head to face the guard.* Just looking at some birds.
Guard.	Oh . . . well you better enjoy it while you can. I'm watching you. (*yawn*) It's time . . . for a well deserved . . . nap. (*then goes over to his chair and sits down*) Who knew how boring . . . these watches could . . . be? Zzzzzz.
Narrator.	Meanwhile, the troopers assemble for the arrival of Governor Videl. General Landmore lines up his men as a helicopter approaches.

General Landmore. Attention to quarters!

Narrator.	The men form into ranks as the helicopter lands. The helicopter door opens, and Zircon steps out onto the red carpet walkway being escorted by two SWAT troopers. They pass by the men lined up in ranks as they walk toward General Landmore.

General Landmore. *salutes Zircon.* Sir (*then drops his salute*), it's an honor having you here.

Zircon.	Long time no see, General. How's the war treating you and the men?

General Landmore. The men are tired, but we managed to stay collective. The morale seems to be moderate; we have had a few turncoats. They have been taken care of though. I have one person who may of be of some interest to you, sir. He's in the brig at the moment.

Zircon.	Perhaps later. How was the retrieval?

General Landmore. It went well, sir. Our best men accompanied by me pulled it off with a hitch. We've occupied most of northern New Havenport already. Their forces had taken out most of our air support, but the ground troops were able to prevent further advances of their forces.

Zircon.	Quite pleasing to hear, General. Let me see what I've come here for.

General Landmore. Yes, sir. (*walks up to a SWAT trooper*) SWAT trooper, go and get the vial from the armory.

SWAT trooper. Yes, sir. (*then walks off*)

General Landmore. *then turns to face Zircon.* Governor Videl, once this war is over we can restore Mesovilla back to the peace that once existed. At least we have the virus vial in good hands now, huh, sir?

Zircon. This is true. You and your men have done well. It's taken us a while to get this, but it was worth it.

General Landmore. I know what you mean, sir.

Narrator. Suddenly, a gun shot goes off coming from the brig area, causing everyone to duck for cover. Then a loud death cry is heard.

Zircon. Where did that come from?

General Landmore. It sounds like it came from the brig. SWAT trooper, let's go.

Narrator. General Landmore and the SWAT troopers enter the cell area to investigate the disturbance. They enter to find the dead corpses of the SWAT trooper guarding the cell that Thornton was in, which is now empty, and the body of the SWAT trooper who went to retrieve the container carrying the virus vial, which is missing as well.

SWAT trooper. *checking on the bodies.* They're dead.

SWAT trooper 1. It looks like the sergeant escaped, and the vial is gone. He must have taken it with him.

General Landmore. I can see that. *Urgh* . . . damn!

Zircon. *walking in.* What happened here?!

SWAT trooper 2. That bastard.

Hopkins. Good lord.

Zircon. General, where is the vial at? I want a good explanation for this.

General Landmore. It's, it's gone sir.

Zircon. Who took it?

General Landmore. Thornton.

Zircon. Him?! So it was him you were talking about earlier? I see . . . I want all of your men to search the area and find him. (*walking outside*) I'm not leaving here until I get that vial in my hands.

General Landmore. Yes, sir.

Dew. *walking up to Hopkins.* What's going on now?

Hopkins. The sergeant escaped and stole the virus vial.

Dew. What?

General Landmore. yelling. I want a search party assembled ASAP! Move it!

Dew. *So he escaped.*

Narrator. As the SWAT troopers all gather their weapons, Dew runs off into the forest up the trail of Mount Darien. An observing SWAT trooper notices this and calls this to Zircon's attention.

SWAT trooper 1. Sir, look. (*pointing at Dew as he is running off*)

Zircon. Where does he think he's going?

SWAT trooper 1. Should we follow him?

Zircon. Hmm . . . that's a good idea. I think I know where he's going. I want to take care of matters here first though.

Narrator. Later on, Dew reaches the chemical facility. He approaches it and comes across four SWAT troopers' corpses laid out on the ground.

Dew. Did they get here before me?

Narrator. With that thought, Dew enters the complex and quickly hurries to Voight's laboratory. He enters to find Dr. Voight lying in a puddle of his own blood. Dr. Voight's body trembles. Dew runs over to him.

Dew. Dr. Voight?!

Dr. Voight. Long time no see . . . SWAT trooper.

Dew. What happened here? Who did this to you? (*kneeling over to aid him*)

Dr. Voight. The SWAT troopers did this.

Dew. So it wasn't Thornton then?

Dr. Voight. No, he tried to save me . . . but my daughter's safety was more important.

Dew. You're dying.

Dr. Voight. We all do eventually. Listen to me; we don't have enough time left. I'll explain to you . . .

Dew. What is it?

Dr. Voight. Governor Videl, he is . . . using you all. The only reason why he wanted to retrieve the virus . . . is to misuse it against . . . the world. We were forced to create this thing . . . We had no intentions of ever using it on our own people. We'll be in dire peril if gets this in his possession. Do you see why we turned against him? He must not be allowed to get it . . .

Dew. I see now.

Dr. Voight. That cretin, he doesn't know himself. He's being played as a fool. Ha-ha-ha . . . Stop Governor Videl . . . It must be done. Forgive me, my love. I wish I would have left this a long time ago . . .

Dew. Who's being played as a fool? Your love? What do you mean?

Dr. Voight. Life is everlasting . . . live it . . . *ugh* . . .

Dew. Dr. Voight? (*then checks Dr. Voight's pulse*) Dead. Damn. I got to find the others.

Narrator.	Dew then exits to continue farther inside. Later on he runs into an injured Hopkins, who is leaning against a wall. Dew approaches him.
Dew.	Hopkins, I'm glad to see you.
Hopkins.	Dew . . . I'm glad we ran into each other . . . hah. (*then coughs up some blood*)
Dew.	Hopkins, you're—
Hopkins.	I know.
Dew.	Not you too. I should have been here sooner.
Hopkins.	I don't know what to tell you, but you should know this. Listen to me.
Dew.	Yes?
Hopkins.	After you ran off, Governor Videl had some of the men to follow you here. They knew you would lead them to the sergeant. They got here a little earlier than you. They found the sergeant, but I couldn't allow them to kill him. We fought them off. I got wounded though.
Dew.	Where are they?
Hopkins.	The sergeant and the woman escaped. I stayed here to give them enough time to flee.
Dew.	Hopkins.
Hopkins.	Do me a favor . . . When this is all over, go back home and take care of Emily for me. I hate breaking promises.
Dew.	Stop talking like that. You'll be fine.
Hopkins.	Tell Emily . . . I'm sorry . . . Dew, you got to live. E-Emily . . . ugh . . . (*then falls to the ground lifeless*)
Dew.	Hopkins . . . HOPKINS! No. I won't let you down . . . DAMMIT!
Narrator.	Dew heads for the roof of the chemical facility and finds Zircon and his escorts holding Elizabeth hostage as Thornton confronts him.
Thornton.	Let her go!
Zircon.	Funny how we meet again.
Thornton.	All that doesn't matter. Let her go I said.
Zircon.	So you finally fell for some girl. (*then sniffs at her hair*) She's pretty.
Thornton.	Damn you.
Zircon.	You tried to run off with my prize, but now I have yours. Maybe we can trade. What do you think?
Elizabeth.	Thornton, no. Forget about me.
Thornton.	I can't do that.

Zircon.   Love is such a weak emotion. Give me the SKT virus in exchange for your woman's life.

Elizabeth.   Don't do it. (*trying to struggle away from the SWAT trooper*)

Zircon.   What's it going to be?

Thornton.   Don't hurt her, or I promise you will suffer. (*takes the vial out of his pocket*) Here it is, as you want it.

Zircon.   Slide it to me.

Narrator.   Thornton slides the virus vial on the ground to Zircon. Zircon picks it up and holds it in his hand.

Zircon.   At last, you're finally in my hands. Thank you. Let the girl go.

Narrator.   The SWAT trooper then let's go of Elizabeth's arm. She runs over to Thornton.

Thornton.   You okay? (*hugging Elizabeth*)

Elizabeth.   Yes. (*hugging Thornton*)

Narrator.   A helicopter approaches out of the horizon.

Zircon.   My ride is here. We're all happy now. (*Then he starts to walk toward the helicopter as it descends to the rooftop of the facility. He then stops and turns around*) On second thought . . . (*then pulls out a handgun and points it at Thornton*) you make me sick!

Elizabeth.   Thornton, watch out! (*Then she pushes Thornton as Zircon pulls the trigger. The bullet hits her in the spine. She falls to the ground*) Oouff.

Thornton.   *getting up.* ELIZABETH! (*Then he runs over to her, kneels down and holds her head in his arms.*) Why?

Elizabeth.   I did it because I love you. (*then holds Thornton's hand*)

Thornton.   No . . . that bullet was meant for me, not you. No. I'm sorry . . .

Elizabeth.   No regrets, never. Life is too short . . . I at least met you. You were the only happiness I had in my life. Thornton . . .

Thornton.   Elizabeth?! (*holding on to her*)

Elizabeth.   I feel at ease now . . .

Thornton.   No, don't leave me now. I'm finally with my soul mate. I can't live without you.

Elizabeth.   Remember me, my love. We will always be one . . . I love you . . . ugh . . .

Thornton.   Elizabeth? (*then shakes her*) ELIZABETH! (*sobbing*)

Zircon.   Damn, I shot the wrong one. *Humph.*

Thornton.   (Rising up) You! (Then pulls out his long sword and rushes toward Zircon) *Arrrrgggghhhhh!*

Narrator.	Thornton stabs Zircon in his arm causing a deep gash. Zircon stumbles back screaming in pain. One of the SWAT troopers shoot Thornton with a rifle, causing him to fly off the rooftop to the water below.
Dew.	THORNTON! (*steps into the scene*)
Narrator.	Dew, out of anger, fights the SWAT troopers and dissembles them. Zircon gets up holding his arm in pain as he tries to stop the bleeding. Dew confronts him.
Dew.	Dog!
Zircon	*then looks in Dew's direction.* Oh, you again.
Dew.	Give me a reason why I shouldn't kill you.
Zircon.	You dare talk to me, your commander-in-chief like that. You have some spunk to question me. It doesn't matter now. Heh-heh-heh.
Dew.	I don't find this comical, Governor.
Zircon.	This is the funny part . . . I've ordered an air raid on this place. There will be nothing left of this place after the bombing. The question is, will you have enough time to kill me before the blast? Perhaps escape and fighting another day is the best option. I'm bleeding to death here, so it doesn't matter to me. What's it going to be?
Dew.	You'll be killing your own military units to, you know that?
Zircon.	Minor sacrifices are needed.
Dew.	You're abhorrent. Dr. Voight was right; all of this was to reach your own personal goals. All for that vial there.
Zircon.	Of course. When the opportunity calls, you got to take advantage of it. This is my property, no one else's.
Dew.	It figures. You political types are always trying to maintain your image and wanting more of this and that.
Zircon.	You must to stay on top. Before my time in office, there were worse than me that was running our government. I'm going to run this country to its true foundations based off of order and law.
Pilot.	Sir.
Zircon.	Yes?
Pilot.	The bomber jets are near; we should leave now.
Zircon.	I see, thank you. I must go now, but it was fun talking to you. Don't die now. Heh-heh-heh.
Narrator.	The pilot begins the helicopter and hovers over Zircon who grabs onto the ladder.
Zircon.	Sorry, maybe next time, kiddo . . . ha-ha-ha.

Narrator.	The helicopter then flies off. Dew quickly hurries to the escape pod room as the bomber jets approach the countryside. Dew finds the escape pod sub and escapes into the Mesovilla Ocean just as the bomber jets drop a nuke wiping all of New Havenport and its residents to ash. The scene shifts back to the present time the next night at the Videl Mansion Estate. All of Zircon's loyalists have shown up in the ball, and security is guarding the doorways checking ID cards. Dew and the others, in disguise, arrive on the scene. They approach the doorway.
Doorman.	IDs please.
Dew.	Here you are. (*going through his pockets and gives the ID cards to the doorman*)
Doorman.	Hmm. (*looking at all four ID cards*) Looks good to me. (*then hands Dew and the others their ID cards*) Enjoy your evening.
Narrator.	The doorman moves out of the way, allowing Dew and the others to enter. Once inside, they enter the huge mansion ballroom filled with Videl's government employee's drinking and chatting.
Rena.	This place is huge.
Cooper.	Makes you wonder where all that tax money goes toward.
Lorenzo.	Living the good life I see.
Cooper.	With all these people here, it'll seem impossible to find Governor Videl.
Rena.	What now?
Dew.	I think it's better we split up for now. Well, at least in two groups.
Lorenzo.	Good idea. Don't want to get lost or caught up in this place.
Cooper.	I guess it'll be me and Rena then?
Rena.	No complaints here.
Dew.	Works for me.
Rena.	We'll mingle in to get a better scope of things.
Dew.	Okay then. Later.
Narrator.	Rena and Cooper walk off into the crowd.
Dew.	Let's party.
Lorenzo.	Party you say? There will be fireworks tonight.
Dew.	Hah. C'mon, let's go.
Narrator.	Meanwhile, upstairs in Zircon's chamber, Zircon is getting ready. Peoria walks into his room.
Zircon.	Peoria?! (*turns around to face her*)
Peoria.	Sir, things are going well as planned.

Zircon.	That's good. Is everyone having a good time now?
Peoria.	Seems like it.
Zircon.	Has Lynch arrived yet?
Peoria.	We've seen him earlier.
Zircon.	Hah.
Peoria.	You want us to dispose of him?
Zircon.	He came in handy when it was needed. As of now, his services are no longer being required. So please see to it, that he is dealt with.
Peoria.	I've already taken the liberty of informing the men to take care of him once they see him.
Zircon.	You always think ahead. It's like you can read my mind. I like that.
Peoria.	*walking toward Zircon.* Great minds think alike. Anything for you (*then places her hand on Zircon chest*) . . . my governor.
Zircon.	Hmm . . . hah.
Peoria.	You're so hot . . . We're alone now.
Zircon.	I just put my clothes on. They can come off fast though. (*then wraps his arms around her waist*) Heh-heh-heh.
Peoria.	I like that (*then kisses Zircon*)
Narrator.	Meanwhile, Dew and Lorenzo continue wandering around the mansion. They exit into the Videl Garden.
Dew.	It seems as if he's not anywhere down here.
Lorenzo.	I guess we should check upstairs next.
Dew.	We'll have to sneak our way up there.
Lorenzo.	Sneaking around as usual.
Narrator.	Suddenly, they hear people arguing on the other side of the garden.
Dew.	What's that?
Lorenzo.	Let's go check it out.
Narrator.	Dew and Lorenzo walk over to investigate the disturbance. They come about as Lynch is exchanging words with Schwartz and two SWAT troopers.
Lynch.	I wish not to be bothered right now.
SWAT trooper 1.	So you don't want to cooperate with us? When the governor wants to see you, you will come.
Lynch.	He's no governor of mine. You're all sellouts. I no longer listen to spineless creatures such as yourselves.
SWAT trooper.	Insurbornate dog! Sir, let's kill him now.
Lynch.	Go figure, you're all the same. Use me, and then dispose of me when I no longer have a purpose.

Schwartz.	Don't take it personally. You did your job well; it's just all about maintaining a proper balance in our economy. Plus, the stunt you tried to pull on the governor yesterday didn't set well with him. It has to be this way.
Lynch.	To hell with you all and your balance. Come and kill me if you want. You'll regret it; I promise that.
SWAT trooper.	Shut up and die!
Narrator.	The SWAT troopers rush at Lynch, within a matter of seconds he lays them out. Schwartz tries to attack him from behind, but Lynch catches his arm and snaps it like a twig.
Schwartz.	*falling to the ground. Arrggh!*
Lynch.	I don't think you completed your objectives as planned. You should have thought more about it before you made your attacks on me. (*then looks over at the SWAT trooper writhing in pain*) I have nothing to lose anymore. You do though!
Narrator.	Lynch raises his foot and is about to stomp on the SWAT trooper's face. Then Dew and Lorenzo appear.
Dew.	Lynch.
Lynch	*lowers his foot down and turns his attention to Dew.* What?!
Schwartz.	W-what, you're still alive?!
Lynch.	Unexpected . . . I see the explosion didn't kill you after all.
Lorenzo.	It did Paca, you coward.
Lynch.	Don't speak of her name ever again. It wasn't supposed to be this way. I've lost everything meaningful to me . . .
Dew.	All because of your act of selfishness, so many are dead.
Lynch.	You don't think I'm sorry for what I have done? I lost my love because I sold my soul. I wanted the best for us, but I was deceived. Now nothing will change the past. I know one thing that will satisfy me.
Lorenzo.	What's that?
Lynch.	My death!
Narrator.	Lynch rushes at Dew and Lorenzo. They are reluctant to fight him at first. In the end, they have no choice but to do so. Dew and Lorenzo defeat Lynch. He staggers back falling to the ground.
Lynch.	Damn you two!
Dew.	Lynch, stop this.
Lorenzo.	There's no point of this, man. We may never have seen eye to eye on things, but we won't kill you.

Lynch.	Why? I deserve it.
Dew.	Listen. Your death will not bring back Paca or anyone else.
Lorenzo.	It's all in the past now.
Lynch.	Ah, that's nice to hear. (*getting up*) I'm sorry for what has happened. I wish I could turn back time . . . Paca was so beautiful . . . our child would have been lovely. Greed consumes us all. There's one thing left to do now. It hurts so much . . . it'll end . . .
Dew.	Hey.
Narrator.	Lynch then pulls out his combat knife and stabs himself in the chest; he drops on his knees.
Lorenzo.	Lynch, no! (*then runs over to him*)
Lynch.	Yes . . .
Lorenzo	*kneels down and hold Lynch.* Lynch, why? What were you thinking?
Lynch.	Like you, guys, said, all those who died won't come back if I died. So let me join them and my love then. Life got so hard after all that has happened; I rather end it this way now. At least I can kill myself knowing I can die having my free will . . . ha-ha. It makes me happy to have known you all lived . . . less guilt now. I appreciate it . . . you, guys, were like family to me. I have to join mine now. This tainted soul is cleansed. Paca, see you soon. We're not all for sale . . . we all can't be bought . . . we're priceless. That was my mistake. No more . . . (*then dies in Lorenzo's arms*)
Lorenzo.	No . . . not again. Lynch.
Dew	*sighs.*
Lorenzo.	Damn Zircon and his lies. Damn him! (*sigh*)
Schwartz.	Ha-ha-ha . . . stupid man.
Lorenzo.	What did you say?
Schwartz.	Anyone can be bought. He was . . . a fool, and died one.
Lorenzo.	I ought to—
Dew.	Lorenzo, he's not worth it. Let him go. We got to take care of other things.
Lorenzo.	You're right . . . I'll take care of you next time.
Schwartz.	I'm sure of it . . . Hah! (*then passes out*)
Narrator.	Dew and Lorenzo walk off. After returning back to the ballroom, they run into Cooper and Rena . . .
Rena.	Any luck on finding Zircon yet?
Lorenzo.	Nope.

Cooper.	We couldn't find him either. I suppose he's not down on any of these levels.
Dew.	We were saying the same thing.
Rena.	You, guys, run into any problems?
Lorenzo.	Lynch.
Rena.	Really? What happened?
Lorenzo.	He went to join Paca.
Rena.	Oh, I see. Was it worth killing him?
Dew.	He killed himself . . . He couldn't bare with the fact of life without her. It's difficult to speak about. I . . .
Rena.	I understand, Dew.
Lorenzo	*sighs*. Into the waves.
Cooper.	Are you all right?
Lorenzo.	I will be.
Announcement Speaker.	All gather front and center. Governor Videl will be making his speech in five minutes. That is all.
Lorenzo.	Now's our chance.
Dew.	Lorenzo, don't start nothing just yet. Let's save the ruckus until the time is right.
Rena.	Please do.
Lorenzo.	I know, I know. I won't.
Cooper.	C'mon, let's go.
Narrator.	They follow the crowd who are all gathered up near the staging area. Seconds later, Peoria comes up on stage and grabs the microphone from the stand.
Peoria.	Ladies and gentlemen, please welcome our governor of Mesovilla, the Honorable Zircon Videl.
Narrator.	The crowd cheers and applauses Zircon as he waves to them and walks toward the microphone stand. He then takes the microphone from Peoria and the crowd quiets down.
Zircon.	Thank you. Thank you all. I am at lost for words here . . . this is quite an emotional moment in our history tonight. I must start off by expressing my gratitude to you all. I thank you all from the bottom of my heart for making this moment possible. I am very appreciative that each and everyone of you had helped in aiding your government on the war against terrorism. If it wasn't for you outstanding citizens of Helix and the people who work to serve and protect our streets; we may not have won this fight. Many lives of those who we had held dear to our hearts in this

	war were lost. But their deaths will not be in vain; because in the end, we have won this thing.
Narrator.	The crowd applauds him.
Lorenzo.	They're so misled. Like sheep led to slaughter.
Zircon.	This is not just a celebration of ending the reign of a disease that was affecting our society. This is my appreciation from me to you, my loyalists.
Narrator.	The crowd applauds him.
Dew.	Appreciation, hah.
Rena.	The masses love to hear only what they want to believe.
Cooper.	Easily influenced.
Zircon.	With this new turn in our society; we will no longer be vulnerable to attacks or living in fear due to the actions of cowards. We will now grow stronger and flourish into a safer and more secure nation. This my people, I promise to you all!
Narrator.	The crowd begins to chant Zircon's name as he smiles. A SWAT trooper then approaches Zircon.
SWAT trooper.	*whispering.* Governor Videl.
Zircon	*turns around.* What do you want?
SWAT trooper.	I have to inform you, sir, of something. This is of importance.
Zircon.	This better be good, I'm in the middle of my speech here.
SWAT trooper.	Lynch is dead, sir.
Zircon.	That's it? Well, good then.
SWAT trooper.	That's not all. Our men were taken out by some intruders that got in.
Zircon.	Intruders?
SWAT trooper.	We're not sure who did this, but it may be the Aurora Blade.
Zircon.	How the?! Find them and take them out *now*.
SWAT trooper.	Immediately, sir. (*then walks off*)
Peoria.	What's wrong?
Zircon.	They're here.
Peoria.	Who?
Zircon.	The Aurora Blade. I want this all secure now. I'm going . . .
Cooper.	He looks bothered by something.
Dew.	He knows we're here.
Lorenzo.	Good. The fun begins now.
Narrator.	Peoria takes the microphone from Zircon as he walks off in a hurry.
Peoria.	Ladies and gentlemen, the governor is feeling quite ill at the moment, so we're going to wrap this ball a little early tonight. If

you all could kindly exit the premises at once. Sorry, folks. Do have a good night. (*Then drops the microphone. She turns to the SWAT trooper*) You, let's go.

Narrator. All the people start gathering their stuff as they exit. With all the people gone, the exits were all locked down, leaving Dew and the others in the empty ball room.

Cooper. Some party this was.

Lorenzo. This is it. (*then begins to run off*)

Rena. Lorenzo, where you going?

Lorenzo. I have to take care of something alone. Let me be. (*then runs off*)

Cooper. Fine time to leave now.

Dew. Damn.

SWAT trooper. *walking into the room along with nine other SWAT troopers.* It was only a matter of time before you street scum had to show up. This time there is no escape.

Dew. Running away is something we don't do. Why don't you make it easy on yourselves and run?

SWAT trooper. Ha-ha-ha . . . We'll see about that.

Dew. You were warned.

Narrator. Dew, Rena, and Cooper battle the SWAT troopers, defeating them quickly.

SWAT trooper. D-damn you . . . *ugh* . . . (*then falls to the ground*)

Rena. I still got it.

Cooper. Too easy.

Dew. Lorenzo . . . (*then starts to run off*)

Rena. Dew, where are you going now?

Dew. Rena, you and Cooper stay here. I've got business to take care of myself. Later. (*running off*)

Rena. Always in a rush.

Cooper. We should follow him.

Rena. I agree. Let's go.

Narrator. Lorenzo continues his pursuit of Zircon, encountering a few SWAT troopers on the way, easily defeating them. Lorenzo finally reaches the rooftop of Videl Mansion and confronts Zircon.

Lorenzo. Zircon!

Zircon *turns around.* Oh, it's the street rat again. Peoria, deal with this.

Peoria. With pleasure, sir. (*then turns to Lorenzo*) I owe you one from last time.

Lorenzo. I have no problems with you. So get out of my way.

Peoria.	Ha-ha . . . I can't do that now. I wouldn't be doing my job now.
Lorenzo.	I guess you didn't learn from the last time.
Peoria.	If you want to get past me, then you'll have to remove me from your path.
Lorenzo.	It's like that? All right, chica, have it your way.
Peoria.	You'll regret this.
Lorenzo.	No regrets here, that died along time ago.
Peoria.	As you should have, like you will now!
Narrator.	Lorenzo battles Peoria and the SWAT trooper alone. He is able to finish them off. After that, Lorenzo then turns his attention to Zircon. Dew reaches the rooftop at this moment.
Lorenzo.	Some people never learn, until the end.
Dew.	Lorenzo, you all right?
Lorenzo.	I'm good.
Zircon.	*clapping*. Now that was impressive. Hah!
Lorenzo.	It's been a long time; finally I'll have my revenge. You murdered my brother so carelessly. Now you will pay.
Zircon.	I did? I've killed so many. After a while it's hard to remember their faces.
Lorenzo.	People like you are the ruin of this nation. Just because you have money, you think you can do as you please. Everyone is equal; no one person is special. We're all human, but we let things such as power and material possessions corrupt us.
Zircon.	How touching to hear that. As if I care to though.
Dew.	I've got you cornered again.
Zircon.	Again? Do I know you too?
Lorenzo.	Dew, what are you talking about?
Dew.	You'll know now. Let me refresh your memory governor. During the Great Civil war, I was once a member of the SWAT trooper elite attached to New Havenport. You had killed my friends and many other innocent people in a nuclear blast. All this to maintain your public image and what really happened there. A certain vial we retrieved . . . Do you remember me now?
Zircon.	Ha-ha-ha. It's coming back to me now. So it was you six years ago that confronted me in New Havenport. Let me guess . . . (*then feels on his scar on his nose*) You were the brat brother who was a pickpocket. You did this to me. It all makes sense now . . . I admit. I killed your brother not out of racism, but it was because I had the power to do so. It's easy to have no

	remorse for people like you. We must rid ourselves of the poor and weak. They are the loose wheel that deprives society of its stability.
Lorenzo.	Who the hell put you in charge of judging that?
Zircon.	The people of course. Blind fools. They don't realize how much freedom they have until they abuse it. I decide what is right and wrong.
Dew.	Get over yourself! You're not God.
Zircon.	True, but the people listen to me though. Things are in order, and it's best that way.
Dew.	Only because of fear, and they are forced to do so.
Zircon.	Like I said, the people obviously know what's best for them. Ha-ha-ha, you both came all this way, fueled by hatred and vengeance to kill me. Look at you two; you're no better than I am. Oh well, I have this! (*then pulls out the SKT virus C vial*) With this, the world is mine.
Dew.	SKT?!
Zircon.	I was able to preserve it for all these years. Soon a new era will begin. Once this virus is unleashed, I shall have complete control over all.
Dew.	I won't allow that to happen.
Lorenzo.	What the hell are you babbling about?
Dew.	I'll explain all this to you later, Lorenzo. It's a long story.
Zircon.	Indeed it is.
Dew.	How could you have the remaining vial if judge Clymer used it on himself?
Zircon.	I gave him a derivative of the SKT virus. When Thornton handed over the virus to me four years ago, there was a written formula contained on the vial. I had my scientist to recreate duplicates. They weren't able to though. I still don't understand why it didn't work, so they created an alternative version of it off of the original samples. So I see that Judge Clymer wasn't so lucky due to it.
Lorenzo.	Too bad.
Zircon.	All the creatures that are roaming around Helix and the rest of Mesovilla are products of the SKT virus. Even my sewerage leech you killed was a product of the toxin. When the derivatives were completed, it seemed as if there was no control over the subjects. There has to be a way.
Dew.	That explains the increase of mutated wildlife as of late.

Zircon.   Mutation is the key to evolution. Soon I shall hold sway over all.

Lorenzo.   Haven't you ruined enough lives already?

Zircon.   You see, to have a perfect society, you need control. This virus will provide that. I will be the father to a new generation of loyal mutated subjects.

Dew.   If that's true, why do you think you can control them? You said it yourself there's a flaw to this virus.

Lorenzo.   You can't control people like that. As humans we have rights and do as we please. We aren't slaves under one ruler; that's what we fight against. We fight for truth, justice, equality, liberty, love, and hope. We are freedom fighters to make a better world than what it is now.

Zircon.   Truth? Justice? Love? All of these are nothing but illusions. Do you know what it was like during the old days? People ran rampant disobeying laws and causing havoc. No order, nothing but pure destruction. The people of those days had it made. Yet they abused their rights to the point where they no longer deserved it. That is why we are under the government rule we have today. If it wasn't for martial law, there would be no order.

Dew.   Some points you make are true. You have no right though to make people's lives miserable for your own personal gain. You can have law and order with the essences of freedom still. It's a proper balance and a fair government as well.

Zircon.   It's too late for that. You two think you can stop me?

Lorenzo.   Believe you me, I will.

Zircon.   Heh . . . It's déjà vu all over again. This time, though, is a little different. No running away now. My dream will become a reality. To hell with individual freedom. The past won't repeat itself. Enough talk . . . (then injects himself with the SKT virus C vial, then slowly begins to mutate into a giant falcon-serpent) Ha-ha-ha. Behold the power I have. All shall glimpse at me. All will . . . kneel before me! Muahaha-ha-ha! You two will be the first to die!

Narrator. Dew and Lorenzo then battle the mutated Zircon. It's a grueling battle. In the end they manage to defeat him. Zircon collapses to the ground.

Lorenzo.   I did it. It's over now. Rest in peace, Steve.

Dew.	That's the end of that.
Narrator.	Dew and Lorenzo begin to walk away from the slain mutated Zircon. The mutated Zircon rises up and is about to swallow them whole as he stalks them from behind. Suddenly, the mutated Zircon head is sliced off in a flash by a mysterious force.
Lorenzo	*turns around.* What the hell?!
Dew.	What's this? *(turns around)*
Narrator.	Dew and Lorenzo run back over to the slain mutated Zircon and confronts a man hiding in the shadows with a long sword in hand. At this moment, Rena and Cooper arrive.
Rena.	Dew.
Dew.	Rena.
Rena.	Whoa, what happened here?
Lorenzo.	I couldn't tell you.
Cooper.	Impressive. The head was cut clean off. This type of execution looks familiar.
Dew.	Who are you?
???.	Ha-ha-ha. After all this time you can't remember who I am?
Cooper.	That voice . . .
Dew.	It couldn't be.
Rena.	Dew, you know him?
Thornton.	*stepping out into the light.* That's right, it's me, Thornton. You remember me now?
Dew.	Sergeant, you're supposed to be dead!
Thornton.	Death would be a reward after all my misery. Time has changed I see. Yet it's perfect for it to begin now.
Dew.	What are you doing here?
Thornton.	I came for what obtains life to nothingness . . . that one elixir of life. *(then he bends down to pick up the remaining sample of the SKT virus C vial from Zircon's slain mutated body)* Thank you, dear brother.
Dew.	Brother?
Thornton.	I never did tell you that I and Zircon were family.
Cooper.	This is a surprise to me.
Thornton.	I see you're still in good health.
Cooper.	What can I say? It could be worse. You seem like you haven't changed a bit.
Thornton.	I've got what I came for, but where are the other three toxins at?

Dew.   There are three more of those?

Thornton.   Yes, but I will soon have all of them. The SKT virus C, G, T, and A will be mine. So now, it must begin. Now it is time.

Dew.   What's your purpose?

Thornton.   Soon the rebirth of the angel will begin. All will suffer the imaginable. "Ring a ring o'roses, a pocket full of poises. Ah-tishoo! Ah-tishoo! We all fall down."

Dew.   What are you talking about?

Thornton.   To find the answer to your question, follow me on a journey. Soon the rebirth will begin. All of you will see . . . paradise is upon us. Ha-ha-ha. (*walking off*)

Rena.   Rebirth?

Dew.   What do you mean? Thornton, wait!

Narrator.   Thornton then disappears into a cloud of mist.

Chapter 2

The Journey

Narrator.	Our chapter begins as Dew prepares to depart onto a cruise ship from Helix harbor. Killbin approaches Dew,
Killbin.	Dew.
Dew.	I didn't expect to see you here. Have you come to see me off? I really don't need a going-away party.
Killbin.	Funny. I'm glad you haven't left though. I need a favor from you.
Dew.	A favor?
Killbin.	It's more of an errand. (*then pulls an envelope out of his pocket*) I need you to give this letter to the alderman in Llivisaca since you're going in that direction.
Dew.	Why?
Killbin.	Since Zircon is dead and no longer in control, I've taken his role as the newly appointed governor of Mesovilla. With that, this country can finally be united again. So, I need you to give this letter to him. It will explain everything to him. (*handing Dew the letter*)
Dew.	What, can't e-mail him the good news?
Killbin.	When Zircon was in office, he cut off all outside communications to the other provinces that were against the Helix capital in the civil war. With this letter getting to the alderman, we can set all connections to that province up again.
Dew.	So you want me to do this for you, huh?
Killbin.	Will you?
Dew.	Sure. (*then takes the letter*)
Killbin.	Things will be different now that I'm in charge.

Dew. How so?

Killbin. You don't trust me? I can see why. I mean, I was once Zircon's loyal advisor. I promise that justice and tranquility will roam throughout Mesovilla once more.

Dew. That would be nice. It's that broken politicians promise though.

Killbin. You'll just have to have faith in me and let time show you. Dew, I have but one more favor to ask of you.

Dew. You want me to walk the dog too? (*sarcastic*)

Killbin. No. I do ask of you this. Whatever it takes, please stop Thornton Videl.

Dew. That I will do. I can promise you that.

Narrator. Killbin nods his head in approval to Dew, and then walks off down the pier to his limo. He gets inside and then drives off.

Rena. (Shouting) Dew!

Dew. *then turns to face Rena.* Rena?!

Rena. *walking up.* Still here.

Dew. *just like before.* I'm glad you came.

Rena. Me too. Where are you off to?

Dew. I have to find Thornton.

Rena. Zircon is dead now, so it's over.

Dew. That maybe true, but it's only the beginning for me.

Lorenzo. *walking up.* He's right.

Dew. Lorenzo.

Lorenzo. I couldn't let you go until I seen you.

Dew. I got a problem to deal with. I'm going to find Thornton and put a stop to his plans of finding those vials.

Lorenzo. I've been thinking about that myself recently. Since Zircon is dead, we've freed Helix. Now the entire world needs to be liberated. I can't let you go at it alone. I'm coming with you.

Cooper. walking up. Sign me in too.

Dew. You too, huh?

Cooper. You had my back during the war, now I must return the favor. Plus you just can't leave without me tagging along too now.

Rena. I will come along as well. All this excitement is worth it. Has been so far.

Dew. You sure of this?

Cooper. Most definitely.

Lorenzo. You know it, man. You're my road dog, so I'm sticking by your side.

Dew.	Yeah . . . it'll be dangerous. But then when has it ever been safe? Ha-ha-ha.
Rena.	Off we go then?
Dew.	Right. Let's go, gang.
Narrator.	After that, the four depart onto the cruise liner and begin their journey out to sea. Our scene starts off as Dew is on the fantail of the ship looking off into the horizon of the Mesovilla coastline. He begins to remember when he was eighteen years old; he is visiting his grandfathers' grave in Twin Pines Cemetery . . .
Dew.	*walking up to a tombstone.* Grandpa *(then kneels down)* . . . you were just here a week ago. I'm going to miss you. Why did it have to be like this? *(a tear falls onto the soil)* I guess . . . this is good-bye. I'll do my best. *(then takes out his grandfather's amulet)* This . . . I will give this to a person that I care for . . . whether it be a friend or love one . . . just as you said. *(then puts the amulet back into his pocket)* After the war ends, I'll come back to see you. I've got to go now. I won't forget. *(sigh)*
Narrator.	Dew then gets off of his knees and walks away toward the cemetery exit. As Dew continues to reminisce, Rena walks up.
Rena.	Dew.
Dew.	. . .
Rena.	Hey, Dew.
Dew.	Huh? Oh, Rena, it's you. Need something?
Rena.	No, I was just trying to see where you were at. I found you. You looked like you were deep in thought there.
Dew.	Yeah, a bit.
Rena.	About what?
Dew.	Nothing much.
Rena.	Hmm . . .
Dew.	It's been awhile since we've had a chance to talk alone.
Rena.	Yeah . . . Hey do you remember the night before you left out to boot camp?
Dew.	I do.
Rena.	I only bring that up because this night reminds me of it.
Narrator.	The scene switches to Twin Pines again as young Dew and Rena meet up at the harbor, just before Dew's departure to the SWAT Trooper Elite Academy.

Rena.   Look at you. I can't believe you're leaving home already. Time goes by so fast; you're all grown up now. It seemed just like yesterday we had first met. Since then, you have learned a lot from me and my teachings of Bojutsu. I am sure it will come in handy some day for you.

Dew.   Time does go by fast. It's been only ten years since then. Wow.

Rena.   It has . . . You'll do just as well with the military. I'm proud of you.

Dew.   Thank you, sifu.

Rena.   You no longer have to call me that. You're training is completed, and we're equal now.

Dew.   Rena it is then. May I ask you a question?

Rena.   Yes, Dew.

Dew.   Before I leave, I want you to have this. (*digging in his pockets*) Here you go. (*then gives Rena the amulet*) It's for you.

Rena.   Dew, you shouldn't have (*holding it*) . . . Why are you giving this to me?

Dew.   I want you to have it. It was given to me by my grandfather. He told me to give this to someone special in my life. So to you, my teacher, here is my token of appreciation for everything you've taught me and better me as well.

Rena.   I will wear this always. (*then puts the amulet on her neck*) Thank you. I mean it, really. I will miss you very much.

Dew.   I will miss you too. I will come back and visit when I can and see you all again.

Rena.   Do what you can.

Dew.   I will. (*then grabs Rena's hand and kisses it*) Good-bye.

Rena.   Take care of yourself. Remember what you've learned, and it will always guide you through the good times and hard times as well.

Dew.   I will never forget.

Narrator.   Dew then walks off with his seabag and walks up the brow to board the ship. Rena stands there as she watches the ship take off waving farewell to Dew, who waves back. Then the ship goes slowly off into the horizon. The scene shifts back to present time.

Rena.   Good memories.

Dew.   They are good memories indeed.

Rena.   When you were gone, I had worried if you were in good health or not. But I knew that you would be fine.

Dew.   I did make a promise to you Sifu that we would see one another again.

Rena.	That you did.
Dew.	The reason why I had survived through that ordeal was because of the training you had given me.
Rena.	It wasn't just my training that did it for you; it was all you in the end.
Dew.	Yes, but there was another reason for that as well.
Rena.	What is that?
Dew.	My heart was set on seeing you again.
Rena.	What do you mean?
Dew.	My love for you.
Rena.	Love?!
Dew.	I've always loved you. Intimate passion burning for you.
Rena.	I never knew you felt like this. Dew, I . . .
Dew.	It's always been like this, ever since I was young. I could never really explain this to you . . . It was . . .
Narrator.	Lorenzo then walks up.
Lorenzo.	Hey, Dew.
Dew	*turns to face Lorenzo.* Yeah?
Lorenzo.	I was looking for you. Did I interrupt something?
Rena.	No, not at all. I'll leave you two alone now. (*then walks off*)
Dew.	Rena.
Lorenzo.	I wanted to let you know, it's almost dinner time.
Dew.	Thanks . . . (*the turns to look at the sea*)
Lorenzo.	You okay?
Dew.	I'm cool. Like she said, it's nothing. I'll be there in a few.
Lorenzo.	Awesome. Later then. (*then walks off*)
Dew.	Hmm . . . love.
Narrator.	The scene changes to Cooper in his room as he is lying in his bed thinking to himself.
Cooper.	If you were all here now . . . Dad. It's been a while since I've been on the water. Ha-ha-ha . . . not seasick this time . . . Mom.
Narrator.	Cooper then begins to reminisce about his past; the day he went on leave to visit his family in Demmin. He enters the living room of the house.
Cooper.	*shouting.* Mom, I'm home!
Mom.	*walking into the living room.* Cooper, you're back. Welcome home son.
Narrator.	Cooper and his mother hug one another.
Cooper.	For a short while, wish it could be longer though.
Mom.	Well, at least you're here though. My little boy. (*then smiles*)

Cooper.	How are things?
Mom.	Well, it's been terrible. I was sent a letter from the Helix capital the other day. They're going to evacuate all of us in two weeks from our homes. What will I do? I have no where else to go.
Cooper.	I'm pretty sure you'll be placed somewhere safer than here. There have been talks about the New Havenport army trying to occupy this area. This is the only part of Demmin that they don't have under control.
Mom.	I just can't leave here though.
Cooper.	You have to.
Mom.	No, I won't. All our family history is here in this house. I won't leave all that behind.
Cooper.	You'll be a memory if you don't. Mom, please leave soon. I have a bad feeling if you don't. I don't want to lose you like we did Dad.
Mom.	You, won't and things will be fine.
Cooper.	Mom, don't be foolish!
Mom.	I am not. I will not leave.
Narrator.	The scene shifts back to present time; someone then knocks at the door.
Cooper.	Mom . . . (*sigh*)
Narrator.	The knock at the door still continues.
Cooper.	?! (*then rising to his feet*) Who is it?
Rena	*enters the room.* I wanted to tell you that it's time to eat.
Cooper.	Thanks for letting me know.
Rena.	Are you okay?
Cooper.	Yes, I am fine. Just drifted off in thought . . .
Rena.	*Dew* . . .
Cooper.	That's all?
Rena.	. . .
Cooper.	Hey, Rena. Hello, you alive there?
Rena.	Yes! I'm sorry; I got lost in thought myself.
Cooper.	You feeling all right?
Rena.	Me? Don't be silly, I'm fine.
Cooper.	Just asking.
Rena.	You should hurry. Before you know it, all the food will be gone.
Cooper.	You're right. I will then. Beat you there ha-ha-ha. (*then walks off*)
Rena.	I am loved . . . *Can I love again? Can I be left alone and disappointed, again? Is this my destiny?* Dew . . .

Narrator.	Rena then exits. The sun sets into the horizon, and the moon appears as the stars come out illuminating the sky. Two days have passed; the cruise ship arrives in Llivisaca pier. The line handlers moor the ship to the pier, and the brow is set in place. Dew and the others, with the crew passengers, begin to depart from the ship. They walk down to the pier.
Lorenzo.	Not a bad cruise.
Dew.	Not at all.
Cooper.	So this is Llivisaca. My first time here. I never thought it would be so tropical.
Lorenzo.	Yeah, humid too. Damn it's hot.
Cooper.	I will have to buy a souvenir here.
Rena.	What now, guys?
Dew.	Since we're here now, I have to deliver this letter for Killbin to the alderman here.
Cooper.	I have an idea.
Dew.	Shoot.
Cooper.	The rest of us should take a break while you go do that. See the sites and all.
Dew.	I suppose so.
Lorenzo.	I like that idea. C'mon, Cooper, let's go do some exploring.
Cooper.	Awesome. Rena, you coming with us?
Rena.	No, I'm fine. I'll stay with Dew for this one.
Lorenzo.	Fine with me. (*then walks off*)
Cooper.	Catch you both later. (*then walks off following Lorenzo*)
Dew.	Me and you now.
Rena.	It is. We should get going to deliver that letter now.
Dew.	Yes . . .
Narrator.	Dew and Rena head to the alderman's house. They eventually find their way there and come to the front door of the house. Dew then knocks on it. The door opens.
Butler.	*opening door.* Good morning to you. How may I help you?
Dew.	We've come to see the alderman.
Butler.	Is he expecting you?
Rena.	No, but we have a letter for him. (*handing the envelope to the butler*)
Butler.	Hmm . . . I see. (*holding the letter*) Come in then.
Narrator.	Dew and Rena enter the alderman's house.
Butler.	I'll give this to him. Please wait here. (*then walks off*)
Dew.	Yep . . .
Rena.	Awkward silence.

Dew. Nice.

Rena. What is?

Dew. The house.

Rena. Oh.

Dew. What did you think I was referring to?

Rena. Nothing else.

Dew. When we were walking here, why didn't you say a single word to me?

Rena. I had nothing to say.

Dew. Something is bothering you?

Rena. No.

Dew. Rena, I . . .

Corot. *walking up.* So, you must be the people Killbin sent?

Dew. Huh? (*then turns to face Corot*) Yes, we are them.

Corot. Glad to meet you, folks. I'am Alderman Corot, and I welcome you to Llivisaca. I read the letter, and I am in total disbelief. Is this true that our world is on the brink of destruction?

Rena. In a way.

Corot. I see that Killbin Janeiro is our governor now. Hah! Times do change. So he wants me to aid you in your progress, to help you find a man named Thornton?

Dew. Yes, that is right. Are you going to help us?

Corot. It's the tourist season now. We've had many people come and go through here. A man named Thornton and with this description hasn't been seen in Llivisaca. Maybe I can be of some assistance though.

Rena. How?

Corot. This is probably your first time here visiting, so you'll need a tour guide then.

Dew. Tour guide? Where do we find a tour guide agency at?

Corot. The agency is north of here. It sticks out pretty well. You should have no problem finding it.

Dew. All right.

Corot. I have a letter you'll need to give to the agency boss. His name is Mr. Rainer. (*then gives Dew the letter*)

Dew *takes the letter.* I guess playing carrier boy is my job all of a sudden. I'll do it.

Rena. Thank you. We'll handle the rest. Come on, Dew. (*walking off*)

Corot. Good luck.

Narrator.	Dew and Rena leave the Alderman's house and head toward the tour guide agency. They enter; a passing tour guide stops to speak to them.
Agent.	You two look lost. May I be of some service?
Dew.	Oh, yes. We've just come from seeing the alderman, and he sent us here to give this letter to your boss, Mr. Rainer. (*then hands the letter to the tour guide agent*)
Agent	*then takes the letter.* That's right, the alderman had called us a while ago letting us know that you two would be on your way here. I'll show you to his office. He's been waiting for you. This way please.
Narrator.	Dew and Rena follow the tour guide agent down the hallway to Mr. Rainer's office.
Agent.	Straight through that door is his office.
Rena.	Thank you.
Dew.	Thanks.
Agent.	Glad I could help. (*then walks off*)
Narrator.	Dew and Rena then enter this office.
Mr. Rainer.	(*chair turned to the window*) Bunch of quitters. I can't believe them.
Dew.	Hmm . . .
Rena.	Who's he talking to?
Dew.	To himself obviously.
Mr. Rainer.	Oh, Mr. Rainer I need a raise. I need more hours. Damn babies! I should have listened to Mother and became a cook.
Rena.	Excuse me.
Mr. Rainer.	He-he-he . . . Huh? (*then turns his chair to face Dew and Rena*) Oh, I thought I was alone. Who are you two, and what are you doing here in my office?
Dew.	We were sent by the alderman.
Mr. Rainer.	That's right; I've been expecting you two to arrive. Alderman Corot told me everything over the phone about your situation.
Dew.	What was this letter for then? (*then hands Mr. Rainer the letter*)
Mr. Rainer.	(*then takes the Letter from Dew*) It has money attached to it. It's to pay for the tour guide agent for you, folks.
Rena.	That was nice of the alderman to do that for us.
Mr. Rainer.	Well, I think it may be of waste though.
Dew.	Why's that?

Mr. Rainer.	At the moment, we have no personnel available. It's the tourist season and we're all booked. I'm really sorry.
Dew.	Just great. What a waste of time this was.
Krista.	(Walks into the room) Mr. Rainer!
Mr. Rainer.	Back already, Krista?
Krista.	I had enough of this.
Mr. Rainer.	What happened now?
Krista.	Those tourists are disrespectful. The children left trash on the bus and gum under the chairs. Some drunk puked all over the place and passed out. This is so frustrating. I don't get paid enough to deal with this type of abuse.
Mr. Rainer.	Calm down, Krista. You know we're short of people at the moment. So we got to manage our wages and deal with this a bit.
Krista.	You know what? I quit! Quit! Quit!
Mr. Rainer.	Now you want to give up on me too, eh? Fine, go ahead then—wait.
Krista.	What?
Mr. Rainer.	I have an idea. I got a new assignment for you.
Krista.	God, what now?
Mr. Rainer.	These fine folks here need our help getting around town.
Krista.	Get someone else to do it. I'm done with this job.
Mr. Rainer.	I have no one else to do this. I need you for this one. You're the best worker I have, don't quit on me now.
Krista.	Best worker? Me?
Mr. Rainer.	Do this task and I'll . . . I'll double your salary. No, better yet, triple it.
Krista.	Really?
Mr. Rainer.	Yes. I beg of you, please do this.
Krista.	Hmm . . . I will. I'll do it. They seem like decent folks.
Mr. Rainer.	Excellent then.
Dew.	We should be going now.
Krista.	Sure. I think you'll love my tours. By the way, my name is Krista Naples.
Rena.	Nice to meet you.
Dew.	Grand.
Krista.	Off we go then.
Narrator.	The scene shifts to Dew and Rena sitting in the back of the tour bus.

Krista.	*speaking into the bus's megaphone system.* To our right you'll see one of the wonderful sights of the Llivisaca shoreline, the golden beaches. Now to your left . . .
Rena.	*whispering.* Wonderful tour this is.
Dew.	*whispering.* I was hoping we could venture around town, instead of being here.
Rena.	Oh.
Dew.	*whispering.* Rena, I have to say something.
Krista.	Excuse me, are you, guys, paying attention to me?
Rena.	Yes, dear.
Dew.	Go on please with it.
Narrator.	Then Krista continues to speak.
Dew.	*whispering.* As I was saying—
Rena.	*whispering.* Dew, what do you find so attractive about me?
Dew.	*whispering.* Beauty, intelligence, and kindness. I admired all of that when I was learning from you.
Rena.	*whispering.* Wow . . . You feel like this for me, really? Hmm . . . I got an idea.
Dew.	*whispering.* What's that?
Rena.	*whispering.* Let's get out of here and find something to do. We do have a lot to catch up on.
Dew.	*whispering.* You want to ditch out on her?
Rena.	*whispering.* I doubt you want to stay here any longer and want to sit through this.
Dew.	*whispering.* Good point. Let's go.
Narrator.	As Krista continues to speak on, Dew and Rena jump out from behind the bus.
Krista.	You, guys, are going to enjoy this next attraction. (*then turns around*) What?! Bob, stop the bus.
Bob.	What's wrong?
Krista.	They left. *Argh* . . . That's it. No one is going to ditch out on me and think they'll get away with it. Bob, stop the bus for a moment.
Bob.	Why?
Krista.	Just do it.
Bob.	All right.
Narrator.	The tour bus begins to slow down then comes to a halt.
Krista.	Get off the bus for a moment.

Bob.   What now?

Krista.   I think we might have a flat tire.

Bob.   You think? (*getting up from the driver's seat, and then walks off the bus*) Things look good here.

Narrator.   Krista then gets into the driver seat and shuts the bus door on Bob.

Bob.   Krista, what are you doing? Hey!

Narrator.   Then she turns on the engine and drives off.

Krista.   So they want to run off from me. Not again. I hate when this happens. I'll find them. *Urgh!*

Narrator.   As Krista drives off in pursuit of Dew and Rena, we find the two at the shopping mall nearby.

Rena.   Great, a shopping mall. We can buy a few things now. It's been a while since I've been out to shop.

Dew.   Do we need any more provisions? We have enough already, don't you think?

Rena.   Where not here for that my pupil. Let's relax for a moment. I know I didn't teach you to be so uptight about things. Let's enjoy the time here. It'll be fun. (*then grabs Dew's arm*)

Dew.   Sure, why not?

Narrator.   The two then walk around the shopping mall and spend most of the day shopping and enjoying the attractions of the mall. Dew and Rena come up to a man taking pictures just before exiting.

Rena.   Dew, let's take a picture.

Dew.   Works for me.

Photographer. Good evening to you two. Would you like me to take a picture of you two together or separate? It's free photo shoot. Interested?

Dew.   Yes, please.

Photographer. All right, sir, now you and the missus get close now. (*aiming the camera at Dew and Rena*)

Rena.   Missus . . . hah.

Photographer. Say cheese!

Dew and Rena. CHEESE!

Narrator.   The camera flashes and takes the picture.

Photographer. Here you go. (*then gives the photo to Rena*) It turned out well, don't you think?

Rena.   *looking at the picture*. It did. See, Dew. What do you think? (*then shows him the picture*)

Dew   *then looks at the picture*. Nice.

Rena   *turns to the photographer.* Thank you very much for the picture.

Photographer. You're welcome, miss.

Dew.   Have a good night.

Photographer. You too, sir.

Narrator.   As Dew and Rena begin to walk off, they hear a large crash coming from outside.

Dew.   What was that?

Rena.   Who knows? I had fun today, Dew.

Dew.   I did too. This made up for all that time now.

Rena.   Oh yeah. As I think about it, you and me never did go out like this.

Dew.   No, but first time for everything.

Rena.   Yeah.

Dew.   We should find the others now.

Rena.   I agree. I wonder what they've been up to.

Dew.   I dunno, but I'm pretty sure they've had fun.

Rena.   Thanks, Dew.

Dew.   For what?

Rena.   Everything.

Dew.   No problem. (*then smiles at Rena*)

Narrator.   Dew and Rena then continue to walk toward the main exit of the mall; Krista appears running up to them . . .

Krista.   (*inhaling and exhaling deeply*) . . . I've . . . I finally . . . found you, guys.

Rena.   Krista.

Dew.   You came looking for us.

Krista.   Yes . . . that was quite rude to run off on me like that. Why'd you do it?

Rena.   We're sorry for that, but we needed to go out and enjoy some time alone.

Krista.   Oh, alone time. You two must be dating then. You sure look older than him, but hey whatever floats your boat.

Dew.   It's not like that.

Rena.   Just good friends.

Krista.   Oh shoot. You could have told me this earlier. I would have stopped for you, guys, to shop. Now as I think about it, I can see why some of the tourists give me pain. My tours are kind of plain.

Dew.   I wouldn't say that.

Krista.   Well, forget about that. I found you all now, so let's get going back now.

Dew.   Might as well then.

Rena.   Hopefully we find Lorenzo and Cooper. (*walking off*)

Photographer. HELP!

Dew.   Where did that come from?! Hold on. (*then runs off*)

Rena.   Uh-oh . . . Dew, hold on. (*then runs after Dew*)

Krista.   C'mon you, guys, I still haven't shown you all of Llivisaca. Dammit . . . wait for me too! (*then follows after the two*)

Narrator.   The scene switches over to the photographer being mugged by thugs.

Thuggish girl. Give us your money! (*pointing a dagger at the photographers neck*)

Photographer. Why don't you believe me? I don't have any money on me at all.

Black Manta 1. He's lying.

Black Manta 2. I say we beat it out of him. Some loose change will fall out then. Ha-ha-ha.

Photographer. I told you already. Let me go!

Thuggish girl. I agree. Let's beat the hell out of this old coot.

Dew.   *walking up*. I wouldn't do that if I were you.

Narrator.   The thuggish girl and the Black Mantas turn their attention to Dew. The photographer runs off.

Thuggish girl. Who are you now?

Dew.   Don't worry about that. Just worry about what I'm capable of.

Thuggish girl. Huh? Ha-ha-ha . . . Oh, so scary. Sod off.

Narrator.   Krista and Rena come running.

Krista.   Boy, you run too fast. I told you hold up. You can't be leaving me behind like that all the time. Hey what's going on here?

Thuggish girl. You?!

Krista.   *exhales sharply*.

Thuggish girl. There is no need for introductions; we are the Black Mantas Society.

Black Manta 2. That's right; nobody dares to stand in our way.

Black Manta 1. Not even the law enforcement dares to contend with us. We own them, everything, and this joint.

Dew.   Is that all? Who are you now?

Thuggish Girl. What?! Who do you think you are? You have some nerve.

Dew.	That man you were trying to mug was clearly poorer than you were. That was lowdown and shameful. What are you proving from doing such things?
Black Manta 1.	*Argh* . . . Elvir, this dude is giving me a headache.
Elvir.	You must not be from around here I see.
Black Manta 2.	I think him and his friends here need to be taught how we run things here. A quick tutorial.
Dew.	I'm a fast learner about things, and master them well.
Rena.	That's true.
Elvir.	*then points the dagger at Dew.* We're going to show you some Black Mantas hospitality. I'm going to gut you good!
Dew.	That's all? I was expecting more of a better threat than that.
Elvir.	Stop sassing me!
Rena.	Geez, always something.
Krista.	Can't we talk about this?
Dew.	You want to make me feel at home? Come on and do it.
Elvir.	Let's get them!
Narrator.	Dew, Rena and Krista battle Elvir and her Black Manta goons. After being defeated, the two thugs run off leaving Elvir all alone. Dew approaches her.
Krista.	Run away, you sissies!
Elvir.	*Ow* . . . my head. (*rubbing her forehead*) Stupid jerk off!
Dew.	Thanks for the warm welcoming.
Elvir,	*backing up into a corner.* Well, I guess you, guys, taught me a lesson . . . Ha-ha. Okay, I was wrong for trying to rob the guy. I promise . . . I'll never do it again . . . you know.
Narrator.	Elvir, with her quickness, springs up from the ground and flips over Dew. With a quick slash with her dagger, she rips Rena's amulet off her neck and grabs it.
Elvir.	Look what I got now. This looks like it's worth something. (*putting the amulet in her pocket*) Maybe I'll see you all again—not! Later, losers . . . ha-ha-ha! (*then runs off*)
Rena.	Dew, the amulet!
Dew.	Damn, she got away. Quick little bugger.
Narrator.	Lorenzo and Cooper then walk up on the scene.
Lorenzo.	Dew.
Dew.	Hey.
Lorenzo.	Glad we found you.

Dew.	Did you happen to see a girl run by just now?
Lorenzo.	A girl? Oh yeah.
Cooper.	She was kind of cute. Why?
Dew.	We had got into a fight with her and her goons a moment ago. She ran off with Rena's amulet.
Lorenzo.	We heard something about a fight going on up here while we were in town.
Rena.	Word travels fast here I see.
Lorenzo.	We were just down the street., so we hurried as fast as we could. I figured if there was a fight, you had to be involved in some way.
Cooper.	We could have been here sooner if we could have gotten pass the wrecked bus outside the mall. Some body obviously can't park.
Krista.	Ha-ha . . . I guess you all won't probably leave until you get that amulet back, huh?
Dew.	No, we must get it back.
Krista.	Well, there's an inn nearby. They know me there, so you'll be able to stay there free of charge. I'll show you the way, come on. (then walks off)
Lorenzo.	Who is this person?
Dew.	Our tour guide.
Lorenzo.	Tour guide? More people coming along for the ride now I see.
Cooper.	What about our pursuit of Thornton?
Dew.	That will have to wait for now. We've got time for that. For now, we're stuck here for a while until I get her amulet back. I can't leave without that thing. It's of value to me.
Cooper.	I see.
Rena.	It's getting late, so it's a good idea to go to the inn and get some rest.
Dew.	Yeah.
Narrator.	Later that evening, once settled in at the local inn, Dew and the others reminisce on the day's events.
Krista.	Things are set up for the night for you, guys. Free of charge. Here are your keys to your rooms. (then hands Dew and the others their keys)
Cooper.	Free lodging, cool. (then takes the key from Krista) I haven't had it like this since I was in the military.
Dew.	takes the key from Krista and puts it in his pocket. Thanks, Krista. I like to know something, what is the Black Mantas Society?

Rena.	Krista, would you know anything about them?
Krista.	I don't really know. They're a shady group of characters.
Rena.	It seemed like to me that girl knew you. Are you sure?
Krista.	I don't know much about them, like I said. Sorry I can't fill you all out on this subject.
Rena.	Hmm.
Lorenzo.	Well, while me and Cooper were in town, we found out some info on them.
Dew.	What's that?
Lorenzo.	The Black Mantas Society is a highly organized crime syndicate who apparently, by the look of things here, runs this whole province.
Rena.	How is this so? I thought all of Mesovilla was controlled by the Helix capital?
Lorenzo.	You would think that, but it seems for us all being in one area fighting corruption, it goes further than we expected.
Cooper.	So this syndicate is under Videl's support?
Krista.	I can answer this part. During the Great Civil War between Helix and New Havenport, Llivisaca supported New Havenport, all from smuggling weapons from the Helix border being shipped overseas, to providing extra personnel to support their forces. When Helix had won the war, the late Governor Videl cut off all support to the traitor providences. This left Llivisaca to be a country of its own. So with no form of government, it made it easier for the low lives to claim their territory. So thus, that is how the Black Mantas Society gained control of Llivisaca.
Dew.	It makes sense. I thought you said you didn't know much about them?
Krista.	About the organization themselves, no. The history of them in our province, yes.
Dew.	Oh.
Rena.	We still need to get back my amulet.
Krista.	If you don't mind me asking, what's the fuss over it? Can't you just buy a new one?
Rena.	No. It's special to me.
Krista.	I see. I'm feeling a little tired now.
Cooper.	Me as well. Maybe we should call it a night.
Dew.	That's a good idea. We'll start our search for them in the morning.

Lorenzo.	We'll find those creeps and get that amulet back in no time.
Dew.	We will. I am off to bed then. (*then walks off*)
Narrator.	Everyone then departs to their rooms and goes to sleep. The scene shifts to Rena's room as she lies in her bed sound asleep. She is then awakened by a rustling noise coming from outside her window from the bushes.
Rena.	Huh?! (*getting up, then walks toward the window*)
Narrator.	Rena then peers out the window to see Krista climbing out of her room to the streets below. Krista then runs off into the sultry scenery of Llivisaca . . .
Rena.	This is odd . . . I wonder what she is up to?
Narrator.	Rena quickly gets dressed and follows Krista. Eventually catching up to Krista through the crowded streets of an ongoing festival, Rena comes to a halt when she sees Krista entering an alleyway. She continues to follow her as she keeps her distance, not to get too close. Rena ends up following Krista all the way to the province landfill as she approaches an abandoned factory.
Rena.	Strange place to go at night.
Narrator.	Rena then continues to follow Krista as she hides behind a wrecked automobile. A man comes outside of the factory to meet Krista. Rena then goes in closer, hiding behind a pile of trash to hear the conversation.
Black Manta.	Long time no see.
Krista.	So welcoming all of a sudden. I was never greeted like this before when I was around. I want to see your boss.
Black Manta.	No greetings back? My, aren't we rude? Ha-ha-ha.
Krista.	Enough of the small talk. I want to see him now.
Black Manta.	I see you're still demanding as before. Well, the boss isn't here at the moment. He's out attending to other matters. Try coming again later.
Krista.	Liar. I know he's here.
Narrator.	Then another Black Manta enters.
Black Manta 3.	What's going on here?
Black Manta.	Krista wants to see the boss.
Black Manta 3.	Really? Well, let her come in. The boss will be happy to see you.
Krista.	I'm pretty sure he will be.
Narrator.	Krista and the two Black Mantas then go inside the factory. Rena then runs over and tries to catch the door as it's closing, but it shuts on her. She then notices an uncovered ventilation shaft and

decides to crawl inside to continue following Krista. Sometime later, crawling her way through the factory ventilation system as she follows the voices of the Black Mantas and Krista, she comes to a stop and sees Krista entering a large throne room. Rena then goes in for a closer look.

Krista.   Ketcy, this has gone on long enough.

Ketcy.   That voice . . . it's been a while sis. I thought I would never see you again . . . (*sitting in a throne*)

Rena.   Sis?

Krista.   Surprises happen.

Ketcy.   How has the world been treating you, my sister?

Krista.   I've been doing well, brother. Well, recently your men and I haven't been getting along.

Ketcy.   Really? Well, speaking about surprises and all, I heard you have some new friends now. Now knowing you, you were never the type to hang around with people you hardly knew.

Krista.   Like I said, surprises happen.

Ketcy.   Ha-ha-ha . . . Still the same. So what has bought you here?

Krista.   I think you know why.

Ketcy.   Ha-ha-ha. Maybe I do. Sister please remember who is running this town. We, the Black Mantas Society, do as we please. We regulate order around here.

Krista.   Yeah, I know. Your so-called order.

Ketcy.   You had your chance a long time ago to stay within the family. We didn't kick you out; you left us. You wanted to do things the honest way, so we let you do that. What does honesty get you these days anyway, if I may ask?

Krista.   A better living than this lie.

Ketcy.   This "lie" has given me power and control. You're here for your friend's amulet? Why come all this way for a total stranger? Why risk your life? I could kill you for trespassing on my property, traitor.

Krista.   You wouldn't kill me, not your own blood. The amulet is of value to her.

Ketcy.   She should have been more careful of her possessions.

Krista.   I will get it back from you.

Ketcy.   How so?

Krista.   My new friends are from the Helix capital. They are the same ones who gave your men the beating today.

Ketcy.	Ah . . . Well, it doesn't matter; they'll be taken care of, as the rest were before them.
Rena.	*I got to get back to Dew.*
Narrator.	Rena quickly crawls through the vent, but because of the lack of support of weight, the vent collapses. Rena then falls out and lands right in front of Ketcy.
Krista.	Rena?!
Ketcy.	Ah?! GUARDS!
Narrator.	Two Black Manta guards enter the room and retain Rena and Krista.
Ketcy.	This was a sorry attempt to ambush me for the throne. Better luck next time, sis. (*then turns to one of the guards*) Put them in one of the holding cells.
Black Manta Guard.	Yes, scion.
Ketcy.	By the way, don't lay one finger on them.
Black Manta Guard.	Of course not.
Narrator.	The guards then take Rena and Krista away. At this moment, Mauvais, Ketcy's servant, enters into the room.
Ketcy.	Mauvais.
Mauvais.	I see we had some quest, scion.
Ketcy.	Unexpected nonetheless. I have a tasking for you.
Mauvais.	I'm here at your service.
Ketcy.	Send one of the men into town. I have a letter I must write up; it's for some new visitors in town. More of a warm greeting, we'll say.
Mauvais.	Right away, scion.
Narrator.	Two hours pass by. Back at the inn, the innkeeper rushes into Dew's room, opening the door as Dew is awakened from his rest instantly.
Inn Keeper.	Sir!
Dew.	?! (*rising up from his bed*)
Inn Keeper.	I'm sorry to have awakened you, but it's important.
Dew.	What's wrong?
Inn Keeper.	I received a message a while ago at the front desk concerning your friends, Rena and Krista.
Dew.	What do you mean? Aren't they here in the hotel?
Inn Keeper.	The Black Mantas have them in confinement.
Dew.	What?! (*then gets up on his feet grabbing his shirt*) I got to get the others. Thank you for bringing this to me. (*puts the shirt on then exits the room*)

Inn keeper.	I've already awakened the other two gentlemen and let them know as well. Hold up . . .
Narrator.	The Inn Keeper follows Dew as he heads down to the lobby of the hotel and meets up with Lorenzo and Cooper, who are waiting for him.
Cooper.	I see you're awake.
Lorenzo.	Just when you thought we were going to take a break.
Dew.	What did the message say?
Inn Keeper.	It said that they wanted you three to go to the Pendragon Restaurant. That's located five blocks east from here. They want to have talk with you all.
Cooper.	I suppose the search for Thornton will have to be prolonged for a bit.
Lorenzo.	Always an adventure.
Dew.	I'm not leaving without them or that amulet. Thornton will wait. Off we go to get into some more fun.
Lorenzo.	Works for me.
Dew.	We're out then.
Narrator.	Dew, Lorenzo, and Cooper then head out to the Pendragon Restaurant. Meanwhile, back at the abandoned factory, Rena and Krista are in the holding cell.
Krista.	Not going anywhere anytime soon.
Rena.	By the looks of it, we aren't.
Krista.	Rena, why'd you follow me?
Rena.	I didn't really trust you. I guess I was wrong though in the end about you.
Krista.	So you heard it all, huh?
Rena.	Yes.
Krista.	It's true, Ketcy is my brother, and he is the reason why Llivisaca is the way it is today. It all started ten years ago for us. We were living in poverty with our mother, who was a drug addict. The times were hard for us growing up, but Ketcy and I always had a positive outlook on things. So eventually, our mother had died due to a heroin overdose, and we were practically left on our own to raise each other.
Rena.	What happened to your father?
Krista.	He died from an over dose of crystal meth before I was born.
Rena.	I'm sorry . . .
Krista.	Yeah . . . so anyway. After the death of our mother, Ketcy went looking for work where ever it was possible; as long as the pay

kept food on the table and a roof over our heads. Although from all that work, it barely did us any good. On one fateful day, a group of thugs were recruiting some new faces for their gang. This was our chances to be free from off the streets and accepted to a new family. My brother had passed all their initiations, and became a member. I had eventually followed right behind him in joining the Black Mantis. As time went by, we were raised by our benefactors, taught the jack of trades of stealing and hustling.

Rena.   Sounds like Lorenzo in a way.

Krista.   A dark veil surrounded us; I began to notice that the corruption we were surrounded by was eating me alive. Ketcy did not notice this; he grew too ignorant and apathetic as he moved up in the society ranks. He eventually became the leader in the end; I could no longer stand living that lifestyle though. The fact of depriving others to satisfy our needs made me sicker as each day passed by. I learned that regardless how much power you have or obtain, it doesn't mean nothing if you aren't happy. So I left them to start a new life on the right foot. I had always remembered where I came from and never forgot it either.

Rena.   I had you figured all wrong.

Krista.   Always nice to know something about people you just meet. Can't always judge a book by its cover.

Narrator.   A Black Manta guard then walks up to the cell door.

Black Manta Guard. Ha-ha-ha . . . Krista, I don't know why you left us in the first place. This could have been all yours. Could have prevented all this that's happening now if you would have stayed here. Silly girl . . . your friends are going to be in for a surprise soon.

Krista.   What are you talking about?

Black Manta Guard. Ketcy and the others are going to ambush your buds at the Pendragon Restaurant. Easy death for them. Won't be too messy, I hope. Ha-ha-ha.

Rena.   Oh, no.

Krista.   We've got to get out of here.

Black Manta Guard. As direct orders from the scion, we got to feed you. I personally think he's being too soft on you being his sister and all, Krista. Well, orders are orders. (*then pulls out a ration from his pocket and places it on the ground, sliding it into the cell*) Well, enjoy your meal. Hah!

Narrator.   The guard then walks off; he unknowingly drops the keys to the cell and exits.

Rena.	Look at this. What luck we have.
Krista.	Go figure. (*then gets on her knees and starts reaching for the key*) Almost got it (*then grabs the key*) . . . Got it.
Rena.	Excellent.
Krista.	*stands up then unlocks the cell door.* We're home free now. Let's go and catch up to the others.
Narrator.	Rena and Krista then exit the cell area, evading the Black Manta guards. Meanwhile, Dew and the others arrive at the Pendragon Restaurant. Two Black Mantas approach them.
Black Manta 3.	We've been expecting you.
Dew.	Where are my friends at?
Black Manta 4.	You'll see them soon.
Black Manta 3.	I suggest for you and your friends not to make a scene here. We've got customers eating here; plus it's bad for business.
Cooper.	What a shame that would be. We'll save the commotion for later.
Dew.	Take us to our friends.
Black Manta 4.	Come with us.
Narrator.	Dew, Lorenzo, and Cooper follow the two Black Mantas inside the restaurant to Ketcy's office upstairs. They enter.
Dew.	Where are they at?
Ketcy.	*sitting in a chair turned to the window.* I'm sorry, but they're not here. So you're my sister's friends.
Cooper.	Sister's friends?
Narrator.	A swarm of Black Mantas jump down from the ceiling along with Elvir, surrounding Dew and the others.
Elvir.	Meeting so soon?
Dew.	I guess so.
Cooper.	Wow!
Elvir.	What does that mean?
Cooper.	It's a shame beauty like yours is so corrupted to petty acts of robbery.
Elvir.	Ha-ha . . . flattery will get you nowhere. Cute. Nonetheless, I guess you all had to show up to die. Such a shame.
Dew.	I want that amulet back!
Elvir.	I haven't forgotten our fight from earlier. So you and your friends want that amulet back really bad, huh? (*then pulls out the amulet putting it around her neck*) Too bad!
Dew.	I have no problem taking it back from you then. (*drawing his bo*)
Elvir.	There are more of us than you three. Be suicidal then.
Cooper.	Crazy.

Narrator.	Dew, Lorenzo, and Cooper battle Elvir and the Black Mantas. They manage to defeat Elvir and her henchmen. Elvir stumbles back to the floor, landing on her hind.
Elvir.	Urgh . . . dammit, not again! (*sits there dumbfounded and dazed*)
Dew.	*walks toward Elvir and rips the amulet off her neck.* Got it back.
Ketcy.	Stupid orphan of society. Bravo . . . I'm impressed.
Lorenzo.	Looks like your men weren't strong enough for us after all. See, in the Aurora Blade, we pick quality over quantity. It's the best choice.
Ketcy.	So you're that famous gang from up north I've always heard about growing up. Most impressive and an honor to have you here in my town. I sense a gang war here. This will be fun. We've never had fun like this before. You may have been able to overthrow the governor, but we aren't as soft as those capitalist pigs were. You're on a whole new playing field now.
Narrator.	Ketcy then pushes a button on his chair, opening a trap door underneath Dew, Lorenzo, and Cooper. They fall to a dungeon below the restaurant. Dew, Lorenzo, and Cooper get back on their feet after recovering from the fall.
Lorenzo.	*getting up.* Different playfield . . . hah!
Cooper.	Where to now?
Narrator.	Suddenly, loud footsteps are heard as they approach the three, shaking the dungeon room.
Dew.	What the?!
Narrator.	Mauvais then enters the room.
Cooper.	You're a big boy.
Mauvais.	Heh-heh-heh, I see it's playtime now.
Lorenzo.	You look a little too big to be playing with others now.
Mauvais.	Humor . . . no time for jokes now. I'm going to stain my fist with your blood. Then we'll see who's laughing.
Dew.	That sounded like a joke to me.
Mauvais.	Sarcasm too. I will be gone with you rodents quick then. *Arrrrrgggghhhh!*
Narrator.	Dew and the others battle Mauvais and defeat him. He comes crashing to the ground.
Dew.	Okay, let's get out of here and find the girls now.
Lorenzo.	Playtime ended too fast for me.

Cooper.	We need to go.
Narrator.	Dew and the others leave the dungeon area back to Ketcy's office. On the way back up there, they encounter a few Black Mantas and easily defeat them. They reach Ketcy's office to find him running off to the rooftop of the restaurant. Then Rena and Krista appear.
Krista.	KETCY!
Ketcy.	*turns around to face Krista.* So I see you managed to escape.
Krista.	We'll settle this here brother.
Ketcy.	So eager to die?
Krista.	Whatever! Llivisaca will be liberated from your menace.
Ketcy.	How so?
Mauvais.	*walking up dragging his left leg.* Scion.
Ketcy.	Mauvais, what are you doing here? Did you get rid of them?
Mauvais.	They got away.
Ketcy.	Idiot! Well, forget about that. We got to finish off the present pest here. The rest of the men will take care of them then.
Krista.	Pest? I'm your sister; listen to what you are saying. Ketcy, stop this now before one of us gets hurt.
Ketcy.	You should have never left. You deserted me! I gave you care when mom died. I looked over you all the time, and you left me when I needed you.
Krista.	I love you, brother, and still do. You could have left along with me so long ago. Why'd you stay?
Ketcy.	The power and security I have is much better than anything such as love.
Krista.	That's a shame (*then shakes head in disapproval*). How can you say such a thing?
Ketcy.	I can because it is true. You don't love me at all. You want this power I have. You will not get it from me!
Krista.	You're freakin' paranoid!
Narrator.	Dew, Lorenzo, and Cooper then run up to confront Ketcy and Mauvais.
Ketcy.	So you made it through my men as well.
Lorenzo.	Can't keep us down, vato.
Dew.	We did, now let's end this.
Ketcy.	No worries. Ha-ha-ha. Ready to die?
Krista.	Ketcy, don't do this.
Mauvais.	You will not beat me like you did last time. CRUNCH!

Lorenzo.   I feel a repeat.

Narrator.   Dew, Krista, and the others battle Ketcy and Mauvais on the rooftop of the Pendragon Restaurant. After dealing with Mauvais, knocking him unconscious, Krista and Ketcy duel. Krista is victorious over her brother who is injured fatally. Krista runs over to her fallen brother.

Krista.   Oh no. Ketcy?!

Ketcy.   Ah . . . well you got through to me now. That was fun,ha-ha. (*exhales deeply*)

Krista.   Save your strength, brother.

Ketcy.   You've become stronger than before. I'm proud of you, sis.

Krista.   Don't worry about that. We got to get you some medical attention.

Ketcy.   I can't deny it when it's over.

Krista.   Ketcy, you'll be fine.

Ketcy.   All those thoughts about when we were younger, they're coming back to me now. Good times, what happened to us? We really did drift apart as time went by, huh?

Krista.   Yeah.

Narrator.   Sirens are heard in the background as police cars rush toward the restaurant.

Ketcy.   All my fun is over now. Nothing lasts forever.

Krista.   My love for you does, brother. Always has even when we were apart. I love you, Ketcy.

Ketcy.   Aww . . . It feels good to hear those words again. Growing up . . . society was cruel to us; we weren't given a chance in the beginning. I look at you, sis, and wish that I could have done things differently. I should have turned away from this lifestyle before it took me over. Well, now I've learned.

Krista.   It's okay, brother, things are fine now. No regrets.

Ketcy.   None at all.

Krista.   You were always stubborn about things.

Ketcy.   I was . . . *ha-ha-ha*. I guess I'll be going away for a while now.

Krista.   Yes, but that doesn't stop my love for you, brother.

Ketcy.   *smiles*. Thank you. I love you too, sis.

Narrator.   Krista then smiles at Ketcy, and they embrace one another. The scene changes to the next day. Dew and the others are about to leave the gates of Llivisaca.

Cooper.   I'm going to miss this tropical weather here.

Lorenzo.	Not a bad place to come back and visit now.
Dew.	I guess it was a nice stop.
Rena.	We did a lot of good here as well.
Dew.	Yes, we did. Now with that done, we're off to pursue Thornton again.
Rena.	She went through a lot to get my amulet back for me. I'll miss her.
Krista.	*running up*. Hey, guys, wait!
Dew.	Huh?! (*then turns around*)
Rena.	Krista, it's you. I thought we would never see you again.
Krista.	I want to come along with you, guys.
Lorenzo.	Really?
Krista.	I gave up my job as a tour guide for a while. So I want to offer my services to you, guys, on your mission.
Dew.	It'll be dangerous.
Krista.	I don't care; I can take care of myself. Since my brother and the Black Mantas are in prison, and the Alderman has total control of the providence now, Llivisaca is secure again. I really have no reason to stay here; plus I always wanted to see more of the world than Llivisaca anyway.
Dew.	Well, as long as you can help, then it's fine.
Krista.	I will.
Dew.	Works for me then.
Rena.	Welcome aboard.
Krista.	Awesome.
Narrator.	With that said, Dew and the others leave Llivisaca and continue onward with their journey. The scene switches to a few days later as we find Dew and the others roaming around the Mesovilla plains only to get caught in an incoming snowstorm.
Cooper.	Hmm . . . it's beginning to snow.
Lorenzo.	All this walking we've done, now it starts snowing.
Dew.	We've got to keep going.
Rena.	I don't know about you, but I'm kind of tired from all the walking. We should take a rest.
Cooper.	It is getting a bit shivery as well.
Krista.	That wouldn't hurt one bit.
Dew.	*coughs*. You're right. We'll have to find some shelter until the weather lets down.
Rena.	Okay.

Narrator.	Dew and the others head toward a cave nearby and camp there. As the group get comfortable around the campfire, Dew stares off into the flames as the others begin to fall asleep. Rena approaches Dew.
Rena.	Dew, how are you doing?
Dew.	I'm good.
Rena.	It's been a while since I've traveled like this.
Dew.	Huh?
Rena.	I meant by that as being out and all.
Dew.	Oh.
Rena.	Nice to get out of that cold.
Dew.	This is true.
Rena.	Well, don't stay up too late in thought. Try to get some rest now.
Dew.	I will. Hey . . .
Rena.	Yes?
Dew.	You okay?
Rena.	I'm fine, why do you ask?
Dew.	Just making sure.
Rena.	Oh . . . (*yawn*) Well, good night, my friend. (*then walks off*)
Dew.	Good night.
Narrator.	Dew stares into the campfire flames more as they begin to crackle. After a while, he falls into a deep slumber. Dew dreams of the first day of his training in the SWAT Trooper Elite Academy. He is lined up in formation with the other recruits. General Landmore walks into the room.
General Landmore.	Welcome . . . welcome, my elite soldiers. Welcome to the SWAT Trooper Elite Academy. You, men, have been chosen to represent our great country. Your individual qualities make you far surpass any other. (*then starts to walk around the recruits*) You're no longer in the care of your families; we are your family now. Your training will be harsh and difficult, but if you make it, it will pay off in the end. We are one collective unit from this point on. United we become; this is a brotherhood. Look out for one another as you would your own. Always be there for your comrades, and never leave a man behind.
Rena.	Dew.
Dew.	Umm.
Rena.	Dew, wake up.

Dew.	Huh?! (*startled*)
Lorenzo.	Hey, man, it stopped snowing.
Cooper.	I thought it would never stop.
Krista.	We should leave now before it starts up again. Trust me, the weather here in the plains are unpredictable.
Dew	*then gets up on his feet.* Right.
Rena.	You look at peace when you sleep.
Dew.	I had a dream.
Rena.	Was it a good one?
Dew.	It wasn't anything of importance.
Rena.	Oh. Well, off we go again then.
Dew.	Yeah . . .
Narrator.	Dew and the others exit the cave and continue their journey. After traveling for a bit, Dew and the others come to a stop as they pass through some old ruins.
Lorenzo.	What is this place?
Cooper.	It looks like this was once some kind of citadel of some sort.
Rena.	Hmm . . . that it does.
Krista.	Actually, this is the ruins of the Priscus.
Lorenzo.	The who?
Krista.	The Priscus. They were a civilization that existed nearly fifty million years ago. Some say that they possessed great magical power and were a highly technological race.
Lorenzo.	So what happened to them?
Krista.	From what I was told when I heard about these stories; the Priscus ended up becoming consumed by their powers which led to their own destruction.
Dew.	How sad that is.
Krista.	Some say that we humans are the "children of Adan and Leva".
Lorenzo.	Who are they?
Krista.	These two were the only surviving Priscus left after the down fall of their civilization. So Adan being the only male left and Leva being the only female left; they together repopulated the world. Kami spared their lives so they could bring bliss back to the old world.
Lorenzo.	Well you put it like that; it makes perfect sense to me now. I'm a believer
Cooper.	I have heard of this as well when I was growing up from my relatives. We as people could learn from their mistakes, and hopefully not make the same ones in the end as they did.

Dew.	Preach it brother.
Lorenzo.	May Kami watch over us all on this journey.
Krista.	I am sure Kami is. (Then smiles at Lorenzo)
Rena.	Ha-ha-ha . . . Where did you hear that from, I may ask?
Krista.	When I was growing up, the town's people always talked about it.
Rena.	Sounds like one of those old wives' tale to me.
Dew.	You don't think it's true?
Rena.	I don't think it is.
Krista.	Say what you want, but I like to think it's true.
Rena.	I see. Well, we should get moving some more then.
Narrator.	The others then walk on ahead, and Dew turns to Rena.
Dew.	Sifu.
Rena.	Yes?
Dew.	Don't you think you were a little rude there?
Rena.	No, not at all. I just personally think the story about the Priscus to be a bunch of hogwash. Who could believe such a thing?
Dew.	Well I obviously do.
Rena.	Hmm . . . .
Dew.	Wait a second; I am a little confused now. You were the same person who taught me to have faith in Kami, and you are the one who gave me a sense of spirituality. But now it seems you are contradicting your teachings by denying all of that.
Rena.	You're taking it the wrong way. I never said I doubted there being a higher power. It's just that specific story I have doubts about . . . that is all.
Dew.	Hmm . . .
Rena.	I'm just a little tired from the walking too. I'm sorry.
Dew.	It's okay. Well, let's get moving then.
Rena.	You don't believe me?
Dew.	I do. I never said I didn't.
Rena.	Okay then.
Narrator.	Dew and the others continue as they exit the ruins. After some time, they reach a small village called Cumbersome.
Cooper.	I guess this is the closest town. We've traveled pretty far. I'm tired.
Krista.	I'm getting pooped myself.
Lorenzo.	Time for a break. We're running low on provisions, so best if we stock up here as well.
Krista.	So this is Cumbersome Village.

Lorenzo.	So many places outside of Helix; this is so new to me.
Cooper.	You've never been here before, Krista?
Krista.	Not at all.
Cooper.	I've never been here either.
Narrator.	A little boy walks up to the group.
Little boy.	Excuse me.
Krista.	Yes?
Little boy.	Are you, people, new here? You look lost.
Lorenzo.	Kind of. We're just passing through.
Little boy.	Do you need help?
Dew.	Actually, we're looking for this person as well. Have you seen any one passing through from outside your village as of late?
Little boy.	Not recently. You, folks, are the only new faces I seen as of late.
Dew.	I see.
Cooper.	There's no point of stopping here then.
Dew.	Well, we'll be going to Twin Pines now.
Little boy.	Twin Pines you say? I used to live there when I was younger. Why are you, folks, heading there, if I may ask? Are you planning to climb Mount Illini?
Dew.	I didn't think about all that.
Little boy.	Hold on . . . I know someone that can help you out with that. Follow me. (*then runs off*)
Rena.	Hmm . . .
Cooper.	Should we follow him?
Rena.	It seems like a waste of time if we do.
Dew.	I think he might be of some use to us. Let's see what this kid can do for us.
Narrator.	Dew and the others follow the little boy through the village until they are led to a straw hut; they then enter it.
Lorenzo.	Some getup this is.
Little boy.	You said you're going to climb Mount Illini, right?
Dew.	I guess so.
Little boy.	*shouting.* Mr. Oilla! Mr. Oilla!
Narrator.	Vilmer enters the room.
Vilmer.	Boy, what did I tell you about yelling? Konrad, what are you doing here so early? (*then turns and looks at Dew and the others*) You brought strangers into my house I see. If it isn't one thing, it's another.

Rena.	We're just passing through, and the young man wanted to assist us. He told us that there is someone here who can help us on some info about climbing Mount Illini.
Vilmer.	Mount Illini?
Dew.	Yes.
Vilmer.	You, folks, want to climb it, huh?
Lorenzo.	Well, yeah.
Vilmer.	Hmm . . . Konrad, go home and I'll see you later. I need to talk to these folks in private.
Konrad.	Okay. Good luck to you, my friends. (*then exits*)
Vilmer.	I can tell you, folks, this; you don't want to climb that godforsaken mountain.
Dew.	Huh? Why not?
Vilmer.	It's a sad story.
Lorenzo.	Why's that?
Vilmer.	Like I said, it's a sad story.
Rena.	Hmm . . .
Dew.	I see where this is going. Listen, all we want is some information about climbing, and we'll leave you alone then.
Vilmer.	You, guys, really want to know that badly, huh? I might as well share my story with you then. Just something to keep in thought. It happened twenty years ago.
Narrator.	The scene changes to Vilmer and his mountain climbing assistant, Aldous, as they set up camp midway up Mount Illini.
Vilmer.	The weather should let up in the morning. (*sneeze*)
Aldous.	We've come this far (*cough*) . . . We're about to make history once we get to the pinnacle of this mother.
Vilmer.	We'll be well-known then.
Aldous.	Ha-ha-ha, this is beautiful.
Narrator.	The wind then begins to pick up.
Vilmer.	Seems like the wind is getting stronger. We should go inside soon.
Aldous.	I'm going to take a smoke; you go ahead. I won't be long.
Vilmer.	Aldous.
Aldous.	Yo?
Vilmer.	I see the headlines now: "Oilla and Ghislain, the men who toppled the largest mountain in the world."
Aldous.	It's got a good ring to it. I like that a lot.

Vilmer.	Yeah. Don't be out too long. (*then walks toward the tent and enters*) Got a long way to go, but almost there. (*then lies down for a nap*)
Aldous.	*screaming*. VILMER!
Narrator.	Vilmer springs to his feet and runs outside from the tent to find Aldous hanging from the edge of the cliff.
Aldous.	Help!
Vilmer.	Shit . . . hang on! (*then runs over and grabs Aldous's hand trying to pull him up*) C'mon!
Aldous,	*hanging from the edge of the cliff*. Don't let go . . . ugh . . .
Narrator.	The weather begins to worsen as Vilmer struggles to pull Aldous up. The wind becomes stronger, and visibility decreases. Vilmer's grip loosens as Aldous dangles over the edge of the mountain. Vilmer tries to regain his grip, but Aldous's hand slips; and he falls to his death.
Vilmer.	ALDOUS!
Narrator.	The scene switches back to the present time.
Vilmer.	After that, I continued my climb up the mountain. I did reach the top, and it was a joyful moment; but I was wracked with sorrow though. It was supposed to be me and Aldous that were going to accomplish this together, but I did it without him. I felt I could've done more to save him. I still feel that to this day. So this is why I will never climb that mountain or any other again. Bittersweet. I advise you all not to do it either.
Rena.	It's all in the past now. You did what you could.
Krista.	It is sad that you lost your friend, but I don't think you should let that one bad experience stop you from climbing again.
Vilmer.	That bad experience is some thing that I wish had never happened, and would like to forget about it. But I can not, so I will never climb again.
Lorenzo.	Dammit, man, get over it already.
Dew.	We do need someone to help us get up that thing. You're the only one that can help us out here.
Vilmer.	I'm sorry, I can't . . . It's best if I don't. Now if you'll all kindly leave, I have errands I must complete today.
Krista.	But . . .
Dew.	It's all right. Thank you anyway for your time though. Come on, let's go.

Narrator.	Dew and the others then exit. Once outside the hut, they talk among each other.
Cooper.	What now?
Dew.	I guess we'll have to climb the mountain ourselves with out his expertise then.
Lorenzo.	Aye, aye . . . I guess freezing to death will be fun. Hah!
Villager.	YEEK!
Cooper.	Where did that come from?
Narrator.	A villager runs up to Dew and friends.
Villager.	Help, help! Please, help me.
Lorenzo.	What's wrong?
Villager.	Konrad, he's in trouble.
Vilmer	*walks outside.* What's all the commotion out here?
Villager.	Vilmer, Konrad is being attacked . . . (*then faints*)
Vilmer.	Konrad! (*then runs off*)
Dew.	Hey, wait a sec.
Narrator.	Dew and the others follow Vilmer to come across Konrad being cornered by a large mutated armor beetle.
Vilmer.	What the heck is this thing?
Dew.	Another mutation.
Lorenzo.	Great, a giant cockroach.
Konrad.	M-Mr. Oilla, help!
Vilmer.	Hold up. Here I come.
Narrator.	Vilmer runs over to Konrad's aid. He picks up a grappling hook that is lying on the ground nearby. Vilmer then throws it at the mutated armor beetle. The armor beetle becomes slightly irritated and turns its attention to Dew and the others. Konrad flees.
Vilmer.	Oh, I think I pissed it off.
Lorenzo.	That you did.
Dew.	Too late to run now. We've got to stop this thing here before it goes off and hurts someone else.
Narrator.	The armor beetle charges at Dew, Vilmer, and the others; and the fight begins. After defeating the armor beetle, Dew and the others walk off. The menace then rises up and quickly heads after a fleeing Konrad.
Lorenzo.	It was playing dead?!
Vilmer.	Konrad, run! (*then chases after the armor beetle*)
Narrator.	Konrad continues to run as the armor beetle is in pursuit of him. Konrad turns around but trips over a tree stump, and the armor

beetle then advances on him. Out of nowhere, the armor beetle is sliced into pieces. Vilmer catches up finally to retrieve the unconscious Konrad. Dew and the others come face-to-face with Konrad's hero, Elvir.

Dew.	So it's you again.
Cooper.	Hello there.
Krista.	What are you doing here?
Elvir.	Surprised, huh?
Cooper.	Not at all.
Lorenzo.	So you were following us this whole time.
Elvir.	Yes. If I may add too, you, guys, walk too fast. It was a pain keeping up with you all. My legs are so tired . . . ha-ha-ha.
Dew.	Why'd you save the boy?
Elvir.	Thanks to you all, the Black Mantis Society no longer exist. For that, I am grateful.
Dew.	How so?
Elvir.	After joining them, I had became corrupted by their cause and totally lost touch with my original intentions of wanting to help those dear to me back home. Now that I am my own person again, I will make up for all that lost time and help out those who need it. With this, I offer my assistance's to you blokes for your journey. What do you say?
Dew.	I don't know about all of that. I must say no.
Cooper.	What?!
Dew.	Sorry, but no.
Vilmer.	What do you mean? This girl just saved Konrad's life.
Dew.	I doubt a thief can be trusted.
Krista.	I agree with him on that.
Cooper.	Oh, come on now, Dew. You and Lorenzo are the same like her.
Dew.	Excuse me?
Cooper.	Well, it's true.
Dew.	You're comparing me and him to a common thief? Why are you defending her?
Cooper.	I'm just saying, you could give her a chance.
Elvir.	Yeah, give me a chance.
Dew.	Yeah right.
Vilmer.	I got an idea. I want all of you to return to my house with me. You as well, Elvir.
Elvir.	Do you have anything to eat perhaps?
Vilmer.	Yes. I was just making breakfast.

Elvir.	Cool.
Dew.	Very well.
Narrator.	The scene changes to a few hours later. Dew and the others with Elvir are waiting outside Vilmer's hut. Vilmer then exits outside to talk to them.
Dew.	How is Konrad doing?
Vilmer.	He's going to be all right.
Rena.	What now, Dew?
Dew.	We're going to Twin Pines.
Vilmer.	Well, you'll need an experienced mountain climber then.
Lorenzo.	You know of someone else?
Vilmer.	Ha-ha-ha . . . don't be silly. I'm talking about me.
Lorenzo.	Oh, now you want to come along.
Vilmer.	Sure do. After fighting that creature, I haven't felt so vigorous in a long time. I will be honored to help in your journey.
Rena.	What about Konrad?
Vilmer.	The village doctor will keep care over him until I return. All I can do is accompany you, guys, for helping me save him.
Dew.	Good then.
Elvir.	What about me. Can I come along?
Dew.	Euh . . .
Cooper.	Dew, come on.
Elvir.	I'll be very useful. I won't get in the way at all. Plus we're no longer enemies now. Just here to lend a hand in something good for once.
Cooper.	She did help us out back there.
Krista.	That is true. All on you, Dew.
Dew.	Who made me the leader of all of this?
Lorenzo.	It's something naturally you have, man.
Dew.	Uh . . . fine. You can come along. No funny business.
Elvir.	I won't. That's a Girl Scout's honor.
Krista.	Something tells me you probably were never in the Girl Scouts.
Elvir.	I wasn't; just trust me. I won't disappoint you all.
Rena.	Twin Pines seem so far away.
Vilmer.	No, my dear. It's a mountain climb away.
Dew.	Well, team, let's go. There's no stopping now.
Narrator.	Then Dew and friends exit Cumbersome Village to continue their journey. A day passes by, and they reach the gates to the providence of Twin Pines.
Lorenzo.	So this is Twin Pines.

Krista.	It just looks like it does on the pamphlet. Well, in person it's more breathtaking though.
Dew.	Home again.
Rena.	Looks like nothing has changed here at all.
Cooper.	We're here at last. So let's take a break?
Elvir.	Sounds good to me.
Dew.	It's been a long walk; we should take a rest. I haven't been home in a while, so I need to go visit a friend of mine.
Krista.	It's not like you get every day to come home. We can go walk around and familiarize ourselves with the area.
Lorenzo.	That's cool with me. Where should we meet up at afterwards?
Dew.	The back gates of Twin Pines. That will lead us to Mount Illini.
Vilmer.	I need to go buy some equipment for our climb then.
Elvir.	I'll go with you.
Dew.	All right then. See you all later (*then walks off*)
Cooper.	What about you, Rena?
Rena.	I personally need some alone time. I have to go somewhere to think alone.
Cooper.	Okay then. Well, see you later. (*then walks off*)
Narrator.	As the others walk off, Rena begins her walk down the streets. After walking a few blocks, she comes to an old run-down schoolhouse. She then enters it.
Rena.	Not so different than we were before . . . memories.
Narrator.	Rena then walks up to a dusty old drawer. She opens it and finds a picture frame lying down. She then picks it up and wipes the dust off it.
Rena.	*looking at the picture*. Kenneth, if you were only here with me now. All of this . . .
Narrator.	Rena then dazes off and remembers the first time she met her late husband, Dr. Kenneth Voight, twenty-four years ago in the province of Marigold at the SWAT Trooper Elite Academy laboratory.
Dr. Eudora.	Ms. Cullen, could you hand me the test tube over there on the table?
Rena.	Yes, Doctor. Which one do you want?
Dr. Eudora.	The one labeled Sulfuric Chloride.
Rena.	Okay. (*she grabs the test tube*) Here you go. (*the test tube slips out of her fingers*) Oops!
Narrator.	Rena accidentally drops the test tube, but in a flash, a young man catches it, preventing it from breaking.

Kenneth.	You should be careful when handling vials like these. Don't want to melt that pretty skin off now, do we? (*then gives the test tube to Rena*) Here you go. (*then smiles at her*)
Rena.	T-thank you.
Dr. Eudora.	Who are you?
Kenneth.	I'm Kenneth Voight. The capital sent me here to serve as assistant for the new project.
Dr. Eudora.	That's right; you're the graduate from Helix University we've been expecting. (*then extends his right hand out for a handshake*) My name is Dr. Alfred Eudora. Pleasure to meet you.
Kenneth	*shakes Dr. Eudora's hand.* The pleasure is the same here, Doctor.
Dr. Eudora.	This is Ms. Cullen.
Kenneth.	Nice to meet you, Ms.Cullen.
Rena.	It's Rena Cullen.
Kenneth.	My, what a beautiful name that is.
Rena.	Thank you. Thank you very much. He-he-he.
Dr. Eudora.	Ms. Cullen was a recent graduate from Demmin University. It seems like we'll all get along well then.
Rena.	Yes, Doctor, I believe so too.
Kenneth.	I agree . . . (*then smiles at Rena*) So . . .
Rena.	Ha-ha-ha.
Kenneth.	What's so funny?
Rena.	I've never seen someone as handsome as you are.
Kenneth.	Really. Well, you're the finest woman I've ever seen.
Rena.	*blushing.* Oh, thanks.
Dr. Eudora.	Well, I think we should get back to what we were working on earlier, Ms. Cullen, and let Dr. Voight get settled in here.
Rena.	Of course, Doctor.
Dr. Eudora.	Dr. Voight, I will show you around the facility and then to your room.
Kenneth.	Yes, Doctor. I'll be looking forward to working along with you, Ms. Cullen. I feel comfortable already here.
Rena.	Me as well.
Kenneth.	Take care. (*then exits with Dr. Eudora*)
Narrator.	Rena continues to reminisce into her past, as the scene changes to six months later as the development of the Priscus project is in its middle stage.
Dr. Eudora.	It took us a while, people, but we did it. Governor Videl shall be pleased with the completion of our gene-enhancing toxin.
Rena.	What were the results so far?

Kenneth.	Be patient, my love.
Dr. Eudora.	I'm glad you asked me that. I'm about to get to that. I'm really excited myself about this as well. SKT (systematic karyotype takeover) virus, this toxin can change a single individual DNA structure by mutating it completely. Enhancing the levels of strength, stamina, and intelligence, this toxin is the ultimate supersoldier formula. The virus in earlier studies had affected the lymphocyte in the subjects as well.
Rena.	Causing faster health regeneration as well. So the subjects undergo an anatomic reconstruction.
Dr. Eudora.	Exactly. This whole time we've spent countless hours and days toiling to make this toxin have paid off. This thing will be able to cure diseases and make our future generations stronger in every aspect than the predecessors. For the demonstration, SWAT trooper, bring in the specimen.
SWAT trooper.	Yes, Doctor.
Narrator.	The SWAT trooper then brings in a caged swine.
Dr. Eudora.	Now our entire earlier tests have been conducted on guinea pigs as you known. Yet that's not close enough to human beings. So with this specimen here has a muscular, skeletal, cardiovascular system relativity close enough to a human being. By birth, our specimen has normal qualities. Yet if we were to alter its genetic structure with our toxin, it will surpass all normal abilities of a normal swine.
Narrator.	Dr. Eudora then takes a sample of the SKT virus into a syringe and then injects the swine with it. The three then stand back and watch as the specimen slowly mutates in front on them.
Kenneth.	Amazing, it's working, Doctor.
Dr. Eudora.	This is amazing, indeed. What does the readings say, Dr. Voight?
Kenneth.	*checking the computer terminal.* The brain matter of the subject has increased 25 percent more; muscle mass has increased by 52 percent. It's really working!
Dr. Eudora.	We've done it. We've far surpassed those scientist who uncovered the human genome and even Thomas Edison's discovery of electricity. This will be in the history books forever! Ha-ha-ha!
Narrator.	The swine then begins to convulse and starts aggressively ramming its head into the bars.
Rena.	?!

Dr. Eudora.	What's going on?
Kenneth.	I'm not sure . . . There seems to be an abnormal increase of brain matter in the frontal lobe; all other areas are slowly declining.
Rena.	What does that mean?
Dr. Eudora.	This isn't good.
Narrator.	The mutated swine then breaks out of the cage after constantly ramming his head against it. Once on its feet, the swine snorts and gives off a painful squeal as it runs towards Dr. Eudora. The SWAT trooper quickly draws his rifle and shoots the swine between the eyes. The mutated swine falls to the floor dead, and Rena stares in shock after what has happened. Rena then continues to remember further into her past. Six years have passed since that day of the SKT trials. This would be the last time she would see Kenneth.
Rena.	Kenneth, put some more thought into this.
Kenneth.	I have my love, and I must continue the research. Dr. Eudora has been expelled from the committee, and the government needs me to do this. They've granted me more money to continue on with the research in New Havenport.
Rena.	Kenneth, forget about it; you don't need to do this.
Kenneth.	I dedicated my life to science so this project must be completed.
Rena.	What about me? Us for crying out loud?
Kenneth.	I love you of course, my dear. I must do my duties though. The virus is finally in its final stage after our restless hours of work put into it. It possibly can work this time with no altering effects.
Rena.	Kenneth, please think of the children.
Kenneth.	I am thinking of them.
Rena.	No, you're not. You're participating in causing genetic genocide; that's what you're thinking about and doing. Stop being selfish.
Kenneth.	Selfish? I am not. Rena, come with me to New Havenport.
Rena.	No, Kenneth. I will not. I don't want that burden knowing what could happen once they start using that on humans.
Kenneth.	I told you the formula has come along way than that mistrial we had two years ago. In science, as you know it, we explore the wonders of nature instead of contemplating about them. Even if we have to alter naturalism itself, it's for the best.
Rena.	I can't believe I once thought like that. That's ignorant.

Kenneth.	I don't want to lose you, but I must continue my work. Rena, will you come with me?
Rena.	I'm sorry, but no. If this is how it must be, and then let it be. I gave you my love; you chose self-consideration. Fate is cruel, but this is for the best. (*sigh*)
Kenneth.	Then it is good-bye to you, my love. (*Then walks away*) This is how it is.
Rena.	Never again . . .
Narrator.	Rena then wakes up out of her daze as she drops the picture frame onto the floor. The glass shatters all over the place. She looks down at the shattered glass lying at her feet.
Rena.	Just like now and before, my life is like this glass that lays on the floor . . . shattered and in pieces . . . ha-ha-ha. Never again.
Narrator.	Rena then exits the run-down schoolhouse. Meanwhile, on the other side of town, Dew comes up to a house. He stops at the door and pauses.
Dew.	It's been a while . . . Is this right of me to come here now? After all these long years . . . I must do this now. (*Then he knocks on the door. He waits for a moment, but no one comes to the door.*) I knew this was a mistake . . .
Narrator.	Dew then walks off; then the door then opens up, and a familiar face greets him.
Emily.	Dew?! Is that you?
Dew.	*stops walking, then turns around to face Emily.* Emily . . . hi. (*then walks up to her*)
Emily.	My god, it's been a long time. (*opens up her arms to hug Dew*)
Dew.	Yeah . . . it's nice to see you. (*then smiles at Emily*)
Emily	*then pulls back from the hug.* You look different . . .
Dew.	You've grown up a lot as well.
Emily.	We should talk. I'm happy to see you . . . so happy.
Dew.	I'm speechless . . . man.
Emily.	Let's go inside and talk.
Dew.	Yes, please.
Narrator.	Dew then enters Emily's house. The scene switches over to the family living room as Dew and Emily converse.
Emily.	This has been a surprise. I thought I would never see you again.
Dew.	Surprises happen here and there.
Emily.	I mean this is a very good surprise though.
Dew.	How have you been?

Emily.   I've been all right.

Dew.   That's good. I see the town hasn't changed too much from when I was last here.

Emily.   When you were last here, I heard that you were in the hospital after that bombing in New Havenport. I did come and visit, but I found out that you had already left. I didn't find out until a week later that you were there.

Dew.   I tried to come by and see you before I ran off. I had some business to take care of though.

Emily.   I see that business of yours kept you away from home for six years. What are you up to these days?

Dew.   Oh . . . I have a few jobs here and there. Mainly caretaking to the poor. Ha-ha.

Emily.   Charity work . . . sounds like something you would do.

Dew.   Yeah . . .

Emily.   Dew, do you have any other woman in your life?

Dew.   No, not me.

Emily.   He-he-he . . . Still my little stud I remember growing up with.

Dew.   Ha-ha . . . I remember when me, you, and Hopkins would sneak out of school to go down to the boat docks and fish.

Emily.   Every Friday that was. Those were the days. I remember those sunsets, sitting there and watching them with you, guys. It was a magnificent sight. Ha-ha-ha, I remember something else.

Dew.   What's that?

Emily.   I remember when your grandfather caught you and my brother going up on Mount Illini.

Dew.   How could I forget that? He was so pissed at us. So many times.

Emily.   Ha-ha-ha.

Dew.   Ha-ha-ha . . . those were the days.

Emily.   The memories we have . . . now since Hopkins is gone, it's been so dull. I miss him a lot and my family's passing. (*sigh*)

Dew.   I'm sorry. When did this happen?

Emily.   It was sometime after Hopkins had died . . . It's okay. They're happier now.

Dew.   Emily, what happened to that guy you was engaged to? I remember you were getting married. Did you ever do that?

Emily.   No. He died in a car accident a few months after my brother did . . . and the rest of my family.

Dew.	Oh . . . I'm so sorry. I wish I didn't ask you that now. Are you okay?
Emily.	It's okay really, like I said things like that happen in life. I dealt with it all these years. Too long it's been.
Dew.	Hmm . . .
Emily.	Dew, why are you back here now?
Dew.	Passing through with some friends of mine. Since we happened to come through here, I thought it would be a good idea to come by and visit you.
Emily.	You always did love the adventure of things. I want you to know something. I've never stopped thinking about you, not once. Every day we've spent together when we were growing up meant a lot to me. It runs through my mind daily, even when I wake up or going to sleep. You're in my thoughts. I had always hoped to see you again . . . Here you are now. Ha-ha.
Dew.	Emily, I . . .
Lorenzo.	Dew! (shouting)
Dew.	exhales sharply.
Emily.	Your friends?
Dew.	Yes.
Emily.	I see you have to go again.
Dew.	Kind of.
Emily.	Are you coming back here anytime soon?
Dew.	I will.
Emily.	Are you sure of that?
Dew.	Emily, I will be back to see you. I wish I had more time to, but . . .
Emily.	I'm just messing with you. I know you will. Thank you, Dew.
Dew.	Emily . . .
Lorenzo.	Hey, Dew! Where ya at?
Dew.	I'll see you later. I will come back. Bet on it. See ya later.
Narrator.	Emily runs up to Dew and gives him a kiss on his cheek.
Emily.	I will be waiting for you.
Narrator.	Dew smiles at Emily then turns away to exit her house. He then steps outside to be greeted by Lorenzo.
Lorenzo.	Dew, there you are, man. Hey, the others are ready to go now.
Dew.	Okay then, let's go.
Narrator.	The group is waiting for Dew at the back gates of Twin Pines. Dew and Lorenzo walk up.

Lorenzo.	I found him.
Dew.	I'm here. We're all ready to go?
Cooper.	No better time than the present.
Rena.	I think it would be a good time now to explain to some of us who just joined us for our journey, to know what's going on.
Vilmer.	I would like to hear this. You, guys, never did explain to me fully about that.
Krista.	I'm all ears.
Elvir.	That would help.
Dew.	Well, let me summarize it then. We're after a man named Thornton. He killed Governor Videl and is leaving a trail of death behind him as well. He's trying to obtain a virus vial, the SKT virus.
Elvir.	SKT?
Cooper.	It's a mutagenic pathogen that can alter a host genetic structure, ultimately mutating them into uncontrollable creatures.
Krista.	Why is this man collecting them?
Lorenzo.	Who the hell knows? He's a strange character I know that.
Dew.	All we know is that once he obtains all four, he will unleash them upon the world. We have to stop him from doing this.
Elvir.	What's he going to do, take a giant syringe and spew it out into the world? Ha-ha-ha.
Dew.	Laugh it up, but this is no joking matter. I've seen what this can do to people. If anyone else thinks this is funny, then turn around and leave.
Elvir.	I didn't mean it like that. Sorry . . . damn.
Vilmer.	I see the seriousness of this. We're all here now, so we must all continue onward. I will be glad to help you all once we get over the mountain.
Krista.	This goes beyond my skills, but sounds like fun to me.
Lorenzo.	Always an adventure.
Elvir.	Well, I'm sticking with you, guys, regardless.
Dew.	Cool.
Krista.	I never thought seeing a mountain up close would be so breathtaking.
Cooper.	Kind of intimidating at the same time.
Elvir.	We're climbing that?
Vilmer.	Yep. It's not that bad of a climb, trust me.
Rena.	We should go then.
Vilmer.	You ready for this, Dew?

Dew.	There's no other way. Yes.
Vilmer.	This brings back memories. Bless us Lord for the climb we are about to embark on. I don't need to lose more friends because of this thing now.
Lorenzo.	We're all sturdy, don't worry.
Dew.	Memories indeed.
Narrator.	With that said the group then begin their climb up Mount Illini. Hours pass by as Dew and the others come one-third up the mountain.
Vilmer.	It's been so long since I did this. I almost forgot how exciting this is.
Lorenzo.	Exciting . . . yeah if you like freezing to death.
Krista.	It's not so cold now.
Dew.	I think we should take a pit stop here.
Elvir.	Let's do that. I'm getting exhausted here.
Narrator.	They climb up onto a ledge of the mountain and then take a stop to rest. Elvir lies flat on the ground.
Vilmer.	Ah, the horizon is still just as amazing as it was twenty years ago.
Krista.	The base is hardly visible from up here.
Lorenzo.	I'm not used to all this climbing junk. I'm a city boy; I'm not made for the outdoors.
Vilmer.	You'll get used to it once you do it some more.
Lorenzo.	Hah. No, thank you. I'll take the good old concrete jungle any day over this. I, at least, I know where my feet are going next.
Elvir.	Amen to that.
Lorenzo.	Err . . . all this climbing has made me a little light-headed all of a sudden.
Vilmer.	That's just the elevation doing that to you. The higher you go in the atmosphere, the less oxygen there is.
Lorenzo.	I wouldn't know anything about that stuff now.
Narrator.	Suddenly, a cloud of mist covers the area.
Vilmer.	This is odd. It's got foggy all of a sudden.
Cooper.	Hmm . . .
Dew.	This isn't fog.
Thornton.	Ha-ha-ha . . . You actually came. (*then jumps out of the fog and lands right in front of Dew*)
Dew.	Thornton.
Thornton.	I see you brought some new friends along too. You were always a persistent one.

Elvir.	This is the guy were after?
Thornton.	I got a little worried you weren't going to show up. I see I was wrong to assume that. I couldn't count you out when it really mattered.
Elvir.	He's talking, and I already don't like him.
Thornton.	Let's play a game, shall we?
Dew.	What are you up to?
Thornton.	If you want to find out, you got to catch me. Ha-ha-ha. (*then he disappears*)
Dew.	Thornton, wait! Damn, he's gone again.
Krista.	Odd man he is.
Vilmer.	We should continue on upward.
Narrator.	Dew and the others continue their climb up the mountain. During the ascension, Dew begins to remember his encounter when he had first came along the trails.
Young Dew.	Hopkins, this way. (*running*)
Young Hopkins.	Wait for me, Dewey. (*running right behind Dew*)
Narrator.	Young Dew stops as young Hopkins catches up to him . . .
Young Hopkins.	What yaw find?
Young Dew.	*picking up a rock*. I found this. (*then shows the rock to Hopkins*)
Young Hopkins.	It's so shiny.
Narrator.	As Young Dew and Hopkins observe the rock, a dark shadow then appears behind them.
Young Dew.	Hopkins, what's that smell? Is it you?
Young Hopkins.	No.
Young Dew.	Did you pass gas?
Young Hopkins.	Nooo . . .
Young Dew.	Liar.
Narrator.	Then they hear a loud growl from behind them as they continue to play with the rock.
Young Hopkins.	Dewey, was that your tummy just now?
Young Dew.	No. I thought that was you.
Young Hopkins.	If that wasn't you, then who was it? (*then turns around*) Gulp! Dewey, l-look!
Young Dew.	*turning around*. Oh boy!
Young Hopkins.	R-run!
Narrator.	Young Dew and Hopkins quickly leap down the hiking trail as the mountain lion chases them down. The mountain lion springs up and knocks Young Dew to the ground, pinning him there. Young Hopkins continues to flee. The mountain lion snares at

	Young Dew and is about to bite him until Grandpa Wilder arrives, battling the beast off his grandson. The mountain lion gives off a whimper and runs off.
Grandpa.	Dew, didn't I tell you not to ever come up here alone? You're lucky I happen to be here. If not, you would have been dead by now. I had the whole town looking for you and Hopkins.
Young Dew.	Sorry, Grandpa.
Grandpa.	You okay?
Young Dew.	Yes, Grandpa. Where is Hopkins?
Grandpa.	He's at the base of the trail. He's all right, but he's parents are very angry at him as well.
Young Dew.	I'm sorry, Grandpa.
Grandpa.	I don't want you ever coming up here again. It's too dangerous. I don't need to have a stroke worrying about you, kids. You mean a lot to me.
Young Dew.	I won't . . . I won't ever again.
Narrator.	The scene switches back to present time as Dew and the others come to another stop point on the mountain.
Vilmer.	Hmm . . .
Dew.	What's up?
Vilmer.	I know it's been a while since I last climbed this mountain. Yet I don't remember this area being here at all. Something seems different about this.
Rena.	Well, mountain structures do change in a matter of years.
Vilmer.	That's true. It's truly been a while indeed.
Narrator.	Cooper looks over at Dew who begins to shiver.
Cooper.	Dew, what's wrong?
Dew.	I feel cold all of a sudden . . .
Elvir.	No shit, look where we're at.
Dew.	It's not that . . .
Narrator.	Suddenly, Thornton appears again.
Thornton.	Good you all caught up now. Finally.
Dew.	Thornton.
Elvir.	Not this jerk again.
Thornton.	Nice to see you all again too. Are you enjoying your climb by the way? Ha-ha-ha.
Elvir.	That's it . . . I had enough of you.
Narrator.	Elvir tried to attack Thornton, but he disappears and then reappears behind her to trip her. She falls to the ground on her face.

Thornton.	Ha-ha-ha . . . Silly child.
Elvir.	*getting up off the ground*. Damn you.
Dew.	Thornton, enough of these games.
Thornton.	This is fun though. Ha-ha-ha.
Cooper.	Thornton, let's end this here and now.
Thornton.	If we did that now, this whole journey would be meaningless. There's much to learn still. (*then turns and looks at Rena*) So much . . .
Narrator.	Suddenly, a loud growl is heard as it echoes throughout the whole trail.
Vilmer.	What's that?
Dew.	Huh?!
Narrator.	A four-legged creature comes running from atop of the mountain down land in front of Dew and the others.
Thornton.	It seems nature wants to meddle in the way of us. Well, I'll leave you, guys, alone. Have fun. (*then disappears*)
Krista.	That's one huge kitty.
Dew.	So it's you again. Go figure.
Elvir.	First we have to deal with that lunatic and now this? Man, what did I get myself into here? I hate cats.
Vilmer.	Mountains lions aren't the friendly cuddly type. We got to get past this thing.
Dew.	There's only one way to do that.
Narrator.	Dew and the other engages the mountain lion in battle. They eventually slay it. Dew and the others continue their climb. After a while they come to the peak of the mountain to find a large opening to an underground cavern.
Cooper.	A large hole. Wonder where this leads to?
Vilmer.	Well, this wasn't most certainly here back then.
Krista.	It looks like some sort of hot spring.
Vilmer.	I bet if we would jump down this thing, the current will most likely carry us down to the bottom.
Dew.	We should give it a try then. Only one way but down.
Narrator.	The group one by one jumps into the hot spring trail, landing into the underground cavern below.
Rena.	*wiping her forehead*. It's humid down here.
Krista.	An underground cavern. I wonder where this leads to?
Vilmer.	I bet this cavern has an exit. That exit will probably lead us outside somewhere.

Cooper.	Let's walk in and see then.
Rena.	Should we, really?
Cooper.	Why not?
Rena.	What if we get lost or it leads to a dead end?
Cooper.	Have we before?
Rena.	Ah . . .
Dew.	Rena, are you okay? Something seems like it's bothering you.
Rena.	Nothing, Dew. I . . . I must be getting tired again. Let's go on and see what we can find.
Dew.	Hmm . . . All right, let's go on forward then.
Narrator.	Dew and his friends continue venturing through the cavern, and the encounter a few hostile creatures. After a while, they find Thornton waiting for them.
Thornton.	Funny how we always end up meeting like this. I see you all didn't become kitty mix after all.
Dew.	Shut up! Enough.
Thornton.	Are you tired of me already? The fun has just begun.
Cooper.	Thornton, you damn fool. Stop wasting our time.
Thornton.	I'm a fool? Ha-ha-ha . . . You know, you are the fools for coming here. The secrets of the past concealed here for so long . . . a tormented child will be free from the bondage of what science has done to him.
Rena.	whispering to herself. It couldn't be . . .
Thornton.	Our love for science brings misery and pain to us all. Misery now has company. (*then disappears*)
Elvir.	Where he go now?
Narrator.	The cavern floor beings to rattle, and something gives off a large roar.
Lorenzo.	I guess we're not out the woods yet.
Narrator.	Suddenly, a deformed muscular man jumps from the raptures to confront Dew and the others.
Krista.	What in god's name is this?
Cooper.	It's another mutation . . . It seems to be human. Rather used to be.
Rena.	No, dear God, no . . . (*then falls on her knees*) It can't be you.
Dew.	Rena?!
Narrator.	The deformed freak then swings at Cooper and Elvir; they dodge back to avoid his hits.
Elvir.	Well, he's not friendly; that's obvious.

Lorenzo.	I see we'll have to bust him up then.
Rena.	Don't!
Elvir.	What?! It just attacked us.
Rena.	You can't . . . He's not a . . .
Dew.	Huh?
Lorenzo.	I don't know about her, but I know we got to stop this thing.
Narrator.	The group rushes at the mutated freak as Rena sits on the ground in disbelief. It was a grueling battle. In the end they manage to slay the deformed freak.
Lorenzo.	Loco.
Vilmer.	That was a workout.
Elvir.	Is he dead?
Dew.	*yelling*. Thornton! No more tricks!
Narrator.	Rena scoots herself near the corpse of the deformed freak.
Rena.	Poor child . . . they did this to you.
Cooper.	Rena, what are you doing?
Rena.	They used you like a dog . . . I should have never left you behind. It's my entire fault. I'm sorry . . . (*sigh*)
Dew.	Rena.
Rena.	I'm sorry . . . So it has come down to this. No more.
Dew.	Hey, Rena.
Rena.	Dew . . . I'm fine. (*then gets up on her feet*) We should go find Thornton.
Dew.	Rena, what's going on? Is there something you want to tell us?
Rena.	I have nothing at all. (*exhales deeply*) No worries. (*then walks off*)
Vilmer.	Weird . . .
Cooper.	We need to watch over Rena more. She's acting strange.
Dew.	Maybe it's just the traveling that's causing her to act like this. She normally would be this way.
Cooper.	Let's just make sure things are all right. I have an odd feeling about all of this.
Dew.	Yeah.
Narrator.	The party then walks off to head toward the exit. After exiting the cavern, Dew and the others find themselves in the province of Marigold.
Rena.	Ha-ha-ha . . . So we are led here. Of course.
Dew.	Huh?
Krista.	This is the providence of Marigold.

Elvir.	We've come this far.
Lorenzo.	Some trip this has been so far.
Rena.	There's no denying it . . . my past is calling for me.
Dew.	What are you talking about? You're hiding something from us.
Rena.	My young pupil, you will know soon enough. I don't have time to explain to you in depth. I know where Thornton is heading. I must do this (*then runs off*)
Dew.	Rena, wait!
Lorenzo.	What's up with her?
Dew.	I don't know.
Vilmer.	This is insane. When I climbed the mountain twenty years ago, none of this was here. It looks like this was manmade, this whole structure of the cavern to lead to here. Things most definitely change throughout time.
Cooper.	So we're in Marigold. As I think about it more now, the only thing that is out here in this providence is the SWAT Trooper Elite Academy.
Krista.	Why would she go there?
Dew.	I don't really know. For what?
Cooper.	What do you think we should do, Dew?
Dew.	We should go after her. I'm beginning to get a bad feeling about this.
Narrator.	Dew and his friends then hurry to the SWAT Trooper Elite Academy. Meanwhile, Rena enters the academy grounds and comes across the bodies of dead elite soldiers. After entering the main building, she roams around for a while until she comes to a laboratory. She enters a room and is confronted by Dr. Alfred Eudora from behind with a handgun.
Dr. Eudora.	I didn't expect to see you ever again, especially here.
Rena.	I thought I would never hear that voice of yours again, Doctor.
Dr. Eudora.	Ha-ha-ha . . . Such a fool to come here at a time like this. I do wish we could have met again under better circumstances.
Rena.	*then turns to Eudora.* Alfred, what's going on here?
Dr. Eudora.	I'm pretty sure you've seen already the bodies of those soldiers splattered about by now. The handiwork of his weapon. It's all come down to this. I knew that spineless yuppie would send someone to kill me off. He's trying to cover his tracks . . . My life work will not be taken away from me. I refuse it!
Rena.	What are you babbling about?

Dr. Eudora	pushes the gun barrel into Rena's back. Don't act stupid with me. You know what exactly I'm talking about. The Messenger of Death is coming soon for me. Then perhaps you're my taker. Ha-ha-ha . . . That's a joke . . . No, not you.
Rena.	"Messenger of Death"? You mean Thornton?
Dr. Eudora.	So you do know. Hah . . .
Rena.	He's here to get the virus vial, huh?
Dr. Eudora.	Now you remember, I see. That's correct, but he will not get it though.
Rena.	Hand it over to me. I'll keep it safe. I assure you of this.
Dr. Eudora.	Sorry old friend, no can do. I rather hold onto this myself, thank you very much. I will not let just anyone get their hands on the SKT virus G.
Rena.	Are you crazy?
Dr. Eudora.	Because of your honey poo, I was put out of a job. I still continued my part of the research. After I heard Kenneth was killed in the bombing in New Havenport, I knew that sly weasel Zircon had taken the SKT virus C. Yet he didn't know about the whereabouts of the other three.
Rena.	Where are the other two at?
Dr. Eudora.	Like I would tell you. That information is too important. I will no longer allow my work of science to be used for other purposes. My work, nobody else's!
Rena.	Alfred, don't be foolish. Your life is endanger. Hand me the vial.
Dr. Eudora.	Like I said before, I can't do that. No hard feelings though. You see I have to protect what's mine. Say hello to Kenneth for me.
Narrator.	Suddenly the room begins to get dark with mist.
Rena.	What the?!
Dr. Eudora.	Huh?! (*turns his attention away from Rena and begins looking around in confusion*) No, it's not . . . H-he's here.
Narrator.	Then Thornton appears.
Dr. Eudora.	You.
Rena.	!
Thornton.	So we meet again, Doctor.
Rena.	Alfred, give me the vial.
Thornton.	*walking toward Eudora.* We should talk.
Dr. Eudora.	S-stay back . . . (*pointing his gun at Thornton*)

Narrator.	Thornton, in a flash, pulls out his sword and slices Dr. Eudora's gun in half.
Dr. Eudora	*falls to the ground. Ugh!*
Thornton.	You know what I've come here for; hand it over.
Dr. Eudora.	Over my dead body.
Thornton.	As you wish. (*then severs Eudora's head off with his sword*) What a shame . . . (*bends over Eudora's corpse, going through his pockets to retrieve the SKT virus G vial*) This is what I wanted. Yes, soon. Elizabeth, soon, my love . . . soon. The stubborn ones always die so easily. Hah.
Rena.	Elizabeth?
Thornton.	*then turns to face Rena.* Well, now, I almost forgot about you there . . . mother of my love.
Narrator.	As Rena stands facing Thornton, the scene switches to Dew and the party arriving at the front gate of the academy grounds.
Dew.	Rena is inside somewhere. We need to split up into two groups to find her. Who's coming with me?
Lorenzo.	You know I will, buddy.
Krista.	You can depend on me.
Cooper.	I guess I'm left with?
Elvir.	Don't take forever trying to figure this one out. I'm tagging along with you. Duh.
Vilmer.	This works for me. Let's get going. Rena could be in trouble by now.
Narrator.	Dew, Lorenzo, and Krista then enter the compound as the others go in the opposite direction to search for Rena. Dew and his companions find themselves surrounded by slain bodies of soldiers.
Lorenzo.	Well, it's obvious that we're going in the right direction.
Dew.	He's been through here.
Krista.	I find it hard to believe that one man could do all of this. Impossible.
Dew.	You'll be surprised. We must keep going though.
Narrator.	After roaming around the Elite Acedemy premises, Dew and his group find Rena and enter the research room.
Dew.	Rena.
Rena.	Dew.
Dew.	Why'd you run off of us?

Rena.	I had to take care of some business.
Narrator.	Krista then notices the headless corpse of Dr. Eudora on the ground.
Krista.	*gasps.*
Lorenzo.	That's what you call taking care of business, huh?
Thornton.	Don't give her too much acclaim; that was all me.
Dew.	*turns to face Thornton.* Thornton.
Thornton.	This is heart warming; the whole gang is here now. You're too late, Dew. I beat you to the punch. (*showing Dew the SKT virus G vial*)
Dew.	*exhales sharply.*
Thornton.	Two down, two to go.
Krista.	What are you doing all this for?
Thornton.	For the rebirth, of course. You'll all witness the Angel of Death's passing of judgment.
Lorenzo.	Rebirth? Angel of Death? Judgment? Please, stop it with your blasphemy. Who do you think you are, God?
Thornton.	That's not important right now, but there is something you should all know. Isn't that right, Rena?
Dew.	What are you talking about?
Rena.	. . .
Thornton.	All that is occurring now is all because of her.
Dew.	Huh?
Thornton.	It was her and her husband, Dr. Kenneth Voight, from the beginning that brought this miserable toxin into the world.
Dew.	Your lies are weak, like you've become. I don't believe a single word you're saying.
Thornton.	You think I would make all this up? Is it really that hard to believe me? Why would you come all this way for me to deceive you with lies? I think somebody is being in denial, hmm?
Dew	*then looks at Rena.* I doubt it.
Rena.	Dew.
Dew.	No . . .
Thornton.	Don't believe me? Then why don't you ask her if it's true or not. C'mon, Dew, prove me wrong. Are you afraid of the truth?
Dew.	I don't believe it. But . . .
Rena.	It's true . . . What he is saying is all true.
Dew.	Rena, why?
Rena.	It happened so long ago. It was a selfish devotion to science. Dew, I . . .
Dew.	Rena . . .

Thornton.	Dew, do you remember when you and the others were pursuing me in the underground cavern right before coming here? That deformed creature you fought, remember him?
Dew.	What about it?
Thornton.	It's also true that my love Elizabeth and that SKT mutation are her offsprings from the early development of the virus. Her own children!
Dew.	What?
Thornton.	Yes, they were used as guinea pigs to test out the capabilities of the virus on human beings.
Rena.	That is true, but that was my husband. I loved my children, but I hated the fact that I left them behind with him so I could live a normal life. I couldn't do anything to prevent that from happening. It disgusted me that science could destroy lives instead of saving it. It was all about war and profit. The mistakes we make in the past eventually catches up to us . . . No more running. I will face my responsibilities for everything.
Thornton.	My Elizabeth, she was taken away from me. Now, my revenge on this pathetic world will pay off in the end.
Rena.	Dew, I should have been truthful with you from the start about all of this . . . I'm sorry.
Dew.	Rena, it doesn't change a thing. I don't care about what happened long ago. The present is all that matters now. We can't change the past; we pay for our actions in the end though. Yet we learn from it and move on.
Thornton.	Ah, forgiveness.
Dew.	Thornton, to think I respected you once and admire how you once fought for the right in life. Now you only want to cause more pain and misery than before. All this death to come . . . I will not allow it to happen.
Thornton.	You're too much. I shall obtain all four soon.
Krista.	You're a true loser.
Thornton.	Says you? Hah! I won't let you nor your friends get in my way, boyee!
Dew.	We'll finish this here then.
Thornton.	Yes. It's been a while since I've fought. This will be fun, just like the good old days during the war. I hear your pain and sorrow already. I yearn for it and will ravish in it. Death is all I live for. Let your death be good!

Narrator.	Dew, Lorenzo, and Krista battle Thornton. The battle is fierce; the three manage to avoid Thornton's lethal blows with his long sword. Dew then goes in as Thornton is distracted by the other two for a shattering blow to his chest with his bo. Dew injures Thornton causing him to fall on his knee.
Thornton.	*Ugh!* That was good. (*exhales deeply*) Annoying gnat! It's not over yet, Dew.
Narrator.	Thornton then leaps with his long sword in hand and is about to spear Dew with it. Rena pushes Dew out of the way; she takes the blow to her stomach. Thornton then pulls his sword out and flips away from Rena.
Rena.	*Ugh . . . (then falls to the ground)*
Dew.	RENA! (*then runs over to the fallen Rena*)
Thornton.	Soon our dreams will be fulfilled. Thus, we'll be one step closer to perfection. Heh-heh-heh . . . (*then disappears*)
Dew	*holds onto Rena's hand.* Rena . . .
Rena.	Dew, it's . . . getting dark . . . *Mmmm* . . . Darn it . . .
Dew.	Hang in there . . . Oh, Rena . . .
Rena.	My . . . it was nice to see you . . . again.
Dew.	Dammit, it's not fair . . . Why like this?
Rena.	Dew, I'm sorry I kept a lot from you . . . I . . .
Dew.	*Shhh* . . . save your strength, sifu. I'll take care of you . . . friends until the end.
Rena.	Ha-ha . . . Dew, we've been through a lot now. This sucks . . . I'm not afraid though . . . *Mmmmm* . . .
Dew.	Why'd you sacrifice yourself for me?
Rena.	You were the only thing I had close to family. I care about you. You saved me so many times and it . . . was my turn to play hero. That's what friends do for one another.
Dew.	Rena, no . . . it should have been me . . . not you. Damn!
Krista	*sighs.*
Rena.	Dew, here . . . (*handing Dew her amulet*)
Dew.	Rena, I can't. It's yours. Why? (*holding on to her hand tight*)
Rena.	I no longer need it . . . Take it and remember me . . . our cause for justice.
Dew.	Stop talking like that. You'll be fine. Rena?! Don't please . . .
Rena.	Our love . . . farewell, my (then starts coughing up blood) . . . friend. Until we meet again . . . live. *Uugh* . . .
Dew.	Sifu?! (*shaking her*) Rena . . . no. REEEEENNNNNNAAAAAA!

Chapter 3

Essence and Vigor

Narrator.   Our chapter begins as Dew is in slumber dreaming of the first day when he arrived at the SWAT Trooper Elite Academy. A bus carrying Dew, Hopkins, and the other recruits pulls up at the academy. Hopkins then looks out the window.

Hopkins.   I can't believe we're here already.

Dew.   Hmm . . .

Hopkins.   *looking out the bus window.* That was a long boat ride here, but the hotel stay made it worth it.

Dew.   Yeah . . .

Hopkins.   *looking out the bus window.* This is where the fun begins.

Dew.   If you want to call it that.

Hopkins.   *then turns to Dew.* You think it's going to be tough for us?

Dew.   I don't know, but we'll see. All I can say is we signed up for this, so it's do or die.

Hopkins.   You're right . . .

Narrator.   The bus then comes to the front gate of the academy. The guards standing watch open the gates; then the bus passes through to enter. The bus pulls up in the SWAT Trooper Elite Academy compound. Dew observes from the window the recruits marching in unison and another group of recruits in the distances active in physical activities. The men then begin to gather their bags and get off the bus. Dew and Hopkins follow.

Hopkins.   Here we go.

Dew.   Oh yeah.

Bus driver.   Have fun now. Ha-ha-ha.

Dew.   Why's that funny?

Bus driver.	This is the place where all the boys go in, and they come out men.
Dew.	Hmm . . .
Bus driver.	What's wrong? You don't look so thrilled. You scared?
Dew.	Not at all. I'm just looking forward to getting this over with.
Bus driver.	Well, you'll have to get past the basic training first, son.
Dew.	That I will do.
Bus driver.	Well, lighten up a bit. You're in the military; you got a chance to prove to yourself that you are the best and represent our country as well. You're the heart and soul of it all.
Dew.	That's touching. Let me guess. You used to be in the service?
Bus driver.	Along time ago. You'll do all right, kid.
Dew.	I will.
Bus driver.	That's the spirit. Here's some advice for you: don't let the bastards get you down. It's all in the head.
Dew.	Thanks, I will remember that. Take care.
Bus driver.	You too.
Hopkins.	Thanks for the ride.
Bus driver.	Hey it's my job. Anytime. You're welcome. Good luck to you and your friend.
Narrator.	Dew and Hopkins then exit the bus. The bus door shuts and the bus drives off from the academy premises.
Dew.	*turns to Hopkins*. Good luck? He made that sound like a bad thing.
Hopkins.	Don't take it personally. He was just wishing us off well.
Dew.	I bet. Well, like you said, let the fun begin.
Narrator.	Dew and Hopkins walk off to join the other recruits. Dew continues to dream on as the scene changes to four months later after he and the other recruits had completed their basic training. The soldiers are enjoying their last night of fun on base before being shipped out to their duty stations. During the party, Dew sits in a corner watching the others drinking, chatting, and dancing. Hopkins approaches him.
Hopkins.	Hey, Dew. What are you doing sitting here all alone?
Dew.	Collecting my thoughts.
Hopkins.	Come on, man, get up and enjoy yourself. Just seeing you over here is making me all depressed.
Dew.	I'm fine.
Hopkins.	This is our last night of fun for a while; you should take advantage of it.

Dew.   There will be other times for that for me.

Girl 1.   *walking up*. Hopkins.

Hopkins.   *then faces the girl*. Hey you.

Girl 2.   Why don't you come over here with us? We want to hear more about yourself.

Hopkins.   Oh yeah? Don't worry ladies; I'll be with you in a moment.

Girl 1 and 2. Okay.he-he-he. (*then walks off*)

Hopkins.   This is going to be fun, oh yeah!

Dew.   Hmm . . .

Hopkins.   Dew, I don't know what to tell you. Just find something to do that's not boring.

Dew.   What maybe boring to you, isn't to me. I just need to think about some stuff here.

Hopkins.   Ok, man. Well, I'm going to go. I must go now and attend to my admirers. See ya. (*then walks off*)

Narrator.   As Hopkins walks off, General Luis Landmore walks up to Dew.

General Landmore. Why the long face there, son?

Dew.   A bit . . . (*then raising out of the chair*)

General Landmore. Wait a sec. You're Wilder's grandson, Dew?

Dew.   You knew my grandfather?!

General Landmore. Yes. Your grandfather and I were in the same unit together during the Liberation War. I remember the last time I saw you when you were eight years old. I use to live a couple of blocks down the street from you. Your Grandfather had invited me over to play poker a few times with him and the other veterans. Do you remember me now?

Dew.   As I think about it more, I do remember you. It's been so long since I last seen you.

General Landmore. I had left Twin Pines to see the world a bit. I got bored sitting around at home doing nothing. It's funny; you're the spinning image of your grandfather.

Dew.   Hah . . . I guess. I thought you were retired?

General Landmore. I was, but after seeing the world and all; I got bored of the civilian life and decided to join the military again to teach the next generation of the elite the skills I had learned when I was in. So I see you're following in the footsteps of your grandfather.

Dew.   Yeah.

General Landmore. He was a remarkable man. I heard that he had passed away. I'm sorry for that.

Dew.   I'm dealing with it. We all have to go someday . . . Yeah.

General Landmore. Well, son, you may of lost one family. You've got the military as your new one now.

Dew.   That's true.

General Landmore. I don't blame you for isolating yourself over here. I never really cared for parties myself too much.

Dew.   Hmm . . .

Sergeant Lahaina. *walking up.* So, General, are we having a good time?

General Landmore. I'm fine. Sergeant Lahaina, how is your night going?

Sergeant Lahaina. It's going well, sir. *(then looks at Dew)* Hello there. I'm Sergeant Lahaina.

Dew.   Lance Corporal Wilder.

Sergeant Lahaina. Nice to meet you. So you got through basic training. You ready for the battle field now?

Dew.   Truthfully, I don't know what to expect, but will survive.

Sergeant Lahaina. I like that. That's what I like to hear from our men. Keep up the morale there son. Well, it's going to be a long war I see, especially this one.

General Landmore. Tell me about it.

Sergeant Lahaina. Well, sir, at least we have the greatest men supporting us out there. I'll be glad to get this over; the sooner the better. General, I heard that Thornton was assigned to your unit.

Dew.   Who?

General Landmore. Yes. I've heard a lot of things about him.

Sergeant Lahaina. Well, from experience, sir, he's a knucklehead. He lacks respect for others, but I have to admit as much as I dislike him, he does get the job done though.

General Landmore. Well, that's all I look forward to doing, getting the job done.

Sergeant Lahaina. I wish you luck with him, sir.

Thornton.   *walking up.* You say that as if I was some kind of trouble, Sergeant.

Sergeant Lahaina. Sergeant . . . what a surprise. We were just talking about you.

Thornton.   That you were, and not in a good way either.

Sergeant Lahaina. Well . . .

Thornton.   It's all right; it's all true though. Like you said, I get the job done. I will do that.

Sergeant Lahaina. Yeah, yeah.

Thornton. I see these are our new "men of war." Ha-ha-ha . . . look at them enjoying themselves not realizing what they are about to endure. The fun is worth it now, but makes you wonder how many of them will go AWOL or even survive the first week during the war. Bunch of slobs.

Sergeant Lahaina. I'm sure they'll all make us proud.

Thornton. If that were so true . . . General, it will be an honor to serve under your unit.

General Landmore. Why thank you, Sergeant. We can use your expertise in my unit. I want you to meet one of my other men in our unit. This is Lance Corporal Wilder.

Dew. Nice to meet you. (*then raises his hand to shake Thornton's hand*)

Thornton. Yes . . . anyway, I must be going now, sir. See you later. (*then walks off*)

Dew. That was rude of him.

Sergeant Lahaina. That's Thornton for you. Well, I must be going now. Nice to have met you Lance Corporal Wilder.

Dew. The same here, Sergeant.

Sergeant Lahaina. Sir, have a good night. (*then salutes General Landmore*)

General Landmore. Same to you, Sergeant. (*then salutes Lahaina back, and Lahaina drops his salute and walks off*) Interesting evening it's been already.

Dew. This is true.

General Landmore. Well, I will be going myself now. Enjoy the party and see you in the morning.

Dew. Yes, sir. (*then salutes General Landmore*)

General Landmore *salutes Dew back and then drops it.* Good night to you. (*then walks off*)

Dew. *whispering to himself.* Grandpa . . .

Narrator. As Dew continues to dream, he goes deeper into his past. The scene shifts to the day of his grandfather's funeral. Dew enters Twin Pines Cemetery walking toward his grandfather's grave. He is carrying a bouquet of flowers; he kneels over to pay his last respects.

Dew. Grandpa, I'll always remember you . . . I will make . . . you proud, and I will live up to you. I won't stop now . . . never . . . stop.

Narrator. As Dew weeps over his grandfather's grave, suddenly a hand pops through the soil and grabs his leg. Dew is startled and tries

	to get away, kicking at the hand. The hand lets go, and then it is Thornton who ascends from the soil and confronts Dew.
Dew.	What the?!
Thornton.	Never stop . . . ha-ha-ha . . . Well, boyee, you better start now! Heh-heh-heh . . .
Dew.	*Ahhhhhh!*
Narrator.	Dew then awakes from his daydream and shudders in the thought he just had. We find Dew in Emily's house in her attic back in Twin Pines. He sits near the window pane as he tries to collect himself. Lorenzo then knocks at the attic door.
Lorenzo.	Dew, you okay? Let me in!
Dew.	Lorenzo . . .
Narrator.	Dew then goes over to unlock the door to let Lorenzo in. Lorenzo then enters.
Lorenzo.	*walking in.* I heard you screaming. You all right?
Dew.	Yeah. I just fell asleep for a bit. It was a nightmare.
Lorenzo.	Looks like you haven't slept too much as of late.
Dew.	I've almost forgotten what that is.ha-ha.
Lorenzo.	Hey, man, I think you should come down now.
Dew.	I need more time to think to myself and atone.
Lorenzo.	Think and atone to yourself? You're going to drive yourself crazy. Come on, man, the others have been asking about you.
Dew.	I am fine, really. I just need to think some more.
Lorenzo.	I think you have done enough thinking as it is. The others are wondering about you. Let's go see them.
Dew.	No. Why should you care?
Lorenzo.	It's not normal for someone to lock themselves in an attic for a week straight to just think.
Dew.	Sure it is . . . I just need time to be alone.
Lorenzo.	I think you've been alone long enough. Listen to me, friend. Rena is gone. She's not coming back anytime soon. You got to realize that. We all have to go someday.
Dew.	It didn't have to be this way though.
Lorenzo.	Well, that's life. She sacrificed herself to save you from harm, and she knew that even in the end. You shouldn't beat yourself up over it, man.
Dew.	Don't remind me.
Lorenzo.	Okay now, my friend, it's time to stop dwelling on the past and move on. You've been doing that too much already. Let's get on going. We still have to look for Thornton.

Dew.	No, I don't want to anymore.
Lorenzo.	Huh?
Dew.	I don't want to risk losing others who are close to me. I can hardly bare the thought that Rena is gone. I . . .
Lorenzo.	I can't believe this.
Dew.	It's too much of a risk . . .
Lorenzo.	Listen to yourself talking. You're quitting on us and yourself.
Dew.	I am not! I just need to reassess the situation.
Lorenzo.	Bullshit, homes.
Dew.	It isn't . . . Leave me be.
Lorenzo.	Well, I don't know about you, but I'm going to stop him myself then. You can sit here like a baby and cry, but I refuse to idly stand by and let that creep do as he pleases. It's your choice, ese.
Dew.	Whatever . . .
Lorenzo.	I see then. Well, I'm not a quitter, unlike you.
Narrator.	Lorenzo then exits. Dew stands there in thought as he begins to question himself.
Dew.	*exhales deeply*, Hmm. I . . . can't do this to myself, or them. No, it's not right . . . He's right. Why am I acting like this? Rena would want me to continue on. Oh, the feeling though of losing more of my friends . . . no. No, I won't give up! No, dammit! It's not over yet! I will continue on . . . for Rena.
Narrator.	Dew then walks out the attic and head downstairs to the living room to meet up with the others who are waiting for him.
Krista.	Dew?!
Vilmer.	Long time no see, stranger.
Lorenzo.	Dew.
Dew.	I made up my min . . . Let's get going. We don't have any more time to waste.
Elvir.	I see someone is feeling better now.
Cooper.	Welcome back, friend.
Dew.	I'm sorry for the wait. I just had to go through some thoughts I had. Well, I can say I'm no longer going to dwell on the past; just look forward to the future.
Lorenzo.	Rena would want that as well. I'm glad you came to your senses. Hey, man, sorry about being so hard on you back there.
Dew.	It's okay, I needed it. I did the same for you when you were down, so it helped coming from you. Thanks.
Lorenzo.	Anytime, man.

Cooper.	Seems like things are back to normal. I was beginning to worry about you there a bit, Dew.
Dew.	No worries; just had to get over some things.
Krista.	So where to now?
Dew.	That's a good question.
Vilmer.	We still have the other provinces to visit in Mesovilla.
Dew.	This is true.
Elvir.	Where do you think Thornton may be going next?
Dew.	I wouldn't know; I'm nonplus on that as well. I know that he's probably still searching for the third vial. Hmm . . . how will we get to those other providences though? They're across the ocean from here and . . .
Vilmer.	I wouldn't worry about that so much.
Dew.	Huh?
Vilmer.	While you had locked yourself away in confinement that attic here, the SWAT Trooper Elite Academy gave us a present to make our trip easier for us.
Dew.	Present?
Elvir.	It'll get us around a lot quicker than us being on foot.
Dew.	What is it then?
Elvir.	Come over to the boat dock and you'll see.
Dew.	They gave us a boat? I don't think we're all going to fit in a small dingy now.
Elvir.	It's much bigger than that now.
Dew.	I got to see this now.
Lorenzo.	While you, guys, are doing that, I will stock up on some provisions.
Dew.	That sounds like a good idea. Hey, wait a sec. Have any of you seen Emily around?
Lorenzo.	Last time I saw her was the third morning here. She was leaving out that day and wanted me to tell you that she was going to be gone for a bit and had to take care of some personal affairs. She didn't go in depth about it, but she left the house in our care.
Dew.	Did she say when she was going to return?
Lorenzo.	Not even that.
Dew.	Hmm . . . that's odd. What could she be doing? I hope she's all right.
Lorenzo.	I'm pretty sure she's fine. I wouldn't worry._

Dew.	Still weird how she just got up and left though. You're right . . . Well, there's no time to put further thought into it. Let's get going to the boat dock then, and we'll wait for you while you collect some provisions.
Lorenzo.	All right then. I'll meet you all there. (*then exits the house*)
Elvir.	Guess we'll be heading out then.
Dew.	Yes. Let's go.
Narrator.	Then the gang exits Emily's house and head over to the dock. Dew and the others come upon the boat dock and approached the moored tugboat.
Dew.	They gave us a tugboat, I see.
Elvir.	We're you expecting something luxurious?
Dew.	No, not at all. Still . . .
Elvir.	Well, this is all we need to get around. It's not like we needed some kind of battleship or something.
Dew.	I see your point. This will have to do then.
Lornezo.	walking up. ha-ha . . . not bad looking at all, huh?
Dew.	You got all the provisions?
Lorenzo.	Of course. Hmm . . . I've never been on one of these things before.
Elvir.	You will now. (*then hops from the pier onto the tugboat*) C'mon then.
Krista.	She seems so excited about this. (*Then hops from the pier onboard the tugboat*)
Cooper.	Oh yeah. (*then jumps from the pier onto the tugboat*)
Vilmer.	First climbing mountains, now out to sea. This is going to be fun. (*jumps from the pier to the tugboat*)
Lorenzo.	Fun . . . *hah!* I hope I don't get sea sick. (*then hops from the pier to the tugboat*)
Elvir.	Hey, Dew.
Dew.	Yeah?
Elvir.	Cast off those marline lines and hop on aboard.
Dew.	Cast off? What are marline lines?
Elvir.	Take the rope off the bit.
Dew.	Oh . . . (*then unwraps the line from the bit and climbs onboard the tug*) Are we going to float aimlessly now?
Elvir.	You'll see. Just follow me (*then runs off to the bridge*)
Narrator.	Dew then looks at Lorenzo.

Lorenzo.	Hey, man, I'm clueless about all this boat business as you are. Let's follow her.
Narrator.	Dew then follows Lorenzo to the bridge. Dew enters the bridge to find Cooper and Elvir talking as they are standing behind the ship's console.
Vilmer.	So many dials and buttons. Modern technology is so great.
Cooper.	Well, we got transportation now. So how do we operate this thing?
Vilmer.	You don't know how to?
Cooper.	No.
Krista.	I surely wouldn't know how to. This is beyond my training.
Lorenzo.	Come on, Dew. You're former military; you can set us a sail.
Dew.	I was apart of ground infantry as Cooper was. I've never had experience operating machinery like this before.
Lorenzo.	Oh damn . . . I sure in hell don't know a thing about boats.
Krista.	Is there any one here that knows how to use this thing?
Elvir.	Excuse me; I think you are forgetting about me here.
Lorenzo.	What do you know about boats, kid?
Elvir.	I can tell you that this type of boat here produces 750 to 3,000 horsepower. Also, the same engine for this tugboat is also used for railroad trains as well. It can maneuver 360 degrees and main use is for pushing other vessels into harbors, and—
Lorenzo.	Okay, okay. I get it. You know your stuff.
Dew.	Elvir, you seem like you have a vast knowledge about boats and all. Get us going then.
Elvir.	Aye, aye, Captain.
Dew.	Don't ever say that to me ever again.
Elvir.	Ha-ha . . . sorry. I've always wanted to say that. I just got a little excited. It's been awhile, but I got this.
Narrator.	Elvir then walks over to the ships console and depresses a button to start the tugboat propulsion. Elvir then goes over to the ships helm and moves the throttle lever up. This causes the tug's speed to accelerate, and the tug begins to shake.
Vilmer.	We're moving?!
Elvir.	I told you I knew what I was doing.
Dew.	You came in handy after all. Elvir, take us on out of here now.
Elvir.	Got ya.
Narrator.	With a steady spin of the ship's wheel, the tug then begins to set out to sea.

Dew.	Well, I guess after a few roadblocks, we're finally on our way again.
Cooper.	Took us a bit there, huh?
Dew.	Yeah . . . (*then looks at Rena's amulet*) No matter what, we got to stop Thornton. Not just to save the world, but in memory of Rena as well.
Krista.	I agree fully.
Elvir.	I can't believe I remember how to drive this thing . . . just like the good old times.
Cooper.	Elvir, how'd you learn to do this?
Elvir.	Oh, it was . . . long time ago. My father . . . he taught me.
Cooper.	Father? I thought you were an orphan?
Elvir.	I am. He's dead . . . He died a long time ago. Yeah . . .
Cooper.	Oh. I'm sorry . . .
Elvir.	No worries . . .
Dew.	Where do we go from here now?
Krista.	Well, we could check out the province of Minerva since it is the closest one to Twin Pines. We just might find a clue to Thornton's whereabouts there.
Dew.	Sounds good to me. Elvir, set a course for Minerva. We have no time to waste.
Elvir.	Aye, aye, Captain. He-he-he . . .
Narrator.	Dew walks over to the captain's chair and sits down in it.
Lorenzo.	Look at you there. From soldier there and now sailor, ha-ha-ha.
Dew.	Yeah, yeah. Don't hate.
Narrator.	The ship then steams off into the sunset of the beautiful Mesovillian horizon as they head toward their next destination. Meanwhile, back in the Helix capital, a van is speeding down a desolate highway. Inside the vehicle are two SWAT troopers; one driving and the other watching over Schwartz who is handcuffed.
SWAT trooper.	I never thought the day you would be in this position, sir.
Schwartz.	Life is full of surprises . . . *hmmm.*
SWAT trooper.	Well, I hope whoever is going to take your place as treasurer now, the pay gets better.
SWAT driver.	Ha-ha-ha. I hear ya on that brother.
Schwartz.	All this time I thought I was doing a good job. Ha-ha . . . Money is what it is all about gentlemen. It makes the world go around and surely nice to have. I at least have seen a lot more than you two ever did.

SWAT trooper. Where you're going, the only bags you'll be seeing is a bag full of dirty laundry.
Schwartz. Heh-heh-heh . . . Good one.
SWAT driver. Pretty funny there, Joe.
SWAT trooper. Yeah. Hey, how long do we have until we make it to the prison?
SWAT driver. Two more minutes, almost there.
Narrator. As the van continues speeding down the highway, a mist suddenly seeps into the van.
Schwartz. ?!
SWAT trooper. What the?!
SWAT driver. Are you smoking back there?
SWAT trooper. No way. (*coughs*)
Schwartz. So it is time . . .
SWAT driver. I think it might be coming from the engine. I'm going to stop the van.
Narrator. The van stops at the side on the road, and the driver gets out the van to check on the engine. He lifts up the hood and investigates.
SWAT driver. Hmm . . . this is odd.
SWAT trooper. *yelling*. Hey, Joe, what's wrong with the engine?
Narrator. As the driver lets down the hood, Thornton appears behind him and smacks the driver in the back of his head with the hilt of his long sword, knocking him unconscious.
SWAT trooper. Joe, everything all right? Joe?
Narrator. The SWAT trooper waits a moment for the response, but doesn't receive one back.
Schwartz. Ha-ha-ha . . .
SWAT trooper. What's so funny?
Schwartz. I wonder if your friend is okay. What do you think?
SWAT trooper. *gasps*. You are one strange man. I'm going to see what's going on out there. You stay here now.
Schwartz. I can't get too far with these restraints on. ha-ha-ha.
Narrator. The SWAT trooper then opens the rear door of the van and takes out his handgun as he creeps around the corner of the van to get a quick view of the surroundings. He notices the driver lying unconscious on the ground. He rushes over to check on him. As he kneels down to tend to his fallen comrade, Thornton appears out of nowhere again. This alerts the SWAT trooper's attention immediately, and he points his handgun at Thornton.

SWAT trooper. Freeze!

Thornton. You're a quick one.

SWAT trooper. Drop the weapon and hands in the air.

Thornton. . . .

SWAT trooper. Did you hear me? Drop it!

Thornton. My hands are full as you can see.

SWAT trooper. Okay, smartass, drop the weapon and hands in the air. Now!

Thornton. Quite the tone there in your voice. Let's see how good you really are.

SWAT trooper. I said drop your weapon and hands in the air. Now! Don't make me do this, pal.

Thornton. You delude yourself. I sense great fear and arrogance in you. "A-tishoo, A-tishoo, we all fall down."

SWAT trooper. What?

Narrator. Thornton then raises his sword up to his face; this startles the SWAT Trooper and he fires the gun at Thornton only to have the bullets deflected. Thornton then slashes the SWAT trooper's handgun in half. The SWAT trooper then tries to attack Thornton, but is knocked out with a single strike to his temple, rendering him unconscious next to the driver. Thornton then walks to the back of the van and opens the door.

Thornton. Long time no see.

Schwartz. It took you long enough.

Thornton. Happy to see me? (*then loosens Schwartz's restraints*)

Schwartz. It depends. (*then rubs his wrist*) That's better now.

Thornton. The time is ripe; much needs to be done.

Schwartz. This is true. Off we go then. (*then looks over at the two unconscious SWAT troopers*) You didn't kill them I see. Are you losing your touch?

Thornton. No, not at all. It meaningless to slaughter those who aren't much of a challenge. Only a true warrior of the same caliber like myself, deserves the honor of death. These peons's lives will be spared and they'll live with the humiliation and face their failures of a sorry existence. Silly humans and their flaws.

Schwartz. You make all that sound like it was some sort of sport. How kind of you to be merciful. I guess you're still human after all and not that killing machine we all know so well. Hah!

Thornton. That's your perception.

Narrator.	With Schwartz accompanying him, the two then disappear into the mist. As they depart, the SWAT troopers regain consciousness.
SWAT driver.	*rubbing his forehead. Ah, ow* . . . my head . . .
SWAT trooper.	Huh? What the?! That bastard . . . (*then gets up off the ground and runs over to check the back of the van and sees that Schwartz is gone*) He's gone?! Dammit!
Narrator.	The scene changes to Dew and the others who just arrive at the port in Minerva Marina. The tugboat slowly comes into the marina as it pulls up along the berth. Then Elvir runs down from the bridge to the decks over to the strobe control and begins to lower the anchor into the water.
Elvir.	Ah, haven't done this in a long time.
Cooper.	This will hold us in place, huh?
Elvir.	As long as the anchor doesn't drag, the sea state is good, and weather calm, no problems for us then.
Cooper.	You sure know a lot about this? I'm impressed. Ah . . . You got to teach me more about this someday.
Elvir.	I will.
Lorenzo.	Land at last. The seas weren't kind to my stomach, but the solid land will be now.
Krista.	So, this is Minerva . . . Nice. It sure looks a lot prettier seeing it in person than on a tour pamphlet.
Vilmer	*inhales and exhales deeply.* Hmm. It may not be the fresh air of the mountains, but the sea air is invigorating as well.
Elvir.	*looking off into the distances at the town ashore.* Home sweet home. This place hasn't changed a bit.
Lorenzo.	We're here now. So what's the plan ya?
Dew.	*walking up.* We should take a break.
Krista.	That's what I'm talking about.
Vilmer.	Not getting straight down to business, Dew?
Dew.	That was quite a long ride, so we all deserve to at least walk around and grab something to eat.
Lorenzo.	That sounds good to me, brother. I'm starving too. Good thinking.
Krista.	I'm with you on that.
Elvir.	*whispering to herself.* It's been a while . . .
Dew.	I think its best while we're here, we should stick together in groups then. So we don't get lost and it's a better way while we're in town to find out info about the whereabouts of Thornton.

Cooper.   That's a reasonable plan. Who's going to stay here and watch the boat?

Vilmer.   I'll stay and keep watch here. I rather stay and observe this gorgeous view of the ocean here.

Krista.   Wow, really?

Vilmer.   Yeah . . . of all my life being on land, I never realized how the other aspects of nature such as the ocean would be so breathtaking.

Krista.   You sound so passionate about it.

Vilmer.   Yes I do. The mountains are a majestic sight themselves, but nature over all is a beautiful thing. Once you get to my age, you begin to notice and appreciate the simpler things in life that surround you. I can say I am rather grateful for coming along with you all. I have seen so much already, this view though . . . amazing!

Krista.   I guess so, but I'm leaving. Lorenzo, you want to come with me?

Lorenzo.   Sure. As long as I don't have to be on this thing a second longer.

Dew.   Let's all meet up back here with whatever info we happen to come across out there.

Lorenzo.   Bet.

Krista.   We'll see you all later then.

Narrator.   Lorenzo and Krista then jump from the tug to the pier and walk off.

Dew.   So I guess it's just us three then?

Elvir.   Hmm . . .

Cooper.   What's wrong, Elvir? You all right?

Elvir.   I'm fine . . . I'll just stay behind with Vilmer for now.

Cooper.   You sure?

Elvir.   Of course. No worries.

Cooper.   Okay then. See you when we get back.

Narrator.   Dew and Cooper then jump from the tugboat to the pier and head off into the town.

Vilmer.   Hmm . . . something looks like it's bothering you, child.

Elvir.   Nothing bothering me. I just needed some alone time.

Vilmer.   It has been a long journey so far.

Elvir.   On second thought, I need to walk to do some thinking alone. I'll be back later. (*then walks over to the rails*)

Vilmer.   Are you sure you won't get lost?

Elvir.   I'll be fine. I know my way around here pretty well.

Vilmer.   Let me guess. You're from here, aren't you?

Elvir.	Stick with that feeling of yours there, you might be right. I just need to take care of some personal business alone.
Vilmer.	I understand. Be careful though.
Elvir.	I will . . . Nothing to worry about.
Narrator.	Then Elvir hops from the tug to the pier and walks off into the town. Sometime passes as Elvir comes along a small busy street and approaches a small orphanage. She comes to a stop and glares at the entrance.
Elvir.	It's been so long since I've been to this place . . . I wonder.
Narrator.	She then walks up to the entrance and enters. She is then greeted by an elderly woman who is one of the caretakers of the orphanage.
Caretaker.	Good morning to you. How may I assist you?
Elvir.	I'm looking for a friend of mine. Her name is Ms. Penway.
Narrator.	Ms. Penway then walks into the room.
Ms. Penway.	Oh?! Well, look who it is.
Elvir.	Ms. Penway, long time no see.
Ms. Penway.	Elvir, it's you. You've come back.
Elvir.	That I have.
Ms. Penway	*begins to smile.* Come here, dear.
Narrator.	Ms. Penway opens her arms to hug Elvir as they embrace one another.
Elvir.	It's nice to see you too. You're still the same kind old gal I remember.
Ms. Penway.	I see you've grown up. How have you been doing, dear, and how did the journey go for you?
Elvir.	Some nicks and bruises, but I'm okay as you see.
Ms. Penway.	Glad you finally returned.
Caretaker.	I remember you now. Forgetful me. It's been a while. Welcome back, Elvir.
Elvir.	Thank you. How are you doing by the way?
Caretaker.	Same usual routine. I would like to stay longer to talk though, but I'm currently in the middle of doing the children's laundry. I shall see you right. Glad you're back. Take care. *(then walks off)*
Elvir.	Nothing has changed at all. It's still the same how I left it. Ms. Penway, how are the others doing?
Ms. Penway.	They're all doing fine. They just left to go to the market a moment ago.
Elvir.	I just missed them, huh?
Ms. Penway.	They'll be back in a few.
Elvir.	I know they'll be happy to see me.

Ms. Penway.	You came back at a good time though. We're having some minor problems.
Elvir.	What do you mean? Please tell me.
Ms. Penway.	The bank is planning to foreclose on the orphanage.
Elvir.	What?
Ms. Penway.	We don't have enough money to support the mortgage.
Elvir.	What about the loans and the money I've been sending?
Ms. Penway.	The money you sent us helped us a bit to pay off the loan from the bank. Though it wasn't enough. Even if we could, that hustling industrialist, Lord Bouzigard, keeps raising the rent up on the orphanage so he can get whatever cent he can out of us. At the rate this is going, we'll be out on the streets.
Elvir.	I can't believe it has got this bad. I should have never left.
Ms. Penway.	You did what you could for us, Elvir. We'll just have to face the facts soon.
Elvir.	No. This is nonsense . . . they can't do this to you and the children . . .
Narrator.	A little girl enters into the room . . .
Betsy.	Elvir, you're back! (*then runs up to Elvir*)
Elvir.	Betsy?! (*then hugs her*)
Betsy.	You came back as you said you would.
Elvir.	Well, I couldn't stay gone too long from you all.
Ms. Penway.	Betsy and the other children always asked how you were doing. I would read them the letters you sent us about your trips. They're faces would get so bright with excitement and joy. I guess we should worry about this problem later on. You must be hungry; do you want something to eat?
Elvir.	Actually I am.
Narrator.	Someone then gives off a loud shriek from upstairs of the orphanage.
Betsy.	What was that?!
Ms. Penway.	Sounds like that came from my room.
Elvir.	Hmm . . . I will go check it out.
Betsy.	Elvir, no.
Elvir.	Betsy, it'll be all right. You two don't worry, I'll be back.
Ms. Penway.	I will come with you. Stay put, child.
Betsy.	Yes, ma'am.
Narrator.	Elvir and Ms. Penway then head up the stairs toward the room where the shriek came from. The scene switches to Ms. Penway's bedroom where two masked thieves are loading their bags with

	jewelry from the drawers. The maid lies on the floor bound and gagged, trying to squirm free of her restraints.
Archer.	That bloody hag bit me.
Darrow.	Stop your whining and help load these bags up already.
Archer.	Yeah, yeah.
Darrow.	Such a baby you are.
Maid.	*mumbling*. You scumbags!
Darrow.	Lord Bouzigard will be pleased with us. (*loading his bag with the valuables*)
Archer.	You think these people would respect the deadlines for paying off a mortgage? Just got to make up for it now.
Narrator.	Elvir and Ms. Penway then enter into the room; the two masked thieves are startled.
Darrow.	Shit!
Elvir.	Hey, jackasses, now what do you think you, guys, are trying to get away with here?
Ms. Penway	*looks over at the maid who is bound and gagged lying on the floor*. What have you done?! (*then runs over to the maid to loosen her restrains*)
Archer.	That damn woman gave us away.
Maid.	Ms. Penway, thank you. These mugs were trying to get fresh with me.
Archer.	We were not!
Maid.	You did so. You touched my boob.
Archer.	I did not.
Darrow.	I told you to be quick with shutting her up. Now look at the mess were in.
Archer.	Now how could I shut the bloody lass up if she bit me finger?
Darrow.	There you go again complaining about nothing.
Archer.	This is me finger here we're talking about, Darrow.
Darrow.	Oh great, genius, you gave us away now.
Elvir.	Darrow?!
Archer.	Wait a sec . . . it couldn't be . . . Elvir?!
Elvir.	Darrow and Archer? What are you two doing here?
Darrow.	Let's get out of here.
Narrator.	Archer and Darrow then head toward the window and jump to the streets below.
Ms. Penway.	Who were those men?

Elvir.	I have no time to explain. I must stop them. I'll be back.
Narrator.	Elvir then runs toward the window and jumps out of it to the streets below in pursuit of Darrow and Archer. Meanwhile, Dew and Cooper just happen to come walking up the street as Darrow and Archer run past them.
Cooper.	Hmm? Someone looks like they're in a rush.
Dew.	Who knows? Well, from the looks of it, no sign of Thornton here as well.
Cooper.	He'll pop up somewhere eventually.
Narrator.	Elvir then comes running up the street and dashes past them without saying a word.
Cooper.	Elvir?!
Dew.	Something is wrong . . . We should follow her.
Narrator.	Dew and Cooper run right behind Elvir into an alley. Elvir confronts the two thieves as Dew and Cooper catch up with her.
Archer.	Great, a dead end . . .
Darrow.	Nice sense of direction, dummy.
Archer.	Now why's it my fault all of a sudden? You followed the dummy, so you're a dummy too.
Dew.	Elvir, what's going on?
Elvir.	These two . . . I caught them stealing from the orphanage.
Cooper.	Stealing from children, that's pretty low.
Darrow.	Hah! They deserve it, bub!
Elvir.	How so? They have nothing of value to you.
Darrow.	They do. Yet we're only collecting the interest that is owed to Lord Bouzigard. They obviously can't afford it in cash, so interest works for us.
Elvir.	You two haven't changed at all.
Darrow.	Still the same smart-mouth brat I remember.
Cooper.	That's enough from you, mister; just hand back the goods now, and this will end peacefully.
Darrow.	Forget about it.
Archer.	Let's get rid of these pests now.
Darrow.	Now you're thinking for once.
Elvir.	I don't want to do this, but one way or another I will get those valuables back.
Narrator.	Elvir, Dew, and Cooper then battle Archer and Darrow. In the end they defeat and cause the two thieves to run off empty handed.

Elvir.	Running off like the jackals they are.
Cooper.	At least we got the valuables back. (*then picks up the bags*)
Dew.	Elvir, what was all that about? Do you know them?
Elvir.	I'll explain to you all later. I need to go back to the orphanage for now.
Cooper.	Orphanage? Is that where you been?
Elvir.	Yes. Come with me and I will explain it all soon.
Narrator.	Some time passes, and the scene switches back to the orphanage. Dew and the others along with Elvir return to the orphanage.
Lorenzo.	So what's so special about this place?
Elvir.	This is my home.
Lorenzo.	Huh?
Cooper.	I didn't know you were an orphan.
Elvir.	Not my whole life.
Krista.	I don't get it.
Elvir.	You can say this place is my second home in a way.
Cooper.	What do you mean?
Ms. Penway.	*walking into the room.* I can better explain everything to you all.
Dew.	You are?
Ms. Penway.	I am Ms. Joanne Penway. I own this orphanage and take care of the children here as well.
Dew.	Nice to meet you.
Ms. Penway.	It is true; this is Elvir's second home away from home. I met Elvir when she was twelve years old. She came to this place to find refuge from her father. I raised her then along with all the other children here. During our years of economical growth after the Great Civil War, we were having problems trying to keep the orphanage open with the heavy taxation on property here in Minerva. Every loan or bill we paid off never seemed enough to pay off. It would increase more and more and thus the cycle repeated itself. We could barely pay off the mortgage for the orphanage to Bouzigard's banks due to this.
Krista.	Your orphanage isn't government funded?
Ms. Penway.	No. Lord Bouzigard owns the foundation that the orphanage sits on. I own the orphanage.
Cooper.	Lord Bouzigard, who is this guy?
Lorenzo.	I have seen that name around town here a lot while walking around.

Elvir.	He is my father.
Cooper.	Your father?
Ms. Penway.	Yes, Lord Miles Bouzigard is the wealthiest man who owns many banks and other institutions here in Minerva, and pretty much owns most of this providence. He was once a member of the old Senate and retired shortly before the Liberation War had broke out. He decided to move down south and acquire land here in this province. The government had pretty much given him the whole province.
Cooper.	This is beginning to make sense now.
Elvir.	Yeah . . .
Ms. Penway.	Just because the Minerva province is a part of Mesovilla, we are a country of our own.
Krista.	Just like Llivisaca.
Ms. Penway.	Yes, but there was order still in our province. We fall under the government rule of commonwealth. This province thrives off of money to maintain a stable economy. For us we were unfortunate though. Times were looking hard, and the orphanage was about to be closed down. So Elvir had decided to go out into the world to find some means of work and help us out with the bills. So she did.
	After finding out the fact she had joined the Black Mantas Society to help us out in our financial runt, I wasn't proud of her choice yet had to accept it. So the money came in through mail. It helped for the time being . . . It wasn't enough in the end though. The children and I prayed that she would make it back to us alive. I felt so sad that I had put such a burden on her, yet she had made that choice to help us out. Nonetheless I waited hoping she would make it back alive, so she is here now. I've never been happier.
Lorenzo.	All this time I thought you were some little punk. I had you all figured out wrong. You've surprised me a lot already.
Elvir.	Funny what you can learn about a person, huh?
Krista.	Why did you leave your father?
Elvir	*sighs*. I left home because of the fact that all my father had cared about was money and regardless who he was hurting to obtain it, he cared less. He began to neglect those around him he had cared for as well. I got tired of it and needed to free myself from that life.

Cooper.	I think if you would have shared this about yourself before with us all, we wouldn't have mistrusted you so much.
Elvir.	You all can think what you want. This is something personal and I don't share my life with many. Plus it wasn't important at the time.
Vilmer.	It took some time, of course, that's with anything, even getting to know others.
Dew.	Well, we know now. So who were those dudes that we fought against? You seemed to have known them.
Elvir.	They were my father's henchmen and . . . my cousins.
Dew.	Really?!
Cooper.	Talk about disruptive families.
Elvir.	Yeah . . . So find out any info on that Thornton fella?
Dew.	None at all.
Lorenzo.	Nada.
Ms. Penway.	Well, it seems to be getting late. Do you all plan to stay here?
Dew.	Actually, we must be going; we have to finish a search for this person.
Ms. Penway.	I see.
Elvir.	Dew, can we stay? It's been a while since I've been home.
Dew.	I don't know . . . but . . .
Elvir.	Dew, c'mon. Please.
Dew.	Thornton might find the third vial and . . .
Cooper.	Dew, we should at least help her out here as well. These people need our help.
Dew.	Hmm . . . Might as well for the time being though.
Elvir.	Yes! Thanks.
Lorenzo.	Another pit stop? Well, traveling like this only comes once in a lifetime.
Cooper.	Better than being in the navy. Ha-ha-ha.
Dew.	I agree on that.
Narrator.	Dew and Cooper then high five one another.
Ms. Penway.	I will set a room up for you all then. For the time being, make yourselves at home.
Cooper.	Thank you kindly.
Narrator.	Ms. Penway then exits the room.
Elvir.	Home again. No place like it.
Lorenzo.	You all right there, kiddo?

Elvir.	Uh . . . yes. I am fine. If you all don't mind, I will excuse myself.
Dew.	No problem.
Elvir.	Just need to think about some things. (*then exits the room*)
Vilmer.	Hmm . . . I sense that the young lady has a lot on her mind.
Krista.	She must be happy to be home, you think?
Vilmer.	Maybe so.
Cooper.	I wonder what's wrong.
Vilmer.	She's probably just trying to get used to being back home again, after being gone for so long. It happens.
Cooper.	I suppose so.
Narrator.	Meanwhile, at Bouzigard Mansion, Archer and Darrow enter Lord Bouzigard's study room.
Darrow.	Lord Bouzigard.
Bouzigard.	Ah, you've come back already. Excellent. Where are the valuables?
Darrow.	My lord, we had a problem.
Bouzigard.	What do you mean?
Archer.	We don't have the valuables, and we ran into trouble.
Bouzigard.	The law enforcement?
Darrow.	No, my lord, we made sure that no local enforcements spotted us.
Bouzigard.	That would be bad for us indeed.
Archer.	She has come back home.
Bouzigard.	Who?
Darrow.	We were attacked by two men and your daughter as well.
Bouzigard.	Elvir?! Ha-ha-ha . . . So she's is still around. Hmm.
Archer.	We were caught off guard by this. Who would have expected this?
Bouzigard.	It all makes sense now. She's returned to save the orphanage . . . ah. She has always been a pain in my ass ever since the day she was born. That child of mine . . .
Darrow.	What should we do about the orphanage, my lord?
Bouzigard.	Well, since they don't have enough to pay for the mortgage, we shall close it down and put all of them on the streets . . . ha-ha-ha.
Darrow.	What about your daughter?
Bouzigard.	For her . . . I have a thought.

Archer.	Hmm?
Bouzigard.	Since she loves those children so much, we need to make an example out of one of them.
Darrow.	How so, my lord?
Bouzigard.	I want you two to return to the orphanage and kidnap one of the children there.
Archer.	Go there again? Those friends of your daughters may be there watching over the place.
Bouzigard.	This is why you two will be cautious about this and not fail me this time. Since we'll have one of the children as hostage, that owner will have no choice to sign over the lease to me. Once that is done, we can tear down the orphanage and start building another one of my banks in place of it. A perfect plan I must say.
Archer.	Crafty.
Darrow.	I bet she'll come to rescue the child though.
Bouzigard.	That is what I want as well. I know she will.
Darrow.	This will be done right away, sir.
Bouizgard.	Perfect way to see her again. Very good. (*then smirks*)
Narrator.	Archer and Darrow then exit Bouzigard's study. Back at the orphanage, Elvir is sitting down by the windowpane in the living room looking out into the starry night. Cooper enters the room.
Elvir	*sighs*
Cooper.	Elvir.
Elvir.	So pretty they are.
Cooper.	What's that?
Elvir.	The stars, aren't they magnificent?
Cooper.	I don't look too much at the sky anymore. I guess so.
Elvir.	Hmm . . .
Cooper.	Elvir, if you don't mind, may I ask you something?
Elvir	*turns to look at Cooper*. Not at all.
Cooper.	Why did you come along with us all?
Elvir.	Like I said before, I wanted to be useful to you all.
Cooper.	Why?
Elvir.	After being with the Black Mantas Society and realizing how I almost allowed myself to become corrupted by selling myself to that evil. I almost forgot my purpose in helping out the children and Ms. Penway back here. I felt coming along with you all, I could make up for all my mistakes I had caused. Just like my

	father, I was overpowered by greed and wanted more. Never again will I disappoint myself like that.
Cooper.	I see.
Elvir.	Being with you all on this trip, so far, has opened my eyes to my errors, and I can only get better from here on out. Foolish . . .
Cooper.	You shouldn't be so hard on yourself. No one is perfect; just needed to remember where you came from, that's all.
Elvir.	Hmm. That really helps me out. Thank you.
Cooper.	No problem . . . ha-ha-ha.
Elvir.	What's funny?
Cooper.	Oh, it's nothing.
Elvir.	Yeah, okay. You got something on your mind there. C'mon, spill the beans.
Cooper.	Oh, I feel good being around you.
Elvir.	Really?
Cooper.	It's your commitment, respect, and love that I feel coming from you. I haven't met someone in a while that's talked so passionately about life.
Elvir.	Well, who was the person last time that you heard talk like this?
Cooper.	My father.
Elvir.	Oh yeah. So when's the last time you seen your family?
Cooper.	Mmm . . . It's been awhile. Actually, they're all dead.
Elvir.	Oh, I'm sorry.
Cooper.	It's okay. It was a long time ago.
Elvir.	I understand if you wish not to talk about it. Well, you always got me near you, until the end.
Cooper.	How so?
Elvir.	As a friend.
Cooper.	Yeah . . . you do from me as well.
Elvir.	Heh-heh-heh.
Narrator.	Suddenly, a loud clatter of dishes breaking coming from the kitchen of the orphanage. Elvir and Cooper then go to investigate the noise. They arrive to find Ms. Penway in tears.
Elvir.	Ms. Penway, what's wrong?
Ms. Penway.	T-they've taken, Betsy.
Cooper.	Who did?
Elvir.	*No, tell me he didn't . . .*
Ms. Penway.	I found this note. (*giving the note to Elvir*)
Elvir.	That bastard! Damn him.

Ms. Penway.	He wants to exchange Betsy for the deed to the orphanage. If we don't, they threaten to hurt her. She's just a child . . . I don't know what to do.
Cooper.	Wow, how sad this is.
Ms. Penway.	I don't want the children to suffer anymore. If he really wants his land, I will give him the deed.
Elvir.	No, he just wants you to do that. He would have won then.
Ms. Penway.	I have no choice too. What about Betsy's well-being?
Elvir.	And of the other children?
Ms. Penway.	She is a child; I don't want them hurting her. I must hand it over to him. This has gone on long enough. We can't go through this forever.
Elvir.	No, Ms. Penway. Don't do it. I will handle this. He knows I'm here now, and I will make this all better once and for all. (*then starts to walk off*)
Ms. Penway.	Where are you going, Elvir?
Elvir.	I'm going to see him and bring back Betsy.
Cooper.	You can't go without me. Hold on.
Ms. Penway.	Elvir! Wait . . . Oh dear . . .
Narrator.	Cooper follows right behind Elvir, who exits the orphanage. Ms. Penway then goes to wake up Dew and the others.
Ms. Penway.	Please wake up, wake up!
Dew.	Huh?!
Ms. Penway.	Are you awake, sir?
Dew.	Yes? Something wrong?
Ms. Penway.	Elvir, she needs your help.
Dew.	What do you mean?
Ms. Penway.	One of the children here have been kidnapped by Bouzigard's men. Her and Cooper went to go rescue the child.
Dew.	Oh boy, I know where this is leading to. How did this happen?
Ms. Penway.	It seems that Bouzigard's men had broken into here and took the child when she was asleep. I . . . I . . .
Dew.	Calm down for a moment. Things will be fine. Where is this place at that they've taken the child to?
Ms. Penway.	It's up the hill from here. It's the large mansion estate in the middle of the city here.
Narrator.	Lorenzo then walks into the room with the others.
Lorenzo.	What's going on?
Dew.	getting out of bed. We've got trouble it seems.

Lorenzo.	It's always like that.
Dew.	One of the children have been abducted. Elvir and Cooper went to that Bouzigard's mansion to rescue the kid.
Krista.	Rest for the weary it seems . . . ha-ha.
Vilmer.	Well, they'll need our help then. Let's go after them.
Dew.	I agree. Ms. Penway, don't worry about a thing. We will make sure the child comes back safely and Elvir as well.
Ms. Penway.	Thank you all so much. Elvir has never had close friends in her life, but you are good people and can see why she stuck with you all.
Vilmer.	Let us go then.
Ms. Penway.	Be safe.
Narrator.	Then Dew and the others depart from the orphanage heading toward Bouzigard's mansion. Meanwhile, Elvir and Cooper enter the mansion's grounds and observe the security guards patrolling the area.
Cooper.	Your father must be insecure about his safety?
Elvir.	Not many people like him as you can tell.
Cooper.	Hmm . . . so how are we going to get past all the security guards there?
Elvir.	Like always, fight our way through.
Cooper.	What?!
Elvir.	We have no time for this. Here I go!
Narrator.	Elvir then runs off into the open as one of the guards spot her.
Guard 1.	What the hell?!
Elvir.	*yelling.* FATHER!
Guard 2.	So this is the girl. You got a lot of gall to pull such a stunt.
Elvir.	First of all I am not a male, and yes I'm pretty bold if you say so.
Guard 1.	Enough talking; let's nab her.
Elvir.	I see you, guys, were expecting me. Good, let's do this.
Narrator.	The two guards then approach Elvir and attack her. She manages to fend them off and knock them unconscious. Cooper then catches up to her.
Cooper.	Elvir, you shouldn't have run off like that. Kind of reckless.
Elvir.	I know, but we got to find Betsy.
Cooper.	I see you took care of them well. I am impressed. Please don't run off on me next time; you can't do this all by yourself. I am your friend here. Come on. Let's do this together, okay? We will get your friend back.
Elvir.	Okay. Sorry about that.

Cooper.	Forget about it; let's go and find her.
Narrator.	Elvir and Cooper then enter the mansion, farther infiltrating it. They eventually come down the main hall to find Darrow and Archer dragging Betsy.
Betsy.	Let me go!
Darrow.	Shut your mouth, you grubby crumb snatcher.
Archer.	I think she bit me earlier. My finger hurts.
Darrow.	There you go once again, always something wrong with you. Such a daisy you are.
Archer.	Well, that isn't nice of you now to say such a thing. Me feelings are hurt.
Darrow.	Oh Jesus . . . I can't wait for our dear cousin to come so we can get rid of this brat.
Betsy.	Lemme go! (*then kicks Darrow in the shin*)
Darrow.	Ouch!
Narrator.	Darrow's grip on Betsy's left arm loosens. She then begins to run down the hall.
Archer.	You okay?
Darrow.	Don't worry about me, you wanker! Grab the girl.
Narrator.	Darrow and Archer then chase after Betsy, and then Elvir appears in front of them. They come to halt.
Betsy.	You came. I knew you would. (*then runs over to Elvir's side*)
Elvir.	Here sooner than you thought, huh?
Archer.	Ah?!
Elvir.	Betsy, are you hurt?
Betsy.	No, I am fine.
Elvir.	Betsy, listen to me. I want you to leave this place and go back to the orphanage.
Betsy.	What about you?
Elvir.	I'll be fine. Me and my friend, Cooper, will take care of this. Please go.
Betsy.	I will. (then runs off)
Archer.	Glad you came, Elvir. Now we can give you the whooping that you deserve for what you did to us earlier.
Elvir.	I don't think I am the one who needs the discipline. You two need it more than I do.
Darrow.	Hah! Just because you have one of your friends with you, won't stop us. Don't take this personally what we have to do. It's tough love, okay?

Elvir.	That's what they call abuse these days. Hah!
Darrow.	*Arrghh* . . . You were always a smartass. That's it!
Narrator.	Elvir and Cooper then battle Archer and Darrow, easily defeating them. Elvir then stands over Darrow, who lies dazed on the ground.
Elvir.	*Humph.* Talk about "tough love". . . .
Cooper.	That takes care of them. We should go back to join the others.
Elvir.	No. I have to see my father now. Please go after Betsy and make sure she is okay for me.
Cooper.	Are you sure?
Elvir.	Yes, please.
Cooper.	Okay then. (*then walks off*)
Narrator.	Elvir then enters her father's study to find him waiting for her sitting on the edge of his desk.
Bouzigard.	Elvir, I see you came.
Elvir.	Father.
Bouzigard.	I knew you would make it. It has been a while since we've seen one another . . . father and daughter finally reunited.
Elvir.	Cut the dramatics, old man.
Bouzigard.	Not so happy to see me after all this time?
Elvir.	Not after all that you have done. Still the same as I remembered. Nothing has changed here at all.
Bouzigard.	You haven't changed at all yourself. Still the same stubborn, sly, rebellious daughter of mine.
Elvir.	I got all that from you.
Bouzigard.	Sarcastic even . . . ha-ha-ha.
Elvir.	Why are you trying to force the orphanage to close down?
Bouzigard.	It's all about the money, my dear. Money makes the world go around, and your friend Ms. Penway owes that to me. I gave them enough time to do that, and that is running short.
Elvir.	You heartless guv; it's an orphanage for god's sake. How can you do this to the children there? Where are they going to go?
Bouzigard.	That's not my problem. Their parents should have never abandoned them in the first place. I do not shed a tear nor compassion to lower-class trash. Survival of the fittest. Like a food chain, and I happen to be on top.
Elvir.	My father, you have become even more corrupted by money. How sad you are. That's why Mother had died of such grief.

198 | David Earl Williams III

Bouzigard.	Shut up! Don't ever bring that up. I told you . . . Hey; I wasn't the one who abandoned you. It was you who had chosen to leave me. You had everything you wanted. How could you turn away from that?
Elvir.	Father, I didn't need materialistic things from you. I needed love and care that a father would give his children and wife. She killed herself because of the pain. All she wanted was love in the end when she was suffering. You couldn't even give her that.
Bouzigard.	What?! No, I did my best for you and your mother. I can't believe you . . . You chose to be with those street scum. Don't blame me!
Elvir.	I at least believed in the good things in life. Money cannot bring happiness.
Narrator.	Dew, Cooper and the others enter the room.
Dew.	Elvir, we're here.
Elvir.	Cooper, Dew?!
Cooper.	Don't worry, Betsy is okay.
Bouzigard.	So, these must be your friends? Are they orphans as well? Ha-ha-ha.
Elvir.	No, Father.
Bouzigard.	Well, you all made it passed my security I see. I will have to show off some of my skills then. See, with money, I've learned from the best martial artists' in the world. You can't be a rich man and be defenseless now. My two hands are weapons themselves.
Cooper.	Such a haughty person you are. We'll end this now.
Elvir.	No, Cooper. I will deal with this on my own.
Vilmer.	Child, are you sure?
Elvir.	Yes, please.
Bouzigard.	I see you want to step up then. Good.
Elvir.	That's right. Let's make a deal. If you beat me, the land is all yours. If I win, you have to let the orphanage off debt.
Bouzigard.	Hmm . . . very interesting offer. I like it . . . I really do. You made a bad choice in doing this, Daughter. (*takes out two daggers from his pockets*) Time to put you back in your place, youngling.
Narrator.	Elvir and Bouzigard then battle one another as Dew and the others stand back to watch. Elvir manages, after a long exhausting bout, to defeat her father causing him to kneel down as he tries to catch his breath.

Bouzigard.	The younger generations always seem to surpass the older ones.
Elvir.	Father, it's over now.
Bouzigard.	That was good . . . I am impressed. All that training has paid off on your end I see. Well done.
Elvir.	Father.
Bouzigard.	*rising up on his feet.* I failed again. You still hate me for your mother's death, don't you? I now see that I have caused too much pain . . . Damn . . . (*then walks over to Elvir*) Do this for me . . . End my sorrow . . . (*then places the daggers in her hands*) Kill me!
Elvir.	Father, no. I don't hate you. (*then drops the daggers to the floor*) I don't blame you for her death anymore. I just want to be a family again.
Bouzigard.	How can you say that? I tried finding a cure to her illness . . . Even with all that money put into it, I couldn't save her. I failed . . .
Elvir.	Father, there will be no more pain. I love you, Father. I don't want to lose you too. You did try to save Mom, and it may not have worked, but she would be happy seeing us together again . . . as family. We're family and that is what matters here. I love you, Father.
Bouzigard.	I feel like a fool . . . I'm sorry. I love you too, my daughter. Thank you for showing me my errors. I am proud of you.
Narrator.	Elvir and Bouzigard then embrace one another.
Elvir.	Thank you, father (*a tear then drops from her eye*)
Narrator.	The scene changes to the next day back at the orphanage as Ms. Penway and Bouzigard wait to greet Elvir and the others off on their journey.
Ms. Penway.	Elvir, thank you so much for all you have done for me and the children. I gladly appreciate your help always. I am in your debt. Thank you.
Elvir.	It's nothing. Just the right thing to do.
Ms. Penway.	You just got here, and now ready to leave us all again?
Elvir.	It's important that I leave with my friends on their journey; the world is at stake here. I will return, I will make sure of it.
Ms. Penway.	(*then hugs Elvir*) Be safe, okay!
Elvir.	I will.
Bouzigard.	Elvir, I want you to take this before you go. (*then hands her his two daggers and some money*)

Elvir.	Your daggers? Why?
Bouzigard.	They may be more helpful to you then me. Use them please.
Elvir.	I will, Father. Thank you.
Bouzigard.	No, thank you. You have shown me my faults and reached through me. I wish it was sooner though. If you're mother was still here, she would be happy for us. I will make sure from now on that all my money will go toward helping others who are in need here in Minerva. I've neglected the people too much, I see. Thank you, my daughter, and wish you a pleasant trip.
Elvir.	Thank you both. (*then kisses her father on his cheek*) Good-bye to you both. Tell Betsy I will miss her too.
Ms. Penway.	I will, don't worry. Farewell.
Narrator.	As Elvir and the others walk off, Ms. Penway and Bouzigard wave farewell to her. After returning to the tugboat, Dew and the others prepare to head out toward their next destination.
Cooper.	You okay?
Elvir.	I am fine . . . just going to miss the place.
Cooper.	Yeah, nothing like home.
Elvir.	Where to now, Dew?
Dew.	Well, since Thornton wasn't here, we can check out Demmin.
Lorenzo.	Demmin? Isn't that whole area a large disposal site these days?
Krista.	These days, yes it is. During the Great Civil War, the New Havenport troops held occupancy in Demmin. Two months after that, the Helix Capital forces had invaded the shores of Demmin, leading to an all-out amphibious assault that lasted nearly six months. Many people's lives were lost, and cities were destroyed as well. Eventually, the Helix capital was successful in ridding the land New Havenport troops, down to the very last man.
Dew.	I was still in basic training when that was going on.
Cooper.	I remember hearing about that . . . all too well.
Dew.	That's right; the Helix capital marked the place uninhabitable after the high levels of chemical weapon detected in the water and air.
Krista.	The place is nothing but a disease-ridding wasteland now.
Lorenzo.	All because of your "glorious governor" then.
Cooper.	Well, guess we won't be going there, huh?
Dew.	Well, to be sure, let's check it out.
Cooper.	Are you sure?
Dew.	You never know. You don't look a little wan. You okay?

Cooper.	Ye . . . yeah. It's nothing.
Dew.	Hmm . . . okay then. Elvir set a course for Demmin.
Elvir.	Got ya.
Narrator.	The tugboat then debarks from Minerva harbor, setting out to sea toward Demmin. After sailing for a few hours, they enter the channel closing into Demmin. The sea state is so rough that the current pulls the tugboat onto the shore of the large disposal site, causing it to shake violently and come to a halt.
Dew.	Whoa! What did you hit?
Elvr.	Nothing.
Lorenzo.	Nice driving there. Why'd you pull onto the shore?
Elvir.	There was nothing I could do; I seemed to have lost control of the steering. Seas must be rough.
Krista.	We're all the way on the shore. I don't think we'll be able to use this as a means of transportation anymore.
Elvir.	Looks like we're grounded here.
Vilmer.	I suppose we'll have to go by foot then.
Lorenzo.	Is it safe to do that? I mean what about the toxins and shit in the air?
Krista.	Over a matter of time, those chemical weapon agents evaporate into the atmosphere. Shouldn't be too hazardous for us.
Lorenzo.	I hope not.
Dew.	She's right about that. We should be fine. We might as well then. Come on, let's get going.
Narrator.	Dew and the others then depart the tugboat to investigate the surroundings of Demmin.
Vilmer.	So this is Demmin.
Krista.	This place is a dump.
Cooper	*exhales deeply*.
Vilmer.	Literally.
Lorenzo.	I thought living on the streets was bad . . . hah. Look at all this junk here.
Vilmer.	You think with modern technology they could find a better way to dispose of garbage?
Krista.	Got to find somewhere to put it.
Cooper.	Reckless . . .
Dew.	I agree on that with you.
Cooper.	A shame; there's nothing left here at all. (exhales sharply) Hmm . . .

Dew.	We should walk on further and see what we can find here.
Krista.	Let's do that.
Cooper.	Yes.
Narrator.	Dew and the others then set forth on roaming around the large disposal site. After encountering a few hostile creatures on the way through their venture, Cooper comes to a stop.
Cooper.	Hmm?
Lorenzo.	Wassup?
Cooper.	This place . . . no. (*looking into the distance at an abandoned rural house*)
Lorenzo.	What about it?
Narrator.	As Cooper continues to stare at the abandoned rural house, he sees a familiar ghostly figure entering the house.
Cooper.	What?! It couldn't be . . . No way.
Elvir.	Couldn't be what, Cooper?
Cooper.	You all must excuse me. I have to check on something. (*then runs off*)
Elvir.	Hey, Cooper!
Lorenzo.	What's gotten into him all of a sudden?
Dew.	I don't know.
Elvir.	We should go follow him.
Lorenzo.	Yeah, man.
Dew.	Vilmer, you and Krista go on ahead. We'll catch up with you all.
Krista.	Shall do.
Narrator.	Vilmer and Krista then walk on ahead as Dew, Lorenzo, and Elvir follow Cooper. Meanwhile, Cooper enters the living room of abandoned rural house. He then comes to a stop to observe his surroundings.
Cooper.	It's still here . . .
Narrator.	The scene switches to Coopers past two weeks after visiting his home. We find Cooper lying in his rack asleep in this barracks back at the SWAT Trooper Elite Academy. Someone knocks at his door, and this awakes him. He gets out of his rack to open the door and is met by a messenger boy.
Messenger boy.	Sorry to wake you. I'm looking for a Mr. Cooper Tyler. Is that you?
Cooper.	Why yes.

Messenger boy. I see . . . I was told to give you this telegram. I am sorry. (*then hands Cooper the telegram*)

Cooper. Sorry? What is this? (*then takes the letter*)

Messenger boy. I will leave you alone now.

Narrator. The messenger boy then walks off. The scene shifts back to present time as Cooper drops to his knees and smashes the soil with both fists.

Cooper. It's all . . . all . . .

Narrator. Dew and the others enter the house.

Dew. Hey, man, what's wrong?

Elvir. You okay?

Cooper. The letter . . .

Lorenzo. What letter?

Cooper. The letter that was given to me on that fateful day that changed my life forever.

Elvir. What happened?

Cooper. I received a letter informing me when the New Havenport forces had invaded this district of Demmin; they tried to force my mother out of this house . . .

Dew. This is your home?

Cooper. She had put up a fight with them, but they killed her for her resistance.

Elvir. Cooper, I'm sorry.

Cooper. Mom, why'd you stay? (*begins to weep*) Why didn't you listen to me? Damn!

Elvir. Hey, man, it's okay. (*then takes Cooper in her arms embracing him*)

Cooper. DAMMIT!

Narrator. A ghostly figure then appears in front of Cooper. He then shrugs away from Elvir.

Cooper. W-what?!

Elvir. Cooper, what is it now?

Ghostly figure. Cooper.

Cooper. Dad.

Ghostly figure. You failed me son. Why did you leave your mother to die?

Elvir. Dad? Who are you talking to?

Cooper. Dad. It can't be . . .

Lorenzo. This shit is getting weird now.

Dew.   Cooper, what is going on?
Cooper.   Dad . . .
Ghostly figure. I thought you would take care of her. You disappoint me son.
Cooper.   I couldn't do anything about her death. I tried!
Ghostly figure. You disgrace me.
Cooper.   I tried!
Ghostly figure. Cooper . . . (*then vanishes*)
Cooper.   Dad! Don't leave me again. DAD!
Narrator.   Elvir then smacks Cooper in the face to bring him back to his senses.
Elvir.   Cooper, stop it. You're scaring me.
Cooper.   Huh? (*bewildered*)
Elvir.   What was all that about just now?
Cooper.   What are you talking about?
Dew.   You were talking to someone just now. Are you all right?
Cooper.   I . . . I am fine. It was nothing. I do feel strange though . . .
Elvir.   Fine my ass. Are you sure you're okay?
Cooper.   Yes . . . thank you for your concern. I am sorry about running off on you all like that. It won't happen again. We should get going now.
Dew.   Would you rather want to talk about it?
Cooper.   There's nothing to talk about. Let's just get going, please. (*then exits the house*)
Elvir.   I hope he's okay.
Dew.   Hmm. Me too. Come on, let's get going.
Narrator.   Dew and the others then exit the house to rejoin Vilmer and Krista, who are taking a rest in a large drainage pipe nearby, hiding from the pouring rain.
Vilmer.   I thought you, guys, would have never shown up. Ha-ha-ha.
Krista.   Things all right?
Dew.   It seems like it.
Lorenzo.   I guess we'll be here for a while.
Dew.   Yeah.
Cooper.   This place has gone to hell.
Elvir.   Cooper, you want to talk?
Cooper.   No. Like I said before, there is nothing to talk about.
Elvir.   Why don't I believe you?
Cooper.   Leave me be. I need to think alone. (*then walks off*)
Elvir.   Cooper.

Dew.	Let him alone for now. He probably needs some time alone. We all do.
Elvir.	I guess. I wish I knew what was on his mind.
Dew.	He'll open up when he is ready to. Give it time.
Elvir.	You're right.
Narrator.	As the group sits to regain their energy, Vilmer then grasps his forehead.
Krista.	You all right?
Vilmer.	Oh . . . yeah. I just felt a little light-headed all of a sudden. Perhaps I'm tired.
Krista.	Might be.
Lorenzo.	We all are . . . especially someone else. (*then glares over at Cooper*)
Elvir.	Yeah . . .
Vilmer.	I guess I'm not as young as I think I am . . . ha-ha-ha.
Narrator.	As some time passes by, the rain comes to a stop.
Krista.	Hey, guys, the rain stopped.
Dew.	Great. We should continue on then.
Cooper.	The sooner the better.
Dew.	Right then. Let's go.
Narrator.	Dew and the others then continue venturing farther through the disposal site. After a few unfriendly encounters with the mutated wildlife, the group comes upon a cliff of the junk pile leading to a dead end.
Dew.	We can't go this way I see.
Elvir.	*looking down from the cliff.* That's a long fall. Sucks to fall from here. Sheesh.
Dew.	I guess we'll have to find another path then.
Lorenzo.	Seems like it.
Narrator.	Elvir, Cooper, and Krista continue to walk as Vilmer comes to a stop.
Vilmer.	Hold on a second.
Lorenzo.	What's wrong?
Vilmer.	Impossible . . . I can't believe it.
Narrator.	Vilmer walks closer to the edge of the cliff and peers over, having a brief flashback of when Aldous fell from Mount Illini. Vilmer jumps back as if he were startled.
Dew.	Do you see something?
Vilmer.	I don't know.

Lorenzo.	Oh great, he's losing it. What's going on here?
Narrator.	Vilmer continues to look at the edge of the cliff and notices a hand grasping onto the soil trying to climb back up onto the surface.
Vilmer.	What the?!
Narrator.	Aldous then appears in front of Vilmer as he hoists himself back up onto the cliff.
Aldous.	Vilmer, my friend.
Vilmer.	This is crazy. How the hell . . . I must be seeing things?
Aldous.	I thought I would never hear your voice again.
Vilmer.	How are you alive?
Aldous.	I can't get a simple hello? How have you been?
Vilmer.	This must be some kind of illusion.
Aldous.	My death echoes in your mind constantly. I can not die until I take back what is rightfully mine. You stole my livelihood from me.
Vilmer.	Aldous, I did everything I possibly could to save you.
Aldous.	Ha-ha-ha. You let me fall to my icy bottomless death. It was all about you, and you wanted the glory to yourself.
Vilmer.	Aldous, that isn't true.
Dew.	Vilmer, there is no one there.
Aldous.	The guilt will rot in you, and you will truly die.
Vilmer.	I don't know what to tell you. I'm sorry.
Aldous.	Feel my pain . . . You will join me soon.
Dew.	Vilmer, snap out of it!
Vilmer.	Dew, stay back. This is my problem; I will take care of this.
Dew.	Huh? What are you talking about?
Aldous.	Come, my friend.
Vilmer.	Let me go . . . This feeling . . .
Dew.	Vilmer?!
Aldous.	End the guilt. Come along with me.
Vilmer.	No more . . . guilt . . . no more . . .
Narrator.	Vilmer then walks toward the edge of the cliff.
Lorenzo.	Hey, man, what are you doing?
Vilmer.	Aldous . . .
Lorenzo.	?!
Vilmer.	It's too much!
Narrator.	Vilmer then attempts to leap from the edge of the cliff, but Lorenzo grabs him before he does and throws him back away from the edge of the cliff to the ground.

Lorenzo.	What were you thinking just now?
Vilmer.	*shaking his head out of daze.* Hey, why'd you do that?
Lorenzo.	What do you mean? You just tried to jump off the cliff a moment ago.
Vilmer.	Why would I try to do such a thing?
Lorenzo.	Are you kidding me?
Vilmer.	I don't recall doing this.
Lorenzo.	Hmm . . .
Vilmer.	Guys, really I don't know what you're talking about.
Dew.	Something isn't right here at all. First Cooper is acting strange; now you.
Vilmer.	I don't. I'm not lying to you.
Dew.	We should catch up to the others now.
Narrator.	Dew and the two then depart the area to catch up with the others, who are waiting for them at a bridge that leads to the province of Tagore. Dew, Lorenzo, and Vilmer walk up.
Elvir.	Hey, guys.
Dew.	A bridge. So where does this go to?
Krista.	The province of Tagore.
Lorenzo.	Tagore?
Krista.	This providence is half of what was Demmin. After the war, they reconstructed half of Demmin, and the other half that we've ventured through was left to be used as a waste disposal site.
Cooper.	All wasn't lost after all. You've been here before?
Krista.	No. Most of the knowledge that I have about the places we've been to so far, is from reading or from other traveler's experiences. I don't know much about this place.
Elvir.	Only one way to find out then.
Lorenzo.	So, are we going on ahead?
Dew.	There might be sign of Thornton there. Let's get going then.
Lorenzo.	What about Cooper and Vilmer?
Cooper.	What about us?
Vilmer.	Yeah?
Lorenzo.	Wouldn't want you two to start seeing mirages again and freaking out on us.
Cooper.	Mirage, hah! Not even close.
Vilmer.	I still don't know what you're referring to.
Dew.	Lorenzo, I think they'll be fine. We should get going though.
Lorenzo.	All right, man.

Vilmer.	*looking at Krista.* I really don't know what he is talking about.
Krista.	I believe you. Probably just exhausted.
Vilmer.	Yeah. Let's get going then.
Narrator.	Dew and the others begin to walk off, but Elvir stops and turns to Cooper.
Elvir.	Cooper.
Cooper.	Yes?
Elvir.	Never mind.
Narrator.	Elvir then walks off to join the others who are crossing the bridge to enter Tagore. Cooper looks back one more time at the disposal site, then walks off to catch up with the others. After entering Tagore, the group continues to explore farther until they come to a stop, observing two druids huddling around a tree.
Lorenzo.	Weird.
Krista.	Who are those guys?
Dew.	Who knows? Let's get closer so we can find out.
Narrator.	Dew and the others then hide behind a nearby bolder to take a closer observation of the druids.
Druid.	Is he here? Did you find him?
Druid 1.	No. He is near though.
Druid.	The master will not be pleased.
Druid 1.	We must find him. This is what the master wishes.
Dew.	Master?
Druid.	The others find him not.
Druid 1.	We're sure that this man is the one?
Druid.	The master knows all. Never doubt that. He is here.
Narrator.	Dew and the others try to go in for a closer view, but Krista accidentally steps on a twig alerting the two druid's attention.
Druid.	What was that?!
Druid 1.	A noise . . .
Druid.	Outsiders!
Lorenzo.	Just great.
Druid 1.	We must dispose of them.
Narrator.	Dew, Lorenzo, and Krista battle the two druids and are successful in defeating them.
Krista.	They weren't too friendly.
Lorenzo.	No kidding.
Dew.	Well, we have no time to put thought on this. Let's get going.

Narrator.	With that thought, Dew and the others venture farther. Meanwhile, back in Helix at Videl Mansion Estate, Killbin is sitting in a chair turned to the window pondering to himself. His secretary then enters the room with a pot of coffee.
Killbin.	Ms. Zeta, did we get any info on the whereabouts of Dew and his friends as of yet?
Zeta.	Not yet, Mr. Janeiro.
Killbin.	Oh.
Zeta.	Would you like some coffee, sir?
Killbin.	Why yes.
Narrator.	Zeta then sets a cup already filled with coffee on his desk. Killbin then picks the cup up and sips it . . . .
Killbin.	Umm . . . very good. I like it. One more thing . . .
Zeta.	Yes?
Killbin.	Keep up the good work.
Zeta.	I shall.
Narrator.	As Zeta is about to exit the room, smoke begins fill it up . . .
Killbin.	Is something on fire?
Zeta.	I don't think so. I will check it out.
Narrator.	Zeta then tries opening the door, but it doesn't budge.
Killbin.	What's wrong?
Zeta.	It's jammed.
Narrator.	Then Thornton appears.
Thornton.	Well, well, well, Killbin. We meet at last.
Killbin.	Thornton?! How did you get in here?
Thornton.	Ha-ha-ha, all so easy. Security isn't what it used to be.
Killbin.	Thornton, what do you want?
Thornton.	Bait.
Killbin.	Hmm . . .
Narrator.	Zeta manages to open the door.
Zeta.	Sir, come on!
Narrator.	Killbin and Zeta then rush out the open door. They dash down the hall and meet a SWAT trooper.
Killbin.	SWAT Trooper, there is a man after us.
Narrator.	The SWAT trooper falls to the ground, and Killbin then realizes he is dead.
Druid 2.	Another waste of life.
Narrator.	Thornton then walks up as the druids contain Killbin and Zeta.

Thornton.	As I was saying . . .
Zeta.	Sir? (*cowering behind Killbin*)
Thornton.	You're all the bait I need. Tie them up.
Druid 3.	Yes, Your Greatness.
Narrator.	The druids then bind and gag Killbin and Zeta. Back in Tagore, Dew and the party enter the city district of the province.
Lorenzo.	Nice-looking place.
Dew.	It does.
Narrator.	An old man approaches Dew and the others.
Old man.	Excuse me, are you, folks, from here?
Dew.	Actually, just passing through.
Krista.	We were looking for a man.
Old man.	Well, young lady, there are a lot of them here. Ha-ha.
Krista.	Oh please.
Dew.	No, not like that. We came here searching for this person that may have passed through here. His name is Thornton.
Old man.	No one by that name that lives here.
Cooper.	A waste of time this was.
Old man.	Well, there were some new faces that passed through here a short while before you all came.
Dew.	Go on.
Old man.	They were the strangest bunch. All dressed up in black hoods.
Dew.	Like druids?
Old man.	Yeah, just like that. I remember seeing this girl with them. She had hair red as fire, skin white like snow, and a nice figure as well.
Dew.	Hmm?
Old man.	They were passing out pamphlets and talking about going on some journey to the world beyond. I was thinking to myself at that moment, these kids must be on some kind of drugs or something. Sounded like one of those crazy cults if you ask me.
Dew.	That woman you said, are you sure about the descriptions you gave me?
Old man.	Oh yeah. You don't see that many pretty faces come through here. In this providence, retired veterans and their families reside here.
Cooper.	Is that all you know?

Old man.	Well, the hooded men were asking me about some man name, Lahaina. I don't know of anyone that goes under that name as well.
Dew.	*Sergeant Lahaina? Emily . . .*
Old man.	I best be leaving you, folks, alone now. If you're all interested to see my machine, my house is at the end of town. Well, good day to you all now. (*then walks off*)
Cooper.	Do you think that man named Lahaina could be Sergeant Lahaina?
Dew.	That couldn't be; he's dead.
Lorenzo.	Who is this guy now?
Cooper.	He was a high-ranking enlisted member in the SWAT trooper elite during the Great Civil War. He disappeared right before the war had ended. He led his unit to raid one of the New Havenport camps posted out the outskirts of Llivisaca. The raid failed though, and his unit was wiped out. Among the corpses, his body was never found.
Krista.	Those druids we fought before we came into town here, they must be the ones searching for this man.
Dew.	Must be.
Elvir.	I don't know about all of that, but the old man's machine he was speaking of sounds interesting to look at. (*then walks off*)
Lorenzo.	Don't get into trouble now. Oh, fuck it. Hold up, I'm coming too. I like to actually see the old man's invention as well. (*walks off to follow Elvir*)
Vilmer.	I think we all should take a look around then. Sounds good?
Dew.	Yeah, works for me. Krista, you and Vilmer go together and let us know what you find.
Krista.	Okay then.
Vilmer.	Let's all meet back here.
Dew.	Cool with me.
Vilmer.	Later then. (*walking off with Krista*)
Narrator.	Cooper and Dew then walk off to begin exploring through town. Some time passes, and the two come to a stop when they observe four druids entering an alleyway.
Cooper.	Odd. You seen that?
Dew.	Yes.
Narrator.	Dew and Cooper then follow the druids into the alley.
Druid 4.	He's here.

Druid 5.	No where to run.
Druid 6.	Hand it over.
Druid 7.	It is required.
Lahainia.	Forget about it. You'll have to kill me before I do that.
Druid 4.	The master demands it.
Druid 6.	Stubborn and dead.
Narrator.	The four druids are about to swarm on Lahaina, then Dew and Cooper jump in. causing the druids to cease their attack.
Dew.	Not today.
Druid 7.	Intruders.
Druid 5.	What shall we do?
Druid 6.	We must rid ourselves of this threat.
Cooper.	Ready for a fight, eh?
Dew.	I guess if that's what they want then . . . sure.
Druid 4.	Master Thornton must be pleased.
Dew.	Thornton.
Druid 5.	Die tainted souls.
Narrator.	The druids then rush at Dew and Cooper; they are easily defeated though in the end.
Druid 7.	We've failed our master.
Druid 4.	We must not be discovered.
Cooper.	Huh?
Narrator.	The four druids then take their own lives by stabbing one another in the hearts with their swords. They fall to the ground dead.
Dew	*gasps.*
Cooper.	Oh god . . . what the hell?!
Lahaina.	I appreciate your help there; I will be going now. (*then tries to creep off*)
Dew.	Wait a second.
Lahaina	*turns around to face Dew.* So what do you want from me? My money? (*then pulls out his wallet and shows it to Dew and Cooper*) It's all I got.
Cooper.	We don't want that at all, Sergeant.
Lahaina.	Sergeant?! How do you . . .
Dew.	No. We've come to talk to you.
Lahaina.	What do you want from me?
Dew.	It seems that those druids there were trying to get something from you. You seemed like you were about to risk your life for whatever it is.

Lahaina.	They were trying to mug me. That's all.
Cooper.	We don't have time for games. No need to lie to us.
Lahaina.	Who are you?
Dew.	My name is Dew Wilder and he is Cooper Tyler. We're after a man you know very well.
Lahaina.	Thornton. How do you know him? Wait . . . I remember you two now. You were part of Landmore's unit. Ha-ha-ha . . . It's been a while. So you want something I have, huh?
Dew.	Something like that.
Lahaina.	I heard after our "great governor" was killed, Killbin took his place. Well, things should be different now since he's running the country. I can't hide it anymore. I suppose it's all right now. (*then takes the SKT virus T vial out of his pocket*) This is what you were looking for, right?
Cooper.	Yes. How did you know?
Lahaina.	I heard that Thornton found the other two vials, and he's sure as hell searching for the other two.
Dew.	Who'd you hear this from?
Lahaina.	My sources.
Cooper.	Don't want to tell . . . hmm.
Dew.	Sergeant, give it to us and it will be in good hands. I reassure you of this.
Lahaina.	Ha-ha . . . Are you sure of this? They almost got their hands on it from me.
Cooper.	We're sure of this.
Lahaina.	Fine then. Take it and protect it with your lives. (*then hands Dew the S.K.T virus T vial*)
Dew.	We will.
Cooper.	Sergeant, don't you think it would be best to go somewhere safe for the time being? There will probably be more of those druids looking for you.
Lahaina.	I would, but I can stall time for you, guys, and let them think I still have it in my possession.
Dew.	You'll be all right?
Lahaina.	Don't worry about me; I will be fine. Just don't let them get their hands on the vial.
Cooper.	We won't, Sergeant.
Lahaina.	I'm not a sergeant any more. Don't fail me soldiers. (*then cracks a smile*) If only your grandfather was here now . . . he would be

	proud. Most definitely. It was good seeing you boys again. (*then runs off*)
Cooper.	Well, we have it now. As long as we have it, it'll be safe.
Dew.	I agree. Let's go find the others now.
Narrator.	Dew and Cooper then walk off to find the others. Meanwhile, back in Helix, Killbin and Zeta are bound to a chair in the master study as two druids watch over them. Thornton stares out the window looking into the city in the horizon.
Thornton.	So many lives there are, and most of them serve such a meaningless purpose.
Killbin.	What do you want, Thornton?
Thornton	*turns to face Killbin.* So curious you are. I think you should know.
Killbin.	If it's about any of those virus vials, I don't know a thing.
Thornton.	I know you don't.
Killbin.	?!
Thornton.	Ha-ha-ha . . . you're just bait to lure out the fish I need.
Killbin.	What are you talking about?
Thornton.	I know by now that Dew and his friends have probably found the SKT virus T vial. So once the news is passed that I'm here holding you hostage, Mr. Governor, he will come and rescue you. Well . . . not without a simple fair trade though . . . being you and the woman's life.
Killbin.	He won't just give it up so easy.
Thornton.	Oh, he will. There are other ways to a man's heart. Something that he cherishes the most.
Killbin.	Well, him and his friends are halfway around the world by now. They won't be here anytime soon. With that, once the men start to notice I haven't left here, they will get suspicious and come looking for me.
Thornton.	It'll just make it more suspenseful, won't it then? Dew will be here soon enough. If there is a way, there is a how.
Killbin.	Insane.
Druid 8.	Master, should we prepare for their arrival?
Thornton.	Yes, do that.
Druid 8.	I will instruct the others, my lord. (*then exits the room*)
Thornton.	We'll be here for a bit then. He will be here soon. I know it.
Narrator.	Back in Tagore, Dew and Cooper meet with Vilmer and Krista at the front gate.

Vilmer.	Well, hello there.
Cooper.	Hi.
Krista.	Well, we weren't able to find anything about Thornton. How about you, guys?
Dew.	We did. (*then pulls out the SKT virus T vial*)
Krista.	How did you get that?
Dew.	We ran into some trouble along the way when we ran into an old friend of ours. (*then puts the vial back in his pocket*)
Vilmer.	Old friend you say?
Cooper.	He used to be a member of the SWAT trooper elite and was being attacked by those druids. We intervened and saved him. Funny how he happened to be carrying the vial on him.
Krista.	Funny how things go. Seems unreal how this is all falling in our laps. As if it was meant to happen.
Vilmer.	It's a good thing we have it now.
Dew.	Yeah . . . Where are Lorenzo and Elvir?
Krista.	They're still at that old man's house, I believe.
Vilmer.	Speaking about running into "old friends," we happen to encounter those druids again. They have a message for us.
Cooper.	So they must work for Thornton then.
Dew.	Message?
Vilmer.	They told us that Thornton is in Helix at Videl Mansion estate, and has taken Killbin and his secretary hostage. He wants us to come there to make an exchange—the vial for their lives.
Krista.	He really wants it that bad.
Dew.	Seems like it.
Cooper.	How are we going to get to Helix from here? We're across the world from there.
Dew.	I don't know, but we should leave soon though. Let's go get Elvir and Lorenzo.
Vilmer.	Yes.
Narrator.	As Dew and the others are about to walk off to find Lorenzo and Elvir, Elvir comes running down the street toward them.
Elvir.	Hey guys. You got to see this . . .
Dew.	If we had time, but we must be going.
Elvir.	Where are we going now? We just got here.
Cooper.	Thornton is back in Helix and has the governor and his secretary hostage.
Elvir.	So we're going to Helix?

Dew.	Yes.
Elvir.	You're crazy; that will take us a while to get there from here.
Dew.	I know, but the sooner the better.
Elvir.	I know of a better way (*then runs off*)
Dew.	Elvir! (*exhales sharply*)
Vilmer.	We should go see what she's talking about.
Dew.	Might as well.
Narrator.	Dew and the others follow Elvir down the streets into a house. They enter and follow her into the basement lab where Lorenzo and the old man are.
Elvir.	Professor, I brought them all here.
Sorenson.	I see, good. I am Professor Gil Sorenson. So you all came to see my device?
Dew.	Device?
Lorenzo.	Yeah, man, this thing is crazy. It's a scientific breakthrough in traveling.
Dew.	I don't get it.
Sorenson.	Your friends here have told me about your current situation, so I think I may be some help.
Cooper.	How so?
Sorenson.	Glad you asked. This device here I created is a teleportation device. Oh yes . . . With present techniques, teleportation is conceivable only with elementary particles, or theoretically, by encoding information about an object, transmitting the information to another place, such as by radio or electric signal, and creating a copy of the original object in the new location.
Dew.	How long have you been researching this?
Sorenson.	At least twenty-six years, my boy. This technology isn't something new. It's been around for quite some time.
Krista.	Does it really work?
Lorenzo.	Hell yeah it does. We tested it on an apple just a moment ago; then whoosh it disappeared.
Cooper.	How do you know where the apple ended up?
Sorenson.	It's called, a GPS (global positioning system) tracker. By homing into the satellites that are in space, the node of the teleportation device and the satellites neural network send information back and forth to one another pertaining to the object or matter that is being teleported to a certain location on the planet. (*then reads the incoming data on the console screen*) By the looks of

	it; that apple of ours ended up some where in the Mesovilla plains.
Dew.	If you can teleport things from here, can you bring them back?
Sorenson.	Well, no. I am still trying to work that part out . . . he-he-he.
Elvir.	The professor here once worked for the Helix government.
Sorenson.	Yes, so long ago. This marvelous invention would have done wonders for the world making transportation so easy. Yet I had to scrap it due to lack of funding from the government, and the first test trials turned out to be a failure.
Krista.	What happened?
Sorenson.	Well, there was an accident.
Dew.	Accident?
Sorenson.	During the first test trial, we used a human specimen, to test out the capabilities of the machine. It was all voluntary, of course. The human matter was semi-transferring; it seemed all was going well. Until the machine had overheated and malfunctioned. I had to quickly reverse the transportation effect and shut the machine down. Luckily no one was killed. After observing this, the government was displeased by the results. In the end, I was out of a job. So I continued my research on quantum physics, and strenuously, after so many years going over the equations and formulas, I have finally perfected it.
Dew.	It seems like a risk if we use this thing. Just because it worked on fruit, doesn't mean it will work on human matter. I dunno.
Elvir.	Well, we have to find some way to get to Helix.
Dew.	Not risking our lives though on some invention.
Elvir.	We have no choice though.
Lorenzo.	Well, if this thing kills us, we at least tried.
Dew.	Damn you, guys. (*shaking his head*) Well, we might as well then.
Sorenson.	So you all are going to use it then?
Dew.	Yes. I hope this doesn't kill us all
Sorenson.	Me too.
Dew.	What?!
Sorenson.	Just joking. Where to?
Dew.	We're going to the Helix capital; Videl Manison Estate.
Sorenson.	Ok then . . . All I have to do is set the coordinates for Helix. (*then types in the coordinates on the keyboard panel*) Ah. Everything is ready now.

Narrator.	The teleportation device gives off a light hum as it starts up.
Dew.	Well, here's nothing.
Cooper.	Yeah.
Krista.	You only live once.
Lorenzo.	We appreciate this, Professor.
Sorenson.	No problem. Just glad to help. Who's first?
Narrator.	Then one by one the professor teleports Dew and his friends to Videl Mansion Estate. Meanwhile, back in Helix in the master study of the mansion estate, a female druid approaches Thornton.
Thornton.	Is he here yet?
Druid.	No, master. I don't think he will be here anytime soon.
Thornton.	Oh, something tells me he will be. All of them. Patience, my child.
Druid.	I hope so.
Thornton.	They will. (then smirks)
Narrator.	Back at the third-floor basement of the mansion, Dew and friends reassemble.
Vilmer.	Ah . . . (feeling himself) Nothing missing . . . whew.
Lorenzo.	That's what you call traveling. Ha-ha!
Cooper.	So the machine actually works.
Elvir.	Told you so.
Cooper.	You did.
Dew.	Seeing it, is believing it . . . for some things.
Krista.	Dew, where do you think Thornton is holding the governor at?
Dew.	It could be anywhere here.
Lorenzo.	Since me and you know this place pretty well, we should split up into two groups to find him.
Dew.	That would be a good idea.
Krista.	Who is going with whom?
Dew.	I'll take Cooper and Elvir.
Lorenzo.	Okay, then it's me and you, guys, then. Well, we should get going then.
Dew.	Be careful.
Lorenzo.	We will.
Dew.	See you later. (then walks off along with Cooper and Elvir)
Lorenzo.	Back here again. I thought I would never miss this place.
Narrator.	Dew and his group then begin their venture through the mansion estate. They encounter a few security bots and druids along the

way, defeating them as they head up each level of the mansion. Advancing farther up, they reach the study and enter. They find Killbin and his security bound and gagged to a chair in the middle of the room.

Dew. Killbin. Cooper, cover us.

Cooper. Got ya. You never know when Thornton may appear.

Narrator. Dew and Elvir then walk over cautiously to untie Killbin and his secretary.

Killbin. *mouth fold falls off.* Dew, it's a trap!

Narrator. Thornton then appears with a sword in hand holding it up to Emily's neck.

Thornton. Dew, over here.

Dew. Thornton.

Thornton. About time you came. Look who I got.

Dew. Emily?!

Cooper. Killbin, leave now.

Killbin. *nods head in approval.* Yes. Zeta, let's go.

Zeta. Yes, sir.

Narrator. Killbin and Zeta then exit the study.

Thornton. Funny how we're always meeting this way, huh?

Emily. He's crazy.

Dew. Thornton, let her go!

Cooper. You damn coward.

Thornton. I think you have something I want that you have. Let's make an exchange.

Elvir. Dew, wait.

Dew. Okay, Thornton . . . just don't hurt her. I got what you want. (*then pulls out the SKT virus T vial*) See.

Thornton. Good . . . now roll it over here.

Dew. Hah, this isn't any different from the first time. (*then rolls the vial on the ground to Thornton. It hits his foot*)

Thornton. The only difference is, you're in my spot and I'm in my brother's spot. Funny how things come about, huh?

Dew. Yeah.

Thornton. *then releases Emily and reaches down to pick up the vial. He then rises up.* Hah . . . Thank you, old friend. One more to go now. This has been so easy. Good work, my child.

Emily. *then bows to Thornton.* Thank you, master.

Dew. What's going on?

Emily.	*stands up straight, then turns to face Dew.* Oh, Dew, you're such a sucker. You've been hoodwinked.
Dew.	You tricked me. Why?!
Emily.	To please my master and heal the world.
Cooper.	Heal the world? Hah!
Emily.	You laugh . . . but you will see.
Dew.	Emily, this man wants to destroy the world.
Emily.	You see it that way, but it will be a new beginning. If you could only open your eyes and see the big picture here. Thornton is the key to our salvation, the path to paradise. He will return our world to the peace it once was. Once the angel is reborn, holy bliss shall reign upon us.
Dew.	No, Emily, open your eyes. He's manipulating you so he can carry out his true intentions. He does not care about all of us. You've been brainwashed with false promises.
Emily.	You deceive yourself.
Thornton.	My children are wise enough to see through your intentions to destroy their beliefs.
Cooper.	My god, Thornton. Do you hear yourself speaking? You're a mad man. Your obsession of gaining power will destroy us all, even yourself in the end.
Thornton.	This is not about power; it is about returning the balance that once existed long ago to this frail world.
Dew.	So that balance involves the meaningless deaths of others? Does that make sense to you, Emily?
Emily.	Regardless of the facts, Dew, I will do as my master wants from me. To better our lives on this miserable planet, I will see to it that my master succeeds in his plans.
Dew.	Unforgivable, Thornton. Whatever you have done to change Emily like this . . . you will pay for this.
Thornton.	Me? She has chosen who she is on her own and what she feels is right. Not my influences at all.
Emily.	Dew, you and your friends will be judged when the day comes. Come join us; you will be saved.
Elvir.	Whatever you're smoking, please let me know what it is.
Emily.	So that's how it is? Hah . . . Nothing will deny my master from obtaining what he wants . . . not even you.
Dew.	How sad you've been taken away from reality. Your brother would have been disappointed in you.

Emily.	How dare you bring him into this.
Thornton.	My child, I've heard enough. Be quick with them; we don't have much time left.
Emily.	Yes, my lord. Dew, you and friends are foolish to rebel against faith. I shall send you to my brother then for that. (*then pulls out her sword*) I won't be let down again. You will die now! (*then runs toward Dew*)
Narrator.	Dew, Cooper and Elvir battle Emily as Thornton watches in the background. Dew manages to subdue Emily by knocking her to the ground.
Emily.	*Ah!*
Thornton.	That didn't go as planned . . . *humph.*
Dew.	*turns to face Thornton and points his bo at him.* Thornton, we'll end this now.
Thornton.	That will have to wait for another time. Well, now . . . she may not have gotten rid of you all. I at least got what I came for.
Emily.	Master.
Thornton.	You served your purpose long enough . . . weakling. You lost your place in paradise for your failure, child.
Emily.	Master, no.
Thornton.	One more vial to go, and soon the Angel of Death will be reborn in the city of lost souls and forgotten dreams. "Ah-tishoo! Ah-tishoo! We all fall down." Ha-ha-ha . . . (*then vanishes*)
Emily.	Master, don't leave me!
Dew.	Emily.
Emily.	Master, why have you forsaken me?
Cooper.	Sheep without its shepherd.
Emily.	I'm all alone now . . . as before. All the promises destroyed.
Dew.	What are you talking about?
Emily.	He had promised me that I would see Hopkins again. He told me he knew where he was at.
Dew.	You believed that? Emily . . .
Emily.	He played me. Since Hopkins death, I haven't been myself. I got into drugs to kill the depression off of losing my brother. It still hurts . . . Why did he have to die? (*then begins to sob*)
Dew.	Emily . . . it's okay now. I'm here for you. (*then holds her head to his shoulder as she begins to cry*)
Emily.	He had promised me he would return. He never did though. It's my entire fault.
Dew.	How is that?

Emily.	I had encouraged him to join the military. He wanted to make our family proud of him. I sent him out to slaughter. When the news came back of the members who died in the New Havenport bombing, that ruined the whole family. My mother died of such grief afterwards. When I met Thornton, I felt the sadness in me dissolving, and there was hope in the words he preached. As with him, I was let down in the end too. If you make a promise to some one, you have to keep it. That is the point of making one, in the first place. Damn! I am sorry, brother.
Dew.	Emily, it's not your fault . . . He knew the consequences when he joined, and did that by his own free will. He wanted me to tell you something right before he had died. I never had the chance to tell you this when I got back to Twin Pines after the war, but hear this now: he loved you and he will always be watching over you no matter what. He would always talk about you daily and how proud he was that he could call you sister. He died for you and everyone else.
Emily.	He said that?
Dew.	Yes.
Emily.	Hopkins . . . (*sigh*) I feel relieved knowing this now, after all these years. He's in a good place with the others now. I know it. (*then looks up at Dew*) Thank you, Dew.
Dew.	It's good you know now.
Emily.	Better than never, huh?
Dew.	Yeah.
Emily.	I don't know what to say after all of this . . . I . . .
Dew.	It's okay.
Emily.	I'm glad we were able to see one another again, really. Now I can join them soon and be at peace.
Dew.	What do you mean?!
Narrator.	She then takes her hand and feels the side of her abdomen and reveals a deep stab wound.
Emily.	I feel it coming now.
Dew.	Emily, no. (takes her in his arms and grasps her head)
Emily.	It's okay, friend, I want this. I may have been denied from my master's paradise, but now I will ascend . . . to another one, to join them all.
Dew.	I don't want to lose you. I lost one friend already, not another one.

Emily.	You'll never lose me if I'm in your heart. You were always in mine . . . Dew.
Dew.	Hang in there; you'll be okay . . .
Emily.	Death isn't the end; it's only the beginning. Life is wonderful; so hurtful though. I repent for all the wrong I've done . . . I'm sorry.
Dew.	Emily . . . NO!
Emily.	It's time . . . now. (*then looks up into Dew eyes*) Dew, I-I . . . love you . . . *ugh* . . .
Dew.	Emily?! (*shakes her*) Not you too . . . (*a tear falls from his eye*)
Elvir.	Dew . . .
Cooper.	*sighs.*
Dew.	This isn't fair . . . Emily. (*exhales deeply*) EEMMMILLLLLYYYYY!
Narrator.	The scene then shifts to later on at night when Dew and the others are back at Rena's house.
Cooper.	All back here again.
Lorenzo.	Seems empty without her being here.
Krista.	Dew, why are we all here?
Dew.	This is probably the best time for me to say this before we all consider continuing on with this journey. This is really important, so please listen up guys.
Vilmer.	I see.
Dew.	I feel responsible for all that has happened so far. I couldn't stop Rena from dying in my place, when it should have been me. Emily, my friend, she died over Thornton's meaningless cause. The rage, the thoughts are burning me up inside . . . I can't deny what I have to do now. I must continue on this journey to stop him on my own.
Elvir.	On your own? Hah.
Lorenzo.	Sorry, bro, we're sticking all with you.
Dew.	No. I don't need anyone else close to me being lost.
Lorenzo.	No, man, we're all in this together. By our choice only.
Krista.	Dew, Rena was our friend too. For granted you may of known her longer, but we did get attached to her as well.
Elvir.	We all miss her. We may not be able to change the past . . .
Cooper.	There is hope for the future though.
Dew.	Guys . . .
Lorenzo.	Like I told you, man, friends until the end. What about everyone else?

Cooper.   No time to turn back now. I'm staying.

Krista.   Well, you need me still; I would feel terrible if you, guys, got lost without me now.

Vilmer.   Well, I made it this far. I don't feel like going home yet.

Elvir.   Don't even ask me. You know I'm coming along.

Dew.   I want to cry. Thanks ya'll.

Lorenzo.   Well, c'mon then, let's get going. We've got a world to save.

Chapter 4

Pure Valor

Narrator.	Our chapter begins as Dew enters through the cemetery gates of Twin Pines. He walks up to his grandfather's grave.
Dew.	It's been awhile since I last visited here . . . If you were only here, Grandpa. I've got a long journey ahead of me still . . . I'm sure we can stop Thornton, but there is part of me that doubts my abilities to do so. I couldn't stop Rena from dying, and now Emily . . . (*then pulls out the amulet as he begins he look at it*) They both died for nothing. If only . . . You told me this amulet was supposed to bring me luck . . . What happened? (exhales deeply) No . . . (*then squeezes the amulet in his palm*) I can't blame what has happened on this or you. What has happened can not be changed now. I must accept that. I can't turn back now. That is the last thing I will do. No more dwelling in the past . . . Look forward to the future, for the better. I will make sure of it.
Lorenzo.	*shouting*. Dew, c'mon, man. Hurry.
Dew.	Hmm . . . my friends are calling for me. I remember when you told me to fight for what I believe in and never give up. I will keep fighting and never stop. I'm going to finish this. (*He then puts the amulet back in his pocket, then turns away from his grandfather's grave and walks toward the entrances of the cemetery. He then turns back around.*) I will keep my oath to you. (*Then he exits the gates.*)
Narrator.	Dew walks out the cemetery and is greeted by Lorenzo and the others.
Lorenzo.	About ready to go, man?
Dew.	Just about. Had to do some last-minute partings.

Krista.   So, where to now?

Dew.   I don't know.

Elvir.   Thornton had mentioned something about returning to the city of lost souls and forgotten dreams. What do you think he could mean by that?

Dew.   Who knows? I do have this feeling though.

Cooper.   I was thinking we should go back to Tagore. We may find some more info there.

Dew.   Sounds good to me.

Cooper.   Thanks to Killbin, he was able to retrieve our tugboat back from the disposal site in Demmin.

Vilmer.   Elvir, do you think we can get to Tagore quicker than before?

Elvir.   It was a little banged up when we got to Demmin, but that shouldn't stop us.

Vilmer.   Sounds like we'll have no problems then.

Dew   *nods his head in approval.*

Krista.   We should all get going then.

Dew.   Right you are.

Narrator.   After that, Dew and the others head to Twin Pines' boat dock, where the tugboat awaits them. They disembark out into the open ocean heading toward Tagore. As the tugboat sails down the majestic ocean scenery, the scene switches inside the bridge of the tugboat. Dew stands in front of the ship's console in thought. Cooper looks over at him.

Dew.   Hmm . . .

Cooper.   Hey, Dew, what are you thinking about?

Dew.   Just glad that I stuck around.

Elvir.   Well, if you didn't, we all would have dragged you back here then.

Cooper.   Ha-ha-ha.

Elvir.   I didn't come along for nothing now. (*steering the ship's wheel*)

Vilmer.   She's right about that. Seems like you're the heart and soul of the group here, Dew.

Dew.   Me, a leader? I guess.

Krista.   I wonder what is ahead for us.

Vilmer.   I couldn't tell you. It's funny how fate brings people together as a group fighting for the same common purpose. God's will is strong indeed. Isolating myself from the world so long has almost made me forget how beautiful it really is. I am glad I came.

Elvir.	I am glad I came too. (*steering the ship's wheel*)
Dew.	Well, just a little bit more to go, guys.
Cooper.	We still haven't found the SKT virus A vial though.
Dew.	As long as Thornton doesn't first, we have a chance of preventing whatever he has planned.
Krista.	Hey, guys, where Lorenzo at? I haven't seen him around lately.
Cooper.	He went outside to the weather decks to get some fresh air.
Vilmer.	Seems like he got used to being out at sea already.
Krista.	Yeah . . . ha-ha-ha.
Dew.	Hmm . . . I think I will get some air too then.
Narrator.	Dew then exits the bridge and heads outside to the weather decks and finds Lorenzo aft of the tugboat leaning against the life rails, gazing into the horizon of Mesovilla.
Dew.	Enjoying the view here?
Lorenzo.	A little bit. I never really noticed how grand the world is. It's so amazing . . . the sky.
Dew.	Sure is.
Lorenzo.	Dew, let me ask you something.
Dew.	Okay, what is it?
Lorenzo.	You think we'll be able to stop that Thornton dude?
Dew.	As long as we work together, anything is possible. He may not be the typical SWAT trooper we're use to battling, but he is human . . . somewhat.
Lorenzo.	We'll find out sooner or later.
Dew.	I am always grateful for you helping me back on my feet after Rena died. You are a good friend, Lorenzo. Thank you.
Lorenzo.	That's what friends are for. Hey, you knocked sense into me too now.
Dew.	Yeah . . .
Lorenzo.	You miss her and the other one, huh?
Dew.	They both meant a lot to me. My teacher and my friend . . . gone. (*exhales deeply*)
Lorenzo.	Well, they're all better off now . . . No more pain. They did help us though in the end.
Dew.	You're right . . .
Lorenzo.	You know Paca and Lynch would have tripped out after the things we've been through so far.
Dew.	They would have.

Lorenzo.   Well, there are always the memories, but I wouldn't get consumed
              in them though. We got the future ahead of us.
Dew.   You're making sense, friend. (*then smiles*)
Lorenzo.   You remember when we first met?
Dew.   It seems like yesterday.
Narrator.   The scene switches to Dew's past when he first met the Aurora
              Blade six years ago. The scene begins as Lorenzo, Paca, and
              Lynch are being chased through the alleyways in the Helix
              capital by four SWAT troopers.
SWAT trooper 1. *running with rifle in hand.* There they are; they're getting
              away!
SWAT trooper 2. Stop!
Narrator.   One of the SWAT troopers fires a rifle in the direction of Lorenzo,
              Paca, and Lynch. The bullet misses them as they eluded the four
              SWAT troopers.
Paca.   *running.* Talk about close.
Lynch.   *running.* These guys just don't let up.
Lorenzo.   *running.* Just keep running.
Narrator.   As the SWAT troopers continue their pursuit of the three Aurora
              Blade members, they eventually end up coming to a dead end.
              They come to a stop.
Paca.   Not looking good.
Lorenzo.   Not here. Come on this way.
Narrator.   Lorenzo and the two then turn around and start running in the other
              direction. They come to a quick stop as the four SWAT troopers
              enter the dead-end alley blocking their way of escape.
Lynch.   Shit.
Paca.   Not looking good at all.
SWAT trooper 1. Nowhere to go now.
SWAT trooper 3. You silly thieves thought you could get away from us? Not
              happening today.
SWAT trooper 2. I smell a reward coming our way. These are wanted men
              here.
SWAT trooper 4. *pulls out his baton.* We promise, we'll go easy on you.
Lorenzo.   Go to hell, you jerk off.
SWAT trooper 3. Ha-ha-ha . . . they never did say we had to bring them back
              alive, huh? (*then pulls out his rifle pointing it at Lorenzo*)
SWAT trooper 2. I don't recall that at all. Blow their fucking brains out.
Lorenzo.   Do your worse homes.

Narrator.	The SWAT trooper is about to pull the trigger until Dew jumps out of nowhere armed with his bo, whacking the SWAT trooper in the head causing him to collapse to the ground unconscious. The other SWAT troopers turn their attention to Dew in shock.
Lorenzo.	Who are who?!
SWAT trooper 2.	Hey, you can't be doing that!
SWAT trooper 4.	This is official government business here. Step off if you know what is good for you.
Dew.	I . . . I usually don't. I am quite hardheaded you see.
SWAT trooper 1.	You're a bold one.
SWAT trooper 4.	Let's get rid of this clown first, and then we'll deal with these punks afterwards.
SWAT trooper 2.	Yeah, he's pissing me off.
Narrator.	The three SWAT troopers rush at Dew, but they are easily thwarted off. Lorenzo, Paca, and Lynch watch in amazement as Dew single handedly defeats them.
Lorenzo.	Damn.
Paca.	Wow . . . I don't know what to say.
Lynch.	He took care of our light work for us. Maybe we should get going before more of those goons show up.
Lorenzo.	No, hold up. He just saved us from those creeps. (*then walks up to Dew*)
Narrator.	Dew stands over one of the fallen SWAT troopers and places his foot on his chest.
Dew.	If I'm a clown, why aren't you laughing? (*then walks away from the fallen SWAT trooper*)
Lorenzo.	Hey, you!
Dew.	*turns to look at Lorenzo.* Hm?
Lorenzo.	What's your name?
Dew.	The name doesn't matter. Just be grateful I was here.
Lorenzo.	The situation was already under control.
Dew.	Didn't seem like that at all from this point of view.
Lorenzo.	If you're going to rub it in then, we didn't need your help at all, pal.
Dew.	All my friends are dead . . . I have none.
Lorenzo.	What? Yeah anyway, thanks for saving our hinds back there. The Aurora Blade is grateful for that.
Dew.	Aurora Blade? You're the ones who are called the freedom fighters of Mesovilla?

Lorenzo.   Well, yeah.

Dew.   Hmm . . . My name is Dew.

Lorenzo.   I am Lorenzo. This is Paca and that's Lynch.

Dew.   My due is done here. (*then begins to walk off*) You know my name; that's all you will get from me.

Lorenzo.   Hey, wait a second.

Narrator.   One of the SWAT troopers regains consciousness and crawls over to grab his hand gun.

SWAT trooper 2. It's n-not . . . over yet!

Lorenzo   *notices the SWAT trooper.* Watch out!

Narrator.   Lorenzo quickly darts over and pushes Dew out of the way. They hit knocking them both down to the ground just seconds before the SWAT trooper fires the gun.

SWAT trooper 2. Damn . . . *ugh.* (*then passes out*)

Dew.   ?!

Lorenzo.   That was close. (*rising up to his feet*)

Dew.   Thanks.

Lorenzo.   Looks like I saved you now. (*then lends Dew a hand helping him back on his feet*) You're lucky I happened to be here.

Dew.   Ha-ha-ha.

Lorenzo.   You like that, huh?

Dew.   Pretty funny. Well, looks like I am in your debt now, buddy.

Lorenzo.   Does that mean we're friends?

Dew.   Always room for more.

Lorenzo.   I think I'm going to like you.

Lynch.   Hey, man, let's roll out before more of those SWAT fucks show up.

Lorenzo.   Yeah.

Dew.   I appreciate you saving me there, really.

Lorenzo.   Anytime, pal.

Dew.   Hah. (*then smiles*)

Lorenzo.   Come on, man, let's go.

Narrator.   Then the four begin to run off as they exit the alley. The scene shifts back to present time.

Lorenzo.   Those were the days . . . Things seem so weird when you look at them from present tense, don't you think?

Dew.   Yeah.

Lorenzo.   Memories . . .

Dew.   *whispering to himself.* Isn't that true.

Lorenzo.	Huh?
Dew.	Nothing, just got lost in thought. We should be arriving in Tagore soon. I'll be on the bridge if you need me.
Lorenzo.	All right, man.
Narrator.	Dew then walks off as Lorenzo continues to stare off into the Mesovilla ocean view. Meanwhile, back in Tagore, Professor Sorenson is taking a nap on the grass underneath a tree on a small hill close to his house. The birds are chirping away as they glide through the sunlit sky. A brisk wind then begins to blow throughout the area, and suddenly, it turns dark. A water droplet falls from a leaf and hits the sleeping professor on his forehead. He then awakes from his slumber.
Sorenson.	*yawns*. That was a good rest. Hmm . . . it's about to rain. Odd, I don't remember hearing anything about that today. Oh well . . . *zzzzz*
Narrator.	Sorenson then falls back to sleep. Suddenly, the ground begins to tremor violently, causing him to awake again.
Sorenson.	Huh?! (*getting off his hind onto his feet*)
Narrator.	The tremors then begin to get worse as the ground begins to start cracking open beneath his feet. Sorenson then panics and runs back to his house. As he runs, he trips over a rock and rolls down the hill back into town. Back out at sea, the waves begin to rise higher than normal and begins rocking the tugboat side to side. Dew enters the bridge as Elvir struggles to maneuver the tugboat through the storm.
Dew.	Elvir, what's going on?
Elvir.	The sea state, that's what. I can't stay on course because of the rough seas.
Dew.	Can we turn around?
Elvir.	Through this, no. (*looking up at the magnetic compass*) Great.
Krista.	What's that?
Elvir.	Something is terribly wrong here. The compass isn't working. (*steering the ship's wheel*)
Dew.	Shit . . .
Lorenzo.	*entering the bridge.* Hey, man, what's going on in here? I almost fell overboard because of your driving, kid.
Elvir.	Not me, it's the sea. (*steering the ship's wheel*)
Narrator.	The tremors continue to worsen as the waves become overwhelming, engulfing the tugboat in it.

Lorenzo.	Oh damn . . .
Vilmer.	I don't think we can make it through this.
Elvir.	Don't say that, I'm trying my best. (*steering the ship's wheel*)
Narrator.	A large tidal wave then comes roaring toward the tugboat, rocking it and causing everybody to fall to the floor.
Dew.	*struggling to get up on his feet*. Damn!
Krista.	*getting up*. I don't think this boat can take it for too long.
Elvir.	*slowly rising up to hold on to the ship's wheel*. I got to try something else. (*then tries to move the ship's wheel, but it is jammed in place*) Oh man.
Cooper.	What's wrong now?
Elvir.	The controls aren't responding. (*then begins pushing buttons on the ships console*) Nothing is now. That last wave sure did it.
Lorenzo.	That doesn't sound good.
Narrator.	Then the ships console begins to spark up in flames.
Cooper.	That's not good either.
Vilmer.	Hah . . .
Elvir.	This is useless now.
Lorenzo.	Fuck this death trap; let's get out of here.
Dew.	To the life rafts!
Narrator.	Dew and the others quickly exit the bridge to the weather decks and flee aft of the boat, where they acquire an inflatable life raft from a chest nearby. The life raft automatically inflates and is dropped into the water, and they all jump into it, drifting away from the tugboat. Moments later, the tugboat begins to sink as the waves consume it.
Lorenzo.	There it goes.
Elvir.	Well, guess we'll be floating there then, huh?
Dew.	Looks like it.
Vilmer.	We're close to Tagore, so it shouldn't take us long to get there.
Cooper.	Yep.
Narrator.	The sea then begins to clam down as the life raft drifts toward Tagore. Sometime later, Dew and the others' life raft washes up on the shore of Tagore. They embark for Tagore observing the destruction of what the tremors left behind.
Lorenzo.	I guess we weren't the only ones affected by the storm.
Elvir.	Not pretty.
Vilmer.	Hmm . . . odd. (*looking down at the ground*)

Elvir.	What's that?
Vilmer.	I wouldn't say the storm did this at all. It looks like an earthquake to me. Look at these cracks in the ground.
Dew.	You're right. This is . . .
Voice.	*yelling.* Help! Help!
Dew.	Huh?!
Krista.	Did you hear that?
Lorenzo.	Hear what?
Krista.	A cry for help.
Lorenzo.	No, not a thing. Don't tell me you're hearing things now?
Voice.	*yelling.* Help me! Over here!
Krista.	That.
Lorenzo.	Oh.
Cooper.	This way.
Narrator.	Dew and the others follow Cooper as he runs over to a pile of rubble where the voice came from. Once on the spot, the group discovers Professor Sorenson, whose right leg is trapped underneath the pile.
Elvir.	Hey it's the professor.
Sorenson.	I thought I wouldn't see you, folks, again.
Vilmer.	Hold on there.
Narrator.	Dew and the others clear the rubble, allowing the professor to remove his right leg.
Vilmer.	You okay? (*checking Sorenson for further injuries*)
Sorenson.	Yes, I am now . . . thank you.
Dew.	What happened here?
Sorenson.	All I remember I was napping on this hill nearby, and then all of a sudden the ground began to shake. I did try to make it back to the house, but ended up falling down that hill there. I obviously didn't make it.
Dew.	The townspeople . . .
Sorenson.	I hope they're all are safe.
Elvir.	Are you okay, Professor?
Vilmer.	I see no other forms of injuries here. It seems that you're okay. Can you walk?
Sorenson.	My ankle is a little sore from it being caught underneath the debris. I think I can . . . Could you lend me a hand?
Narrator.	Vilmer then hoists Sorenson up on his feet.

Sorenson.	Thank you.
Cooper.	*facing Dew.* Perhaps we should go back into town and check up on the townsfolk.
Dew.	Yes. Let's do that.
Sorenson.	It's strange though. This region of Mesovilla has never experienced an earthquake; those are usually more active in the northwestern region of Mesovilla.
Vilmer.	That's true. The magnitude of the damage from the looks of it here looks to be a 5.6 or larger.
Sorenson.	Those only occur every one hundred years though.
Dew.	What could have caused this?
Vilmer.	Perhaps a shift in the earth's rotation field.
Lorenzo.	I don't know about all of that, but . . .
Narrator.	Suddenly, the tremors start again.
Krista.	Oh no.
Cooper.	Maybe it would be best to get going now.
Lorenzo.	No need to tell me twice.
Vilmer.	Up to higher ground. We'll be safer there.
Narrator.	Dew and the others—along with the professor, who is being carried by Vilmer on his shoulders—continue running upward as the tremors continue to get worse. Suddenly, something begins to emerge out from the distances causing the ocean to rumble more violently. The wind then becomes unbearable as the tremors do as well. Once Dew and the others get up on higher ground, they witness the province of New Havenport rising from the depths of the Mesovilla Ocean, now floating over Tagore. They stand dumbfounded on what has just taken place.
Lorenzo.	Earth's rotation field, huh?
Vilmer.	I can't explain this at all.
Sorenson.	Phenomena!
Krista.	It's an island.
Dew.	The city of lost souls and forgotten dreams.
Cooper.	New Havenport.
Krista	*turns to face Dew.* How?
Dew.	I don't know . . . I have this feeling.
Lorenzo.	I thought that place was wiped off the map.
Elvir.	Bloody hell.
Dew.	For some reason . . . I can feel Thornton has something to do with this.

Lorenzo.	You think he's there waiting for us?
Dew.	No doubt about it.
Sorenson.	This breaks the laws of gravity and science entirely. This is amazing.
Elvir.	Well, we know where he's at now; we should go after him then.
Krista.	How are we going to get from here to there?
Sorenson.	My teleportation device, of course.
Krista.	Oh yeah. I almost forgot.
Dew.	It didn't kill us the first time; should be okay the second time.
Sorenson.	I hope so.
Dew.	What?
Sorenson.	*Hee-hee-hee . . .* I'm joking. Just some scientific humor.
Dew.	Funny.
Sorenson.	On a serious note, we should get back to my house.
Lorenzo.	Sounds good to me.
Narrator.	Dew and the others follow the professor as they head back into town while the eerie presence of the New Havenport province floats above Tagore. The scene changes back to the professor's house in his basement laboratory, where Dew and the others gather.
Krista.	Seems like all the townspeople are unharmed.
Elvir.	That's a good thing the earthquake didn't kill anyone.
Lorenzo.	One less thing to worry about. Now we've got to stop that bastard Thornton.
Sorenson.	*viewing the power gauge of the teleportation device.* Oh darn . . .
Dew.	What's that?
Sorenson.	Oh my . . . (*checking the fuse panels to the teleportation device*)
Elvir.	That doesn't sound good.
Sorenson.	Hmm . . .
Lorenzo.	Is it still going to work, Professor?
Sorenson.	Well, the machine works, but there is no power source left. (*looking at the fuse wires*) It seems the wires are burned out. It must have happened when the earthquake had hit us, or perhaps the first time you all used my machine.
Dew	*sharply exhales.*
Krista.	There's got to be a way.
Sorenson.	Hmm . . . I got it. I will energize it using the backup generator to be sure, and then you all will be off on your way. (*then unhooks the wiring to the teleportation device*)

Dew.	Great.
Cooper.	No time to waste now. Coming down to the end.
Narrator.	Sorenson then hooks up the cables from the backup generator to the teleportation device. He then flicks on the switch to the control panel as the teleportation device gives off a low hum.
Sorenson.	Ah, it works. Good. (*observing the power gauge*) We've got about 85 percent of power now. This will be enough. All I have to do is set the coordinates for New Havenport now. (*then types in the coordinates*)
Elvir.	Hey, Prof, you're going to be okay?
Sorenson.	Oh, don't worry about me, young lady. I will be fine. I'm still alive, aren't I?
Elvir.	True.
Sorenson.	I don't know how long this will stay up. You all should go now. It's all ready.
Dew.	All right ya, let's go. Thank you, Professor, again.
Sorenson.	No problem and I hope the trip doesn't kill you.
Dew.	What?!
Sorenson.	I kid, I kid. Have some humor, I'm old. *Hee-hee-hee.*
Dew.	Yeah.
Elvir.	Appreciate it.
Narrator.	Then one by one the professor teleports Dew and his friends to New Havenport moments before the machine loses power, shutting down all the electricity in the house.
Sorenson.	Good luck to you all.
Narrator.	Back on the desolate streets of New Havenport, Dew and friends reassemble.
Vilmer.	Whoa!
Cooper.	I'm still all here.
Lorenzo.	Now that's a rush!
Krista.	Just like a roller coaster.
Dew.	I'm surprised I'm still alive as much that old man makes jokes about death. I tell you, he has it out for me. Creepy bastard.
Lorenzo.	Ha-ha-ha.
Elvir.	Don't take it to heart now. I think he only does that because you doubted if the machine would work or not.
Dew.	Well, yeah.
Lorenzo.	Well, we're all here. What now, Dew?
Dew.	Got to find Thornton first. Stay alert, ya'll.

Cooper.	Never a dull moment.
Vilmer.	*staring into the sky*. Hmm . . .
Krista.	What's wrong, Vilmer?
Vilmer.	It's strange, the sight of the sky here.
Krista.	Looks like the aftereffects of the radiation from the bombing is still in the atmosphere.
Dew.	It's only been six years.
Vilmer.	Aldous . . .
Krista.	Radiation takes years, even centuries to clear up from the atmosphere and soil itself.
Cooper.	Poisons that we humans dish out . . . hah.
Krista.	I just remembered something now.
Dew.	What's that?
Krista.	I remembered when I was younger, I heard stories about the few surviving veterans from the Great Civil War who filed complaints to the government that they were having hallucinogenic episodes.
Cooper.	. . .
Dew.	Really?
Krista.	These people who were going through this, their mind would shut off while they were awake. As if they were in a daydream state; then they would begin to trip out. Well, after the government conducted evaluations on the veterans, the doctors concluded that it was due to being exposed to immense amount of radiation during the war.
Lorenzo.	Those chemical weapon agents you mentioned earlier, I thought the Helix capital used them to kill off the opposition.
Krista.	Yes, they did. Yet with all the other agents that were disbursed into the environment during the war, they must have synthesized together, creating a new chemical that triggered the hallucinations.
Cooper.	That was all?
Krista.	Well, along with that, it was also triggered by some sort of traumatic experience in the individual life in the reports as well.
Dew.	Repressed emotions, huh?
Cooper.	Hmm . . . interesting.
Dew.	What happened with the victims that went through these episodes?

Krista.	Most of them went insane and were locked up in asylums, unfit to live in society. For the few that caught it on time, they were treated with medication to repress the pain. They received huge compensation for that as well.
Dew.	Always easy to cover up the things we do.
Cooper.	You think money will make up for the pain?
Krista.	Of course not.
Elvir.	What does this have to do with any of us?
Vilmer.	I understand now . . . the grief I held over Aldous death and being exposed to the chemical weapon agents that were in the air in Demmin caused me to start seeing things. It wasn't real at all . . .
Krista.	Exactly.
Vilmer.	I will no longer dwell on things that were. What could I have done to save Aldous then?
Lorenzo.	I believe you did your best.
Vilmer.	True . . . Well, I will not let the guilt of what could have been destroy me. I tried my best. It's all really clear now. Time to let the feelings go. You're never too old to learn any thing at all.
Elvir.	Cooper was affected too.
Cooper.	Was I?
Krista.	Regardless if he was or not, it's all in the mind pretty much.
Lorenzo.	Why weren't any of us affected by the chemical agents then? So does that mean Cooper and Vilmer will go insane as the others did?
Krista.	The toxins that resided in the air in Demmin aren't as strong as they were first disbursed during the war. I think Cooper and Vilmer will be fine. The reason for the rest of us being not affected by the toxins is because we have no kind of repressed emotions for the chemical agent to trigger. It depends on the individual.
Lorenzo.	That makes sense.
Elvir.	Well, if that's so, who says this isn't all real? What if we're all imaging all this right now?
Dew.	You're being too silly now. You can't say this isn't real where we're at right now. We're here in New Havenport, and Thornton is waiting for us.
Krista.	I think I figured that out pretty well.
Cooper.	Fitting to return to this place.
Elvir.	Cooper.

Cooper.	*facing Elvir*. Elvir, I'm fine.
Elvir.	Why do I not believe you?
Cooper.	Ah . . . (*turns away from Elvir to face Dew*) We should get going. Thornton awaits for us.
Dew.	Might as well then. Let's get a move on, ya'll. (*then walks off*)
Elvir.	Humph.
Narrator.	Dew and the others begin their journey through New Havenport. After encountering a few hostile creatures and disposing of them while roaming through the city, they come to a stop after seeing a man who appears to be Thornton, who is facing the other direction looking into the horizon of Mount Darien. Dew and the others approach him.
Dew.	*walking up*. Thornton.
Thornton.	*facing away*. Oh, it's you. I see you're finally here. Good.
Dew.	No more games. We end this here. (*then draws his bo out*)
Thornton.	You're so eager to fight me. Is it because your mentor's death or your close friend's?
Dew.	Both.
Thornton.	So strike me down then. I didn't intentionally mean for them to die. Rena happened to be in the way when I was trying to deliver that fatal blow to you. After all, she knew exactly what she was getting herself into. Not my fault for other people's choices.
Dew.	You lied to Emily, saying Hopkins was alive.
Thornton.	Oh, but he is . . . in spirit.
Dew.	No kidding.
Thornton.	Nonetheless, he can be resurrected along with many others. We can bring eternal paradise back to this world.
Dew.	We?
Cooper.	You again with that blasphemy.
Thornton	*then turns to face Dew*. Have you ever stopped to enjoy the wonders of nature and its beauty?
Dew.	What are you talking about?
Thornton.	This world was once magnificent before our very own existence. It can be like that again. Though mankind daily defiles the very fabric that is paradise . . . Isn't this place proof enough of that?
Dew.	It is.
Thornton.	Every time I feel her getting closer, her spirit is calling me.
Dew.	Elizabeth, you mean?

Thornton.	Yes . . . the rebirth will begin soon enough, and the Angel of Death will be reborn. She will pass her judgment and all shall feel her wrath. Death for their sins. The rise of a forgotten civilization will be the resurrecting grounds of the ancient force that will hold sway over all you pathetic life-forms.
Dew.	So collecting these viruses and bringing a plague among the world will be atonement for mankind's sins?
Thornton.	Ha-ha-ha . . . no. The viruses are the elixir of life itself.
Dew.	So you're trying to bring her back to life? What does Elizabeth have to do with all of this?
Thornton.	She is quite different from me and you.
Dew.	How so?
Thornton.	She has powers beyond imagination, something we as humans can never fathom. Elizabeth could sense things out of people, how they were feeling and thinking as well. This world is full of sadness, and she wanted to heal it then. She hated what this world was becoming. All the sadness, pain, greed . . . we will bring bliss back to this world soon.
Dew.	What is she?
Thornton.	In time you will understand. When she is resurrected, all will bare witness to her magnificent glory. You all will all bow to the Angel of Death and be judged.
Elvir.	You want to bring your girlfriend back to life (*sarcastic*). How romantic.
Lorenzo.	Sorry, ese, that's not going to happen.
Thornton.	*Humph.* Silly creatures. Well, I need a good warm-up. (*then vanishes*)
Dew.	Thornton?
Krista.	Where'd he go? (*looking around*)
Lorenzo.	I don't know. This vato is pissing me off. (*looking around*)
Dew.	Keep your eyes open. I know he's still around.
Narrator.	As Dew and the others continue looking around for Thornton, he then appears from above, leaping down at them knocking Dew and the others to the ground.
Thornton.	Hmmm . . . You all forgot to look upward. You people these days, with your lack of faith. Ha-ha-ha.
Dew.	I know one thing you'll be lacking though. (*getting up on his feet*)
Thornton.	What's that, Dew?

Dew.	Your life.
Thornton.	Oh, such harsh words. You, guys, are no fun . . . Well, let's get down to business then, shall we?
Elvir.	I thought he would never ask.
Thornton.	Good. (*then draws his long sword*) A-tishoo! A-tishoo! We all fall down.
Narrator.	The battle begins as Dew and the others rush in at Thornton. The battle is fierce as they receive their share of damages at the hands of Thornton, who evades most of the group's attacks. In the end he is overpowered though. Thornton then falls to his knees, gripping his ribs.
Thornton.	Good . . .
Dew	*inhales and exhales deeply.*
Thornton.	Hmm. I seemed to have underestimated you all a bit. You may have got the best of me this time (*then smirks*) . . . but this isn't over yet. (*then vanishes*)
Lorenzo.	Running away already? Pussy . . .
Elvir.	Well, we took care of that bloody bloke.
Dew.	Wait a sec.
Narrator.	Suddenly, Thornton reappears hovering over Dew and the others in midair.
Thornton.	See me now?
Vilmer.	Watch out!
Narrator.	Thornton then fires a projectile from his hand at Dew and his friends below. They quickly dodge it; the projectile hits the ground causing it to crack open and Dew and his friends to plunge into the sewers below.
Thornton.	Hah . . . see you all soon. (*then vanishes*)
Narrator.	Meanwhile, the others awake to find themselves in the sewers after the long fall.
Lorenzo.	*getting up on his feet.* That Thornton dude . . . What a chump.
Vilmer.	Is everybody all right?
Krista.	I'm fine.
Elvir.	Some day this has been. (*dusting herself*)
Cooper.	Where is Dew? (*looking around*)
Vilmer.	I don't see him around.
Krista.	You think he probably fell somewhere else?
Lorenzo.	Could be.

Elvir.	Where?
Cooper.	Could be anywhere. I think we should split up into groups to find him.
Lorenzo.	Sounds like a good idea to me.
Krista.	We'll be able to find him quicker.
Lorenzo.	All right . . . I'll take Krista and Vilmer with me.
Cooper.	Elvir and I it is.
Lorenzo.	Whoever comes across Dew first, be sure we all meet up later again.
Elvir.	Got ya.
Cooper.	Let's get going; he may need our help. (*then walks off*)
Narrator.	Cooper and Elvir then walk off in search of Dew. Lorenzo, Krista, and Vilmer then begin their search as well. Meanwhile, we find Dew lying unconscious in a pile of rubble, dreaming that he is back in Twin Pines standing in front of his grandfather's house.
Dew.	Huh?! (*then begins to look around*) Wait . . . How did I get back here? Where is everyone?
Narrator.	He then begins to hear a distinctive laugh coming from the house.
Dew.	Grandpa . . .
Narrator.	Dew then walks up to the front door, turns the knob, and enters the living room. He then continues to look around in confusion.
Dew.	Lorenzo, Cooper, Krista, Elvir, Vilmer? Where are you, guys? Anyone here?
Narrator.	Dew's grandfather then steps out of the kitchen and enters the living room.
Grandpa.	Dew.
Dew	*then turns to face his grandpa.*
Grandpa.	I see you finally came home. It's been a while, young man.
Narrator.	The scene changes back to the sewers as Cooper and Elvir aimlessly continue their search for Dew. Cooper then comes to a stop.
Cooper.	. . .
Elvir.	Huh? (*then stops walking*) What's wrong, Cooper?
Cooper.	I need to rest.
Elvir.	Sure, we'll take a break then. We've been walking for some time. My dogs hurt. *Hee-hee-hee.*
Narrator.	As Cooper and Elvir sit down for a break, Cooper, sitting on the edge of the walkway, peers into the sewerage water. As

	he continues to look, the ghostly figure of his father's face appears.
Ghostly figure.	Cooper.
Cooper.	*startled and then jumps back.* Dad?!
Elvir.	What's wrong?
Narrator.	Cooper then looks at the water again.
Cooper.	It was him.
Elvir.	Your father is it?
Cooper.	Yes.
Elvir.	Cooper, ignore the feelings. They're not real like Krista said.
Cooper.	I . . . I can't do that.
Narrator.	The ghostly figure appears again waving to Cooper to follow him as he walks off . . .
Elvir.	Cooper?
Ghostly figure.	Son.
Cooper.	Dad . . .
Elvir.	Cooper, snap out of it.
Narrator.	The ghostly figure continues to wave at Cooper to follow him.
Cooper.	Don't leave me again.
Narrator.	The ghostly figure then continues to walk farther off into the distance.
Cooper.	Wait!
Narrator.	As Cooper starts to go after the ghostly figure, Elvir steps in his way.
Elvir.	Cooper, don't do it.
Cooper.	I must.
Elvir.	Why? Can't you let those feelings go? You have nothing to regret. Why do you hold onto them?
Cooper.	It's because I failed to do as I promised. I must see him now. (*then runs off behind the ghostly figure*)
Elvir.	Cooper, don't go. We still have to find Dew. Cooper! (*exhales sharply*) Wait for me then.
Narrator.	Cooper follows the ghostly figure into one of the tunnels. He then approaches him.
Cooper.	Dad, I am here now.
Ghostly figure.	Cooper.
Cooper.	I can't be hallucinating this.
Ghostly figure.	Cooper, you failed me.

Cooper.   I've heard that before already from you, Father. Why do you torture me?

Ghostly figure. You do it to yourself; I wanted the best from you.

Cooper.   I know . . .

Ghostly figure. You had promised me you would have taken care of your mother; you left her to die though.

Cooper.   No . . . I didn't. I did what I could, Father, and Mom made her choice in staying there.

Ghostly figure. It wasn't enough

Cooper.   It was the best I could do.

Ghostly figure. Deep down in you, you wanted things to be turn out different. You could have made that happen.

Cooper.   I did want it to happen for the better, yet I did what I could. I accept the reality of it now. When I was younger you demanded so much from me, and that fueled me to live up to what you were. I did that, but I'm not perfect; neither were you. Things happen the way they turn out; I did what I could. This remorse I carry for her death will not destroy me anymore.

Ghostly figure. Take in the misery, feel it.

Cooper.   You're not real; you're not my father at all. Leave me alone, false specter. I will not do this to myself anymore.

Ghostly figure. Let it rot in your mind.

Cooper.   No!

Ghostly figure. *in Cooper's mother's voice.* Why'd you leave me to die? (*screaming in pain*) End it.

Cooper.   No! No! No!

Ghostly figure. *in Cooper's mother's voice.* Failure.

Cooper.   This isn't happening . . . (*inhales and exhales deeply*) I will not let this continue. Krista was right; I am the only one who is to blame for holding on to these feelings. I must let them go. There is only one way now. I must be rid of you for good!

Narrator.   Cooper then battles the ghostly figure mentally. In the end he overcomes the burden of guilt that he carried for so long, causing the ghostly figure to dissolve into nothingness. Cooper then falls to the ground as Elvir enters the tunnel.

Elvir.   Cooper?! (*Then she runs over to him. She kneels down to lift his head up to her lap.*) Cooper, wake up! Cooper?!

Cooper.   *opening his eyes.* Elvir . . .

Elvir.	Cooper, I thought you were . . .
Cooper.	No, not me . . . hah. I'm going to be fine. All is lifted.
Narrator.	Elvir then smiles at him. Meanwhile, we find Lorenzo, Krista, and Vilmer wandering around through the tunnels of the sewers as they look for Dew.
Krista.	I really don't know where we're going.
Lorenzo.	I'm clueless as you are. We do need to keep looking for him though.
Vilmer.	He's got to be around here somewhere.
Lorenzo.	I say we take a break for a moment, and then we'll continue the search for Dew.
Vilmer.	Might as well.
Krista.	You think Cooper and Elvir found him yet?
Lorenzo.	Who knows? Hopefully they're not lost as we are.
Vilmer.	We'll find our way out of here eventually.
Lorenzo.	Yeah.
Narrator.	As they sit down to take a rest, Lorenzo notices the nearby wall vibrating.
Lorenzo.	The hell?!
Krista.	What's wrong?
Lorenzo.	*pointing.* The wall there, it looks like its moving.
Narrator.	Vilmer and Krista then look in the direction where Lorenzo is pointing at. Vilmer and Lorenzo then walk over to investigate the wall. The vibrations stop.
Vilmer.	It looked like it was moving a bit.
Lorenzo.	It just stopped though.
Vilmer.	That's odd. Something isn't right here . . .
Narrator.	As Lorenzo and Vilmer continue observing the wall, the sewerage water nearby begins to bubble. Krista turns her attention in that direction.
Krista.	Hmm?
Narrator.	Suddenly, a large sewerage leech pops up from the water to stand in front of Lorenzo and his group.
Krista.	*startled and quickly jumps to her feet.* Oh dear.
Lorenzo.	Holy shit.
Vilmer.	It looks like one of those mutations again.
Narrator.	The sewerage leech then gives off a loud roar.
Vilmer.	Somebody must have been sleeping well . . . hah.

Krista.	So much for a breather.
Lorenzo.	Well, not out the woods yet, I see.
Narrator.	Then the battle begins as Lorenzo, Krista, and Vilmer battle the sewerage leech. After defeating the leech, which collapses on a wall nearby, revealing a new path for them to transit through.
Vilmer	*inhales and exhales deeply*. Whew.
Krista.	That was tough.
Lorenzo.	We should hurry and find my mans soon.
Vilmer.	Yes.
Narrator.	Lorenzo and the others then continue their venture through the newly formed path to find Dew. The scene switches back to Dew's subconscious, as he finds himself confronted by his grandfather in his house back in Twin Pines.
Dew.	How is this . . .
Grandpa.	Real? Real as you make it. What is real lies in your heart.
Dew.	This can't be happening.
Grandpa.	It is though.
Dew.	Am I dead?
Grandpa.	Do you feel dead?
Dew.	Euh . . . no.
Grandpa.	Come here and give your grandpappy a hug. (*then opens his arms for embracement*)
Narrator.	Dew walks up to his grandfather with some hesitation and then hugs him.
Dew.	Is it really you?
Grandpa.	Yes, Dew. I missed you so much and finally, together at last.
Dew.	I have too, Grandpa.
Narrator.	Then they cease the embrace.
Grandpa.	Look at you. You've grown so well. Time has gone by so fast; just yesterday I remember how short you were. (*then smiles*)
Dew.	I have so much to tell you. We've got a lot of catching up to do.
Grandpa.	There will be time for that later, but first thing is first though.
Dew.	What do you mean?
Grandpa.	We must prepare you for the battle to come. I'm here to provide that.
Dew.	You're helping me in what way?
Grandpa.	To make you stronger . . . mentally.
Dew.	How so?

Grandpa.	You carry so much weight on your shoulders, feeling lost of things. You really don't know what will happen; every thought that consumes your mind is negativity. Uncertainty will hold you back.
Dew.	That's not true.
Grandpa.	I know you well; denial of not being afraid of losing those who are close to you will destroy you in the end.
Dew.	Well, that's not . . .
Grandpa.	You fear it though.
Dew.	You're . . . right. What happens now?
Grandpa.	A test.
Dew.	I don't understand.
Grandpa.	To fight yourself.
Dew.	What do you mean by that?
Grandpa.	Let go of the memories and what-ifs.
Dew.	I-I can't do that . . . no.
Grandpa.	It's the only way for you to let go of those feelings of rage that lies within you.
Dew.	It still hurts though. How can I?
Grandpa.	Fight them. Let it go. The things that have happened and we can't control, you shouldn't blame yourself for it. Understand that fear leads to anger, and you're heading down that road.
Dew.	Hmm . . . how right you are.
Grandpa.	No matter what happens, it will be fine in the end. Keep the faith in things. All the others had faith in you too, Rena and Emily.
Dew.	Yes . . .
Grandpa.	All you got to remember is this: stay strong and never quit. Nothing is easy. Life was never meant to be. All on how you make it. Stay focused.
Lorenzo.	*shouting.* Dew!
Krista.	*shouting.* Dew, where are you?
Dew.	*looking around.* Hmm . . . my friends.
Grandpa.	Go to them, lead them.
Dew	*nods head in approval.*
Grandpa.	Never forget what you've learned here now.
Dew.	I won't. Thank you, Grandpa. I . . .
Grandpa.	You have the valor now; you will be fine. (*then turns to walk away*) We will meet again someday. Until then, live life and don't waste a single moment of it. We'll all be there waiting for you.

Dew.	Where?
Vilmer.	*shouting.* Here he is. Hey, guys, I found him.
Grandpa.	Where else? Follow your senses and you'll know. Farewell. (*then vanishes*)
Narrator.	Dew then shuts his eyes with a smile on his face. The scene switches over to Lorenzo and Krista running over to Vilmer, who finds Dew lying in the pile of rubble. Cooper and Elvir then enter the scene to rejoin them.
Elvir.	There you, guys, are.
Cooper.	Elvir, over here.
Narrator.	Cooper and Elvir then run toward Lorenzo, who is standing over the unconscious Dew being attended by Vilmer.
Elvir.	You found him.
Cooper.	Is he going to be all right?
Vilmer.	We will see. (*then continues to check his vitals*)
Narrator.	Dew then begins to move around. This startles Vilmer.
Dew.	*Ugh-ugh.*
Krista.	He's okay.
Vilmer.	Dew, can you hear me?
Dew.	*eye lids then opens.* Mmmm . . . I'm . . . I'm fine. (*then looks up at Vilmer and the others*)
Lorenzo.	Glad you didn't die on us.
Dew.	Yeah, I know. (*then gets up on his feet*) That was some fall . . . *oow.*
Vilmer.	If you're feeling fine, we should find a way out of here then. What do you think?
Dew.	Yeah, I'm cool.
Elvir.	Let's get out of this place then.
Narrator.	After that, Dew and the others wander through the sewers, some more looking for an exit. They eventually find one leading outside to the front gates of the city.
Krista.	The light at the end of the tunnel.
Elvir.	It's about time we found our way out of there.
Lorenzo.	That smell was getting a little too unbearable. Nice to get some fresh air.
Cooper.	I don't know which was worse—breathing in the crappy air down there or out here.
Dew.	Well, I'm glad to have made it out alive. That's all that matters.
Vilmer.	I suppose that Thornton fellow isn't in the city limits anymore.

Lorenzo.	Guess not. Where could he be now?
Dew.	I have a good feeling where he could be at.
Cooper.	You're thinking what I am thinking?
Dew.	Yeah.
Krista.	And that is?
Dew.	Mount Darien. He's at the chemical facility. It's located on the midpoint of the mountain.
Cooper.	He's waiting for us there.
Elvir.	Ah, more walking to do. Great.
Vilmer.	The more the better, I say.
Dew.	No stopping now. We've come this far; might as well continue it. Let's get going.
Narrator.	Dew and the others exit the New Havenport city limits and begin their trek up Mount Darien. After wandering a bit up the trail, they encounter a few mutated wildlife, easily defeating them. Some time passes by. Dew and the others come to a bridge where across from it lay the remains of the chemical facility. They all come to a stop.
Cooper.	Still standing.
Dew.	Looks as if it was rebuilt.
Elvir.	We can take this bridge to get there, so we should cross.
Dew.	We can do that.
Narrator.	Dew and the others begin to cross over the bridge. Then out of nowhere, three druids come leaping to the bridge, blocking them from proceeding farther.
Lorenzo.	Them again.
Druid 10.	The time has come.
Druid 8.	We won't allow you to intervene.
Druid 9.	You must die. (*then draws sword*)
Elvir.	*Humph* . . . we'll see about that now.
Cooper.	How easy to be manipulated to die for someone else's obsession.
Lorenzo.	You, guys, are loco. Die crazy then.
Narrator.	The druids then swarm to attack. Dew and the others are able to defeat them in the end.
Druid 8.	We've . . . failed . . . *ugh*.
Elvir.	That's the end of them.
Vilmer.	Shall we be going?
Dew.	Yep.

Narrator.	Dew and the others then cross the bridge to approach the chemical facility. They then come to a stop to prepare for what lies ahead.
Vilmer.	This is it.
Lorenzo.	We've come a long way.
Krista.	So what now, Dew?
Dew.	I was thinking we should split up into two groups.
Elvir.	Who's going with whom?
Dew.	Since me and Cooper have been here before, we'll take whoever.
Cooper.	Fine with me. So who are you taking with you, Dew?
Dew.	Good question. I think I'll have Elvir and Lorenzo with me.
Cooper.	It's come down to this. No matter what, I will see it out to the end. (*then walks off*)
Krista.	Funny how I met you all. I was supposed to guide you all to just one place, and look how long I stuck around. Well, no regrets. (*then walks off*)
Vilmer.	I've accomplished so much in my life, seen so many sights in my time. Out of all that, that doesn't compare to the thrill and pleasure I have gotten from aiding in your cause. Until the end . . . Be careful now. (*then walks off*)
Elvir.	Well, Dew, you can count on me. No way to leave you all now. Nope.
Lorenzo.	Dew, you and I have been road dogs for a while. I value our friendship, and for the honor of Aurora Blade, we'll see it to the end that Thornton is stopped. Let's do this.
Narrator.	Dew, Lorenzo, and Elvir enter the chemical facility to begin their venture through the large complex. After wandering through the facility, Dew and his group enter the cargo room to find a cargo elevator.
Elvir.	An elevator.
Dew.	Seems like Thornton isn't anywhere on this floor, so let's check the ones below.
Lorenzo.	Yeah, man.
Narrator.	Dew and the group enter the elevator, and he selects to take it to the second-floor basement. The elevator then begins to move.
Dew.	On our way now.
Lorenzo.	This is all too easy.
Elvir.	Isn't it always?

Dew.	Well, stay alert, just to be on the safe side.
Narrator.	As they descend down the shaft, the elevator suddenly comes to a halt.
Dew.	Huh?
Lorenzo.	Why'd it stop?
Elvir.	Dew, try pushing it again. We might start moving again.
Narrator.	Dew then walks up to the control panel and pushes the button. The elevator still doesn't move.
Dew.	It's not working.
Lorenzo.	Something up here.
Narrator.	Suddenly, a large security pod comes hovering over Dew and his group.
Security Pod.	Intruder alert! All trespassers will be eliminated! WARNING! WARNING!
Narrator.	Sirens go off.
Lorenzo.	I guess they know we're here now.
Elvir.	So much for surprising them.
Dew.	No time to soak on it now. Let's end this quick.
Narrator.	The battle then begins as the security pod comes swooping down at Dew and his group. The security pod begins shooting laser beams at the group, but they are able to dodge the attacks. Dew comes in and delivers a blow with his bo to the security pod radar sensors, knocking it out of commission. In the end, they destroy the nuisance. The elevator then begins to become operational again as it descends down the shaft.
Lorenzo.	Piece of junk.
Elvir.	We're moving again.
Dew.	*puzzled*. Strange . . .
Lorenzo.	What's up, man, you look bothered?
Dew.	It's crazy . . . Why would that thing be here?
Lorenzo.	Well, obviously, to prevent us from going further.
Dew.	No, not that. I'm saying that those things were scrapped years ago during the civil war due to malfunctions in the internal programming. So they said.
Lorenzo.	Who knows? But it looks like it was operational now.
Dew.	There's more to this than it is . . . Something is telling me.
Elvir.	This is getting weirder by the moment.
Dew.	We'll figure this out later. Hopefully, we'll run into the others soon.

Narrator.   The elevator descends down the shaft and gets to its destination.
              Dew and his group depart from the elevator to begin their search
              through the second-floor basement. After walking a bit, they
              eventually encounter Cooper and the others.

Dew.   Guys.

Cooper.   I see you all made it safely.

Vilmer.   We were wondering what was taking you guys so long to get
              here.

Dew.   Ran into a few snags on the way, but no scraps here.

Krista.   Cooper was beginning to worry us; we almost started to come
              look for you all.

Vilmer.   I would say all that worrying from Cooper, was the concern for
              Elvir well being.

Elvir.   Really?

Krista.   *Hee-hee-hee.*

Cooper.   I don't know what you're taking about.

Narrator.   Elvir then blushes.

Vilmer.   Guess you all didn't find Thornton yet, huh?

Dew.   No.

Elvir.   We're all here now. So what now?

Dew.   I think it's best we stick together now.

Lorenzo.   I wonder where this dude is at?

Vilmer.   He's got to be somewhere here.

Cooper.   If I remember clearly, the SKT research lab is somewhere on
              this floor, isn't it, Dew?

Dew.   That's right, it is. He hasn't found the fourth vial yet, so we can
              end this now.

Lorenzo.   Well, what are we all standing around for, homes? Let's go greet
              him then.

Narrator.   The group reunited again then heads off to find the SKT research
              lab. Some time passes by before Dew and the others come across
              the entrance of the lab.

Cooper.   This is it.

Dew.   Like it was before.

Lorenzo.   Let's go in and kick some ass then.

Krista.   I wonder what is in store for us. No time for the cold feet now.

Elvir.   Ready to go, guys?

Dew.   Well, this is it.

Narrator.	Dew and the group enter the research lab as the doors automatically open. After they all enter, the doors quickly slam shut behind them. Elvir walks toward the door to see if it will open. It doesn't.
Elvir.	Someone doesn't want us to leave.
Dew.	I bet.
Narrator.	Thornton then steps out from the shadows into the opening to confront them.
Thornton.	Dew.
Dew.	Thornton.
Thornton.	I see you all are here. Finally, we can celebrate the rebirth together.
Dew.	None of that nonsense matters. (*then draws his bo*)
Cooper.	Dew, wait.
Dew.	We end this now.
Narrator.	Dew then dashes at Thornton to attack him; out of nowhere, Schwartz appears with a Taser gun and fires it at Dew, which causes Dew to fly back, hitting a wall. The others run over to Dew's aid.
Thornton.	Ha-ha-ha.
Cooper.	*checking on Dew.* Dew, you okay?
Dew.	Ah . . .
Lorenzo	*turns to face Schwartz.* Schwartz, what are you doing here?
Schwartz.	You missed me, huh?
Narrator.	Dew then gets up on his feet as Cooper and Vilmer help him.
Schwartz.	You weren't expecting to see me again, were ya? Hoo-hoo-hoo . . .
Narrator.	Thornton then notices Rena's amulet lying at his feet.
Thornton.	What's this? (*bends down to pick up the amulet*)
Cooper.	What is going on here?
Schwartz.	Questions that I have an answer to. First things first; got to reap the rewards. (*then walks over to Thornton*)
Thornton.	Here you go (*handing Schwartz the amulet*)
Dew.	Rena's amulet. Give it back!
Schwartz.	Thank you. (*then takes the amulet from Thornton*) I can't give back this precious now. After all these years, finally the search has ended.
Lorenzo.	What are you talking about?

Schwartz.	It's simple, my boy. I have finally obtained them all.
Dew.	Obtained them all?
Narrator.	Schwartz then opens the amulet and pulls out the SKT virus vial A.
Cooper.	The vial?!
Dew.	?!
Schwartz.	Yes, this must come as a shock to you all. You had it this whole time and never realized it. Ha-ha-ha . . . hidden in this amulet for all these years.
Dew.	How did you know where it was?
Schwartz.	It's such a long story, but I might as well share it with you all before the end. It all started twenty-four years ago, I had funded what seemed to be a promising investment in the beginning. Our society at that time was still recovering from the aftermath of the Liberation War even after the reconstruction of the country was completed. The nation was in some what of a runt as we were trying to maintain the proper balance in our health care, military, weapons, education, and science programs. The government had spent billions of dollars separately into these programs; mainly into the science programs that seemed to look as if it was turning out to be a waste of the nations assess. One example of this was Professor Sorenson's teleportation device along with many others. However, there was one that would be more promising and reinsuring. This project was known as the Priscus Project.
Krista.	The Priscus Project?
Schwartz.	Yes. At the time, there were three scientists assigned to develop the SKT Virus: Dr. Alfred Eudora, Kenneth Voight, and Rena Cullen. They spent six months developing the virus strain. Two years later, the project would turn out to be a complete success. At this moment it had seemed that I was on the verge of financial success. Then thirteen years later, the Great Civil War had begun. That would be the beginning of my misfortune. With Zircon Videl being inaugurated into office to serve a life term after the passing of his father; I had the vials split up among four people I could trust until the day came to retrieve them once more. Thanks to the actions I took, he never knew of the existences of the other three vials. Dr. Alfred Eudora had the SKT virus G; Dr. Kenneth Voight held the SKT virus C originally

before Zircon had murdered him for it; Sergeant Lahaina, along with his unit, raided one of the other labs in New Havenport and discovered the SKT virus T vial then he disappeared with it in his possession. Of course I can't forget about the man who I had considered as a brother and very close friend . . . the man who I gave the SKT virus A vial and amulet to—your grandfather, Dew.

Dew.   What?!

Schwartz.   While he served in the SWAT trooper elite, he worked alongside me as my bodyguard and friend. I gave it to him because he vowed to protect it, even if it meant his life.

Dew.   Hmm . . .

Schwartz.   I went to visit him one night to retrieve the vial and amulet from him. This was six years ago.

Dew.   Six years ago, that was when . . .

Schwartz.   Yes, before he had died, and you went off to the elite yourself. As I was saying, when I arrived to see him, I demanded for the vial. But he had misplaced it, so he said. He had actually found out the capabilities of the virus and refused to return it to me. So I had attempted to bribe him, but he had chosen the latter end of that deal. After all those years how close we came, he was going to rat me out to the government. I couldn't allow that to happen. Dew, your grandfather's death wasn't an accident.

Dew.   What do you mean?

Schwartz.   He had run off from us knowing his life was endangered. That accident of his wasn't by coincidences as your mother and father had suffered. No, I ran him down. Hah, such a shame. He was an impressive soldier, loyal to the country's purpose to the end. If only he had joined me . . .

Dew.f   *inhaling and exhaling sharply.*

Narrator.   Dew clinches his fist in anger and is about to take a step toward Schwartz, but Cooper holds him back.

Cooper.   Not yet, Dew. Not yet.

Dew.   This bastard killed my grandfather.

Cooper.   Dew, no. Wait.

Lorenzo.   That's dirty, really. (*shaking his head in disapproval*)

Schwartz.   The power we have, with money, you can do anything.

Krista.   There's no happiness in that.

Schwartz.   Who needs that? Ha-ha.

Vilmer.	The greed and ambition has corrupted your soul, all because of power. How low you are.
Schwartz.	Well, it has helped me to get where I am now, and much more. The vials aren't the only things that are of value here. (*then squeezes the amulet in his palm*) The amulet . . .
Dew.	What does the amulet have to do with any of this?
Schwartz.	This amulet was discovered four years before the development of the Priscus project. An archeologist from the University of Helix along with his students went out to the Mesovilla plains to record data on the constant land shifts that took place there. During one of the observations, a violent earthquake struck the area which revealed a lost civilization treasure. It looked to be some sort of ancient ruins that were buried underneath the soil there. It took months to dig up the ancient ruins, yet they were able to salvage the ancient scriptures that were in good condition at the time of discovery. The writings were hard to decipher at first; but in time after careful study, they broke the code. It seems that the ancient beings known as the Priscus lived fifty million years ago. They were a highly technological advance race that had invented a many number of things. Out of all their inventions, the amulet was of great importances to them and very sacred. It had protected their empire from evil spirits, disease, and economic ruin. For such a highly advance race, they were quite superstitious. After a while the Priscus began to misuse the powers of the amulet, and this led to their own destruction.
Dew.	Those times sound no different from the present.
Schwartz.	But there were two lives that were spared by Kami after the downfall of the Priscus civilization.
Lorenzo.	So the story of us human's being the "children of Adan and Leva" are true.
Schwartz.	Yes they are. With every generations passing, our genetic structure had changed drastically falling short of the "glory" that Adan and Leva had possessed within them. They were of a "pure race"; but with only two of them left to repopulate the world, the chances of their offspring's, you and me, possessing the same powers as they did, were slim. Frailty and ignorance's was Kami's cruse on the human race due to the actions of the Priscus . . . but that will soon change.

Dew.　　　　How so?

Schwartz.　　After learning about this information, I had attempted to unlock the power of the amulet. That obviously didn't happen. Ha-ha. As I had mentioned before, the Priscus had elements within their bodies that could withstand the powers that the amulet radiated. For a human to extract such immense power, it would kill them. It almost did me the first time around. As my frustrations grew ever so more with the days passing, I eventually came up with a brilliant plan that would solve this issue. If a normal human being couldn't bask in the powers of the amulet, a child from recreation probably could.

Dew.　　　　Cloning?

Schwartz.　　Precisely. After the discovery of the ancient ruins, we were able to find traces of the Priscus DNA there. The SKT research team created a child from scrap. Two members of the team volunteered to be used as specimens themselves to aid the cause of science.

Dew.　　　　Dr. Voight and Rena.

Thornton.　　Yes.

Schwartz.　　By using the gene manipulation method, they used their own DNA cells splicing them together to construct a perfect child, a child who mimics all the qualities and abilities that the Priscus had. This child's name was Elizabeth.

Dew.　　　　It all makes sense now.

Thornton.　　The SKT viruses were developed from her DNA structure. They carry the Priscus mimetic information in them. For a normal person to be exposed to the viruses, it would result in death, in some cases mutation.

Dew.　　　　What about her brother?

Schwartz.　　He unfortunately was the end result of a complete failure. So better than to throw the specimen away, we tested various toxins on him.

Cooper.　　　Like a guinea pig.

Elvir.　　　　Sick.

Schwartz.　　The SKT viruses are prone to attack specific cells in the body to alter an individual DNA. Our bodies cannot withstand these invaders, so the white blood cells tries to fight them off. Well, in the end process, the white blood cells are overtaken by the pathogens. Only one whose body is pure can withstand the power

	of the amulet. In the beginning, the viruses were planned to be used on our soldiers in increasing their strength. A supersoldier in other words. Well, because of the mutation factor, it was hindered. Zircon found out the hard way. Regardless though, this will be the evolution of our species.
Lorenzo.	Evolution? Bullshit, man, you're going to be killing millions with this. Someone blinded by greed would never see that. You're foolish as Zircon was.
Schwartz.	Say what you must, but this is the future; and now is the time.
Thornton.	I think that's enough of the lecture. I kept my end of the deal; now your turn to live up to yours.
Schwartz.	Of course . . . as I promised.
Narrator.	Schwartz then walks over to a covered capsule and then uncovers it, revealing the frozen body of Elizabeth in cryogenic sleep.
Dew.	Is she alive?
Schwartz.	Her physical self, no. She's not entirely dead though.
Cooper.	That doesn't make sense.
Schwartz.	After the bombing here, Zircon had sent in a biological waste cleanup crew to dispose of any evidence that could have been left over that the bomb did not wipe out. They came in and found her corpse. The immense amount of radiation in the atmosphere could melt skin like it was butter underneath a heat lamp.
	Extraordinary upon the discovery, there weren't any signs of radiation poison or a mark on her body. She fell into a coma due to taking a bullet to her spine, but her healing factor made it possible for her to live. She was quickly retrieved and brought back to the Helix capital. I had her frozen in a cryogenic chamber. She wasn't the only thing they found left alive.
Dew.	Thornton, you mean?
Thornton.	Yes. I was able to survive only because I had injected myself with a small sample of the SKT virus C before my immediate death at the hands of my brother. My body was able to sustain life due to the radiation from the bombs that was dropped.
Schwartz.	He did suffer the psychical effects from the bomb blast; I had Dr. Eudora fit him with an exoskeleton suit that increased his speed, strength, and endurance. Along with that, to heighten his abilities as my effective soldier, I had implanted in his right thigh a small chip that would give him the means to teleport

anywhere in a certain radius. We had perfected the technology that Professor Sorenson had failed to do in the first place.

The years passed by, and I was beginning to fear that Zircon would sooner or later discover the existence of the other vials. That day when you, Dew and the Aurora Blade, showed up at the warehouse and blew it up, you did me a favor. That place, not just being the storage for all the collected tax money from the citizens, it was where the main operation for the development of the SKT virus C samples was. That halted Zircon's plans indeed, and you gave me more time than expected. With that happening, I had the girl's body moved back here after the reconstruction of the chemical facility, and Thornton sprang into action to watch from the shadows what Zircon was up to. After all this, my money didn't go to waste after all. With her, she is the way to immortality.

Thornton. Now with all in place, the rebirth of the Angel of Death and a new beginning.

Cooper. All this pain . . . for your stupid vision.

Thornton. This vision will become a reality, and we shall be together again.

Dew. Why did you have Dr. Eudora killed off?

Schwartz. He ran off with the SKT virus G vial and was planning to use it as a bargaining chip against me. He knew by doing that how important it was to me and what I would do to get it back. Well, rather than negotiating for it and giving into his demands, what a better way for him to die for his betrayal.

Krista. Was it worth it, all the deception and pain you caused?

Schwartz. It was.

Vilmer. You're a degenerate.

Dew. *shaking head in disapproval.*

Schwartz. All has gone as planned; now to carry out the next step to all of this.

Narrator. Thornton touches the display glass of the cryo chamber, looking at Elizabeth lying in slumber. He slides his hand up and down the display glass touching her face.

Thornton. The time is ripe now, my love. (*then turns to face Schwartz*) Schwartz, give me the vials so I may revive my beloved.

Schwartz. Oh, I can't do that.

Thornton. Really? Why is that?

Schwartz.	You see, the only reason I kept you around this long was to do all the dirty work for me. See, I have what I have now. I will become the ultimate being and rule over all as I see fit. I did keep my promise in the end; you have your frozen girlfriend, and I have the power I need now. Your services are terminated now.
Narrator.	Schwartz then points his Taser gun at Thornton and fires it at him. The bolt from the gun knocks Thornton to the ground knocking him unconscious.
Dew.	?!
Schwartz.	I guess you aren't the killer you once were after all. Ha-ha-ha. Damn fool, he thought I was going to serve his purpose of resurrecting her. I will become the god now.
Lorenzo.	How are you going to do that? Like you said, a human being coming in contact with those viruses would die.
Schwartz.	I underwent gene therapy throughout the years, and I had samples of her DNA grafted onto mine. I've been preparing for this for so long. Once I inject the vials into me, this will unlock the power source of the amulet. I will have reached the zenith of all organisms.
Dew.	Not if I have anything to do with it.
Schwartz.	It was so easy getting you all here. You all can be the first to die at the hands of a god. Now I will crush you and—
Elvir.	Yeah, yeah! You know you speak too much, just like a woman.
Schwartz.	You dare to interrupt a god?
Lorenzo.	Get over yourself.
Schwartz.	Hah . . . Well, let's get the show on the road then.
Narrator.	Schwartz then puts the amulet on his neck and pulls out the four vials.
Thornton.	*slowly getting up*. Not . . . yet!
Narrator.	Thornton then dashes at Schwartz as he is about to inject himself with the vials. He draws his long sword and, with a flash, slices Schwartz's head off. The four vials drop to the ground and Rena's amulet as well.
Krista.	*gasps*.
Narrator.	Schwartz's severed head falls to the ground, then his corpse.
Dew.	?!
Lorenzo.	He's not coming back from that.
Krista.	Ah, what a terrible way to die.
Vilmer.	Good riddance's to bad rubbish.

Cooper.	Stupid yuppie.
Dew.	Rest in peace now, Grandpa.
Elvir.	Well, one less asshole to worry about.
Thornton.	*looking down at the headless corpse of Schwartz.* Schwartz, like I said, I never kill lesser life-forms . . . for you; you're an exception to the rule. (*then bends over to pick up all four of the vials and the amulet*)
	I have them all now, my love. Soon the rebirth will begin. (*puts the amulet on his neck*) No time to waste now. (*then vanishes*)
Dew.	He's gone. Damn.
Krista.	We've got to stop him.
Vilmer.	Where do you think he went, Dew?
Dew.	I don't know, but we better start looking quick.
Narrator.	Suddenly, a large crane comes down and grabs the cryo capsule. It then lifts it up into the air and begins to carry it off into a room above.
Lorenzo.	Where's it going?
Elvir.	Looks like there is a room up there. See? (*then points up in the direction of the room above them*)
Dew	*then looks up.* Yeah. Come, ya'll.
Narrator.	Dew then runs off, and the others follow him to the room above the research lab. The scene switches to Thornton, who awaits the arrival of the cryo capsule in the room. The crane lowers the capsule to the ground, and Thornton then approaches it.
Thornton.	Finally, the time has come. (*He then takes out the four vials and begins to look at them.*) "Ring a ring o'roses, a pocket full of posies. Ah-tishoo! Ah-tishoo! Ah-tishoo! We all fall down."
Narrator.	Dew and the others then enter the room running up to confront Thornton.
Dew.	Thornton.
Thornton.	*then turns around from the cryo capsule to face Dew.* Ah, we're all here at last. No more interruptions now. Yes, the time is ripe.
Cooper.	Thornton, stop this at once. You don't know what will happen if you go through with this.
Thornton.	Oh, but I do. We will rejoice together in the glory, and we will be saved.
Dew.	Saving us by destroying the human race? Ridiculous.
Thornton.	You say that now. (*then turns to face the cryo capsule*) Elizabeth, it's time for you to awake.

Narrator.	Thornton enters the four vials into a slot on the cryo capsule, and then all four are injected into the frozen body of Elizabeth. Seconds later, the cryo capsule begins to shake and then gives off an eerie glow from within.
Thornton.	It's beginning . . . Ha-ha-ha.
Lorenzo.	Damn, we're too late.
Elivr.	What are we going to do now?
Dew.	I don't know.
Narrator.	As the cryo capsule continues to shake and glow, the room then begins to fill with smoke that seeps out from the cryo capsule.
Cooper.	What the?!
Krista.	Guys, watch out!
Narrator.	Then the capsule hatch blows off from the condensed pressure within, flying toward Dew and the others causing them to fall to the room below. The room is then entirely covered with smoke. Moments later, the smoke begins to clear up and reveals Elizabeth's body falling out of the capsule. She's on her knees. Thornton then runs over to her aid.
Thornton.	*squats down to hold her head in his arms.* Elizabeth?!
Elizabeth.	. . .
Thornton.	Did it work?
Elizabeth,	*opening her eyes and, looking up to see Thornton. Mmmm . . .* T-Thornton?! Is it really you?
Thornton.	*then smiles.* Yes, my love, it is. It worked, you're alive. Ha-ha-ha.
Elizabeth.	Thornton, I've missed you.
Narrator.	Elizabeth and Thornton then embrace one another for a compassionate hug.
Thornton.	I had missed you too. It's been so long, but at last we are together again.
Elizabeth.	As promised.
Thornton.	I could never forget about you.
Elizabeth.	Oh, Thornton.
Thornton.	My love . . .
Narrator.	They then stop hugging, and Thornton helps Elizabeth up on her feet. They begin holding hands, staring into each other's eyes.
Elizabeth.	I feel like . . . I've been sleeping forever. To awake to see you again, it's a relief. I'm sorry I've kept you waiting, my love.
Thornton.	It was worth the wait.

Elizabeth.	I will never leave you again, my love.
Thornton.	Yes.
Elizabeth.	Fate is strange. Two soul mates brought together to be split apart from one another, then now to be reunited. The beauty of life and death.
Thornton.	From here on out, we'll be together.
Elizabeth.	Forever. This place . . . I feel so much sorrow, so much pain . . .
Thornton.	It is time then, my love.
Elizabeth.	Let's heal this world now.
Thornton.	Together.
Elizabeth.	Two soul mates . . .
Narrator.	As Thornton holds on to Elizabeth, the amulet gives off a flicker of light.
Thornton.	One force.
Elizabeth.	One desire, one determination.
Thornton.	One being, one whole self, one everlasting love.
Elizabeth.	To meld as one, unchained by fate, one destiny, one chance.
Thornton.	Forever as one.
Narrator.	Thornton and Elizabeth then kiss as the amulet gives off a large beam of light that gradually consumes their bodies in its ethereal essences, and they begin to meld as one. Dew and the others in the lab below regain consciousness, and they are confronted by the newly formed entity.
Thornliza.	Because we are one being, one god, one ruler over all. We are Thornliza. Ha-ha-ha.
Elvir.	*getting up on her feet*. This looks bad.
Vilmer.	What is this abomination?
Lorenzo.	Well, it's certainly no God.
Cooper.	The Angel of Death.
Krista.	Any ideas, guys?
Dew.	I know one thing though; it's not over yet.
Lorenzo.	This is it then, huh?
Elvir.	Yep.
Dew.	We're all here now. Come on ya, let's do this.
Thornliza.	Ha-ha-ha. All who dare to defy us will suffer the unimaginable. Soon you, humans, will pay for your sins. All kneel before us. We are the deity who will determine the course of all, and our

	judgment upon all. Soon the holy bliss will roam throughout the world again, cleansing all.
Dew.	By destroying life itself you mean?
Thornliza.	You, humans, don't deserve nothing more but death. You, humans, abused your free will. Now we shall correct your mistakes and start anew. The knowledge of the Priscus flows through our veins. "Purify this world, save them all." We can hear the souls of the damned crying to us. No more sorrow and pain. We are invincible. We are omnipotent.
Elvir.	You may be all that now, but we won't let you destroy our world.
Cooper.	The madness ends here. No more blood and sinew.
Thornliza.	You inferior life-forms. You dare challenge us? We are eternal. You will suffer for your ignorance. You all will be the first be to be annihilated from existence.
Lorenzo.	Naw, that's not going to happen, ese. I'm going out like a real G. I don't care what you say now; the outcome is going to be much different. I'll see to that, believe it.
Krista.	I'm not going to lie. I'm a little scared. Well, it won't stop me from fighting though. This world may have its ugliness to it, but there is beauty in it as well. I won't allow you to destroy that. Just forget about it.
Cooper.	I've lost many friends and my family in the past. I'm not planning to join them anytime soon. I still want to live life. I have no more guilt about what could have been. I'm free now from the pain of the past. I will see to it that you will suffer the unimaginable. There is hope still.
Elvir.	This is all for the children back home and my father. I will see them again. I will fight my best for them all. I'm ready to go.
Vilmer.	I've been all over the world; I've met so many people. Life is too short to waste it. When this is all over, I'm going to be looking forward to living life all over again. Yeah, the right way. I got to do that.
Dew.	All the pain, the drama . . . it comes down to this. This is the end of the long journey. No matter what . . . I won't stop either. In memory of Rena, Emily, Hopkins, my grandpa, and for the future's sake, you will go down. Let's go, everybody.
Thornliza.	Ha-ha-ha. "Ring a ring o'roses, a pocket full of posies. Ah-tishoo! Ah-tishoo! Ah-tishoo! We all fall down."

Narrator.	Dew and the others then draw their weapons and rush at Thornliza to begin the final showdown. Thornliza unleashes powerful attacks against Dew and the others, causing them to sustain minor injuries. However, this didn't stop them, as the group continues to fight using all their might against the omnipotent entity. In the end, after a long, strenuous battle, Dew and the group are able to overcome Thornliza.
Dew.	*inhaling and exhaling deeply.*
Elvir.	Is it over?
Thornliza	*kneels down.* Impossible . . . We are invincible. We can't be . . . (*body then begins to spontaneously combust into flames*) NOOOOOO! (*falls to the ground writhing in pain*) *Uuuuuuurrrrrrgggghhhh!*
Vilmer.	What a pity.
Elvir.	Well, that's that.
Lorenzo.	Glad that's done with.
Thornliza.	You inferior creatures. (*getting up slowly on its feet while engulfed in flames*)
Dew.	Geez?!
Lorenzo.	Still alive?! What gives?
Thornliza.	We are eternal. (*then begins to walk toward Dew and the others*) You'll all suffer. DIE! (*then shoots off a projectile aimed at Dew*) Ha-ha-ha.
Cooper.	Dew, watch out!
Narrator.	Cooper quickly pushes Dew to the ground to avoid being hit by the oncoming projectile. Cooper is then hit by the projectile himself and is knocked to the floor. Thornliza begins to combust into larger flames and wails in pain.
Thornliza.	*Ahhhhhhhhh!* We won't . . . perish alone. We are one . . . ugh . . .
Narrator.	Thornliza then collapses onto a nearby console, crushing it. Dew then runs over to the fallen Cooper to check on him.
Dew.	Cooper?!
Cooper.	. . .
Elvir.	Cooper, you okay? (*then checks Cooper for further injuries*)
Cooper.	I'm fine.
Dew.	Why'd you do that? You could have been killed.
Cooper.	I still owed you one.

Elvir.	Cooper, you stupid jerk, don't ever do that again. I was starting to worry about you.
Cooper.	So you actually care for me?
Elvir	*blushes and smiles.* Just shut up. I'm glad you're fine.
Cooper.	Heh-heh-heh . . . funny how history just keeps repeating itself with all of us, huh? Well, at least my ankle didn't get the worse of it this time around.
Dew.	Can you move?
Cooper.	I'm a little sore, but I'm still kicking.
Narrator.	Dew then lends Cooper a hand as Elvir helps him up on his feet.
Dew.	All good?
Cooper.	All fine here.
Narrator.	An alarm then goes off indicating that a self-destruct sequence has been activated and the time remaining.
Vilmer.	Hmm . . . that's not good.
Lorenzo.	No kidding. (*then turns to face Dew*) Sorry, dudes; I hate to ruin your Kodak moment, but we need to get going. Time is ticking away.
Dew.	Yeah, let's do that then.
Krista.	Well, how are we going to get out of this place?
Dew.	There should be an escape pod room around here still. If my memory serves me right.
Elvir.	Let's hope it does.
Lorenzo.	Lead the way, man.
Narrator.	Dew and the others then exit the research lab and head for the escape pod room. Finally reaching the room as time continues to tick away, they find one pod left.
Elvir	*exhales sharply.* Just our luck. One left.
Krista.	Shucks.
Vilmer.	We'll all have to fit in there then. (*then walks up and climbs into the pod*)
Lorenzo.	No time to be picky. Time to go.
Narrator.	As the others walk over to the pod and climb into it, suddenly, Thornliza comes crashing into the room knocking down the door panel and falling to the ground with it. This catches Dew and the others' attention as Thornliza crawls slowly toward them.
Thornliza.	Dew . . .
Dew.	*gasps.*

Elvir.	*exhales sharply.* You got to be kidding me.
Thornliza.	It's not over, Dew. Not . . . yet!
Vilmer.	Pretentious little bugger.
Thornliza.	*inhaling and exhaling rapidly.* "Ring a ring o'roses, a pocket full of posies. Ah-tishoo! Ah-tishoo! Ah-tishoo!"
Lorenzo.	Dew, come on. Let's go, man.
Thornliza.	*then rises up on its feet and looks up at Dew.* "WE ALL FALL DOWN!" *(then begins to run toward Dew)* *AAAAAAAARRRRRRRGGGHHHHHHHHHHHHH!*
Dew.	I would like to stay, but got to go.
Narrator.	Dew then leaps into the escape pod along with his friends, and it is launched out of the chemical facility into the air, plunging into the Mesovilla Ocean below. The self-destruct sequence then goes off moments later causing a massive explosion, and it disintegrates the entire Chemical facility to ash as the providence of New Havenport crashes into the ocean below. After all the dust clears up, we find the escape pod drifting in the middle of the Mesovilla Ocean. The hatch on the escape pod then opens as Dew and the others take a peek of their surroundings.
Elvir.	So . . . is it over now?
Cooper.	It is. Finally.
Krista.	That's a relief.
Lorenzo.	Never thought I would be so happy to see the sea again. *(then inhales and exhales deeply)* Ah.
Krista.	You're not seasick?
Lorenzo.	No, not at all. Feeling good.
Vilmer.	Knowing that you're alive makes you feel like that.
Elvir.	What now, Dew?
Dew.	Can't really say.
Vilmer.	Hmm. So we're stuck out here for the time being. Some adventure this has been. Of all that we've been through, I'm glad I came along.
Elvir.	Me too.
Cooper.	The way things look now, we can hope we get to land soon or end up drifting aimlessly out here. To end up like that . . .
Dew.	Well, we still have hope.
Lorenzo.	That's all there is.
Krista.	Come on, guys, just be happy that we're still alive. We just saved all of humanity for crying out loud. So what if we die out here

and no one finds us. It doesn't matter. Just knowing the fact of what we did does.

Vilmer. I couldn't have said it any better. You're right.

Dew. Together, until the end.

Lorenzo. Until the end, pal.

Narrator. Dew then smiles at Lorenzo.

Cooper. No regrets at all.

Elvir. None here either.

Narrator. Elvir then grabs Cooper's hand and holds on to it. As Dew and the others continue to drift around in the Mesovilla Ocean, a helicopter appears from the distance.

Krista. Hey, guys, look! (*then points in the direction of the helicopter*)

Lorenzo. We're saved.

Cooper. There is hope always in the end.

Narrator. Dew and the others start waving at the helicopter to signal it in their direction. The helicopter approaches them.

Pilot. *speaking into the helicopter intercom system.* Are you, folks, okay down there?

Krista. *yelling.* Yes!

Narrator. Then Professor Sorenson pops his head out the passenger side of the helicopter and waves at Dew and the others below.

Elvir. It's the professor. (*then waves at the prof*)

Dew. A sight for sore eyes. (*then smiles and waves at the prof*)

Sorenson. *speaking into the helicopter intercom system.* Hold on a second; we'll be right down there to get you all.

Narrator. The helicopter then hovers over Dew and the others. The cargo door of the helicopter opens, and Professor Sorenson drops a ladder that they use to climb aboard onto the helicopter. Once Dew and the party are onboard, the helicopter flies off back into the sky.

Pilot. *navigating the helicopter.* Everyone here?

Krista. Yes, we're all here. Thank you for your help.

Pilot. No problem.

Vilmer. This old man needs a nap . . . tired.

Dew. So you came to our rescue again.

Sorenson. I had a feeling you all may have needed it again.

Elvir. How did you know where to find us?

Sorenson. I figured I would come after you all since you, guys, had no way of getting back. I got a little worried after seeing the explosion of New Havenport; I didn't want to think you all had perished when that had happened. So I had to be sure of that, and we kept searching for you all. We've been flying around for an hour until the pilot had spotted you all. I just couldn't let you all die out here after all you've done for me.

Elvir.	Thanks, Prof.
Lorenzo.	Yeah, homes, you saved us back there.
Dew.	So, is there enough fuel left in this thing?
Sorenson.	No.
Dew.	What?!
Sorenson.	I'm kidding. Ha-ha-ha.
Dew.	You're a weird man . . . but, funny. Ha-ha-ha.
Elvir.	Ha-ha-ha.
Sorenson.	So, where you, folks, heading now?
Dew.	Only one place . . . Home.
Lorenzo.	Home sweet home.
Vilmer.	Nothing like it.
Krista.	That's enough excitement to last me a lifetime.
Dew.	You can say that again . . . (*Then whispers to himself*) Home sweet home. Maybe now. It's probably worth going back. Maybe now, I can find my bliss, my role in life. Maybe the time is right . . . yeah.
Cooper.	Dew, you okay?
Dew.	I am. (*then smiles*) Let's all go home. We all deserve that the most.
Elvir.	Sounds good to me.
Narrator.	Dew then turns to the window and looks out into the horizon at the clouds.
Dew.	Farewell to you all. Someday . . . someday we'll all meet again as we promised one another. But not yet. (*sigh*) Just not yet. Someday, all of us . . . again. (*then smiles*)
Narrator.	The helicopter then flies off into the sunset. Meanwhile, back on the shores of Tagore, the water washes up calmly onto the shore below, carrying the amulet along with it. The amulet drifts onto the sandy shore, and the water washes it back into the ocean. The amulet then gives off an eerie glow.

THE END